Intelligent Design: Revelations to Apocalypse

J. M. Erickson

Intelligent Design: Revelations to Apocalypse

http://www.jmericksonindiewriter.com

Editor: Suzanne M. Owen
Cover design: Cathy Helms, Avalon Graphics, LLC
http://www.avalongraphics.org/
Formatting: Polgarus Studio

Publisher: J. M. Erickson
http://www.jmericksonindiewriter.net

ISBN: (Paper back) 978-1-942708-15-5
ISBN: (MOBI Format) 978-1-942708-13-1
ISBN: (ePub Format) 978-1-942708-14-8

Printed in the United States of America

Other works by this author

Action/Adventure Thrillers

Albatross: Birds of Flight—Book One (Revised)
Raven: Birds of Flight—Book Two
Eagle: Birds of Flight—Book Three
Falcon: Birds of Flight—Book Four
Flight of the Black Swan

Action/Adventure Science Fiction

Future Prometheus I: Emergence & Evolution—Novellas I & II
Future Prometheus II: Revolution, Successions & Resurrections—Novellas III, IV & V
Intelligent Design: Revelations
The Prince: Lucifer's Origins
Intelligent Design: Apocalypse
Rogue Event

What Reviewers Are Saying About...

Intelligent Design: Revelations...

"Intelligent, complex, riveting, and with surprising twists, *Intelligent Design: Revelations* was an unexpected treat for me... The technology and advancements were believable and yet almost feel ahead of its time." - ***Indie Book Reviewers***

"Well-written and suspenseful, Erickson's story blends scientific theory with fast-paced action in an adventure that should have its fans practically sitting up and begging for a sequel." - ***US Review of Books***

"...it is to Erickson's credit that he fulfills the absolute criteria for a proper science fiction novel: i.e. science made into fiction—and that should be very enjoyable to sci-fi purists seeking out this exact kind of work." - ***Self-Publishing Review***

"...wonderfully absorbing science fiction novella presenting existential questions that occupy the reader's mind long after the book has been put down." - **Suzanne Owen,** ***Independent Editor***

Intelligent Design: Apocalypse...

"Amid this fantastical setting, the narrative reads as sharply as an SAS thriller with efficient, no-nonsense heroes and heroines who understand the full and terrifying impact of the decisions they make." - ***Readers' Favorite***

"The author's soaring imagination and mastery of technical jargon are on full display in this tale of impending interplanetary destruction that would seem to be shattering, yet may not in fact be as catastrophic as one might first imagine." - ***US Review of Books***

"The writing is very good—intelligent, suspenseful, descriptive and disturbingly honest." - ***Indie Book Reviewers***

"...The dialogue is well-crafted and meaningful and the characters fully reveal their humanity as they interact with one another and react to events that are life-changing and beyond control." - **Suzanne Owen,** ***Independent Editor***

List of Characters

Andrea Perez, or Perez the Younger—Former MIT doctoral student of holographic and light spectrums, she is now a resident on the planet Terra. As an "Earther" on an alien planet, she is of the engineer-warrior class, tasked with keeping the planet's holographic emitters running to keep the planet Terra hidden from Earth. She has been on Terra for years and has become accustomed to its martial law that parallels ancient Rome's.

Anthony Perez, or Perez the Elder—Former army captain who worked as a trauma specialist in the Department of Veterans Administration, Perez is a recent arrival to Terra. Previously, he worked on preparing Earth for the revelation that another planet with a developed civilization existed within the Sol System, but had been well hidden. He originally ran the Epsilon Team Six, an all-Terran-female SEAL team, but turned it over to his friend Roberta Josephine Riesman when he was injured.

Christine Reich, CEO and President of Reich Enterprise—A wealthy German industrialist, billionaire, and philanthropist who used to be known as Roberta Josephine Riesman, PhD, a former army major. Her last position was as executive director of Readiness and Disaster Logistics in the Federal Emergency Management Agency's Office of Response and Recovery. She adopted the Reich persona when she learned the truth about the hidden planet and when her close friend Anthony Perez was injured and left Earth to reunite with his daughter Andrea on Terra. She is the leader of a special ops team, Terran Epsilon Team Six—made of Lux, Pax, Vespere, Bella, and her master computer, the Keeper—that is now focused on keeping humanity alive on Earth.

General David Farrell—General in the United States Army who runs a specialized unit in the communication, spectrographic analysis, and guidance division of NASA. He searches for intelligent life within the Sol System. For years he has followed leads from "lost" documents, documents with corrupted dates, "missing" files, and disappearing witnesses. He suspects a cover-up about an invisible planet that affects gravitational pull on all the system's planets but that cannot be seen.

Chief Inspector Arthur Bradley—From New Scotland Yard. Works with his team—Officer Virginia "Ginny" Spenser and Officer John "Jack" Middleton—to locate missing persons and solve riddles on international cases. Works with General Farrell and has spent a great amount of time searching for an escaped nemesis, Sir Phillip Pierce, and the wealthy though elusive Christine Reich.

Master Architect Janus—Leader of the "Old Ones," a group that survived the collision of Gemini's Alpha and Beta dwarf planets sixty-seven million years ago deep within Mars's crust. Janus and his companions, Olympia and Athena, plan to start a family. He was a great architect of the once-thriving Martian civilization and led junior architects, such as Iris of Venus and Hades of Terra, to populate the Sol System with different species of hominid. His leadership helped all the planets, even Earth, survive the initial destruction from the great collision. As the Martian population now dwindles into extinction, Janus and his master computer, the Keeper, foresee an all-too-familiar astronomical event: another extinction-level collision is about to begin. Once again, Janus must warn the others to prepare for the coming apocalypse, which will either lead to the annihilation or the next evolution of each species.

Setting

Terra—A tidally locked planet obscured from Earth by the sun and holographic emitters that cloak its existence; it is larger than Earth and keeps an opposite orbit. It is a martial-law society based on Earth's ancient Roman culture of 1.9 billion hominids, which bear a striking resemblance to Earth's Neanderthals. Terrans live underground, along the equatorial line that leaves half the planet in perpetual darkness and the other side in perpetual light. The holographic emitters are failing, and its existence is about to be revealed to Earth.

In the beginning was the Word, and the Word was with God, and the Word was God.
The same was in the beginning with God.
All things were made by him; and without him was not any thing made that was made.
In him was life; and the life was the light of men.
And the light shineth in darkness; and the darkness comprehended it not.
There was a man sent from God, whose name was John.
The same came for a witness, to bear witness of the Light, that all men through him might believe.
He was not that Light, but was sent to bear witness of that Light.

—John, 1:1–8, King James Version, Earth

In the very beginning, before the great collision, there were Mars, Venus, and Terra.
We were the Old Ones. We believe we were the very first created by the Originators.
We developed and created various carbon-based hominids in our own image and artificial intelligence to reflect our own. We stretched out from our Martian cradle to populate and create new civilizations. This was all to imitate our creators, the Originators. They were our creators, the ones we strived to emulate. The ones we followed to the stars.
And when the time came for us to leave before the end, before Collision, most of our kind left to find the Originators.
Few, so very few, architects and master computers created arks for our creations.

—Hades, 1:1–9, B.C., Great Library, Terra

Revelation

Novella I

Sixty-Seven Million Years Ago

Prologue

In the Beginning—Mars

When it is obvious that the goal cannot be reached, don't adjust the goals, adjust the actions steps - Confucius

"Just Beautiful. Unusually quiet, but beautiful nonetheless." Master Architect Janus stood on his balcony, gazing over the miles of well-maintained but desolate homes in his near empty city. The lots, arranged in neat rows, contained two to three-story rectangular homes interspersed with gardens and small farms. The Originators had constructed the planet's cities to accommodate twenty million inhabitants with privacy and space. The arrangement of well-marked roads, arboretums and gardens made the Martian landscape aesthetically simple and pleasing, well designed in both form and function. Canals laid out in a grid pattern ran throughout the plateau, their order in stark contrast to the irregularity of the occasional rivers that cut across the land. Four-story pyramids glimmered throughout the cityscape.

Strategically placed by the waterways, they provided decentralized energy generation via water and solar. The sun set, plunging the planet into a reddish blue twilight, and birds flew squawking from their nests in search of their evening meal.

"Not much food, I fear, for the birds of prey," Janus said. "It does sadden me that while we were able to collect the majority of the planet's species over the past century, we are leaving many behind." He leaned on the balcony railing and took another sip of coffee from his high-grade plastic mug.

Two birds took flight from a rooftop and swooped on a small pack of rodent omnivores that had become more daring in the absence of Martians and other prey. The birds seized one of the smaller rodents, but the rodent pack turned on the attackers.

One of the birds barely escaped. The other lifted the struggling rodent into the sky.

That was close. There will be no love lost when that species disappears, Janus thought while watching the rodent pack reorganize and move onto an unsuspecting garden. He turned and took a slow step from the silence of the outside world into his office, where a low but constant flow of computer voices reciting different data streams, observations, and conclusions played over the office intercom just as they had for centuries. No seats surrounded the large empty work tables in the center of the room, but benches lined the surrounding walls along with potted vegetation, bound books, paper star charts, planetary models, and a sea of color-coded tablets. One uneaten plate of food, a bottle of wine, and an empty glass sat on a bench amongst analytical equipment and paper-bound records. Janus sauntered over to the bottle of wine and poured himself another drink.

"Ah, Keeper, once again it is you and me, a handful of other stubborn old scientists, soldiers and the old left," he said just loud enough to be heard above the computer voices. "It is sad that after a millennium of preparation, I still wonder if we did everything we could to preserve life in this quiet corner of the galaxy."

He closed his layered work robes over his tall, thin frame and, with a full glass in hand, walked around his office, listening to the planet's master computer running billions of computations on the planet, colonies, and the solar event poised to happen at any moment. The master computer's female baritone stood out from the other computer tones as unmistakably in charge of the entire artificial intelligence of the planet.

"Master Architect Janus, I wish you would reconsider evacuating with the others. Both the Venus Keeper and the junior Architect of Earth request you join them. Your demise here is not necessary and it … it pains me that you will not leave when you could live," the Keeper said in its resonant, feminine voice.

Hmm … the beginning of emotion? Maybe she will survive and even reach sapience, he thought as he reviewed the number of cryogenic stasis chambers below. Though he had made his decision to stay long ago, he nodded as if he were actually considering it.

"No. I have no offspring, no spouse and no relatives. I have been in this workspace for two hundred years and in the field for another hundred years. I took over for Master Architect Lucius, who took over for Master Architect Guiana. They were of this world just as you are, Keeper. I cannot leave this world any more than you can. And besides, are there not cryogenic stasis chambers well below the surface?" He sipped his wine.

"Experimental. The liquid bonding and temperature only preserved the last subject for thirty-two thousand annual rotations," the master computer said.

"Only thirty-two thousand rotations? That's quite a bit of time. Experimental? What are your metrics for success? A billion annual rotations? Your demand for perfection surpasses even my predecessors, and we know how Architect Lucius was."

"Yes … Master Architect Lucius was demanding, critical and often correct even when his ideas were unconventional and far from the norm, but I digress. Please, Master Architect Janus, a ship awaits you to leave at any moment. I can report on the final days and moments here should they come as expected. The ship is designed for long range, long term cryogenic sleep. You can join the others who left long ago to find the Originators." She spoke with more emotion than he expected.

Persistent, and single-minded … Impressive.

"No, Keeper. Enough of this unresolvable discussion.

When the time comes, I will, with the others, retreat to the chambers for safekeeping." He walked towards the balcony, his mind racing again as thoughts of things to do and check on flowed through his head.

"By the way," he said, "I'm curious that with all my planning and efforts to salvage this solar system, why did you take it upon yourself to attempt to terraform Terra along with Junior Architect Hades? Why would you move ahead with such an unlikely plan on that tidal-locked planet, closer to hell than hope? If I did not know better, I would have guessed that Architect Lucius was still milling around here, or that he left a hidden program." He gazed out the balcony window and sipped his wine, hoping that his efforts to distract the master computer worked. The computer background voices and the quiet dialogue of internal programs on the intercom comforted rather than distracted him after all their years together. Yet, ironically, his one voice easily distracted his longtime master computer, colleague and friend.

"While primary efforts to relocate the majority of our indigenous species to Venus while we transform Terra are running well ahead of schedule, Earth's indigenous life has made it difficult to relocate the excess there. The massive warm-blooded omnivores have made havoc of our efforts, and the air quality still needs work, though minimal. Effort to transform Terra is low on the list but necessary should Earth not be a viable place for the excess overflow from Venus ..." the Keeper said.

Janus interrupted her. "So you allowed Architect Hades

to create a warehouse on a planetary scale. Based on the manifests of terraform equipment and fission producers, there is more than enough power to simply heat a contained environment along the terminal line rather than create a habitable world. Am I right?"

"Yes. But Junior Architect Hades is young and ambitious. He did, in fact, keep your ideas as a backup plan should things go awry. However, like many his age, he prefers to dream big and take risks."

"And he took the rodents and their favorite mushrooms to Terra? Was this part of an experiment or does he have a fondness for fanged, long-scaled, tailed omnivores and fungi?" He watched the rodents methodically ravage the unattended garden.

"Architect Hades has taken a number of species, animal and vegetable, to see which species could exist underground in harsh conditions and darkness. He believes he can orchestrate an ecosystem where he can create a source of food, the omnivorous rodents, for higher order species should the proposed food chains collapse, such as a planetary disruption to food transports, supplies and commerce."

"Smart for sure but dangerous—the fungi and rodents will multiply and live anywhere. He would be better served to focus on transforming and let those species die out." Janus found it difficult to conceal his natural dislike for both species. He cringed at the thought of needing to eat either one if necessary.

"I suppose there's also a good reason why Hades

collected every large scale holographic emitter on our planet? Does he have any idea how the public would've responded if they were here to witness this act? They are difficult to construct and more difficult to move. I suppose I should be grateful he left mine alone."

"Architect Hades is convinced that with a continuous supply of energy the holographic emitters will bend light just beyond our visual range."

Janus calculated the creativity required and the probability of success in converting holographic emitters from projecting light particles to bending them and pushing them to either end of the light spectrum. After a moment, he chuckled.

"Once again, creative. He would need to utilize a power source as great as the terraform equipment, but he could do it. Risky, but he could cloak physical objects on a planetary scale, especially with Terra's dark side of ice as a reflector. Provided he doesn't blow up the planet. Very risky."

"Yes."

But why he would want to do this? Because he can? Was I that foolish when I was young?

"Speaking of taking risks, please remind Architect Iris to slow down her titration of the Venetian atmosphere. I am concerned she's moving too quickly and could inadvertently create a runaway greenhouse effect. That would be bad."

He stood, taking in the sight of his Martian home, and thought of something else to convey to Iris, about another young ambitious Junior Architect.

"She has been warned repeatedly on this matter … Wait. Wait. Architect Janus, please look …" Janus heard the Keeper speak, but the sky already drew his attention. A brilliant light filled the Martian twilight and, as it faded, a few lights flickered on in the empty cityscape—the homes of those citizens who had decided to stay. Janus took a deep breath, and his shoulders and the top of his back relaxed as if they'd been waiting for this moment, this catastrophic, extinction-level event.

"I take it the dwarf planets Gemini Alpha and Beta finally collided. I expected it to happen next month. I hoped their gravity wells might survive this pass. How their orbits became suddenly destabilized in the first place is beyond me, just as it was to my predecessors." Janus calmly continued to watch the light fade and the sky return to its darkening reddish blue tint.

"Not all the predecessors. Master Architect Guiana believed that it was 'the will and hand of the Originators,' though she lacked scientific support," the master computer said.

"It was her faith, Master Computer, not science that provided her answer, the answer that satisfied her to the last days of her life. Still, I thought there might be a little more time …"

"Your assessment is accurate. In regards to the early destruction of the planets, it was the extreme gravitational pull of the twin planets' close proximity that ripped their cores apart. Our sensors have captured dramatic images of each planet's final moments. I will forward these events and recordings to the Keepers. The others will appreciate the scientific significance of this rare occurrence."

Though the Master Keeper's artificial intelligence often precluded emotion, Janus thought he detected emotion in her voice—sadness. *Our time is close to an end and another story is about to begin without us.*

"Even with all our advanced technology, we could not keep the planets from destroying themselves."

"It was not through lack of trying," she said.

Janus smiled and started to take another sip of wine but stopped with a sigh at the compassion in her voice.

If only there was more time ...

"I'm guessing that extinction level debris will hit us in three days." He wasn't afraid. He, like everyone else, knew the end was coming. They'd had years to choose whether to leave or stay, and he'd decided, like Hades, the junior architects, all of them, to witness this phenomenon and see if they could save the viable worlds. Most left, few stayed. He'd made peace with his decision years ago.

"Unknown. It will take less than a minute to determine a timetable and where we will be hit. The impact craters will be impressive. Even with the debris on the other side of the Jovian planets, I speculate, based on their size and number of strikes, that nothing will survive on our planet's surface. I am also concerned based on the timing of this collision that Earth may be in the line of impact. Venus should be clear and the Sun will easily protect Terra," the Keeper said.

"That's ironic. The least habitable planet is safely

protected behind the sun while Earth's monsters rule the planet, but … if a series of meteors large enough to wipe out the species but not destroy the atmosphere struck … it would give a narrow opening to transport mammalian life to Earth after the initial fallout."

"The gravitational disturbances could affect Terra's orbit as well as ours. They could alter the planetary axis as well, changing the climates and biosphere of each planet in unique ways."

"Yes … the effects of a massive impact may eliminate the dinosaurs and provide an opportunity for new, more viable sapient life similar to our own," Janus said.

"Architect Iris will take full advantage of that," the master computer added.

"But no rodents or fungi … please tell Hades to spare the planet." He turned from the balcony and marched to the center of his office, wondering if his sarcasm would be lost on the computer. "If your data collection is complete, please simulate the destruction of the Gemini planets with a projection of debris field, trajectory and the inner and outer planets' orbits," he said.

Within seconds, the architect's simple office mutated into a star field with the planetary bodies of Earth, Mars and Venus in position around the sun while images of the Jovian planets, Jupiter and Saturn with all of their moons, hovered in front of him. Just beyond them, two small planets close in mass to Mercury and in different orbital planes looked as if they would miss a collision. A sudden explosion of light sent a shock wave of debris in all directions.

"The energy released from their collision is impressive," Janus said.

"Yes."

"And based on the positioning of the Jovian planets, most of the debris will strike Jupiter and Saturn."

"But not all of the debris. Those planets' mass will pull in a substantial portion, but Earth, Venus and our world are exposed."

"And Terra is behind the sun." "Yes."

"Maybe just enough debris ... end simulation," Janus said. The solar system dissolved around him and, once again, he stood in a simple office. After a moment of reflection, he strode to one of the desks.

"Based on your rate of walking and accelerated heart rate and blood pressure, I am guessing that you are revisiting transforming Earth based on the possibility that its life might be destroyed?" the Keeper asked.

"Yes."

"It is possible that should the dinosaurs survive, they might evolve into sapience, similar to mammals."

"Possible. But, based on computer projections, I believe Earth's atmosphere is slowly choking them into extinction. This cataclysmic event could clear the planet for another attempt for another species," he said as ideas flooded his mind.

When Janus stepped in front of his workstation, four monitors emerged from below the desk: and two keyboards and two stacked tablets appeared from a concealed drawer.

Simultaneously, the other desks revealed various sized monitors, elaborate displays of key tasks and holographic images suspended in space. He looked at each screen in turn. They recognized his retina and gaze, and started sorting through various programs.

"Right now those carnivorous monsters will destroy everything that is smaller and unarmed. And while Terra might be out of harm's way from asteroids and the debris field, the heliosynchronous orbit that keeps it out of Earth's view might change in the course of millions of years. But that's for you to see should you and the other Keepers survive," he said absently as numbers and equations flooded his head.

"Sadly, unless I am able to perfectly titrate the cryogenic plasma solution, preserving you and the others for that long will be impossible. I will need a DNA sample when you have a chance. You do not much care for these dinosaurs, especially the carnivorous ones. You know they did not evolve from our rodents?" the Keeper said with more than an inflection of humor; something Janus would have considered thoroughly had he more time.

But why does she need a DNA sample?

"Yes, I don't care much for dinosaurs or rodents. And we only have three days before we're destroyed, so we'd better get started."

His hands flew between the keyboards and the monitors flashed with different graphs, equations, columns of numbers and maps. Images changed with a look at the monitor and a gesture of his eyes.

"Of course, if you leave now, you would be able to see the project through after our demise and keep the novice architects focused on their duties for years to come," the Keeper said.

"I'm impressed with your persistence." *Though not surprised*, Janus smiled at the fact that his master computer said nothing in response.

"If the stasis chamber works, I might be revived someday to see the results first hand," Janus said to fill the void, while considering the material he needed to figure out his ecological problem.

"Perhaps, should the stasis chambers, underground power sources, control mechanisms, and the planet's crust survive the impacts."

Janus began to draw up plans for a Keeper on Earth.

"I will leave if you do, Keeper."

"You know I am unable to leave this world; I am a part of it. While there can be records and images of me, I cannot be removed and relocated due to my connection to Mars."

"And that's the same reason I will stay. My roots are here, on Mars, in this room, with you, doing my work. Even in certain death there is hope for new life."

"I assume your response is an emotional construct that is not amenable to logical debate," the Keeper said.

"You are accurate." The Master Architect thought of yet another opportunity that could spring from the approaching disaster.

Present Day – A Few Years Ago

Chapter One

Fact is Stranger than Fiction - Earth

Life is really simple, but we insist on making it complicated - Confucius

This is such bullshit! Andrea Perez thought. Arms and legs folded, Perez had spent two hours sitting in a twelve by twelve spartan interview room with two silent federal agents. The growls of her hunger pangs pierced the silence, and she regretted not eating her chocolate glazed donut or the cinnamon muffin before she'd set her experiment. The simple experiment had involved light beams, prisms, ice, and new experimental holographic equipment sent by MIT. While it had taken hours to set up, the test would have taken only twenty seconds to complete had the school's dean not shown up with the department chair and three agents flashing badges and spewing the words 'national security.' She hadn't thought to take her food on the way out. It didn't seem like a viable option at the time, and it wasn't as if she were in any danger of starvation.

At least she had her good lab coat on; the others were too small and stained with everything from grit and oil to pizza sauce.

The doorknob turned for the first time in two hours, and Perez spun around, eager to hear a voice, any voice, but preferably one that would tell her what was going on. So far, she'd only had the sound of the fluorescent lights and her stomach to keep her company. An older man in full military dress entered the room.

"Dr. Perez? Thank you for waiting. I know this is a little out of the ordinary, but I think after the meeting you'll understand the necessity."

Tall, physically fit and with very nice blue eyes, 'older' may have been too much. *Seasoned maybe; mature.*

"Let me guess: national security reasons."

"Exactly."

"What's really going on here?" Perez demanded as she stood.

"You don't have the right to hold me. Why did these guys take me out of my lab?"

"I know it must seem odd to you."

"No … why would it be odd? Three FBI dudes show up at my lab, flash their badges and whisk me away. And the dean and department head just keep saying 'don't worry,' as they wave me off. Who are you people, and what do you want?"

"Please, Dr. Perez…"

"I'm not a doctor! I'm a doctoral student. What the hell?"

The soldier held up his hands as if surrendering.

"Okay. Please sit down, Ms. Perez, and I'll explain everything."

Perez stopped and consciously unclenched her fists and jaw. She took a deep breath and sat. Another loud, protracted hunger pain broke the silence. After two hours of sitting in a small, blank office with two silent FBI men who were totally unresponsive to any questions, her blood was boiling. An image of her dad flashed in her mind along with a sudden sense of concern. He was a military man who practiced clinical work with the Veterans Administration.

"Does this have something to do with my dad? What do you want from him? He's had enough shit happen and doesn't need to be pulled into anything you people have to offer."

Perez sat away from the small table with her arms folded and her legs crossed; her body language made it clear she was not happy to be in the room. The officer shook his head and sat on the chair opposite her, then took off his cap and pulled his seat into the desk. He made eye contact with the FBI agents and they moved towards the door. Perez locked her eyes on the new arrival and spoke in an even, sarcastic tone.

"Hey, guys? Thanks for the conversation. Let's do it again soon."

To their credit, they left the room as silent as they had been for hours.

Who the hell are these people? Tension tightened her

shoulders, neck and arms. Even her face felt tight.

"Again, I apologize for the secrecy and the strange way we had to move, but it was necessary to ensure that we secure your work so you can continue ..." the man said.

"I'm not talking to you or anyone until I have a name and a clear explanation of why I was brought here against my will and without reason. I want to know, right now." She kept her tone low and calm, but anger laced every word.

"I will explain everything, Ms. Perez. As crazy as it will sound, I'll tell you everything, but please let me finish before you ask any questions. Once you hear everything, you'll have to figure out what questions to ask, because once you find out what's going on, you'll grab your balls."

Perez's eyes widened at the mention of what she would grab, and she fought to keep a smirk off her face.

The officer's face flushed and he spoke quickly to recover his equanimity.

"My name is Lieutenant Colonel David Farrell. I run the communication, spectrographic analysis and guidance division of NASA's space exploration and the search for intelligent life. My job covers a lot of areas, and I work with a lot of brilliant scientists around the world—China, Russia, India, and any other country, no matter how small, that has a telescope, computer and bright people."

Spectrographic analysis? There's a whole department that looks at light? And here I thought I was the only nut looking at it.

"As you can imagine, working on such areas with

different governments can be difficult, but in this case it's necessary." Farrell broke eye contact and looked at his hands. Perez noticed the change, something her father always told her to look for when people were talking.

Was it a mark of anxiety, or an indication that he was hiding something?

"You know, Ms. Perez, we live in a world of dualities. On one hand, we have technology that can pick up chemical compositions of planets outside our solar system, and we can now grow and transplant human organs. There are space probes in deep, interstellar space, and we can tell when and how many times our planet wobbles on its axis," he said, still looking at his hands.

"At the same time," he continued, "there's a cult in Ireland who believe there are aliens living among us. In another part of the world, we have a madman who's president of a powerful country looking to retake former territories in an effort to rebuild an empire. Finally, we have a pandemic of religious violence to determine once and for all whose god is the most just and benevolent."

Perez frowned. Confusion, a feeling she loathed, and frustration at his digression replaced her anger.

"What does this have to do with me?"

Farrell held up his hand to stop her. It did, but he stayed silent for a few seconds before he spoke again.

"Ever since Galileo looked at the stars, we knew there were other worlds out there. Other giant minds came, and they were able to pinpoint where we fell in our constellation, how our planet's orbit affected our world, and where to look for new discoveries. When the space age started, we led the charge into space. The *Apollo* missions, *Luna 16, Mariner 10, Spirit* and *Opportunity, Voyager, Messengers, New Horizons*, all of them, and many more you and the public don't know about, all set out to chart, investigate and discover everything at our front door and beyond. When we look out, there are so many possibilities in other galaxies. And when we look close to home, we find that Mars once held an atmosphere and water, and a couple of moons near Jupiter and Saturn hold possibilities for life. Nothing else, or so we thought." Farrell's voice trailed off as if he were thinking of something to add.

Perez listened to every word, so focused on what he said that her body unfurled and leaned on the desk towards him, waiting for him to continue.

"Over the past thirty-five years, we've picked up unusual variations in our orbit and other small changes in Mars and Venus. They were minute at first but clearly there. In the last ten years, this variation has become predictable, measurable, and clearly indicative that a large body of something out there is affecting our planet's orbit. Nothing dangerous, but clearly there is another factor, on a planetary scale."

The room fell silent. Perez noted her shallow breathing, took a deep breath, and shook her head as if to break some kind of spell. "No way! Are you drunk? Is this some kind of psychological game or an elaborate joke Dr. Vincent came up with?" Perez wiped a hand across her suddenly hot and sweaty brow.

Farrell continued as if she had said nothing.

"Fifteen years ago, a series of probes and satellites were sent to specific coordinates to observe this disturbance. That's after we reviewed millions of images, new and old, from all the probes, missions, and satellites from every country capable of space flight. We found nothing, or rather we *saw* nothing, nothing visual occupying the space we pinpointed. Direct observation was initiated and the *Veritas* probes were launched. When the first one got to its designated location, we lost all contact. When the second and third got into place, all seemed to work well until they initiated spectral analysis and x-rays, then they went dark. The third probe did send back data, and for just a nanosecond we thought we had something, but then some kind of computer glitch happened, and the data was lost. The fourth *Veritas* probe blew up on the launch pad," Farrell added more to himself than to her.

"You're not joking, are you?" "No. No, I'm not."

Holy shit ...

Farrell looked at her. "We re-routed a couple of satellites and old probes to our mystery disturbance, but they experienced some kind of problem or their data was useless for some reason or other. China and Russia experienced the same problems. And now, for the last eight years, the internet is alive with chat groups and forums talking about 'Planet X' on the far side of the sun."

"They're in on this too?"

"Yup. They got similar results."

"Jesus ..."

"The South Koreans successfully launched their own probe. They were able to shoot a light beam in the general direction of the anomaly and got a measure of curvature before it went dark."

"Curvature? The light bent?"

"Yes. The light's particles curved as if affected by a large planetary body. When the curvature of the light beam was measured, it was extrapolated that only a planet larger than Earth would have the gravity to do that."

Stunned, Perez looked directly at Farrell. He held her gaze and continued.

"We have another set of probes getting ready to launch in the next four years with an array of spectrograph equipment and an unparalleled number of telescopes and measuring devices. In addition, we're establishing a manned launch so we can have direct human observation. All of this in spite of a major economic downturn, a recession that will dwarf the Great Depression. We are doing this as we exit two wars, and the danger from terrorism and maniacal leaders lurks everywhere. A world of dualities."

"If all our satellites, probes and shit haven't been able to see it or snap an image, what will sending people to observe do?" Perez's anxiety had kicked into high gear, and sweat broke out on her forehead, armpits and small of her back.

"We're not going to just look for it. We're beyond that now. Everything points to something being out there. And whatever it is, a massive asteroid, planetoids, moon or whatever, we're going to land on it and bring a piece of whatever it is home."

"You're going to … to land on an invisible planet?"

"There's something out there. If it's real, we can land on it."

Perez blinked. Her eyes and throat felt dry. It might have been only two minutes of silence, but it seemed longer before Perez continued.

"There can't be another planet in our solar system. We'd have seen it. It's just not possible."

"I've been doing this job for too long, Ms. Perez. There's been a lot of smart people, a huge amount of money and technology thrown at this, and yet the mathematics and physics don't lie: there is something as big as a planet on the other side of our Sun that's ducking us. And when I mean it's ducking us, I mean it's actively hiding. Either it exists at a spectrum of light we just don't see naturally or it's artificially created to keep us from seeing it."

"No, no, no … Now you're talking science fiction, or an advanced civilization or technologically gifted species that's hanging out in our solar system. Come on!"

"Absolutely, Ms. Perez, and it's here, too, on Earth."

"What? It can't be…"

"It's all true. When we've been able to get data to our servers and computers, there's always some kind of data incompatibility issue or information degradation that makes the information, images, everything useless. And government sponsored projects to advance surveillance have had their imaging and spectrograph equipment destroyed, hindered, or blocked. Ultimately, their plans disappear or are so badly altered that they too are useless."

Perez held up her hands as if trying to slow the conversation and its inevitable train wreck.

"Colonel, what you're saying is … well, it's just too incredible. I mean, it means there's some kind of world just beyond our line of sight that's able to bend light waves so it's invisible. And now you're saying there's some kind of conspiracy as well. That someone's messing with our technology to make sure we don't see what's there." Saying it all out loud did not make it sound less crazy as Perez had hoped.

"Do you hear yourself?"

"Sure do. Have for years. It takes a while to believe, but when you and others say the same thing all the time, it becomes as real as it gets."

"A conspiracy on Earth too?"

He answered without hesitation.

"Absolutely. All your notes, designs, and all electronically-stored documentation of your project disappeared this morning."

Perez was on her feet in milliseconds. *Years of research, thousands of hours work, all gone!*

"What? Are you bullshitting me! That's not remotely funny!"

To Farrell's credit, he remained calm and still, and allowed the burst of emotion to pass as if he had been in that very situation before. After a moment, he nodded and motioned for her to sit down. Once she'd settled and her heart rate had slowed,

he spoke in the therapeutic tone her father had used to calm his clients.

"Yes, Ms. Perez. All your work saved on the university's server system, external backup system and cloud started to degrade into an unintelligible mess or disappear altogether. Since we've been monitoring your work, we saw it happening, re- routed and manually inputted some of your backup files to old thumb drives. We also dispatched the local bureau to pick you up before anything happened to you."

Shit.

Farrell looked at his hands again.

"What do you mean?" Perez asked. "What happens to the people that do what I do or make advances on this problem?" She sat in her chair with her arms folded over her chest, very aware of her clothes absorbing her sweat.

Again, he replied immediately.

"They disappear, fall off the planet. Even their electronic footprint disappears as if they were never here. Even when they're in protective custody, or witness protections, they still disappear. INTERPOL and Scotland Yard have been all over this for the last three years. The lead guy at Scotland Yard is convinced there's something systemic, so tied into our computer systems that we are missing something."

"Maybe he's wrong ..."

"Bradley? Arthur Bradley from Scotland Yard?

Wrong?" Farrell said with more emotion than she had heard for the entire interview. "Bradley is many things, but he's not wrong here. He's the guy who found the patterns with the computer and people disappearances. No, he's not wrong. I wish he was."

More silence. Throat dry and breathing deeper, Perez thought she would have more questions but only managed one.

"What happens next?"

"We're going to go into the next room where there are a bunch of stenographers using old manual stenotype machines and scientists with pens and pads of paper that are going to write everything you say about your project down. Your work is remarkable and that's why we're moving fast. If the data breach's speed is any indicator, your work may hold the key in seeing the invisible," Farrell replied.

After a moment of silence, Perez could hear the fluorescent light again in addition to her breathing. Her growling hunger pains had gone. "A whole planet? An entire world just outside the visible spectrum?"

"Yup, and that's not the interesting part."

"What? A whole planet next door and we can't see it, and that's not the interesting part? Jesus, Colonel! What's enough to pique your interest?"

"I don't think invisible planets occur naturally. Who's running the technology to make an entire planet invisible and why are they hiding?" Farrell returned to looking at his folded hands.

“What happens to me after I give you everything?”

“You go into witness protection. A place where there’s lots of wheat fields, in the middle of nowhere. No computer or internet. Just books, lots of books if you like.”

Perez sat still. Her world and life had completely changed in mere hours.

Shit.

Present Day

Chapter Two

Dreams Do Come True - Terra

Choose a job you love, and you will never have to work a day in your life. – Confucius

Cold rain washed over Andrea Perez. She stood, feeling chilled and drenched, in the middle of a cornfield with her slipper-clad feet sinking into the mud. A huge, black bird-shaped ship hovered silently mere feet above the ground. Three small females stood before her. Their sleek black jumpsuits seemed at odds with their large jaws, sloping foreheads, and broad faces.

"Obviously, we are not from around here," the redhead said.

"I thought aliens would have really big heads and speak telepathically?"

"Why do Earthers say that when it is clear that they are the giants? But enough. For you to be safe, we must go," the woman said. No coercion, no force, just a statement.

Still, she hesitated.

"Safe? From who? Farrell?"

"No, not him. He is determined and committed to the truth, but he means you no harm. Others are not like him. And if we were able to find you with ease, they surely will."

"My dad? He'll be alone?"

"No, he will not. He understands and wishes you well. He will join you but not before his work is done."

"What work?"

"Preparing Earth for the truth. We need your help as well."

"Why me?"

"Our holographic emitters are failing. We need your help."

Reassured, Perez smiled and approached the ship's extended ramp with confidence. "I'll miss the rain," she said.

Why will I miss the rain … there's no rain on Terra? Lightning. Ice. Caves. Underground … There's only rain on Earth. I'm not on Earth.

Perez's consciousness returned as her recurring dream of her last day on Earth faded. She sat up, jolted to the present. She'd had far too many mushrooms and 'special' cabbage dishes that, though they filled her quickly, made her very sleepy. After years of combining those two foods, she should expect such dreams.

Perez blinked and stretched in her seat. She'd fallen asleep at her work station in her small quarters. A series of old blueprints for terraform equipment that had been converted to energy for the Terran community's life support systems and holographic emitters lay on the table. The first thing she'd done when she'd arrived was to recommend periods of taking the cloaking field offline when Earth satellites and probes weren't around. She found it ironic that she was one of the key conspirators on a hidden planet that Farrell had alluded to so many years ago. Now, fully awake in the present, she noticed a water stain where her head had been, right beside her empty plate and cup. She wiped her mouth. Yes, she'd drooled as she slept.

"Now, that's really unattractive," she muttered.

Though still dressed in her plain brown slacks, and black and reddish tunic, she wanted to pull off her shoes and crawl into bed just feet away. Her quarters had been built for women of less than five foot three; she was lucky to have two rooms and her own semi-private bathroom with attached bathing area.

"Just when you thought college dorm life was bad."

Her knife, affixed at her waist, gave her the feeling that she had to be somewhere else—she only took a weapon when leaving her quarters. She glanced at the piles of large books, tablets, and paper charts stacked like pyramids around the room. A flash of Terra's spinning molten core, unusual on a tidal-locked planet, popped into her head. She often wondered how a still planet could generate such a powerful magnetic field solely by the planet's core. It was fascinating how Terra's spacecraft used magnetic fields for landings and launches.

"Wait! The launch! Crap!"

Perez raced out the door and into the narrow common hall in a bid to make her appointed time. Low lights ensconced and scattered throughout the residence core allowed her to see and wave back to her neighbors and coworkers, who all lived next to each other in a honeycomb structure made of stone.

"Late for another meeting, Perez?" an unusually large-jawed woman said with an even larger grin.

"Thanks for overstating the obvious, Hydra!"

She wove in and out of small pockets of people, all with pale white skin and dark brown eyes. Being a full head taller than her new peers made her stick out in a crowd, and even after all her years here, she still wasn't used to her lean body. If she exercised as Clematis had suggested, she would become even fitter, could perhaps even become an athlete. Once the first of three flights of stairs came into view, she no longer needed signs to guide her through the elaborate community. She sprinted up the staircase as a siren began to screech. The sound of spinning turbines and other machinery hummed constantly throughout the subterranean world, and periodic sirens marked changes of shifts, announcements, and, rarely, warnings. This siren proclaimed a shift change that meant in a few seconds mobs of people would fill the corridors, preparing either to arrive for their shift or to go home, eat, dance or hunt. Her breath grew ragged and her leg muscles tightened with the effort, but she was determined not to miss her meeting.

"Not again … I swear I won't hear the end of it."

A group of scientists, identified by their green sashes, gathered just ahead of her. They waved their tablets and spoke with great enthusiasm, while just behind her, another group carried sharpened spikes, spears and other edge weapons for a hunt.

"You'd think … that with all the advanced technology … they'd have invented elevators or escalators," she gasped while running up her third flight of stairs. Though not completely out of breath yet, her hope that she'd reach Legate Legionis Clematis and Dux Cloelius dwindled.

I bet they're already gone. What the hell, Perez. Lay off the vegetables and mushrooms!

Despite almost fifteen years of acclimating to her new home, Terra's gravity still strained her human body. Terra was only slightly larger than Earth, considered by most of her peers as negligible, but they didn't have to live with the change for the rest of their lives. She wondered if she'd live beyond a hundred like these people—more time to learn more languages, origins and maybe even find a new power source for the emitters.

Perez, comfortable now with the array of edged weapons and firearms they carried nearly all the time in their subterranean world, dodged more clusters of females clad in various browns, black and reddish colors. Her own knife bounced against her hip.

Damn! Forgot my sidearm again! I'll regret that one of these days.

She entered a larger space brightened by light reflected

through large skylights. Unique markets, food dispensaries, drinking establishments and places to sit lined the sides of a wide foyer. Though reminiscent of the old markets of Earth, the ornate, colorful sculptures, free standing or embedded in large stone archways, resembled those of ancient Rome. But while ancient Rome had fallen on Earth, here, Rome's origins and life remained commonplace.

So much to still learn still, she thought as she sidestepped a group of adolescents and avoided crashing into a weapons rack. Edged weapons were so familiar in public that she hardly noticed the first aid kits, fire extinguishers, atmosphere alarms, and racks of knives for killing the planet's large rodents.

I really have to learn more maneuvers, she thought as she continued her jaunt past more newly installed racks. The monsters had become more brazen recently. Finally, she saw the two women. They'd stopped to wait for her in the congested walkways. She realized that with an entire civilization built underground—three level structures on the surface and three below the crust—elevators for people were not really necessary. Feeling as tall as a giraffe in the land of lions, she could easily spot the Terran-Earth mixed children. Even as adolescents, they were taller than the native Terran. Perez enjoyed her transition into a society that valued height and strength almost as much as teaching and learning. As a scientist and an ambassador from Earth, she held the title of Immunes, a direct derivation from Latin meaning a soldier with at least one specialization.

Her pink sash, one of five on the whole planet, indicated the high regard in which they held her—a scientist responsible for fixing a failing cloaking system for the planet.

New arrivals from different parts of Terra looked sideways at her; even though the proportions of her limbs and trunk were nearly identical to theirs, they perceived her Earthly thick build and short stature as thin and tall. Her thick, dark-brown hair, which fell below her shoulders, was truly an anomaly among the shorter red-haired women and the few Terran men. Her narrower head with a corresponding jaw, higher cheek bones and an average human skull with its high forehead all differed from her Terran counterparts with their heavier brows, sloping foreheads, and flatter craniums that jutted out more towards the back of the neck.

But what really turned heads was her brown skin, signifying her heritage from Earth's sub-Saharan Africa, along with her European-genus blue eyes. These features indicated that she came from a world where one could be in the sun without fear of immediately dying.

"In the land of the blind, the one-eyed giant will be king, "she remembered her dad often said. *I wonder if this is about him. Have they moved up the plans? It really would be great to see him sooner than later.*

Finally, she stood before the women and bent over to catch her breath. Her original assessment of being out of shape dissolved as she realized she'd run at least a mile in about nine minutes. Back on Earth when she was out of shape, she could've run half a mile in the same time, then would've promptly thrown up.

Legate Legionis Clematis and Dux Cloelius looked up from their stone-like tablets, one green and the other purple.

"Minor Perez! We are so happy you made it." It hadn't taken Perez long to get used to the title 'minor' meaning younger. They referred to her dad as seniores. *He'd hate that.*

"You must have run to catch us. But I see you have neglected your sidearm. That is dangerous," Clematis said with a smile as she put her tablet in her tunic and planted her hands akimbo.

Cloelius produced a canteen of water and offered it to Perez. Clematis nodded in approval. Perez straightened and took the canteen.

"But … but you never carry a firearm … only knives …" she said between gasps of breath.

"That is because I've been battle tested. I killed two rattus with one spike and a spear. No need for me or Cloelius to carry a firearm. Someday, you will face the challenge, and it will be decided then," she said enthusiastically.

Perez drank the opaque liquid, a salty-sweet syrup mixture that both quenched thirst and gave energy.

"I … must … catch my breath … first."

She focused on her breathing and pushed the thoughts of large rats, or rattus as Terrans often called them, out of her head. I think I'll stick to walking in well-lit, well-populated areas before I take that challenge, she thought.

"You are a special one, Perez. But we must go. The launch dance is already in progress, and the Centurions and Milites have already boarded *Silent Star Falling*. They await our arrival." Clematis began their mile trek to the launch bay with Cleolius, Perez and other high-ranking officials in tow.

"There must have been a change in plans for the mission to be moved ahead to now." Perez handed Cloelius's canteen back with a thank-you nod and fell into step with the smaller officers, one a general and the other a leader, though she was still not sure who was who.

The military here had rank and order but no saluting, barking orders, or rigid behavior. Military order was somehow inbred as prescribed and predictable behaviors, part of their nature as a species. They had no need to remind each other.

Her father would love it here—a clinical person's dream come true. He would wish he'd pursued that anthropology course he started ... Her mind hit a dark wall. Her smile faded and her heart sank as her last memories of her mother and brother flooded her mind. Years after their deaths, her father had finally pulled out of his depression and attended some anthropology courses at a local college, something her mom had done when she was younger.

"Do not grieve, Perez. The Keeper of Atlantis believes she can ensure safe passage for your father to the extraction zone. She is just being cautious in moving it up. She wants to make sure she gets the supplies to us even though we have what we need for probably centuries to come. Nonetheless, I do hope she has provided your planet's chestnuts in the cargo. They are remarkable! How you humans simply let them grow on trees and fall to the ground is beyond me."

"Thank you for your reassurance." Perez followed the women through the crowd of people who stood or sat around the foyer, talking, laughing or singing in groups. Some peered into their own uniquely-colored tablets, and some told stories as they sharpened their weapons and drank a version of coffee.

They walked past multiple shops, but Perez no longer looked away from the skinned rattus hides that hung near the market place. Scaled tails with sharp edges at the ends, and their size—as large as dogs—distinguished them from the common Earth rat. They lived underground and were not only the primary source of meat protein but also, and more importantly, hunting them provided a way to prove yourself and advance in station and rank. Most Terran citizens survived their hunt for the *norvegicus rattus*, but some fell to the packs and never returned. And sometimes, the creatures would come up to the foyers and take a child or unsuspecting Terran. Hence, everyone always carried weapons. You could count on two things with Terrans: hunting and dancing, with rituals to match for every situation.

Just as you'd expect from cave dwellers!

"I wonder why you Terrans love chestnuts so much,"

Perez said.

"Does it have something to do with your Earthly ancestors? A kind of DNA-loaded thing that still lingers?"

"I do believe you're right, Perez," Cloelius replied thoughtfully. Her expression indicated there was more to come.

"There are many references made of them in the ancient articles, and our own Keeper has thoroughly explained what they are and the role they played in our development. Sadly, like so many things we left behind, chestnuts, bark and lemons … dogs are the ones I think we all miss the most."

Lemons? Yuck!

"Not being outside? Being stuck in these caverns? I thought that would be the thing you'd miss the most?" Perez asked.

Clematis took her time answering, just as all Terrans did.

"Maybe the open fields for the hunt, too, and tracking the herds, chasing them and finally capturing them. The rattus hiding in the depths of the caverns are not the same, for sure. But then the Keeper reminds us that there are places on the Earth where it is very cold, and the elements harsh, yet the Earthers live on the surface rather than embedded in the ground. I love it when our cloaking field is off, and we can view powerful storms from our underground world in safety, comfort and peace. And where day and light collide on the surface, we can watch Terra's beautiful twilight with wind and fire on the day side, and ice and lightning on the night side … just glorious! A perfect place."

"Except for the rats." Perez felt for her sheathed knife as she eyed a very large rodent skin and tail hanging near a stove— possibly five feet long, with a full snout of teeth in its skull and an additional four feet of tail—truly a monster rat from hell.

Vile and disgusting.

"Yes, except for them. Cunning, smart and clever," Clematis said with a smile.

Perez nodded and pushed the rodent image from her mind's eye. They navigated around even more people on the cavern's third story arboretum—an open design supported by huge stone columns and flavored by the smell of cooked meat and vegetables wafting up from the open market below. The increasing number of teenage males intermingling with the larger number of young women surprised and pleased Perez. The boys' reddish, dark hair and taller stature, the expected result of cross-breeding, made them easy to pick out. Efforts to replenish the male species seemed to be progressing better than expected.

The purplish sunlight of the never-ending Terran twilight filtered in from the narrow skylights above. With the planet tidal-locked with its sun, the inhabitable zone on planet Terra stretched across the longitudinal equator of perpetual day and night. Perez had been in one of the few places on the planet where one could look over the surface, and the perfect positioning of the few exposed, low-lying buildings to seize solar energy for powering the holographic emitters had impressed her. Failing millions of years old machinery, not lack of sunlight, caused the problem.

Perez never thought she would miss day and night, but she did—rain too. She wondered what the Terrans would do if they experienced the total light of day and the darkness of night. She remembered that they'd really liked the rain.

"The Keeper asked us to bring extra rations for eight people, especially dried meat and fish products and preserves," Clematis said.

"It saddens me that the Keeper will continue to stay on Earth even to the end. Her action is consistent with the Great Keeper. Unfortunately, her rationale does make sense. Of all the humans on your planet, she is sure your father has found one that can help the Earthers understand their predicament and maybe even our existence." Clematis helped Cloelius open the heavy doors that led to the busy walkway to the launch pad.

Heavy drums beating in the distance echoed through the cavern, and the closer they approached the next vaulted cavern, the louder it got.

Seriously … Dancing and drums?

"I hope to talk to the Keeper, and my father, someday. But I suppose I'll need to take the journey to earn my own stone tablet, with my own color, I presume, before I can do that," Perez said.

Clematis smiled and nodded. "I suspect that your own

curiosity and need to know will propel you on your journey without you even knowing it. You have been on many journeys and paths with your work and searching, but I think there is yet a bigger one you harbor."

Perez nodded as if she understood everything Clematis said, but she wished the Terrans would speak bluntly.

Why the riddles?

"It will be good to see my father, though, after all these years."

Near the entrance to the launch pad, a group of soldiers and scientists moved in rhythm with the music, holding knives, swords and other spear-like weapons above their heads.

With the clash of modern technology and primal music, Perez was surprised not to find a roaring fire pit with one of those rodents cooking on a spit …

Yuck! Now that's an image I have to get out of my head. Good job, Perez!

Cloelius stopped at the opening to the launch bay.

"I understand that your father has thoroughly embraced our natural diet and habits and can make this trip, though he still has difficulty with keeping step and dancing. Still, his ability to lift his own weight and to square off with Centurion Dea Data at his seasoned age is impressive, especially on Earth with all those poisons, distractions and dangers."

The humming and circular dancing of the families, soldiers, and scientists overshadowed even the powerful resonance of the beating drums. A group of Terran humans dressed in plain uniforms performed a tribal dance with edged weapons in hand, while a huge black spaceship in the shape of a raven stood on a launch pad in the middle of a cavern supported by huge stone columns. Pyramid-shaped buildings two to three stories high filled with still more scientists and flight specialists surrounded the ship. They held an uncanny resemblance to the significantly larger pyramids of Earth's Egypt, and she'd seen similar structures throughout Terra and along the terminal line on the surface. The Terrans had housed their holographic emitters in the same simple design, perfect for surviving the violent weather—fierce winds, explosive lightning, and constant thunder—of the tidal-locked planet. If it wasn't for the planet's powerful magnetic field, the surface of the planet would have long since been destroyed by solar winds and space debris.

"Perez?" Clematis said. "You have noticed these structures before and yet you have done no research as to their origin and why they appear on both your worlds."

Perez turned to face the woman and smiled at her words, confirmation that the Terrans truly accepted her as part of their world.

"You know, it'd be easier to simply tell me the origin of our worlds. Your practice of having your young and curious seek out their answers from the library themselves doesn't seem efficient, especially when I have no stone to access the Keeper." Perez tried to drown out the drums and public announcements. She already knew the answer Clematis would provide. Still, Perez enjoyed the shock she gave when she made such a bold statement.

"And deprive you and the curious of their journeys? Simply tell you? That confounds the process of truth. It would be quite a disservice to hinder one's natural growth that way. If we were at war or in danger, then it makes sense. But we have not been at war for thousands of years because each of us takes our own path to finding our place. We go as far as we wish, but we all go; we are not told. And based on my experience of you, Perez, I suspect you will go very far in your journey. If we have learned anything from the Earthers, it is that they do not do well with letting mysteries lie. They seek the truth at all costs—good for the seekers who stay on the path. The knowledge, however, is lost on those who simply observe without the benefit of taking the road to understanding." Clematis smoothed her tunic and adjusted her weapons, obviously preparing herself for something important.

"So I have to find my own answers … just like my dad would always say," Perez said.

"Yes."

Suddenly embarrassed that she had been on Terra for fifteen years and had learned only about its unique history, Perez decided to find out not just the origins of Terra and the planet's connection to Earth but also the origins of *everything* in her solar system, and to do it well before her father arrived. She tried to cut herself some slack; after all, she was a stranger in a new, undiscovered world far from home and needed to find her place. She remembered her shock and awe when Lieutenant Colonel David Farrell had first told her of the possibility so many years ago … *I wonder how he's doing. I bet he'd like it here—kind of his type of people.*

"So be it," Perez said, more to herself than to Clematis.

Her friend turned to her and smiled as widely as her large jaw would allow. The size of the Terran's jaw and teeth still amazed Perez. *No wonder they could eat chestnuts like peanuts.*

"Excellent! So you are beginning yet another journey. Great things you will find. Difficult at first but wonderful once you see the tapestry of it all." Clematis took a deep breath and walked towards the front of the waiting ship.

Perez looked back for Cloelius and found her in the middle of one of the dancing rings. At the base of the ship, the centurion, captain of the vessel, stretched out her hands and cried, "*Datum est verbum?*"

Is the word given? Perez understood the phrase as requesting permission to depart.The centurion waited dutifully in her dark-red flight suit while the din of the drums and Terran voices escalated. Clematis stretched her arms above her head and belted out the expected phrase: "*Datur est verbum!*" *The word has been given.*

With that, the drums increased even more, the centurion retreated onto the ramp below the bird-shaped ship, and it closed as the launch pad's heavy mechanical gears and hydraulics slowly lifted the ship to the ceiling of the cavern, hundreds of feet above them.

Unbelievable … this never gets old.

The huge black ship rose silently in the air, looking like

a falcon waiting to fly. After just a few minutes, while the dancing and drumming escalated even further, two large doors opened above the cavern. Wind flowed inside until the bottom of the launch pad sealed the opening with a loud clunk, leaving the ship on the surface. A minute later, the roar of engines carried through the reinforced metal launch pad and drowned out the sounds of drums and humans.

Cloelius came up behind her. "Perez? The pad will remain at the surface for a couple of hours to ensure that fuel residue, flames and vapors are cleared away by the atmosphere above."

A public announcement broke through the din, and the drumming and dancing stopped. "*Qui me fecit, stella cadens circulum. Deinde cum dicit: quod stella cadens tacita consequi orbis!*"

A burst of cheers erupted and the drumming and dancing resumed. Perez took her time to translate the literal meaning in her head: "Mission Leader, Leader Ennius reports that *Silent Star Falling* has achieved orbit. Repeat: *Silent Star Falling* has achieved orbit.' It is a great day for us all."

Perez glanced around. Everyone was getting into the music and dancing. She joined in, but struggled to keep in step with the shorter, red-headed, pale-skinned, dark-eyed Terrans. *Latin, German, French … those were easy to learn. But dancing? I need more practice.*

Chapter Three

Ashes to Ashes—Earth

Our greatest glory is not in never falling, but in rising every time we fall. – Confucius

"…Yours in the Kingdom and the Power and the Glory, I of the Father, and of the Son, and of the Holy Spirit; both now and ever, and to the ages of ages. Amen."

Roberta Joanne Riesman refocused her attention to the priest's prayer. With so many prayers in a period of three hours, she had lost herself in thought.

"I knew so many things about him," she said softly. At forty-five, it wasn't her first funeral, not by a long shot, but it was the longest she'd ever experienced and the closest she'd endured in a long time.

"…Glory to the Father and to the Son and to the Holy Spirit. You are our God, who went down to Hades, to loosen the pains of the dead that were there; Give rest also to the soul of Your servant, O Savior …"

She sniffled. There were so many things she didn't know about him.

Other wakes and funerals had moved her with their stories of a wonderful life, or a young soldier taken too soon. Last week, three firefighters in Yellowstone.

And next week? Does it matter?

Her shoes sank in the moist grass. Dark skies hung about her with no likelihood of clearing. The empty trees, muffled sounds of restrained sobs and coughs made everything so real. For any other funeral, she could have gone for an early morning run to shake off the pain, but she knew she could run forever and the pain would persist. This was not a normal funeral.

"Hiaki …"

Riesman wondered if the priest swinging incense around the closed casket indicated the end of the service. His low, somber voice drew her in and helped her hope that her lover had found peace. She had not and never would. Never again.

"…O God of all spirits and of every flesh, who did trod down death and overcome the devil, bestowing life on this Your world, to the soul of this Your servant, Hiaki Nakamura, departed this life, to You Yourself, O Lord, give rest in a place …"

Riesman looked beyond the priest to a throng of darkly dressed family members and friends of Dr. Hiaki Nakamura, brilliant mathematician, statistician, and theorist. A mild- mannered soul whose warm gaze, kind eyes and soft smile had melted her heart years ago when he joined her team. After years of working with him, she'd found her vacations annoying and had joined him in the field whenever he headed to a disaster area. His voice, humor, eyes, and touch held her heart with no chance of escape.

He can't ... I just can't believe he's gone.

"...establish the soul of His servant, Hiaki, departed from us, in the testings of the Just; give him rest in the bosom of Abraham; and number him among the Just, through His goodness and compassion as our merciful God." The priest finished with the incense and now held Mrs. Nakamura's hand, consoling her, while she and her two grown daughters stood by the closed casket.

Still monitoring her own breathing, Riesman's hot tears fell again on her cheeks.

She found a well-worn tissue and wiped her eyes beneath her sunglasses. She didn't need them to block out the sun but to cover the bloodshot eyes that would betray the depths of her despair. He'd been more than a friend, just short of a soul mate. The weeping widow and two daughters with their families aroused a mixture of grief and guilt. In an effort to distract herself, she rewound her conversation with her administrative assistant around an hour ago.

He'd reported that the FBI seal flashed across Nakamura's computer screen, denying access. Hiaki's sudden death probably prompted the response. It wasn't unusual for them to confiscate computers when someone from FEMA or Homeland Security died as a result of an accident, but Hiaki's heart attack, while tragic, was of natural causes according to the reports. As to what was on the computer, they had shared more secrets than the average employer-employee, so its loss did not concern Riesman. Suddenly aware that she was staring at the family, she looked away. The priest had finished, and already a long line of people queued to bid their last farewell. If she hadn't been his boss, she would have left immediately.

You deserve better than that, Hiaki. I just wish we had more time.

One of her aides touched her gently, startling her from her thoughts. He held the umbrella for her and, with a nod, gestured her to move.

"Thank you, Peter."

Her aides and protection detail were quiet, respectful, and, most of the time, invisible. Just as she liked it. She wiped her eyes and cheeks again and scanned the surroundings. Many people, dressed similarly to her detail, gave the same impression of being invisible. A man and woman to her left watched an interaction beyond her line of sight. Riesman sighed.

What's the FBI doing here?

Unable to see what they were observing, Riesman reined in her wandering mind and focused on her feet. The wet grass was difficult to navigate, and the warm weather out of place for November in Cambridge, Massachusetts. With every step closer to the casket, her heart slowed and her breath shortened, as if an elephant was sitting on her chest. Riesman tried to shift her thoughts to the climate, to work, to anything but Hiaki and his family just ahead.

Hiaki's smiling face with his caring eyes appeared in front of her.

Why did you leave? Years of super storms, flooding in the mid-west and Texas, volcanic activity in the Pacific Rim, melting polar caps … we were supposed to find the answers … something to do with miscalculating the planets' orbits. Hiaki. Why?

She blinked her eyes, his face melted away, and she realized that she was shaking Hiaki's grieving widow's hand.

"I am so sorry for your loss, Dr. Nakamura. Your husband was a great scientist," Riesman said, unable to look her in the eye, and grateful that her dark glasses hid her shame. The widow's grip surprised her. Mrs. Nakamura gave Riesman a forced smile, then her eyes drifted to the casket.

"Thank you so much, Dr. Riesman, for coming today. Hiaki spoke very highly of you. He was fortunate to have a boss and friend like you for so many years." The widow continued to hold her hand and gaze at the casket. Riesman's mouth tightened and more tears brimmed in her eyes.

Oh God! Please help me!

Unable to say anything or to escape the woman's grip, Riesman's desperation built and her knees grew weaker by the second. Mrs. Nakamura finally released her hand and looked at her.

"I know you can only stay for a short time, so I put you

near the back of the luncheon with some former co-workers. I hope you don't mind." The widow's deep, brown tear-filled eyes swallowed Riesman up.

She fought the urge to flee and forced herself to smile, nod and then repeat the same sentence to everyone else down the family line: "I am so sorry for your loss. Please accept my condolences."

It was the longest three minutes she'd experienced in some time. Her mind was running wild, trying to find some excuse to avoid going to the luncheon, when she caught sight of an older, light-skinned Hispanic man who looked familiar. He stood in the distance engaged in an intense conversation with a well-dressed, regal-looking man. A young woman who might have been his granddaughter stood beside him and held the man's arm.

Riesman moved onto the road to obtain a better vantage point and noticed the two FBI agents watching the men as well. After a moment, she remembered why the man looked so familiar, and had he not been engaged in an argument, she would've run over and given him a huge hug. Suddenly, the couple left. The Hispanic man called after them in a tone laced with hostility—unusual for him from what she remembered.

"We're not done here, *Sir* Pierce."

He made the sarcasm quite clear. Riesman slowed her pace until she was sure she had accurately identified him.

No way! It's impossible!

She stopped around eight feet away and stared at him while others worked their way around her. Other than the

FBI, no one else had noticed the hostile interaction.

"Do you know him, ma'am?" her driver asked.

"Yeah. As I live and breathe, I know him," she replied, pleasantly surprised by the chance meeting. She picked up her pace again and stopped before him. It took him a moment to realize who she was, then his anger evaporated, he smiled, and she embraced her old friend.

"Captain Anthony Perez! I never thought I would find you here! How are you, old man?"

She pulled back to take a better look, surprised at how fit he looked for his age. His arms, chest, and back felt as if they were made of stone. Even his face and neck had the chiseled look of a young man.

"It's been a long time, Bobbie Jo." In a matter of seconds, her old friend's therapeutic voice eased her feelings of emptiness and guilt. She stepped out of his embrace and took him all in—black suit and tie, crisp white shirts, very short black cropped hair with only small patches of white betraying his age.

"Whatever you're doing, I need to get some. I saw you over twenty years ago …"

"Twenty-three years, but who's counting? I've been lucky with good genes and time for exercising."

"And writing too, I hear."

"One published book does not an author make," he said sheepishly.

"Kind of the right thing, in the right place at the right time," he added.

"I bet sales went through the roof when the New York

Times called your work uplifting, enlightening, and thought provoking," Riesman teased.

He nodded and looked down while he walked, his hands thrust into the pockets of his buttoned suit jacket. Even his voice sounded stronger than she remembered.

"That book is about fifteen years old and it was unusually successful. It allowed me an opportunity to forge ahead with a small practice and teaching. Still, you're right. I did find some time per day to exercise, and I eat pretty well."

"Well, it's great to see you in spite of the circumstances."

A sudden onslaught of emotions threatened to consume her, so she tried to find more questions to avoid her sadness. Unfortunately, she stalled as she remembered that Perez's son and wife had been killed in a tragic car accident nearly twenty years ago when he dropped off the map. She thought he had a daughter but was afraid to ask. When his book came out, she'd found the courage to call him. He'd been gracious and kind, but graver than before.

"So, did you know Dr. Nakamura through work?" he asked, just as she was about to ask him the same question.

"Yes. He worked on my team. And how about you?" she asked quickly.

Breathe, Roberta. Just breathe.

"I worked with his wife several years back. A family matter on her side."

Riesman glanced at him. Out of the thousands of discussions in the office, over dinner and breakfast, or in the bedroom, nothing registered about any family member having a mental health issue.

"Are you going to the luncheon? I plan on staying very briefly myself," he asked.

Her driver held her car door open. She still couldn't think of an excuse not to go, but her final answer surprised her.

"Yes."

Perez smiled before walking away.

"I'll see you there, Bobbie Jo."

She watched him go, noting his determined yet relaxed gait and square backside. Though more than two decades had passed since they'd worked together at the Veterans' Administration Hospital, she didn't remember him being so solidly built. The two FBI agents followed him at a distance. While baffled as to why they were following her former boss, his physical appearance struck her as even stranger.

He's got to be late fifties or more. How can he look like he's thirty? I should read his book.

Peter's voice brought her back. "Are we going to the luncheon, ma'am?"

"Yes," she replied as she got into the car.

"Have Diane look at my afternoon schedule, too."

"Yes, ma'am."

After adjusting her nylons, she shed her jacket, wiped her shoes on the car mat, and noted with pleasure that her driver already had the air-conditioning on. Tablets, papers, and folders full of unfinished work spilled from her open brief case and spread across the seat. Now she had one more anomaly to figure out.

What was Perez doing here?

Riesman pulled her mirror, eyeliner and lipstick out of her handbag. After a few minutes of applying makeup, she stopped.

"When you age, you're supposed to look older, right?"

Chapter Four

Sands of an Hour Glass—Earth

The cautious seldom err. - Confucius

"I gather you're not a fan of the man and woman you were talking to?" Riesman took the last bite of her garlic mash potatoes.

"Sir Robert Philip Pierce," Perez said with contempt. "He's a traitor and a miscreant; too good to be so, and too bad to live." He looked out the restaurant's window.

Riesman's eyes widened. Several times during their conversation he'd sounded as if he were reading from a classic book when a simple yes or no would have sufficed. She'd held onto his every word despite the noise of people talking, his quoting, and the three glasses of wine. She picked up her second cup of coffee and blew on it.

"What? He's a miscreant?"

Perez's eyes shone as he slipped into his old teaching mode.

"Sorry, Bobbie Jo, but I have a history with this guy. And I wish I could say I composed that saying, but

William Shakespeare got to it first. I think it was one of the Richards plays, maybe *Richard II.* I'd rather talk about anything but that sack of crap."

"Okay. Then tell me how come you look twenty years younger?"

She'd taken two gulps of coffee before it looked as if he might respond; a surprising length of time to answer what she thought was a simple question.

"What is it? Steroids or something?"

"Nope. I eliminated all processed foods and I've focused on exercise."

Since nothing more followed, Riesman leaned forward and extended her hands, palms up, as if asking, 'Well?'

"No. That's it. Really. I wish there was more."

"There's more, but you're not saying it. Come on, Anthony—I was born at night, but it wasn't last night."

"Do you remember our ward unit's psychologist? She was Indian and always messed up phrases like that. You know, she would say something like, I was born at night, but it was yesterday. Now what was her name…?"

"Stop, Anthony! You're stalling and doing a piss poor job at it too," Riesman said. "Usually, I'm not so vain, but I'm in my mid-forties, and I'm killing myself to stay healthy and looking young. Yes, I said it: looking young. But you look younger than I remember twenty years ago. Not to be biased, and I may be projecting, but for a guy who has to be in his sixties, I would have mistaken you for late thirties."

"Just thirty?"

Riesman put down her coffee, folded her arms, and waited.

"Did I mention that I spend about three hours a day exercising?" he said.

"No way! There is no way you can convince me that exercising every day and eating nothing but natural, unprocessed food has halted your aging, or rather reversed your aging in your case. It's not my first day on the job, Anthony. I'm not that young, impressionable trainee who's just showed up on the admissions' unit, accepting without questioning your word as gospel."

Riesman spoke a little louder than she wanted to. Fortunately, the noise level from the full restaurant covered it. Okay. Less wine and more coffee, she thought and lifted her cup.

"Yeah … she was funny," he said.

"Who?"

"The unit director. I said, the only easy day was yesterday, and she'd mess it up later and say, the only hard day is tomorrow."

Riesman put down her coffee and looked at him.

"Are you done?"

"Ah yes, the old days of me telling you to just do it are forever gone. You never did strike me as the kind of woman who'd just follow orders. It's a good quality, you know," he said.

A waiter appeared with a thermos of fresh coffee. He refreshed her coffee and took her dinner plate away. Perez waved off an offer of coffee. Riesman noticed that his drinks and appetizers remained untouched, and he'd only picked at his food.

"I would never expect the Executive Director of Readiness and Disaster Logistics in FEMA's Office of Response and Recovery to accept at face value any statement so fantastic without the required data and analysis to support it," he continued.

Riesman sipped her hot coffee and observed him closely. He looked out the window. The thought that her former boss and mentor knew her present position, role, and title at the Federal Emergency Management Agency made her uncomfortable.

How could he know that when they'd assigned her new title just three weeks ago with an internal memorandum? It hadn't appeared on the organizational chart.

Rather than ask another question, Riesman pulled a clinical strategy from her mentor's own treatment strategies and said nothing. The din from the luncheon guests rose, and he too remained silent for a few moments. Then he smiled even more. Clearly, he'd picked up that she waited for some kind of response. Whether deliberate or not, Perez did go on, but not in the expected direction.

"Flour, sugar, chemicals, all that stuff I cut out fifteen years ago. High intensity exercise, especially weight bearing, in combination with eating non-processed food, has made a profound difference. Add to that teaching, helping people, and biblio-therapy, I can truly say that the stress in my life has dropped off to nothing."

"Biblio-therapy? So you've discovered another

treatment strategy?"

"No, Bobbie Jo. I wish. Biblio-therapy is another way of saying I've been writing. Freud was the one who discovered the art of writing down a stream of unconscious to get at neurosis, traumas and such. In other words, it helps when I write."

"Speaking of writing, I did see that your book, while highly regarded, was quite short."

Darn! I jumped to another subject. There was more. Man, my clinical skills have rusted.

"Eighty-two pages. Long enough to get my point across, and short enough for people to actually read it without skimming and scanning."

"Well, it did work well, and it was inspirational. How did you come up with your title … what was it?" Riesman stopped with her coffee half way to her lips.

"*Life's Directives: Twenty Ways to Live a Healthy Life.*"

He picked up his phone.

Two things struck Riesman at the same time: first, his expression had become remote and dark at the mention of his book, and the size of his smart phone was larger than any she'd seen before. Too big for a smart phone, it had to be a tablet.

"When my daughter died and I was left alone, I had a choice to make, live or die. As simple as it sounds, I needed a reason to live. After a great deal of soul searching and looking at everything possible, I found some inspirational Roman artifacts, and they became the impetus for writing my book," he said in a matter-of-fact tone as he looked at the tablet.

The news of his daughter's death stunned Riesman. How could all that happen to one guy? And how had she missed such a tragedy? Her friend's entire family had gone, and she felt ashamed that this was the first she'd heard of it. Guilt, sadness, and anger at herself swept over her leaving her sad and empty. How could a man who lost both his children and a wife, albeit more than fifteen years ago, appear so serene and focused? Could she ever achieve the same level of equanimity?

Living without Hiaki was going to be unbearable. She glanced at Hiaki's wife and daughters—a life she would never have. She shook herself out of her despair and turned back to her old mentor. Perez was touching his screen. After a moment, he tucked it back in his pocket with one hand and placed his napkin on the table with his other, then stood without a word. Peter's sudden appearance startled her.

"Director? Administrator Damon needs to speak with you. It's urgent," he whispered in her ear.

Riesman frowned. With the number of directors in the chain of command between her and the administrator, why would he contact her? What disaster could have happened for him to call her directly? She stood, anxiety rising, and turned to excuse herself, but Perez embraced her in a hug.

"Looks like duty calls us both. If you're not doing anything next week and find yourself in Massachusetts, come on over for Thanksgiving. I'm having a couple of colleagues over for dinner, dance, and fun. No pressure. Just if you're around."

Her anxiety shifted to curiosity. She nodded but wondered how Perez knew that work had called. He might have guessed, but it could have been a family emergency.

"Ma'am? We have to go," Peter said.

Perez's firm grip fell away. He smiled and turned to leave before she could respond.

"Hope to see you soon, Bobbie Jo," he said without looking back. A sudden urge to ask for more details almost set her after him. He'd disappeared through the exit already, and by the time she made it to the veranda, he was getting into the back seat of a large, high-end green sedan with tinted windows that obscured the occupants. The car moved as his door closed and drove out of sight.

"Is everything all right, Ma'am?" Peter asked.

"Yes … everything's all right," she replied, but she couldn't help feeling as if something was completely wrong.

Chapter Five

No Win Scenario—Earth

He who learns but does not think, is lost. He who thinks but does learn is in great danger. - Confucius

There's absolutely no sound in this office, Riesman thought. She sat on a leather couch, staring at a large plasma television embedded in the mahogany paneled wall in front of her. Closed captions flowed in large print beneath continuous images of the national and international news. The pair of smaller monitors flanking it showed local coverage of disasters occurring around the US.

She could see why Administrator Damon never had to visit any disaster areas, unless it was at the White House. Riesman stood to shake the cramps from her legs, and, for the third time, walked the perimeter of the office and examined the dozens of presidential citations and congressional awards. Then she listed all the ways her ten by ten office with its generic faux wood and plastic veneer differed from his thirty by thirty foot office with its polished pen holders, heavy oak furniture and matching rugs and drapes.

She still wore her black funeral attire and had the smell of old, dry coffee on her breath. An escort had whisked her off to the Administrator's office as soon as the private jet landed, and the male secretary had brought her straight into the office, so she'd had no time to reapply her makeup and freshen up. While brusque, the secretary was kind enough to bring cups, a thermos of coffee, and a message that she would need to wait some time until he arrived.

The time would've passed quickly if her smart phone had worked in the office. The only time she'd stepped out of the office was to get a signal.

"Your phone is not rated or equipped to penetrate the signal dampening fields," the secretary had said. "You also don't have clearance to use any phones here. I am sorry, but could you please return to the office," he added

He hadn't sounded sorry. Riesman had returned to her seat and fumed about all the mystery and the time she was wasting. She also thought about her interaction with Perez and the bureau's clampdown on Hiaki's computer.

And why is there a dampening field in this office? A new protocol?

A caption caught her eye on the main news channel. General David Farrell, in full uniform, was giving an interview. Riesman returned to her seat, picked up her cup of coffee, and resumed reading the captions. Farrell, a man of mystery with an even more mysterious series of projects, all associated with space, was very high up in the Pentagon and never gave interviews. He sat calm and at ease with his hands folded on his lap, shoulders rounded, and face relaxed.

Interviewer: "…you haven't denied the existence of another celestial body affecting our orbit. That said, do you acknowledge that there is something out there?"

Farrell: "I can't confirm or deny what's out there. But what I can say is that we're eighteen months away from launching a series of manned exploration missions, including two to Mars. "Interviewer: "So you're not willing to confirm or deny Planet X's existence, but at the same time, American tax dollars will fund a mission for something you're not willing to say is real?"

Farrell: "I think I just said that. But let me say it another way. Whether there is or is not a Planet X, we will soon find out. If no Planet X exists, we still have a problem as to why our orbit is slightly off kilter. If there is a hidden planet, then we have our answer and life goes on."

Interviewer: "But how would it be possible not to see it? We've had spacecraft of all sorts out there. You'd think we'd have seen it by now."

Farrell: "Yup. You'd think that …"

"Good evening, Ms. Riesman."

She jumped at the Administrator's voice, spilling some of her coffee on herself, the couch, and the rug. As usual, Administrator Richard Damon had arrived with two other people, a younger man and woman, right behind him. All three wore the same dark suit, shirt and similar accessories.

The man and woman weren't the same two people she'd seen at the funeral, but they looked similar.

Riesman put her cup down and stood to shake his hand.

"Good evening, Administrator."

"Good evening." He walked to his seat, reading on a tablet.

She retracted her unshaken hand and took a seat closer to his desk. The Administrator introduced the other two people without looking up from his tablet.

This is one the most bizarre and rude situations I've been in for a long time.

"These are Special Agents Arthur Harper and Donna Lee. They're helping us with our internal investigations," Damon said.

Internal investigations? On who? What is going on here?

"They've been working on the Nakamura and Perez case for years."

Riesman's heart jumped and her breath came up short at the mention of Hiaki Nakamura, Anthony Perez and internal investigation all in the same breath. Riesman wished she had better control over her emotions; she'd be terrible at covert operations.

"What? Why is Hiaki under investigation, and what does Anthony have to do with him, or anything?"

Damon looked up from his tablet and stared at Riesman. Her emotions had apparently taken him by surprise. Though embarrassed by her own reaction, she maintained the eye contact, not in the mood to back down.

“Agent Harper? Agent Lee? Bring the director up to speed, please,” he said as he broke eye contact and returned to reading.

Agent Harper was a handsome young man with well-manicured hands, a warm smile and just a hint of musk and sensuality—a candidate for dating had she been fifteen years younger. He approached with a tablet and held it in front of her.

“Director? Do you know this woman?”

Riesman looked at the image of a serious looking young woman, maybe in her early twenties, surrounded by computers and white boards filled with all kinds of equations. Her mocha skin color, blue eyes and long curly hair made a striking and familiar picture, but no name popped into her head. “She looks familiar, but I don’t have a name.”

“Her name is Doctor Andrea Perez,” Lee said.

Riesman looked again. The woman had a different eye color and lighter skin but the same shaped face, jaw line and eyes as her father, Anthony Perez.

“This has to be years ago. He told me that she died …”

“Who told you that?” Agent Lee asked.

Riesman sized her up: handsome and well put together like Agent Harper, but less familiar and kind. She looked back at the picture as she formulated her answer.

“Anthony Perez told me this no more than six hours ago. We attended the funeral and luncheon of Dr. Hiaki Nakamura earlier this morning.”

"We know you were there, Director," Harper said.

"This picture was taken about fifteen years ago," Lee said. "Dr. Perez was a brilliant scientist in the area of spectrograph analysis and light, and how they might be bent or manipulated. She was on the cusp of rewriting some key equations that would have changed the way we think of light."

"Dr. Perez had taken the mathematical works of Newton, Einstein, Hawking, Guth … all of them, and produced a series of formulas that would not only change our understanding of the world but also give us the right tools, calibrated the right way, so we could see things that we couldn't before," Harper added.

Riesman frowned.

Things we couldn't see before?

"Like when the *Hubble's* lens was repaired. The entire universe opened up," Lee said.

"Okay. But she's gone, right? And what does it have to do with Dr. Nakamura? He was a mathematician and statistician in light and wavelengths."

Her mind bounced back and forth between Perez, his daughter and Nakamura. The confusing new data was too personal and close to her heart.

"Dr. Perez was not into astronomy either, and she's not dead," Lee replied. "Missing? Yes—she's been missing for the last fifteen years. And her connection with Dr. Nakamura—he continued her work. He made progress where everyone else had failed."

Riesman's balance wavered as she tried to process all

the information at once. Harper produced another image. This time of her beloved Hiaki sitting on a park bench with Anthony Perez right beside him. Both men looked very serious, as if they held the world on their shoulders. Riesman reached out to touch the tablet, but Harper pulled it away.

"This picture was taken three months ago when you and Dr. Nakamura were staying at the Queen Anne Hotel in Montreal," he said.

Riesman's gaze dropped to the floor, her face and neck flushed with heat. She thought her pale Wyoming skin and blonde hair must have looked like a genetically altered Maine lobster with white limbs and hair.

"How long have you known?"

It took all her courage to look at the Administrator. He stared at her— unlike the first part of the meeting.

"Probably right from the beginning, five years ago, but that's not important," Lee replied.

"What is important is that Mr. Perez was in contact with Dr. Nakamura three months before he died. His daughter went missing while working on a contract with NASA and the Department of Defense. And Mr. Perez tells you that she's dead. We have looked everywhere for her. It's as if she's fallen off the planet. And, after all of these coincidences and mysteries, Mr. Perez shows up at Dr. Nakamura's private funeral, specifically arranged by us and kept out of the paper, internet and everything. Mr. Perez is in the center of a great deal of mysteries." The last line was said with great sarcasm.

"Then why don't you bring him in?"

"Because Perez is not who we want. We want his sponsor, Ms. Christine Reich."

Riesman, frowning in confusion, glanced from Harper to Lee and settled on Damon.

"What? Do you mean *the* Christine Reich? No one's ever seen her. She's a ghost. And how is Anthony connected to Reich?"

"We're not sure. But Andrea Perez's work had another sponsor, Reich Enterprise's telecommunications branch, along with NASA and DOD. Again, it was there that she was on the cusp of something great, and then she disappeared, along with every piece of her work. Reich's officials blamed corporate espionage, but her lab, computers and home were so thoroughly destroyed that it's hard to really believe that an outside corporation had anything to do with it. We won't bring Perez in unless we are sure he's connected to Reich and get some leverage on him," Harper explained.

"And that leverage is you, Director Riesman," Lee said. "He did ask you to join him for Thanksgiving, right? He said there would be some friends there." The question was rhetorical. Riesman focused on Damon. Dry sweat stuck to her clothes, and a chill ran down her back. Processing the information had drained her, but she managed to pull some moisture into her mouth and croak out some words.

"You … want me to spy on Anthony and his guests at Thanksgiving?"

Exposed and confused, Riesman waited for Damon to

respond to her directly. Based on everything that had transpired in the past twelve hours, it must have been evident that she wanted some answers. It took Administrator Damon a moment to answer, albeit carefully and slowly.

"Roberta, Drs. Perez and Nakamura were the best minds this country had ever developed. We as a government and as a country invested time, money, resources and access to classified data so they could advance the human race. And just when the deliverables are within reach, they disappear and die. Behind all of this is one woman—a German national, private industrialist and financier, Christine Reich. A woman of multiple talents, heavily resourced and thought to be the wealthiest woman in the world. And yet the world's best intelligence agencies can't even get a picture of her, nor can we find any record of her past, school, church, parking violations, nothing. Now we have an opportunity to connect all the players. And you are the one person he seems to trust. If we have an opportunity to get them all together, including even a chance of meeting this mystery woman Reich, then the answer is yes, you will be spying next Thursday on Thanksgiving. It will be for flag and country. But if it helps, we are not interested in Perez, just his guests and some answers."

It took a moment, but Riesman nodded as if she acquiesced. Her thoughts and heart were still with Hiaki—his warm smile and soft eyes.

"All right." Judging by the quick looks they exchanged,

her answer had taken them by surprise.

"All right then, Director Riesman. I assume you know this is classified at the highest levels and is not to be shared with anyone outside of this room," Agent Harper said.

"Yes."

"We will be in contact with you, starting on Monday, to go over questions and fit you with wires for tracking and listening," Lee said.

"Yes."

The room remained silent then, so she stood with her bag, nodded and waited to be dismissed.

"You know your way out, Roberta," Damon said.

"Thank you."

Riesman turned and walked slowly to the door. She noted, as she passed through the administrative assistant's office, that the assistant was also elegantly dressed and manicured. After leaving the antechamber, she walked in silence down the series of hallways, mechanically producing her badge, bag and herself for inspection at the several checkpoints throughout the Homeland Security building. Fifteen minutes later, she sat in the back seat of her car, with a different driver and protection team, all of them immaculately dressed with similar accessories and manicured hands. Riesman looked out the window with multiple thoughts running through her head. Every time she rewound the conversation, she got stuck on the same couple of things.

Why is the Department of Defense involved? A weapon? What do Hiaki and Anthony have to do with all this?

Chapter Six

Entrapment—Earth

When anger rises, think of the consequences - Confucius

What's happened to you? You're not this man. I don't know this guy.

Riesman stared at the primitive artifacts scattered on Perez's walls and tables. She moved closer to the mounted spears, easily seven feet long with heavy-looking metal tips and different colored feathers at the other end. The level of detail was impressive. After close inspection of other edged weapons, Riesman stopped and really looked around. Various flowers in pots attached to large columns gave the only hint of life in the spartan living room. Paleolithic era weapons and shields hung on every wall, interspersed with, and in stark contrast to, the abstract art scattered throughout the apartment. Expansive floor-to-ceiling windows overlooked the Boston Gardens, and the strong smells of honey, cinnamon and lilac filled the air. Rock and roll played too loud for her liking.

"It's another world."

Perez and his three other guests worked as a team, laughing and chatting in German while they cleaned and put away the Thanksgiving dinner plates. All three were short women with varying shades and length of red hair, and all three wore loose-fitting turtle-neck blouses over black tights. They gyrated to the music as they worked.

Riesman sipped the wine she'd brought as a gift along with a purchased, baked apple pie. She still had no idea why Perez was with them. Money, not looks, was her clinical analysis; roommates for the expensive piece of real estate—a penthouse in Boston proper.

Riesman looked out the grand windows. The building lights flickered on as the city skyline darkened.

She sipped more of her second glass of expensive wine, uncomfortable both with her task as a spy and where Agent Lee had put the tracking/transceiver device. Riesman walked around, hoping that both gravity and Kegel moves might help, but she only made it worse. She took another sip and tried to distract herself by analyzing the three women.

With red hair and large, dark eyes, they didn't fit the German stereotype of the tall, blonde, blue-eyed Aryan. They had the robust quality though. Uniformly five feet in height, they had a broad, square build with muscular legs and arms. Riesman tried to look closely without being rude. Their facial features were not very feminine. All three had sloping foreheads, broad faces, broader jaws, and expansive eyes, set back and well protected by their brows. If it wasn't for their hair, they'd have quite an exposed overhang, Riesman thought. Images of *Neanderthal* humans came to mind.

I got to say that for chicks who are pretty homely, they sure act like they're the hot models around town. You got to respect that.

Riesman smiled and sipped her wine, glad that she fell well within the American ideal. Feeling suddenly self-conscious of her own appearance, she smoothed out her elegant, midnight-blue pencil dress and chided herself for being catty and shallow.

The women, still dancing to the music, placed desserts, tea and coffee on the table while Perez finished cleaning the kitchen. The setting and people were so surreal that she found herself forgetting why she was really there. The transceiver's location reminded her. She walked around the room again. It still didn't help.

Who are you, Anthony? Was it the loss of your entire family that changed you into who you are now, whatever that is? Are you in some cult? What happened to that simple, overweight, gregarious guy?

She realized she was staring at Perez. He fiddled with his small tablet—or was it a large phone?—clearly immersed in something. He'd never struck her as a technophile, but he'd never been far from his tablet all night, and it was the oddest one she'd ever seen: very sleek lines, no ports, almost like a smooth piece of marble. When its screen was off, it looked like polished stone.

Her gaze wandered to the set of primitive weapons that hung on the wall above his head, then to the martial statues on the table beside him. When she refocused on him, he was nodding and talking quietly to himself or his tablet. He made eye contact and walked over.

"I'm sorry for the delay, Bobbie Jo. Are you ready for dessert?" he asked.

Riesman pointed to his tablet.

"I've never seen a tablet like that. Can I take a look?"

He raised an eyebrow and blinked, as if taking a moment to understand what she was asking. A strange look crossed his face, then he smiled and handed her the tablet while offering to take her wine with his other hand.

"It's a little heavier than it looks."

She exchanged her wine for the tablet. It did feel heavier than she expected, and unlike a regular tablet or smart phone, had no visible buttons, slides, or controls. Both sides looked and felt like a polished, flat stone—perhaps light marble or granite. She'd never seen anything like it before. She turned the phone over again, looking for the screen housing.

"The screen is on the other side and is activated by you looking at it."

"Oh? That's pretty high tech for a therapist like you."

Riesman looked at the stone, and a low, green light began to pulsate slowly. She held it firmly in both hands, and warmth flowed through her fingers, but the rich green light intrigued her more. The more she looked, the deeper into the depths of the object it drew her. The light grew, and her fingertips heated further, but it aroused curiosity and puzzlement, not alarm. A vivid sensation came over her of a dark, warm, protected cavity, then a constriction followed by a rush of cold air that embraced her whole body. A cough, a sharp slap on her buttocks, then an image of her mother's beautiful blue eyes looking down on her.

Mum? You're so young …

More images and sensations flew by. She saw herself as a little girl entering kindergarten, falling off her bicycle and being picked up by her father and sister in third grade, the strong smell of cow manure, and the rush of riding her favorite horse. She saw herself delivering her first calf on the farm, followed by driving her family's tractor in the corn field on a brutally hot day. She saw and felt the neighbor boy's very first kiss. Middle and high school flashed through her mind, as did her first orgasm. Cold days, hot nights, and warm beer came and went, as did visions of her first day in officer training; all the ways to a firefight in Iran. The flashes came faster, and so did the days and nights of her past: some tender visions, others of dead friends and soldiers. She felt intensely throughout the experience: happiness, pain, tenderness, fear and sorrow. A vivid image of meeting Perez arose, and one of her running her first clinical group, followed by completing her doctorate and explaining to her parents why she was not moving back to Wyoming.

More visions came—various assignments, friends and lovers— and only slowed at her appointment to FEMA and the news of Perez's family tragedy. They sped up again with tense, sad moments at her mother and father's funeral, and she watched her nieces and nephews grow before her eyes. The visions slowed again at her last lovemaking with Hiaki, attending his funeral, lunch with Perez, her meeting with the Administrator and agents. Finally, she saw Agent Lee making sure that the audio devices and internal tracking system was as comfortable as any large tampon.

Riesman shook her head. The green light blazed brighter. Her hands shot to her eyes, and the tablet clattered onto the floor. Her knees weakened, but Perez's strong arms caught her before she fell.

"I got you."

She rubbed her eyes and blinked. It worked well. Her vision cleared quickly and the heat subsided from her fingers.

"What the hell was that, Perez? Thanks for the warning …Does … does it always do that?" It took her a moment longer to regain her balance, sight and wits.

"Only sometimes," Perez replied.

"It can give me a nasty static shock on dry days like this." He checked that she could stand alone, then stepped away.

Static shock? Are you kidding me? It was something much more than that.

Perez picked up the tablet and looked at it briefly. Surprisingly, the glossy surface displayed no finger prints, and no dents or damage from its drop to the hard marble floor.

"I'm sorry, Bobbie Jo. The tablet also has a

biochemical defense mechanism. I thought I'd turned it off, but by your response, I expect you experienced a series of emotionally powerful images, important ones, I bet?"

"Are you kidding me? It's like I experienced my entire life's highlights in seconds. So if someone unauthorized holds it they get a here's-your-life show while you tackle him? You're kidding me, right? Wouldn't a biochemical knock-out zap be easier?"

She tried to make light of the event, but when she rewound the moments just prior to holding the tablet, she remembered how Perez had put her drink down to free both hands, almost in preparation to use them if necessary.

She concluded that it wasn't a mistake. She glanced beyond him to the three women. They looked at her with stunned expressions. Riesman took the glass of wine back, glad that she didn't make a total spectacle of herself.

"*Um Himmels willen, Terra und Erde! Die blonde Gigantin hat eine Verwandtschaft zu unserem Stamm. Das hätte ich nie erwartet,*" one of the women said in a surprised tone.

Great! Here comes the German again.

"*Einverstanden! Wieso ist sie so groß geworden, nachdem sie so viel verarbeitetes Mehl und Getreide gegessen hat? Denk nur, was passieren würde, wenn sie sich gesund ernähren würde! Denkst du, daß die Gigantin noch größer wäre?*" the other woman asked.

"You know, Anthony, this speaking German is getting pretty old," Riesman complained.

Perez rolled his eyes at the women's exchange as if he

understood them. The pygmy women had spoken German all through their time together. They spoke English occasionally, but only to ask her to move or tell her where to sit. This exchange had been the most she'd heard from them, and she was sure they were talking about her.

"*Sie kann kein Deutsch, meine Damen. Seien wir nicht unhöflich,*" he said as he led her to her chair at the table.

Riesman shot a look at Perez. She'd never heard him speak another language other than Spanish, and even that was rare.

German! You speak German? You live in a Boston penthouse with three women, walls covered in primitive art, and you speak fluent German. Who the hell are you?

"*Unglaublich! Sie kann die Sprache ihres Stammes doch überhaupt nicht? Armes Ding, siehst du, Milites Lux und Vespere? Sie hat ihre Vorfahren, ihre Abstammung vergessen und sie tötet sich langsam durch ihre Ernährung. Ich wette, sie möchte lieber in der Sonne liegen als sich zu verstecken und sich von UV- Strahlen zu schützen. Armes Ding. Und sie hat noch mindestens acht Prozent des genetischen Codes unserer Erbschaft?*

Erstaunlich!" Dee Dee said in a tone of contained enthusiasm as they sat down for dessert.

"Please," Perez said with a look as he took his own seat.

"Sorry, Immunes, I will focus. I thought Riesman knew German because of her last name. I apologize, Riesman," Dee Dee said in perfect, though heavily accented, English. For a moment, Riesman found herself unable to respond or move. She couldn't tell if the reason was the experience with the tablet, the revelation that at least one of the women spoke English and Perez spoke German, or the use of certain words such as 'immunes.'

Does that mean she heard my pygmy comment earlier? Shit!

Riesman replayed when she'd said it, her volume, and where everyone was at the time. She tried to push down the embarrassment and focus on something else. Perez dipped his spoon into some earth-colored, graham-cracker-textured dessert. She tore her eyes from the vile plate, and tried to repeat the word she hadn't understood.

"Immunes is a title from Latin that means something like a specialized soldier, such as Special Forces."

"Latin? As in dead language?"

"Yup. Roman Empire, Tacitus, Cicero, Caesar. Oldies but goodies."

"And it means specialized forces like a Delta squad?"

"Delta, Omega and Epsilon. All trained for specialized missions. That's what immunes means. Kind of cool, huh?"

"*Epsilon* Team? Really? An all-*woman* 'Delta Force?' That's just a myth; some Navy SEAL guy's fantasy," she scoffed.

"Maybe not here, but other governments might have such a force."

Riesman was about to continue when she noticed that she was the only one having a piece of the apple pie. Perez took a tiny sliver—a no-thank-you-but-I'm-not-interested-in-this-food size her mother had trained her to take when confronted with offensive food. To her surprise, he'd taken a larger helping of the dirt-like substance the other women ate so eagerly. The large quantity of food the women ate amazed her. The Thanksgiving meal had been composed of protein rich meats and fowls of all sorts, followed by legumes and vegetables—no starches to speak of. She'd asked one of the women about the drinks and learned that they contained no alcohol but lots of blueberry and blackberry juice. It tasted more like pure extract than a sugared drink. The women also used large thick bowls for their dessert; similar to what they'd used at dinner. Riesman sighed and tried to figure out why she was getting very angry.

"So does anyone else want some pie I …?"

All three women said no before she could get the last syllable of her question out, as if she'd offered them poison. Worse, they pulled their own dessert closer as if she might take it. As if she wanted that pile of dirt!

"What are you eating?" she asked in an attempt to contain her surprise and rising anger. The women frowned and looked at each other as if trying to figure out what she was saying. Again, Dee Dee spoke for them all.

"Why, it's baked chestnuts with crushed almonds, and coconut soaked in its own juices with cinnamon and lemon topping."

Riesman's jaw slackened. At first, she thought the woman must be joking, but the other two women returned to eating their treat with gusto.

My God! What have I've fallen into here?

Riesman put her fork down and looked around the table. She was not used to being the odd one out, or being ignored or avoided. Her jaw clenched and her heart rate rose. She picked up her wine glass, swirled the contents for a moment, and then, frustrated, plonked it down with more force than necessary. Thud. The others turned their heads at the sound. She closed her eyes and organized her thoughts.

"What is your problem with me? Why would you speak German when clearly I'm an American, and you can obviously speak the language?"

"*Est-ce que la géante préférait-elle le français?*" Vespere asked.

"*Non …je ne pense pas qu'elle puisse parler français non plus. Pourquoi ces gens ne peuvent pas apprendre les langues de leur monde?*" Lux said to Vespere.

"What! What is that? French? Now you're speaking French?" Riesman's voice rose.

"Ladies! That's enough! Stop badgering her. She's a guest and that's discourteous," Perez said, then he turned to Dee Dee.

"Milites Vespere and Lux! Silence!" she said with authority to the other women. Silence filled the room. Riesman looked at all of them before turning to Perez. He sat quietly with his elbows on the table, hands folded beneath his chin, looking down at the table.

"Anthony, what the hell is going on here? This isn't you. You lived in the suburbs and had … normal friends. These women don't belong here. You don't belong here with them, in this apartment. You couldn't have changed that much. I know you had losses …"

Sadness filled her heart at the thought of her own loss; Hiaki dying, gone forever. She would have continued, but Perez's head snapped up when she mentioned his loss. He sat back and glared. Riesman blinked; never before had he directed anger at her.

His eyes narrowed, jaw line tightened and he placed his hands on the table.

"And you know my pain, Bobbie Jo?"

The kind, gentle soul she thought she knew dissolved in front of her, leaving a hardened effigy. He stared through her for a moment, then looked at his hands and uneaten dessert.

Riesman wanted to reach out, but he looked up again, less hard and more of the person she had known for years, but still different.

"There are some things that are bigger than us. Things greater in scale and scope that dwarf our own problems, tragedies, hopes and dreams. Visions of the future can only be fully grasped if we look beyond ourselves and see that we are only part of a larger plan, a small cog in a machine."

"What do you mean?"

"I mean bigger truths that once known will shake the very core of our existence," Perez continued. "While our own planet sits on the very doorstep of its own demise, it's not the biggest problem to humanity. Deadly, dangerous, extinction level events bubble just under the surface of the planet's crust, and they're the least of our worries. The biggest narcissistic injury is yet to come. There are only a few people, very few, who can prepare our government that will in turn prepare a nation and world for the biggest existential answer to a long- standing question: are we alone? We've never been alone. The one who knows this carries great despair and responsibility to act outside the norms, beyond the laws and above all else, to teach a race of people not to strike out in fear and anger but to sit back and learn. So different is this from our nature. We attack what we don't know. It takes a special type of person to lead the way and convince a planet to save itself and its soul. This is big, even bigger than my personal loss." Perez fell silent and looked through the windows to the Boston skyline.

Riesman stared at him, unable to understand his words or look away from the man and the dark abyss into which he fell. She wondered if he were crazy. She wanted to say something reassuring and comforting but couldn't think of anything that could counter his eloquent tirade.

The younger woman, Lux, caught her off guard when she spoke clearly in a thickly accented, low tone but in perfect English. "…'His very existence was improbable, inexplicable, and altogether bewildering. He was an insoluble problem. It was inconceivable how he had existed, how he had succeeded in getting so far, how he had managed to remain—why he did not instantly disappear.'"

Riesman's mouth slackened yet again, and she stared at

the woman, stunned by her ability to verbalize her own thoughts, truly capturing the moment.

Vespere, who nodded as if she approved of the statement, answered an unasked question. "J. Conrad's work, *Heart of Darkness and the Congo Diary.* A fine choice, Lux. I was thinking more J. Milton's *Paradise Lost* quote of 'Yet he who reigns within himself, and rules passions, desires, and fears, is more a king,' but then I think the better setting would be on Venus than Earth."

Riesman's eyes widened even more.

Just when you thought things couldn't get any stranger!

Perez smiled and returned to his calm, kindly self. He shook his head, pulled out his tablet and placed it on the table while Dee Dee spoke to the two younger women.

"Your growth here and experience will serve both of you well, Milites Vespere and Lux. I will miss you. I feel much better leaving you both here to continue the work and the replacements' training. Still, I long to see my family, to start teaching and continue my own journey. My departure will mean your promotion to Immunes."

"Thank you kindly for your patience and time, Centurion," Vespere said and bowed her head.

"You will be remembered along with my kin. Your words have been my life," Lux said.

Okay… this is crazy! Venus … Earth? Centurion and leaving… Quoting Milton and Conrad … all right, everyone, it's been nice getting to know you all. Time to go!

Riesman pulled her napkin from her lap, plopped it on the table, and stood ready to leave, but Perez's even tone and matter of fact words caught her attention.

"All right, ladies, it looks like the authorities will be here in thirty seconds. Five agents and an unarmed man in the back, also an armed helicopter coming in from the east about one klick out. I'm guessing it's for suppressing fire if necessary. Local law enforcement has already set up a perimeter in the front and back, leaving exits gamma and omega open. Entry will be the front door. They'll probably use flash-bangs."

Riesman's heart jumped several beats, and sweat burst through nearly every pore of her body.

How did he know they are coming? And why are they coming? Falsh-bangs? She'd thought this was only reconnaissance.

"Did the Keeper deactivate Riesman's devices?" Dee Dee asked. The three women stood in unison, pushed their chairs in, and stood behind them while Perez did the same thing.

"What? How do you know about that?"

"All but a tracking device located… really, Bobbie Jo? They made you put one there?" Perez said, pointing below her waist. Riesman's mind went blank and heat flushed her face and neck.

"Well, now, that is inappropriate," Lux said with disgust on her face.

"So much for dignity," Vespere added.

"Stop it! How … how could you know that?" She suddenly wanted to cover her front as if she were naked.

Perez made a hand signal and the women lay on the

floor, closed their eyes and covered their heads while he continued. "All right, ladies, it's going to happen soon. I hope you got a plan for that rotor, Dea Data?"

"Yes, though timing and placement will be critical."

The mention of flash-bangs was enough to convince Riesman to imitate everyone else. She lay on the floor, facing away from the door with her head covered and her eyes squeezed shut.

"Good … I'm guessing flash-bang in five, four, three, two, one …"

Riesman covered her ears and waited. She was about to look up when the front door crashed open, lights flashed, something popped loudly, and heavy feet ran towards them, shaking the floor. The events would've completely disoriented and immobilized her had she not been prepared. All she could think about amidst the noise, yells to remain still and something pressing on her body was how Perez saw this happening and with such detail.

What, or who, is the Keeper?

"Get up!" a man yelled.

The smoke and smell of discharged electricity made breathing difficult and her movement slow, but two strong hands pulled her off the ground and stood her on her feet. Riesman blinked, but it didn't clear her disorientation or stop her eyes stinging. A man bound her hands roughly in front of her. The room spun around her, making her unsure of her footing. The other women were crying.

"It's nice to see you're in one piece," Administrator Damon said, his calm demeanor at odds with the previous chaos. At least the blast hadn't compromised her hearing. The smoke cleared enough to reveal Damon standing in the middle of the mess surrounded by Agent Harper and men in expensive-looking suits, body armor and assault weapons.

"You could have knocked, Administrator. I'm sure Mr. Perez would have let you in."

Because somehow he'd known they were coming.

"Perhaps ..." Administrator Damon said.

"Agent Harper, please release the director and the women. I think we have the prize. Not the big one but...

"Absolutely."

A loud pop pierced the air and blood splattered across Riesman's face and dress. Stunned, she stared at the mess with wide eyes. One of the women screamed, and she looked up in time to see Damon fall to the ground. Shock rooted her to the spot, but the other women's cries pushed her to speak.

"What's wrong with you, Harper? You just killed my boss!" she blurted out. She glanced back and forth between the dead body, Agent Harper and Perez, and after a few moments realized she'd stopped breathing.

"Merck! Daniels! Shut those ugly pigs up," Harper said.

Ignoring her, he stepped over Damon's body, his smoking semi- automatic handgun still in hand, and stood in front of Perez. Fired by adrenalin, lack of air and shock, Riesman stepped towards him, but someone yanked her back into place. Another man struck Dee Dee from behind, sending her face first to the floor. Everything moved so fast and changed so suddenly that it was impossible to take it all in. Riesman decided to focus on one thing at a time. She watched Harper, who continued to stare at Perez.

"Nice job, Jones. Teach Merck and Daniels not to hit like girls later, please."

Perez, bound like her and with a cut above his eye, remained silent and returned Harper's gaze without flinching. Riesman tried to figure out what to do next to stay alive—a difficult task with her dead boss and Dee Dee's still body just feet away.

"Captain Anthony Martinez Perez, after years of soul searching, research and interrogations, I think *you* are either the mysterious Christine Reich, or you know exactly who she is and where I can find her."

A menacing smile grew on Harper's face until a floodlight from a helicopter streamed through the panoramic window. Its beams gave an eerie look to the shattered apartment, and the rotors shook the plate glass.

"Harper? It's Lee. Get the package to the chamber. The locals are getting curious. No need for the others," a disembodied voice said from a small transceiver on Harper's tactical vest. Without taking his eyes off Perez, he gave the helicopter the thumbs-up.

No need for the others … Riesman thought, realizing that she had just attended her last supper. *They're going to kill us.*

The helicopter moved off, and Perez said something to

Harper that took her off guard.

"Just like you killed Dr. Nakamura, Agent Harper? It wasn't an accident."

Riesman's heart jumped. Her eyes locked on Harper. Her breathing slowed. Her head spun and her knees weakened. She felt as if she were going to throw up.

Memories of laughing with Hiaki over breakfast in bed no more than two weeks before he died flooded her inner eye until she forced them down. Her boss's dead body confirmed that Harper could do it, but he gave no indication that Perez's accusation was correct.

"You killed Hiaki?" Her voice lacked strength, but her bound hands balled into fists. Harper faced her, paused for a moment, then stepped towards her as if he were going to say something, but instead, he turned suddenly on Perez and struck him with his handgun. Blood gushed from a large gash above his injured eye, and he crumpled to the ground.

Riesman gasped. "Anthony!"

The sound of Vespere and Lux's crying heightened.

Perez blinked several times. "Yeah, you're a real scumbag." he said defiantly.

Harper extended both hands as if he had won a prize fight.

"See, everyone. I told you this old guy would be strong, unlike that pathetic piece of shit, Nakamura. Man, the crying, weeping and begging that weak old man did was an embarrassment."

Riesman's shock turned to rage. Determined to kill

Harper, she struggled against her bonds and tried to strike him when he drew near, but her guard restrained her.

"Yeah, this old guy won't have a heart attack like Mr. Hiaki Nakamura." Harper, his tone mocking, exaggerated each syllable of her dead lover's name.

"I'll kill you."

"Maybe, someday, but not today. Merck, let Daniels watch those crying bitches, and get the drugs and guns. Time to make this look like a party gone bad." Harper walked to Perez. "And get the tracker out of Riesman. We don't need her anymore, either," he said casually, as if he were ordering takeout, then he pulled Perez off the floor with the assistance of the guard who stood above him. Someone yanked her from behind, and strong hands gripped the back of her neck and arm.

"Don't worry, Director, I'll be quick."

She pulled away and spun to face him, preparing for a fight, but the guard no longer stood on the floor. Her eyes widened and her jaw dropped. One of the knives she'd admired earlier protruded through his body armor and lifted him off his feet. Riesman backed away from the fearsome weapon. A blur raced across the room and smashed into Merck's back. His thighbones crashed into the dining room set. Riesman flinched from his high-pitched screams.

"Christ! What?"

Thrown from behind, the man with the knife in his chest crashed into another guard. Dee Dee cut Merck's screams short by cracking his exposed head open on a dinner bowl. Perez wrestled over a gun with his guard, and Riesman stepped forward to help him, but Harper blocked her way. She jerked her bound hands upwards and struck his gun hand. The weapon discharged. She grabbed his gun with both hands, expecting a struggle, but his arm lost strength, and he fell on top of her.

"Get off me, you bastard!" She shrugged him off, ready to strike again, then gasped at the sight of the two swords that cut deep into his torso, eviscerating him. Horrified by the gore, she turned in time to see Lux flick her wrist at the man struggling with Perez. A large knife magically appeared in the man's chest. His death throes tightened his finger on his weapon's trigger and set off a volley of bullets.

"Shit! Full auto!" she yelled, rolling out of the stream of bullets. But his line of fire followed her. She smacked into a pillar, thinking that she'd lost any chance of escaping death, but the man's gun arm suddenly separated from his body. Behind him, Vespere dropped a machete and helped Perez up. Behind Vespere, another man rose off his feet, swung upside down, and crashed to the floor.

Adrenalin flooded her body, and Riesman's mind spun. How had three tiny women killed five highly trained assassins in under a minute?

Beams of light flooded the plate glass windows, and they exploded with a burst of gunfire from the helicopter. Riesman hugged the floor behind her pillar as bullets flew everywhere. She caught sight of Dee Dee flashing rapid hand signals. Riesman followed her gaze. On the other side of the room, Vespere and Lux held their former attackers' assault weapons and opened fire. The helicopter backed up but continued to shoot. Luckily, the apartment's columns were more than decorative, but the hail of bullets still ate into them, trying to get at Vespere and Lux.

Riesman raced to Perez, her eyes widening when she saw Dee Dee run full speed at the helicopter, poised to hurl the spear she'd admired earlier. The helicopter moved closer, blasting the column Vespere and Lux used as cover. Dee Dee slid to a stop and hurled the javelin. The missile sailed through the apartment's broken glass and smacked into the helicopter's cockpit, shattering the protective canopy. Riesman figured it hit either the pilot or co-pilot/gunner, because the helicopter stopped shooting and veered downward. A moment later, it crashed into the ground a few floors below and exploded, sending up an impressive plume of flames and smoke.

Bodies littered the silent and shattered apartment. Had she not fought in skirmishes in Iran and had Naval and FEMA disaster training, she would probably have retched. Riesman counted the bodies and stopped at Harper. Even amid the horror, she still hated him.

"I guess it was your time to die, you asshole." A firm hand on her shoulder pulled her back to reality.

"We must go," Dee Dee said. Vespere helped Perez to his feet, and Lux headed towards the bedroom area. Dee Dee cut Riesman's binds.

"Are you Epsilon Force? The all-female Delta Force I

said was bullshit?" Riesman felt strange, analytical and removed from the surreal scene of death and destruction.

"Yes, but not here. Time to leave."

Hands free and recovering faster than she expected, she followed Vespere and Perez to a bedroom on the other side of the apartment. All three women had removed their outer garments and now wore form-fitting black attire with various leather straps and belts in key areas that exposed their svelte but muscular forms. Dee Dee walked before her and Lux came back to cover the rear.

"You changed," Riesman said.

"You noticed. Time for you to lose those shoes. I have no idea how you women wear them." Lux grabbed Riesman's feet and, having no energy to fight for her one hundred and eighty-two dollar high heels, she let the woman rip them off. What would the next steps be? she wondered. *Go to the police? The FBI? Who?*

"A spear was your weapon of choice?" Perez said weakly to Dee Dee.

"A highly crafted, augmented javelin with reinforced shaft and copper tip, yes, the spear was my first and best option. I regret I will never get it back and that the Earthers will not appreciate its craftsmanship." Dee Dee opened up a large trapdoor that led to the floor below.

Now that's really weird … just like everything else.

Dee Dee helped Perez down first, then Vespere spun her around and, using a large knife in one sweeping blow, cut a high slit in her beautiful dress.

"Hey! You could have killed me," Riesman said,

looking at the height of the slit. As expected, it allowed her to move freely, but Riesman discovered that wasn't the primary reason for the ruined dress.

"Are you going to make me take that tracking device out of you, or are you going to do it?"

"Oh." Riesman squatted down and searched for the end of the device but felt very awkward and exposed. After turning slightly for more privacy, she produced the little transceiver/transponder and held it in her hand for Vespere to see.

"I don't want it for a keepsake, Riesman. Throw the thing over there."

Heat flushed Riesman's face—of course she didn't want it! She tossed the device against the wall, then wiped her hands on her ruined dress and was about to ask where they were going when Vespere's small, strong hands pushed her off balance. She fell, but instead of hitting the floor, she plummeted through the trapdoor, barely clearing its edges, and landed firmly in Lux's cable-like arms.

"You can afford to miss a meal, Riesman. All that sugar, rice and processed food will do you in," she said as she pushed Riesman off. Vespere jumped through the trap door and landed solidly on her legs. The heavy door closed above them.

"Thanks for the warning." No one replied, and Riesman wondered if they understood sarcasm. She followed the others across an empty room and through a door into the public hallway. As soon as they stepped into the common area, Dee Dee, who was helping Perez, pulled a fire alarm. Sirens screamed and red lights flashed.

The hallway began to fill with nervous people evacuating, and the group walked away from the elevators and into another apartment. Once inside, Dee Dee turned to Vespere.

"Blow the apartment."

She produced a small device that emitted green light, flicked a switch, and pressed a button. The light changed to red and a huge explosion rocked the building above them and to the far right. They moved on before the shaking and sound subsided.

"Okay. So you're an Epsilon Force from where? UK?" Riesman asked under her breath.

"We are not from around there either," Vespere said.

"Let me guess … the apartment was set to blow. So you were prepared," Riesman continued, aware that her familiarity with Seals helped her adapt quickly from Thanksgiving dinner conversation to an elite commando unit on a mission.

"Yes," Lux replied.

Perez and these women left nothing out, nothing to chance and made no mistakes. And they killed an entire FBI strike team. But they couldn't be FBI. They'd planned to kill her, and the three women, just like they had Damon and Hiaki. Riesman wondered what she'd fallen into.

Lux opened a closet door and pushed the back wall. It opened into another part of the building, where they walked through more empty apartments. Once in a different public hallway, Vespere pulled another alarm. People came out in waves, and Riesman and the team flowed onto the street with everyone else.

Outside, large numbers of people milled around, and in the confusion, they didn't notice three small women wearing all black helping an injured man and a barefoot woman covered with blood. Riesman glanced behind her. A large police barrier obstructed the road nearly half a block away. Above her, helicopter wreckage was embedded in the third floor, and two stories above that, the penthouse burned. Brilliant yellow and white flames curled skyward and spread across the entire top floor. *Impressive.*

She turned her gaze to the front and walked on with Lux at her side. "Where are we going?"

"To a very fast vehicle," Lux replied.

"And that fire back there?"

"A little something-something I concocted to not only burn rapidly but to such high temperatures that it should melt metal, bone, teeth and everything around it. They won't be able to identify anyone. If they know we were all there, they should believe that we are all dead. Hopefully, they won't make the connection unless they find the trap door, which was at the epicenter of the blast." Still smiling at her handiwork, she opened a car door and assisted Riesman into the back seat with Dee Dee and Perez. Lux and Vespere climbed into the front. Dee Dee, observing Perez closely, removed blood-soaked bandages and replaced them with clean ones. Only then did Riesman realize that Perez had been hit.

"Oh my God!"

"Not to worry, Riesman. Two bullets cleared vital organs though one looks like it collapsed a lung. If we get him to the ship quickly, he should be fine once we clear the landing zone. Vespere, go to the emergency extraction zone on the island; we are going to the old fort in Boston Bay. *Silent Star Falling* has made all of its pickups and is already preparing to land, but it has only five windows to accomplish this between the Earthers' aircraft traveling over it and the possibility of pursuit. There is a small landing craft exposed to open ocean that will take you to the yacht."

"Excellent! We'll be able to go fishing. I love the ocean," Lux said as the car took off at a fast clip.

"The chart, course, and supplies are all in place. Once I leave, take the new Milites and Dr. Riesman to the new location and continue with the preparation. Also, the Keeper apparently left three pounds of chestnuts for you both in the boat."

"Praise the Keeper and may she have long life!" Lux cried.

Riesman swam in a sea of information with no idea of what to do. Should she make a break for it once the car stopped, or continue on with them? After all, throughout everything, Perez and these women could have let her die—a couple of times. But they hadn't. She looked at Perez. He appeared to be unconscious. It hit her how brutally Agent Harper had killed her boss right in front of her and brazenly admitted to killing Hiaki. She realized that the people she could trust might be only the ones with her right now.

"Dammit," she said quietly.

Chapter Seven

Silent Falling Star - Earth

Virtue is not left to stand alone. He who practices it will have neighbors- Confucius

“I'm sorry for all of this, Bobbie Jo.” Perez spoke with difficulty from where he lay on the back seat of the car.

Riesman knelt beside him with the door open, her back towards a large open field. His face had swollen, and bandages and compresses covered his body. “Don’t talk, Anthony. You’re working on one lung ...”

Perez frowned as if trying to remember something. “It makes sense that you take over ... Roberta Joanne Riesman: retired Major, Executive Director of Readiness, Disaster Logistics, Office of Response and Recovery at FEMA, US Office of Naval Intelligence, Ph.D. Psychology, MPH ... it makes sense ... you’ll understand the issues ... the disaster, hysteria ...” he muttered.

Not knowing what to do, she put her hand on his shoulder. It seemed to bring him back to the present, and they sat quietly for a moment in an empty field in the middle of an abandoned fort in Boston Bay.

"Just rest, Anthony. I guess help is coming," Riesman said. He nodded and closed his eyes.

She surveyed the open, desolate field tucked at the end of a peninsula. A Civil War fort stood in ruins on a nearby hill overlooking the vacant field and ocean. Light swept across the sky from the automatic lighthouse beside it, and faint light from the Boston skyline bled through the fog. Riesman took a deep breath, and the refreshing smell of sea salt, ocean and some kind of flowers eased her tension.

I'm alive.

Only the constant flow of air traffic heading over the island into Logan International Airport marred the setting. The roar of engines moved from a distant hum in the east to a loud thunder as they passed low overhead, and then faded as the planes coasted in for landing. Always another plane followed right on their tail.

Dee Dee stood by the driver's door staring at her tablet while Vespere and Lux organized back packs, five of them by Riesman's count.

This is an operation. Some kind of extraction, she thought. *How many times have I been here … usually with my own gear and boots …*Cold rose through the soles of her mangled shoes, and Riesman's heart grew heavy as she tried to figure out what to do next.

As if reading her mind, Perez spoke quietly but clearly.

"You know you can never go back, Bobbie Jo. Those people back there are killers. They killed Hiaki and your boss with ease. You and the other girls were on the list, and I would have joined you shortly, I'm sure."

"I can go to the police. I have friends in D.C. …"

"And then the same people that set your boss up, interrogated Hiaki, and killed them both would find you. They would assume you know something."

Riesman raised her voice above the airplane noise.

"But I don't know anything!"

"I know that, Bobbie Jo. I know that," Perez said. He took in a deep breath and continued. "But they don't. And these are the kind of people that don't like loose ends. The people who sent that hit team don't know how much or how little you know, and they won't be happy until you're dead."

Riesman tried to find fault with his logic, but considering that she'd escaped death less than two hours ago after being compelled to be a part of entrapping a German national, Perez's analysis seemed accurate.

"But what about my family? My sister and nieces …" Yet another plane rumbled in the distance.

"They'll be safe if you're presumed dead. If they think you're alive, they become bait."

Perez shuffled across the seat towards the door. Taking the cue, she assisted him outside, and he leaned on the car facing the field, looking settled but tired. The sound of the plane overhead receded and, surprisingly, none took its place. Riesman looked east and didn't even see any navigation lights.

"Looks like my ride is here. Do me a favor and hold onto this until I get back." Perez handed her his tablet. "I may get a new one, but I want you to hold onto this because it belongs here, and it will help you with some answers. I'm going to be gone for a while." She frowned.

"Anthony? What are you saying?"

"Right now it's rebooting and should be back online in about a week. The transmissions are weak and it desperately needs recharging," he explained.

Though reluctant to touch it in light of what happened last time, she took the tablet. The night had grown strangely still, the roar of descending planes having ceased. She turned and looked east again—no oncoming planes, just an empty field.

She turned back to Perez with a frown. He took another deep breath, as if the prior conversation had exhausted him, and pointed directly upward. She looked up and gasped, eyes wide, heart suddenly racing. Above them, a massive, black bird silently descended. Riesman took a step back, shaking her head in disbelief. A moment later, landing gear emerged from the smooth, black ship.

Earthers, Terrans, Venus, not alone in the universe … spaceships? Another planet?

"Holy Crap! My God! What in God's name is that?" Riesman said with bated breath.

Dee Dee provided a casual explanation of the vehicle in standard military, minimalist vernacular while she assisted Perez.

"An interplanetary, stealth spaceship typically used for observation, surveying, immediate evac, and pickup runs. Minimal weaponry so it's very fast while having a guidance and landing system that uses the Earth's molten core and magnetic field as a means of landing rather than the usual chemical fission thrusters required on Terra and Venus. Due to Earth's rapid rotation, the magnetic field alone will suffice for lift off."

Slack jawed and wide eyed, Riesman watched the massive ship settle on landing struts, and felt a sudden need to go the bathroom.

"Immunes Vespere and Lux—you're now in command. If all goes well, I'll see you both in ten years or less. Good luck and instruct your Milites well," Dee Dee said as she helped Perez to the opening ramp. Both women stood silently at attention and placed a closed fist over their heart in salute.

This can't be happening! A spaceship? For real?

"Bobbie Jo? Bobbie Jo—go with Vespere and Lux. They'll make sure you're safe. Once the tablet recharges, it'll tell you what you need to know. Then you can make your own decisions," Perez said.

Slowly, Riesman recovered from the shock. With Dee Dee's support, Perez ambled to the ship. Two other women that looked just like Vespere and Lux passed them at the edge of the ramp.

"Let me come with you." Riesman spoke out of desperation, not even sure what she meant. Dee Dee and Perez stopped and looked back at her, obviously as surprised as she was for asking.

"Hiaki is dead. I'll have to hide and never see my family. There's nothing to stay here for," Riesman blurted out as tears filled her eyes.

Perez motioned her closer.

"Bobbie Jo, if you hear what the Keeper tells you, you may decide to take a path that will create an entirely different and more important life than you could ever imagine. I'd hoped to be around, but this is your place, here on Earth, while I need to be elsewhere with my daughter. As long as you have the Keeper and your team, you'll never be alone unless that's the journey you take."

Riesman shook her head. His words hadn't reassured her, and she had too many unanswered questions. Where was his daughter? And who is this Keeper?

"Have faith in yourself. Trust me, you're the right person for this. Even if they call you Giant, the role you'll play with this planet's history is monumental. You're actually trained for this kind of change, both the real dangers and the more ...existential one."

He and Dee Dee ascended the ramp, and it started to close. Riesman stepped out of the way, feeling suddenly alone, empty, and exhausted. The ramp closed, and the struts silently retracted.

"No ... don't leave me here alone."

"You're not alone, Riesman. You do not have to be unless that's what you wish." Vespere said in a quiet and unusually gentle voice. Riesman turned. Vespere was looking up, watching the large ship slowly ascend as quietly as it had descended.

A few moments later, the black spaceship was nearly invisible, and planes flew in again from east to west.

Riesman's gaze fell to the ground. She felt as if she were going to weep.

What am I going to do?

A familiar voice jolted her.

"Vespere! The new Milites—Bella and Pax? They have never been on the sea, which does make sense, considering! They are in for such a treat," Lux said from behind her. She looked back to see the two new women donning the packs she'd seen earlier.

"Is it true about how there are chestnuts and lemons that fall from trees and are just left there?" the new soldier, Bella, asked eagerly.

"All true. And there is more, including great fishes in the ocean which you will see. Now we must go—the chestnut and lemons await us on the yacht, but we must clear the bay and be in open ocean before daylight," Lux said.

Riesman glanced at her tablet. It looked like a solid piece of black stone.

"I can imagine that this is all confusing, Riesman."

She looked up. Vespere held another pack, opened for her to see shoes and clothes inside.

"At the very least, take these clothes and come with us for a short while, until the Keeper talks to you. Then make your decisions," she said in a calm, kind voice.

Riesman glanced from her to the clothes, then took the backpack. What other option did she have? Vespere turned her back to give Riesman privacy.

"Thank you." Riesman put the heavy backpack down

and took out a warm jumper and track pants—much more appropriate than her torn dress for going on a yacht.

"Yes, but in all fairness, I suspect that like many of you Earthers you are nearly hairless all over … which is simply too much for me," Vespere said. The disgust in her voice was so obvious that Riesman stopped in mid-stride to rewind the last comment to make sure she understood what Vespere said.

"Well, of course, I have some hair on my legs when I don't shave, but the only hair I have is—"

"Please, no more! The image of a hairless woman is difficult to get rid of once envisioned. I would like to enjoy my breakfast tomorrow."

An airplane roared overhead. Riesman shook her head in amazement and went back to changing clothes. Three hours ago, she'd wanted to leave an awful Thanksgiving dinner to get away from these people. Now she was going on a cruise with female ninjas from a silent spaceship.

And it's my being hairless that's a crazy thought? What have I gotten myself into?

Chapter Eight

From Hell's Heart – Terra

I hear and I forget. I see and I remember. I do and I understand. - Confucius

Andrea Perez, hands deep in her pockets, walked to the Great Library with a heavy heart. She figured it had to be after Thanksgiving on earth. The Christmas stuff would be out in the malls—baby Jesus in his crib, the three Wise Men surrounding the Son of God, and carols floating in the air.

Unable to sleep, she'd taken to getting up early and doing her new calisthenics routine. Normally, she would wait until the fourth shift broke from work, but today was different. She'd discovered that there was more to the solar system than Terra. More than the hand of God. Mortal beings, not God, designed life as she knew it.

"Is there a God?"

The dark carpeted walkway, empty and quiet, hushed her voice. The fourth shift had hours before their morning meal when the first shift took their place, and the sentries had passed her twenty minutes ago near the residence habitat. She walked with measured steps, thinking of the past, present and future—dark thoughts that matched the concourse's low lighting.

Jesus Christ's birthday. Son of God.

It was easy back then with only one planet and no intelligent life anywhere but Earth. And humans were the ones made in God's image.

But now … What else am I going to find? Were we a mistake, too? Her anxiety increased with every step towards the library and its books that challenged her notions of herself and her place in the universe.

Bad enough that there is Terra, but life on Venus too?

Perez stopped. She'd been so busy with her existential thinking that she'd lost track of where she was, and it felt strange to see the food courts and markets closed, but a quick scan of the area confirmed that she was on track to her destination. She noticed new edged weapons—short swords, javelins and serrated knives—with their impressive blades placed in breakaway clips hanging on racks throughout the hall, an indicator of either a great hunt preparation or a recent attack by the huge rats.

Rattus! I hate those things.

She glanced down and felt along her waist. "Dammit! I forgot my sidearm again. When are you going to learn, dumbass?" But her fingers found her sheathed combat knife, a gift from Dux Cloelius for her journey and protection. She walked on and picked up her pace at a rustle behind her. She remembered her conversation with

Clematis and the recent increase in rattus attacks. Perhaps such a late sojourn to her studies wasn't a good idea.

Perez stopped a hundred feet from the library. An air vent just to the left of the door hung off its hinges, as if pushed from the inside.

"Dammit."

Perez backed away to the weapons rack she'd seen several feet back. She kept her eyes peeled for any movement and cocked her head, listening, but the continuous vibration of the air and heating machines made it difficult to hear anything subtle. When she reached the weapons rack, the tension in her chest eased a little. She grabbed two large, serrated blades just as a loud, guttural scream pierced the stillness.

"Percutiamque vos monstra!"

"Dammit!"

Perez's grip tightened around her weapons, and she moved in the direction of the yell, eyes darting everywhere. Glass shattered below her level, followed by the sound of breaking wood, perhaps a chair or table. Without thinking, she ran down the flight of stairs, taking several steps at a time. She burst onto the lower stores level and caught her breath at the sight of a young Terran girl, maybe a teenager, waving her weapon at four rats the size of large dogs with ugly tails that doubled their size. She'd seen skulls, skins and tails of these creatures hanging up to dry, but their similarity to the smaller versions on her former planet surprised her. Only their huge size made them grotesque and evil monsters, and seeing four of them surrounding a young woman pushed Perez from shock to disgust to loathing and hatred. Anger burst from her heart and she let go a scream of her own.

"No!"

She ran, clutching the hilts of her blades, into the battle. Her first blade crashed into the back of one rat as it turned to face her, and her second blade struck out at the rat's nose. For a moment, Perez felt disoriented, as if she'd bumped her head, then something stung her right side. She ignored the sensations, yelled again, and struck out at the retreating creature. To her satisfaction, it scurried away with one of her blades sticking out of its back.

Screw you, bitch!

With one out, she shifted her focus to the others. Two of the rats slunk off, startled by her appearance, but the third seized the moment of distraction and snapped at the young woman's hand. Her blade clattered to the ground, along with three of the fingers that had gripped it. The woman grimaced but didn't scream. She just tried to grab her fallen weapon with her other hand, while the rat devoured her fallen fingers.

Perez, shocked by the girl's stoicism, yelled and tossed her remaining edged weapon to the girl, then drew her combat knife. Perez glanced at her small weapon and realized she needed more. Without a thought, she grabbed a broken chair leg and attacked the rat as it made a run at the girl. Though losing blood, the girl, clearly well trained with edged weapons, slashed out at the rodent who'd taken her fingers. After tasting blood and flesh, the rat looked determined to kill her.

"Hodie non turpis linguis! Not ever, you scum!" Perez yelled as she advanced to the woman's side, but before she got there, another rat appeared and scurried towards her.

Perez screamed and swung the chair leg into the creature's legs. She heard a bone break. The rat snapped and she backed away, but she struck the creature repeatedly in the head until it stopped snapping. The injured rat stepped back, favoring its broken leg. Perez lunged and shoved her knife in the monster's eye. It screeched and flailed around, tail swinging. Perez jumped aside but the rat's tail brushed her left side and ripped her pants, cloak and skin. Nonetheless, the creature slunk off with her knife embedded in its eye.

She stared defiantly at another rat that watched from the distance, and it fled along with the other two. Down to her chair leg, Perez turned to the injured girl. She looked very pale and her movements had slowed.

Blood loss, shock—shit!

The rodent hunched down, hips up, eyes focused on its victim, preparing to attack. With a scream, Perez raced in, drawing the full attention of the rodent. It bared its ugly teeth, stiffened its tail, and wriggled its haunches, about to spring. Only the young woman stopped it. She jumped on top of the creature and drove her blade deep into its back. The rat jumped, knocking the girl off, and swung around, trying to bite the blade protruding from its back. Perez swung her chair leg like a bat and made full contact with the creature's head, but her club, though solid, broke in two. Only a makeshift wooden stake remained. She grasped it firmly, but her leg began to go numb and her head ached. The young woman lay face down on the ground, not moving.

Not good.

The dazed and bleeding rat backed away from Perez and turned to the downed girl. Without hesitation, Perez stepped between the predator and its prey. She waved her stake and crouched low, bracing herself for another attack. She looked for the best place to strike. Though slowing, the rat appeared determined to have its meal.

"The underbelly … I'll get her fingers from your stomach, you bitch!"

The creature crouched lower, once again poised to attack. Just as Perez thought she would get her shot, something struck the rat from behind. It vectored to the side and slammed into a group of tables and chairs where it remained, unmoving. Two spears and a throwing knife stuck out of its body. Perez breathed a sigh of relief and looked around for her rescuers.

"Ad arma!" A group of women yelled from the floor above.

The sentry group … thank God.

Satisfied that the danger had passed and help was en-route, Perez fought the banging in her head and growing pain in her side and limped towards the young woman with one leg trailing. The numbness was spreading.

"It would've been so much easier if you had your sidearm," she said to herself. She made it to the young woman and turned her over to make sure she was still alive. Not sure, Perez ripped off her blouse's sleeves and made a tourniquet for the woman's wrist. Every time she looked down to attend to the woman, something dripped from above, and she wondered where it came from. The first responder arrived with her weapon still drawn. She stopped and stared wide-eyed. Perez finished her work on the injured girl, then looked right back at the staring woman.

"What …" Perez started to say, but the effort winded her.

Three more women arrived. They too stared at the scene, jaws slackened as if in awe. The first woman's expression changed from surprise to a broad smile at their reaction. Perez ignored them and took a deep breath for the first time since the battle. She felt drained; her leg felt dead, her side was on fire, and her head hurt. She put her hand on her head to see what was dripping on her and assumed the warm liquid was sweat. She tried to speak, but her voice sounded different.

"That young woman is hurt and she needs medical attention. Now."

Perez lowered her hand and stared, eyes widening at the blood and hair smeared across it. She did remember feeling disorientated at one point, as if something had hit her. Perez looked back at the woman. She'd sheathed her weapon and the other three had gone to take care of the young woman and look for the other rats.

"There will be such a lore about this, Earther. You have

no idea what you have done. You are now Terran—battle-hardened and bound by blood to a noble name," she said solemnly.

Beyond her hand, a pool of Perez's blood puddled around her injured leg.

"Oh hell," she said, recounting how many times she might have been struck.

The woman continued speaking, but Perez, swimming in confusion, didn't register the words. Her eyesight tunneled, and she felt as if the floor rushed up to meet her. Strong arms stopped her from crashing into the ground. Tiredness overwhelmed her and she drifted off.

Chapter Nine

New Mission – Earth

Real knowledge is to know the extent of one's ignorance - Confucius

Riesman turned over in her snug bunk. Resting had given her a chance to put the Thanksgiving events behind her or, at least, to take a break from thinking about them. She'd already slept a couple of hours, but her new alien women friends were singing and dancing above deck louder than usual. Under normal circumstances being on a yacht anchored at Bimini just west of the Bahamas would be enjoyable, especially in December, but restlessness, anxiety about the future, and knowing things she preferred not to know about spoiled it for her.

"Really? A hidden world with more of those people?" she said aloud, her voice competing with the festivities above. Satellite news and internet reports that she and Administrator Damon, along with a number of guests, were presumed dead from a horrific fire made everything seem more real. She snickered at the constant reports from a Christine Reich's spokesperson in Hamburg who reported that 'Ms. Reich never made her flight out to be at that party,' and that she was 'saddened by the terrible events.'

Lucky you. Several dead, assassins killed, intended victims MIA, and world's biggest secret revealed. It's the best flight you ever missed.

But the four women on the boat distracted her from the truth of that night. The new arrivals acted like children in a toy shop, delighted by their fresh experiences—the ocean, chestnuts, lemons and fish. Meal times had a festive atmosphere, filled with laughter, singing and talking about their own planet, Terra.

Riesman learned that the tidal-locked planet on the other side of the Sun had advanced technology to hide it from Earth, but the technology was failing. If she hadn't seen the spaceship silently landing and lifting off, and the similar, though alien, nature of the women around her, she would've thought such ideas meant she was high or psychotic.

Yet, it was all real. She knew, but the rest of the world didn't, and it would be chaos when it found out.

How could Jesus Christ save another species when he was the human son of God? And Genesis? We're supposed to be special, a chosen people in the image of God.

In addition to the existential dilemma, the aliens liked to walk around naked. They couldn't do it on their home planet, but Earth was apparently ideal for the lack of clothes. And to Riesman's surprise and chagrin, they took great pride in their bodies. It took her several days to learn not to stare. Nearly every part of their bodies had hair except for their breasts, the majority of their face and neck, and the back parts of their limbs. The hair on their head was thick and coarse, while their body hair appeared fine and silky. She discovered that her walking around in a one piece bathing suit was just as revolting to them. To reduce the mutually discomforting visual images, Riesman spent much of the day topside, enjoying the sun and clearing her head with either Lux or Vespere, while the others slept, rested and worked below. Unfortunately, that meant they typically stayed up at night, all night, navigating the vessel and partying as if on spring break. The days slipped by, and they stayed very close to Bimini. It finally dawned on Riesman to ask why they were there.

"This may be overwhelming," Vespere said.

"Really? It may be 'overwhelming?' After seeing an interplanetary spacecraft and everyone talking about their home planet being on the other side of the Sun, I don't think there's much more that can surprise me," Riesman said honestly.

Vespere's sigh indicated that she was choosing her words carefully.

"This site still holds an active Keeper's communication node. The Keeper of Earth was located in a land your people called Atlantis. When it was swallowed by the ocean, all of its secrets, teachings, and population were killed, leaving only a partially functioning node, a remote computer. The tablet you hold is a portal or mini-computer that accesses this node. Since it was in constant use for the last decade, it shut down. Once this happens, the portal, or what you have been calling the tablet, needs to be brought here so it can recharge, update and reboot. That's why we rushed to get here. This is why we stay, other than the beautiful location and weather." Vespere stopped and sat quietly.

Unable to find words, Riesman sat with the sun warming her shoulders and neck and stared at the naked, hairy Vespere and her beautiful ocean backdrop. Eventually, she nodded and went below deck to sleep. Perhaps she was suffering from heat stroke.

"Atlantis … the City of Atlantis? See what happens when you think you've heard everything," she said. Riesman hoped that sleep would help her perspective.

She slept well beyond dinner, and, once awake, decided to stay in her bunk in an attempt to fit another puzzle piece with everything she'd learned to date. Her fear of how the general population might deal with the revelations of a new planet, a new species and its relationship to Atlantis, tired Riesman in spite of the dancing and singing above decks, and her eyelids started to close. They flew open when electric blue light suddenly illuminated the small room.

"Roberta Joanne Riesman. Thank you for transporting me to this location for rebooting and recharging," a calm female voice said. Riesman bolted upright, narrowly missing the cabin's ceiling. The tablet Perez had given her glowed.

"Updates are complete, and we can now leave this location. Would you like a mission briefing?" the voice continued.

Bleary-eyed and still sitting on her bunk, Riesman took a moment. "What?"

The tablet's light subsided to a low intensity dark blue. Riesman turned on the light. The tablet looked different; blue rather than the glossy black she remembered.

It speaks … and it changed color.

"Immunes Riesman. You are obviously still confused, either from your sleeping or the entirety of these past events that have resulted in you needing to give up one life for that of another. I will take the initiative and provide a very brief synopsis of the mission," the voice said.

"All right," Riesman said cautiously. She slipped from her bunk and stood over the tablet, watching the images that accompanied the voice—DNA coding, physical structures of humans along the evolutionary line, and then two worlds, Earth and another that looked less hospitable.

"You may call me Keeper, as I am the portal to the last remaining power node of the Earth's only Keeper in Atlantis. I should remain functioning for the next decade depending on use. Here is a summary:

"There are two habitable planets in this solar system remaining from a total of four. Terra was an experimental habitat that was never expected to survive but has persevered as a result of the Terran Keeper, the Architects and Eco- Scientists. It is inhabited by a species similar to humans you know as Terrans. These Terrans are a separate hominid species from planet Earth. They may appear as derivatives of what you would label as Neanderthal, but this species predates human development on this planet. The original Terran species developed on Venus until the cataclysmic events created by its greenhouse effect necessitated their relocation to Terra permanently. As Terra's original species died out, the eco- scientists groomed the present Terran species to inherit the planet.

The events that destroyed Mars, home of our creators, the 'Originators,' also wiped out the dinosaur species of your planet and accidentally furthered Earth's development. The planet's atmosphere stabilized approximately sixty-three million years ago, and the Eco-Scientists moved five hominid species to Earth in the hopes that one of the species would survive and thrive. Ultimately, the planet yielded one species. However, for a period of time, two coexisted and interbred. The groups you refer to as Neanderthal from Europe and southwestern-central Asia, and Homo-sapiens that evolved from Africa, produced offspring that left mitochondrial remnants that exist at an estimated point zero-zero-zero-one-three. Your mitochondrial remnants exceed that baseline, making you the closest ambassador between the humans on Earth and Terra …."

Though she found the information fascinating, Riesman shook her head with frustration.

"What does it matter? Why is it important? Why did Hiaki Nakamura have to die? What does this have to do with the women topside and Perez?" she blurted out.

The outlandish history of Mars, Venus, dinosaurs and Neanderthals filled her mind with more outrageous thoughts than she'd ever dreamed could exist. Without hesitation, the Keeper answered the questions in a calm, low tone.

"Your sharing the mitochondrial remnants is important because you have a connection to both planets that is valued by the more technologically advanced civilization of Terra. Further, in eight point five years, part of Terra will move out from the solar glare of the sun, making it visible for the first time in Earth and Terra's history. While it has been able to use the sun and a sophisticated holographic imaging device to hide the planet, the machinery required to keep the planet invisible is failing. It has required periodic shutdowns to repair but its ability to remain perpetually active is no longer possible. It will take Earth two point three months to discover Terra if its cloaking system were to fail. Dr. Nakamura's work in light, prisms and energy was on track to discover this technology. Terra wanted to bring him to their home planet with other humans to assist in repairs. He was contacted but refused to leave."

"Why?" Riesman said more than asked.

"He wouldn't have been afraid. My God! He would have leapt at the chance of a new world…" She saw his caring face with dark, penetrating and smiling eyes. How he made her so happy.

"He reported that he did not want to leave you," the Keeper said.

Riesman's heart sank and her eyes filled with tears. She couldn't move or speak. Hot tears hit her cheeks, lips and bare feet. Her mouth quivered and her knees weakened. She had no idea how long she remained that way, and only when her sniffling stopped and her crying slowed, did the Keeper's voice return.

"Once Dr. Nakamura understood the nature of his work and how Terra's discovery would affect an unprepared Earth, he agreed to destroy his work. Mr. Perez was sent to assist him in that endeavor. Once Immunes Perez discovered his relationship with you, both he and Dr. Nakamura accurately feared for your life."

Another wave of sadness washed over her at hearing both names.

They both cared for me?

"Further review of your medical file, history, and family of origin search found a remote possibility that you possessed mixed heritage. I confirmed this when you made contact with me on November twenty-third, two thousand and twenty-three. Once Dr. Nakamura's death was confirmed, your safety was compromised. Immunes Perez made contact with you in the hope that the people watching you would use you to get to him. Their ultimate goal is to find Ms. Christine Reich. The events that occurred on Thanksgiving were initiated and perpetrated by rogue agents of the United States federal government. However, Immunes Perez and his Terran team orchestrated their role. Its purpose: disrupt their efforts, create the illusion of your death, and to clear a path for you to take over as team leader vacated by Immunes Perez."

Riesman stood silently over the dimly-glowing tablet, considering the implications of the last sentences. The tear tracks on her face dried as she took in the information and processed it as if it were a complex puzzle.

"How do you know these things? How can you be sure of all these things when you're from an alien world?"

"Due to an unexpected event, we discovered Johann Christian Reich twenty-three years ago—"

"You mean *the* J. C. Reich of Reich Enterprises?"

"Yes."

"What do you mean 'you discovered him'?"

"The Terran survey ship, *Clear Ahead Horizon*, suffered systemic computer failure resulting in loss of orbit. The crew abandoned ship but not before setting the ship to self-destruct upon crash landing to ensure secrecy. This occurred in Tunguska, Siberia, Russia on Earth time-line July 30, 1908."

Something about that location is familiar. I thought that was a meteor blast?

"The eight survivors were able to remain unnoticed and covert. However, with the advent of World War Two, it was evident to the survivors that Earth technology was advancing faster than expected. The team reorganized itself and drew up new mission parameters: locate the Atlantis power node to bring me back online; re-establish communication with Terra; locate Earthers who would be in a position to understand the situation, and use our advanced technology to create an identity that would allow us to monitor all communication, access all computers and artificial intelligent creations, and access all critical commercial, military, educational and scientific forums world- wide."

"You did it, didn't you?"

"Yes."

"So when history says that Reich created the light-bearing principle that changed the way computers think…"

"We were the ones that assisted in that project as a means of tying into all future operation systems and allow Immunes Reich to increase his wealth."

Riesman's head spun as she tried to remember what else the elusive J. C. Reich did in the world of technology and computers.

"It's involved in every computer on the planet now," she said.

"Yes."

"And he created the 'Licht Lagersoftware.' the 'Lucifer' software…"

"Yes. This software is key in harnessing the computer power from a computer's hard drive memory into amplifying the working memory, RAM, of any computer. Processor speed increased exponentially. J. C. Reich's transition from using my knowledge and mathematical advances moved from predicting profitable stocks in the United States to an actual technological advancement. As a result, J. C. Reich was able to move his already amassed fortunes into controlling shares in the foreign equivalents of Microsoft, Apple, Android and MaxDrive operating systems as well as acquiring these same companies' suppliers. The net result was an increase in his vast wealth and resources, as well as placement of Lucifer software in every operational computer on the planet in two thousand and eight."

"Just before the world-wide recession …" Riesman said. "He was able to move all of his money into commodities to hold its value as stocks crashed. And when they were at their lowest, he bought them all … stocks in computer, software, military suppliers, universities …"

"Yes."

"But didn't he die?"

"His fictional death was recorded to have occurred on July twenty-third, two thousand and ten, as a result of a heart attack. This left Christine Reich as sole heir to his empire."

Fictional death?

"Let me guess, J. C. is alive and well?"

"He lives as Joseph Collins in Maui, Hawaii. He adopted Terran life style and has halted his diabetes, maintained optimal weight, and reversed his high blood pressure. While he still drinks more than the recommended amount of wine per day, he is active and reports that he is having the time of his life."

"How does Perez fit in here? I mean, this is pretty incredible …"

"His daughter, Andrea Perez, specialized in

spectrograph science and gravity."

"And you found this out."

"My artificial intelligence and access points are spread over the entire planet. This includes, but is not restricted to, the US Department of Defense, NASA, the National Security Agency, the Chinese Ministry of State Security, and hundreds more databases and servers that are thought to be impervious to security breaches."

The Keeper's voice was calm, matter of fact, and emotionless as it reported on how it had breached every security and defense agency in the world. Riesman stood still and watched the corresponding images and events that the tablet relayed, including visuals from top secret bases that were rumored to exist around the world. After a few moments of silence, save for the dancing and music topside, she began to fully appreciate that this tablet had a back door to everything. The Terran software increased processor speed and was in every operating system, which meant that any private or public agency with the need for top grade computers would have it by default.

"Damn," she said. "Who is Christine Reich?"

"Christine Reich is a virtual creation, the fictional orphaned niece of J. C. Reich. Long before his reported death, I created a virtual footprint and put all his documents and assets under her control. The top ones are Reich Enterprises' computer companies, pharmaceutical companies, import-export companies, and specific electronic firms. She is real to the world but is solely virtual."

Riesman sat on the edge of her bunk, her head swimming with espionage, false identities and alien computers and worlds. She pulled the blanket over her shoulders and said nothing. She felt lost, alone, and completely out of control.

Now what?

"So what do I have to do with this?"

"Your participation is voluntary. Immunes Perez believes you to be a capable person, but he did not wish to commit you to the mission unless you wished."

Riesman's heart and mood lifted. She smiled at her painted toes and felt a glimmer of hope. "I can walk away if I chose?"

"Yes. I will need to provide a new identity and a substantial amount of financial resources for you to live well and in obscurity abroad."

"A *substantial* amount of financial resources? You mean I'd be rich?"

"Yes."

"Okay."

Visions of living in France jumped into her head. She could smell the cafes, feel the expensive clothes and fast cars, and taste the wine, cheese and croissants.

"I wish you'd told me that part first." Her voice sounded light and clear.

The visions and sensations were perfect until she remembered her family, Anthony Perez, and Hiaki Nakamura. Her thoughts turned dark at the memory of Agents Harper and Lee killing her boss, and intending to kill her. Now that the option of leaving was a viable recourse, Riesman asked a question she did not expect to ask:

"And what if I stay?"

The Keeper spoke as evenly as before.

"You would take on the virtual life of Christine Reich. You would complete the primary missions, which are twofold: warn your world of the impending natural disaster of the significant release of methane gas emanating from the reduction of ice and permafrost in the North and South Poles and initiate steps that need to be taken prior to this catastrophe, and facilitate Earth's discovery and processing of Terra's discovery."

Methane gas? Riesman's FEMA director persona took over. She jumped off the bunk and picked up the tablet.

"What do you mean, 'methane gas?'"

"Immunes Riesman, before I proceed, I need to know if you are inclined to disembark from this proposed mission or to engage it. The choice of this journey is yours."

The Keeper's matter of fact tone bothered Riesman.

"So … before I hear anything more, you want to know if I'm in or out."

"Yes. Immunes Perez chose you because he felt you would also address a number of other objectives."

"Like what?"

Images of destitute children, women, and families, all in pain and distress flowed across the Keeper's screen. Riesman's eyes knitted.

"What the hell is this?"

The Keeper stopped the disturbing flow of human horror and focused on a group of apparently well-off people.

"Disrupt a child trafficking operation posing as an adoption agency in Moscow, Russia. Disrupt human trafficking, prostitution and drug operation in Beijing, China. Disrupt and terminate flow of child slavery via Sir Robert Phillip Pierce of Pierce Industries, London, UK…"

"Hold that image," Riesman blurted out.

A regal-looking man dressed as an elf and surrounded by very young girls dressed in sheer gowns filled the screen. He smiled, but the girls did not. Perez had looked at the same man at Hiaki's funeral with intense disgust and vehemence. The reason was now clear.

"Child slavery … *Sir* Pierce."

"Yes."

Her anger swelled and she had to consciously release her tightening grip on the tablet's edges. The music and dancing above seemed to escalate as the question settled in her brain. Her confusion and ambivalence faded and the motivation that emerged caught her by surprise.

Do I want to get back at the people who killed Hiaki? Do I want to save these kids and do a little good in the world? she thought as more dossiers of 'bad' people flowed across the screen.

"I could live in peace … in France …"

"Yes," the Keeper answered as if it were a question.

Riesman looked into the blue glare in her small cabin

and struggled with conflicting thoughts. The urge to run was palpable.

"I don't know," she whispered.

Chapter Ten

Revelations – Terra

You cannot open a book without learning something. - Confucius

"How could I have been so blind to it all? Why did I wait so long to ask the bigger questions?" Andrea Perez said. She stood akimbo at the apex of the largest pyramid on the planet's surface in front of several feet of transparent stone windows, looking into what appeared to be a star field and empty space.

She turned and looked at the world clock and calendar on the wall several yards behind her. It announced that it would shut down the planetary cloak field in five seconds. Maintenance and repair would have to be completed in five days. Perez took these precious moments to relax in full knowledge that she and the other scientists would probably be on their feet with the engineers for that entire period.

She turned back as the rocky Terran landscape dotted with pyramids of all sizes materialized in the window. Her reflection, appearing leaner and more muscular than before her battle with the rattus, overlaid the view of the rocky surface.

Perez, wiser and battle hardened, stood prepared to fight, holding the hilts of two long serrated knives. Her old combat knife, retrieved from the rats by the Terrans, sat against her thigh. To complete the ensemble, she sported a handheld laser capable of eight individual shots that could cut through diamond in seconds. She'd never been without her firearm since her release from the infirmary.

She shifted focus back outside before her gaze reached the reflection of her scarred head. To her left, windswept rocks, sand and periodic pyramids glistened in the sun of the perpetual day. She thought about the revelations she'd dug up and shook her head in disbelief that she'd not pieced it all together sooner. In an effort to think of something else, she shifted her gaze to the perpetual darkness on her right where more low-lying pyramids stood against bitter winds and crackling lightning bursts. The flashes illuminated a great frozen ocean in the distance.

She took the precious moments while she waited for Clematis to reflect on her discovery of the solar system's origin. She'd spent many hours locked away in the Great Library and other libraries, including the Keeper's Chamber. Terra's world computer still worked and provided images that fleshed out the illustrations and diagrams the Terrans had produced to preserve the story.

Many times she'd cried tears of joy and sadness; she'd felt bursts of understanding and then moments of darkness and confusion. Climbing aboard an alien ship to another planet was nothing in comparison to her latest discoveries.

She'd been so busy learning the new science, technology and languages that she'd only looked at Terran's history before, not the others. But after Terra came Venus. Her Terran friends and colleagues watched her with great enthusiasm and brought her food and water, as if she were tracking her meal on a great hunt across the Serengeti.

After her battle with the rattus, Perez felt part of an exclusive club. As a result of her journey, as the Terrans called it, they suspended her duties with the holographic emitters and planetary cloaking. Terrans of all ages told the lore of her battle with the Magna Mures, Great Rats, as if she were a great warrior. The young woman she'd saved, daughter of an Elder, who'd sneaked out to look for a male friend, also achieved warrior status for her part in the fight. Both of their roles were great enough to propel them into lore, witnessed by the sentry group and the young woman's sister. Perez had come of age, and the story would transcend the ages. Whether she liked it or not, she was the adopted kin to the powerful warrior clan House of Ferris. The powerful matriarch, Dimitra, was far from pleased to have her join the family but Perez did save her daughter, Vista. It was a matter of honor now.

The Battle of Delta Mezzanine they called it—sounds good, but it was more a skirmish than a battle. How long ago was it? After Thanksgiving but before Christmas ... Christ's birthday ... Son of God...

After the incident and her recovery, she'd returned to her research and discovered that Terrans were expected to endure at least six journeys. She'd already completed three, leaving procreation, teaching, and death on the to-do list. She changed her view from the right to the left and back again while different thoughts jumped around in her head. Along with the wisdom gained from her research came the pain of not being special.

"Intelligent design," she said quietly.

Though she focused on a series of lightning strikes across the frozen sea, she sensed that Legate Legionis Clematis stood behind her. Her flowery odor and her light footsteps gave her away. After her battle with the rodents, her senses had become acute, honed to even the slightest of air movements. Even the constant hum and vibrations of the underworld's machinery didn't obscure them.

"I understand the wisdom of the journey. I'm almost embarrassed at my asking you to tell me. Now, with still more to learn, I'm both at peace and excited," Perez said to Clematis, still watching the elements rage silently outside while the powerful winds, thunder and hail reverberated under her feet.

"There is no need to be embarrassed, Perez. Always the curious ones are the most impatient. Your Earth origins clearly reinforce both your curiosity and your impatience. Your discipline harnessed them both and brought you to this part of your long journey. The relentless speed and vigor you pursued it with is beyond even the youngest of our youth. Amazing, I say. And in the middle of it, you endured a battle, fought alongside a Terran, saved her life by nearly forfeiting your own, and then you went back to your research. We are proud of you, Perez. Please, though, tell me what you found. I am curious as to how far you went."

Clematis sounded like a child about to hear a great story. Perez turned to look at her. She realized that her journey was never in isolation; her colleagues and friends were there with her all along.

"While the information and data of your journey is known to me, it's your interpretation that escapes us all. Your understanding is unique from ours as we have always been on Terra. You bring the perspectives of two worlds, and that is a journey that we cannot take without your help."

"My help?"

"Yes, Perez. One of your other journeys will be to teach what you have learned from your perspective. But please, tell me your insights." Clematis walked to the middle of the small room and sat cross-legged as if awaiting an interesting story. Perez joined her on the floor as shadows of lightning danced across the reinforced walls of the transparent stone windows. Perez rearranged her various weapons and sat beside her, wondering where to begin. Unable to cross her left leg due to the deep wounds still healing from the rat tail, she kept her legs straight.

"Please, Perez, do what the Earthers do so well—

summarize and give the key points. I do not wish to spoil the full breadth of the story when you start teaching it to us later. I look forward to it."

My God, I've missed so much. How we've all fought our nature back on Earth; instant answers and no time for the stories.

"It started with your love of chestnuts, pyramids, and your physical appearances," Perez began.

Clematis's eyes grew wide.

"I knew that would be the starting point! Please, tell me more," she asked.

"I'd always assumed that both Terra and Earth must have shared a common history at some point. The physical phenotype of the Terrans was consistent with an ancient species of hominids we called Neanderthals. We believed the species died out thirty to forty thousand years ago. The Terran's skull, the short, strong stature, large jaws, dense bones and powerful muscles and facial structure all led me to believe this, and that my species was the superior species. But Terrans are not Neanderthals.

Rather you are an alien hominid, close in DNA but distinctly separate and Venusian in origin, relocated by yet another alien species."

"Yes! But then what made you revise that thought, other than you spending time with us?" Clematis asked.

"I'm embarrassed to say that it was less my observations for the last fifteen years and more my deduction, later supported by those now obvious facts. I was really slow," Perez said.

"Slow, thorough, it does not matter. How did you get to your conclusions?"

"I discovered that while us Earthers' intelligence is in our frontal lobe, the Terran's intellectual center is concentrated in the parietal lobe, safely tucked below the head rather than right up front."

"Oh. I never would have thought that's how you discovered the truth."

"Yes. That was why the doctors were so concerned about my head injuries." Perez pointed to her scarred head. It held a metal plate where a rat's tail scale had lodged during the fight. She often touched the chain around her neck where the two inch scale hung. A memento pulled from her head, the claw hung like a trophy. It had launched a fashion trend of rat scale and claw necklaces.

"But your Neanderthal species were the original Terrans. The ones we replaced," Clematis said. Perez shook herself to refocus.

"Yes. To some degree, my discovery was accidental. But when I also discovered that the genetic percentage of Neanderthal and Terran DNA were nearly identical, I realized that the Neanderthals were the Terrans that had made it to Earth. For a period of time we all co-existed there. And for a short time, there was interbreeding which left a genetic marker in many of us hominids as well. The medical test you have here can identify these markers. We might have this technology now but we didn't when I was on Earth. While there is no Neanderthal DNA code in people from Africa's sub-Saharan plate, it must have been something when I showed up with my dark skin, Terran body and Earth-like head."

"Oh yes! We had never seen such a unique distribution of our DNA so clearly present in a dark Earther such as you," Clematis said.

"Well, you can thank my multiracial heritage for that. Clearly, there is more European influence than my parents and I thought. So once I realized that our species co-existed, I had to re-evaluate our very existence on Earth and the probability that we came from elsewhere."

"Yes. The fourth planet from the sun. What do the Earthers call it?"

"Mars. It's funny too; all of our myths, stories and even some of our science clearly point to it being an older planet that had life. Our best science fiction literature suggests an advanced civilization living on Mars, an idea supported by ancient writings throughout our history. Still, once I found the Keepers' old logs on Mars, I felt foolish for not seeing it before." Perez rubbed her temples. She had a lot to keep her busy: charts, books, two-dimensional images, and ancient Keepers' logs all meticulously copied by hand in Latin. And while her appreciation and understanding of Latin grew in leaps and bounds, she never found out how Latin, a language from her own planet's ancient history, ended up on Terra.

Unless Latin originated here, on Terra. Maybe Mars?

"And what do the Earthers think of Mars?"

"There's nothing there. There was a great civilization

there once, a Martian Master Keeper's on the surface even, but not today. Not on the surface, but underground there remain survivors of a great species called Architects and Master Keeper. I should have seen this. When you have stories of Martian invasions, hieroglyphics and ancient drawings that point to an older civilization on a red planet, you'd think we'd pick up on the clues. But anyway, I'm impressed with how the Keepers understood the dangerous nature of the universe and thought to colonize Earth, Venus and Terra. Almost prophetic when you think about it," Perez mused.

"I have always come to believe that their motivations to avoid extinction via meteor impact made sense. With two dwarf planets' orbits on a collision course between Mars and the Jovian planet, the Keepers must have known when the collision would happen and the likelihood of the ensuing planetary destruction. The asteroid belt put them in grave risk."

"Too true. The foresight, though, and the engineering and compassion to set out and populate new worlds is truly inspirational."

"Almost inspirational enough to write about it in a book? What the Bible called 'The Great Flood,' 'End of Days' and the 'Four Horsemen of the Apocalypse?'" Clematis said. While Terrans were not known for sarcasm, they still had the capacity for it.

Perez pinched her nose, ostensibly to relieve sinus pressure. Clematis's jab at Earth's religions didn't surprise her.

"Don't be mean. We got the stories right, for the most part. We just didn't have the advantage of having a Keeper to fill in the context, and we left out the other books that explained key points of the Bible. Not bad for a species that had to do it all from memory."

"Like I said, the Earthers do not do well with unanswered mysteries. I have always been impressed with how your species did get much of it down in a book, a series of books, without the assistance of a Keeper. But then that's the tragedy of it all," Clematis said with sadness.

"Yes … when the end came for Mars, it wiped out Earth's Atlantis, home of the Keepers, and after millions of years—well into the era before the Egyptians—it finally sank into the sea. It is so sad and unfair …."

"Yes. And Venus … such a lush, beautiful world the Keeper tells us, the gem of all the planets. I am amazed that much of Earth survived unscathed, with the exception of Atlantis. Almost as if it were deliberately destroyed. An experiment perchance."

"Maybe. I wonder what things would have been like if we'd had a similar Keeper."

"It is amazing that your kind managed to prosper without one. A great experiment! Meanwhile, the Sun protected Terra, a desolate planet with nothing but caverns. I have often wondered, if the Keepers had been able to finish terraforming this planet, might it have been as beautiful as Venus?"

"It would have been better, but I'm guessing that since

Terra always has the same side facing the sun, it would've taken an additional tens of thousands years on top of the tens of thousands they had to finish the job. I think your subterranean world, the location along the terminus line, and an ocean filled with life, protected by miles of ice, has served you well. The Keeper's regeneration of Terra's magnetic field and reduction of methane and sulfur from the atmosphere is impressive," Perez said.

Visions of massive, interconnecting machines that tied into a majority of the planet's pyramids from the planet's poles filled her head as she imagined what it would be like to switch the planetary machinery from holographic illusions and life supports to terraforming again. The noise, heat and energy would be tough and the power consumption huge.

Is there going to be enough power to keep the underground world going and keep the emitters online? Perez wondered. *Maybe they'd planned to finish the project later and then seed the planet.* She guessed they'd run out of time and had decided to preserve an underground habitat rather than create one on the surface.

"I think hiding from Earth is a good idea. On top of the culture shock of your planet's existence, Earth would colonize Terra if it was in prime condition. It wouldn't be long before humans showed up, planted flags and took it all over. Bad enough that our presence will be discovered soon, at least Terra looks like a desolate, hostile and dead planet. Even then, you know us Earthers ..."

Perez's heart filled with anxiety at the thought of

various Earth governments pooling resources and setting out to conquer a new world, just as Columbus did.

That didn't turn out so well for the Native Americans now, did it?

If Earth was at a tipping point, the human race would be more desperate and see the Terrans as a primitive species and a problem to be eliminated.

"Absolutely! That's where we once again share a lot in common. No matter how inhospitable the land is, we can live there. We can live anywhere. But tell me, Perez, would our existence if known to our Earth cousins be so bad?" Clematis asked.

Perez answered as if their very lives depended on how quickly she shared her concerns.

"I think it would be devastating for the nine billion people on Earth. If they were to take the same journey I did, the majority of them would understand and make changes to save their own world. But religious zealots would feel threatened if they found the Keeper's knowledge and data. Humans don't do well when fundamental aspects of their understanding changes. The basis of many religious and philosophical beliefs would become unhinged, emotions would run amok, and the knowledge that we Earthers are not alone and not unique would first shock and then anger us. Many would lose their fundamental belief in God and codes of ethics."

"Like the Judea-Christian's Ten Commandments and the Tenants of the Koran," Clematis said.

Perez pressed on, feeling an urgent need to warn her

friend and her adopted world of a waking giant.

"Yes. As incomplete as they both are, these codes of good behaviors might be tossed aside by those who come to believe that there is no God and that we are not unique."

Anxiety and fear took hold of Perez. Her own belief that more existed after death suddenly left her, and she felt alone in the universe.

"That is all possible, Perez, but doesn't our existence reinforce the presence of God or a Divine Creator?" Clematis asked.

Perez felt as if she'd hit a wall. The idea that good or reassurance might come from the discovery of aliens just across the solar system or that humans might embrace a newly discovered world with another similar species never occurred to her. Only Earth's consistent history of conflict when one country saw opportunity with another came to mind—wars over politics, economics, and religion.

"Did the Keeper tell you where they came from?" Clematis asked.

Lightning reflected off the walls of the silent room.

"No. The Keeper reported that its earliest memories were the discovery of Mars and its teeming ecology and bio-systems of life." A suddenly realization dawned.

"Life was there before they arrived."

"So how was the circumstance for life created on Mars before the Keepers' arrival?"

Perez smiled. Some of her unasked questions possibly had answers. "It looks like I have to ask more questions," she said.

"Good, Perez. It may be time for you to join my journey as I have been searching for that answer. I would like to find it before my final journey so I can tell my kin and all the other Terrans." Clematis stood, ostensibly to leave.

Perez, surprised by the invitation to join her on an important journey, followed her lead, though with some difficulty as her leg had stiffened.

"What questions have you been trying to answer?" she asked. Clematis's eyes widened slightly.

Let me guess … it's obvious.

"Just tell me, Clematis. I'm exhausted, hungry and thirsty."

Perez took time to straighten and regain feeling in her leg. She rubbed her thin face, then ran her hands through her not-so- clean hair, avoiding the new growth near her scars. Fortunately, Clematis took pity on her and answered.

"I want to know who created the Architects and the Keepers. Where did they come from? They had to come from somewhere, right? We call our creators the Originators. Who are they?"

Perez stopped to consider the simple question. Her hands went to her knife hilts and her eyes narrowed. In the finest tradition of Earth humans, she hadn't focused on the most important questions, the ones that could yield a more unifying answer. "Hmm."

Clematis didn't wait for an answer. Apparently, she

had more immediate things on her mind.

"But before that journey, I hope your father brought bushels of chestnuts. We will know soon, as *Silent Falling Star* will be here in the next several hours."

"What?" Perez's voice rose. "You let me rant and rave all this time and forgot to let me know that my father will be here soon?"

"I did not forget, Perez. I chose the right time to tell you, which was now."

"Hmm." Perez rolled her shoulders. She could feel her leg again, and it had been good to talk about all this. "Lead the way, Clematis. I need to get clean and prepare for the drums and dance."

"Excellent, Perez! Maybe you can take the lead in the dance?"

Clematis was already opening the hatch in the floor to the staircase below.

"Maybe I will." Perez shook the stiffness out of her sore leg and prepared to follow.

Chapter Eleven

Reunited – Terra

Things that are done, it is needless to speak of…things that are past, it is needless to blame. - Confucius

"Your father, Perez the Elder, continues to improve, Perez the Younger," Centurion Dea Data said.

Perez stood close to the semi-transparent cryogenic tube where she could see him sleeping. Relieved that her father was all right, she was glad there was a simple solution to distinguish them since first names were nonexistent on Terra.

Oh Dad. What were you doing?

Perez paused at the thought that she looked very different as well in not just years but also in wear and tear.

Wait until he sees me…

Dea Data, or "Dee Dee" as she was called by Clematis, continued with her summary.

"We were able to remove the projectiles with ease and repair his lung. The swelling in his face has substantially subsided while he was in cryogenic stasis. To ensure his steady recovery and acclimate his body to Terran's gravity and atmosphere, I made the decision to keep him in stasis while we adjusted his chamber during his return."

Perez nodded but remained focused on her father. He had more gray hair, but other than the bruising near his temple, he looked very healthy and even younger. Perez felt Clematis's reassuring grip on her shoulder. Cloelius looked on.

"Thank you, Centurion. And thank you for taking care of him all these years back on Earth. He looks remarkable considering all he's done and what he's gone through."

"He is a tough brute. Disciplined, focused, tenacious—I swear he is full Terran," Dee Dee said.

Perez looked back at Dee Dee and was going to ask her a question, but Dee Dee was looking over her shoulder and smiling. Perez followed her gaze, as did the others. A large Terran male, tall and very broad, drew the women's attention. His casual gait and beautiful smile made Perez feel safe. With Terran males in few numbers, seeing one was rare. The group watched him stretch out his arms and envelop Dee Dee in an embrace.

Perez looked away to be polite, but Clematis and Cloelius did just the opposite. They looked, vicariously experiencing the embrace. Not sure what to do, Perez opted to pull Clematis and Cloelius's voyeuristic stare away and remind the couple they were still in the hangar with hundreds of staring women.

"I've seen very few males here, but he's the first I've seen that is … I don't know … muscular?"

"That is because he is one of the older ones, joined to several women for our procreation efforts. When he's not involved with his tasks, he is teaching combat maneuvers, ethics and physics. He is quite the specimen," Clematis said.

"And he's quite a looker too; he has hair everywhere and his physical prowess is legendary," Cloelius added. A hint of envy and admiration glittered in the woman's eyes.

"And he wants to talk to you later, Perez. The story of your battle with the rattus horde intrigued him, and he wants to hear more about your tactics, about how you beat back four rattus; a first, by the way," Clematis said.

"It was actually two on three; one rat stayed out of the fight and I caught one by surprise while the other was already engaged …"

The couple's conversation drew Perez's attention, and she moved to the other side of her father's stasis chamber to listen in.

"Don't ruin a good story with facts," she heard one of them say.

"…Well, I am impressed that my sisters will let me have you for three whole weeks, undisturbed, after my absence for a decade. How kind," Dee Dee said sarcastically.

The way the couple hugged and smiled at each other reminded Perez of her father and mother … *a lifetime ago.* She reached out and touched the transparency just above her father's face.

"Now, Dee Dee, be kind. I tried to get more time, but

your sisters are not as flexible or as generous as you. Still, forget about them and come home. I have prepared a return meal, and the family will join us in two hours," he said.

His virile build and deep voice impressed Perez. It matched his persona.

"I must oversee the cargo manifest first and debrief on the mission." Dee Dee's expression grew sad.

Clematis took a step towards the couple.

"No, Centurion Dea Data. Dux Cloelius, Minor Perez and I are here for that task," she said in a warm voice.

"You are to go home with your betrothed now."

"We are?" Cloelius asked. Her expression matched Perez's surprise.

"Yes, Centurion. We have this covered. Welcome home. We will find you should we have questions." As if to finalize the act, Clematis produced a tablet and stylus and began to go through the ship's manifest.

Dee Dee's eyes widened. She smiled and bowed with her closed fist over her heart. Perez saluted in return. Dee Dee grabbed her mate's hand and they left, talking together with sparkling eyes and excited gestures while dozens of people arrived to dance upon the ship's return.

They do find reason to dance.

"That was very kind, Clematis," Perez said.

Two women dressed in medical uniforms walked up and gave quick bows.

"Yes, Clematis. You were very kind to speak for *us*. Very kind, indeed," Cloelius said without enthusiasm, as the medical team lifted Perez's father from the stasis chamber.

"Well, that is partially true. I do have a vested interest in seeing firsthand what *Silent Star Falling* has brought to us from Earth," Clematis said.

The medical team transferred Perez's father to a transporter and took him to the medical center.

"I'm sure there will be … My word!" Clematis's eyes widened and her mouth hung open.

"What is it?" Perez asked.

Clematis said nothing. She focused on the ship's manifest for moment, then pushed the tablet into Cloelius's hand and waited, grinning and hopping from one foot to the other while casting covetous glances at the ship.

Now what? Fresh lemons? A barrel of chestnuts? No—I bet it's a barrel of honey.

"What's going on, Cloelius? I've never seen her so excited."

Perez joined Cloelius's search of the manifest for something obvious, Perez reading slower due to the Latin. She saw Dee Dee's name and realized that her name, Dea Data, meant having been given by God. Distracted, she shook her head to focus on the ship's cargo.

"Other than chestnuts, lemons, tomatoes, and several tons of live haddock and salmon ready for transplanting … I can't … Oh. Now I see it. Oh, Legate Legionis Clematis! You are such a child at heart!" Cloelius said.

"What is it?" Perez asked.

Cloelius looked at Perez. Her face softened and her smile grew.

Well, at least it's good news.

"Puppies, Perez. The centurion has several species of puppies in stasis. Large breed dogs we had heard of from your planet—German Shepherds, Basset Hounds, and other hunting dog species. That is why she requested the extra stasis chambers and food for the trip back. It's been nearly two centuries since we lost our last pack. We now have our dogs back, Perez. It's such a great day for us all!"

Cloelius's expression made it clear that something big had changed on Terra forever.

"Oh … great … I hope all of you people know what goes into taking care of these creatures. I wonder if their poop will be heavier here. Yuck!"

Cloelius ignored the comment and walked to the ship with the deliberation of one approaching a sacred altar. Perez's father loved dogs, but her own memories were mostly that of taking the dog out to poop and picking up the mess. The day she'd left home for college was the day she escaped dog duty. But in the spirit of celebration and understanding the joy these creatures would bring to the people of Terra, she stood tall with her hands on the hilts of her blades and conjured up some enthusiasm for the dogs' arrival.

"Praise the Creators and God bless us all!" she said with emphasis. The dancers continued their jubilation, the drums beat louder, and a vision of full-sized dogs appeared in Perez's mind.

Next time those rat bastards come out again, they'll have to deal with dogs too.

Perez felt for her sidearm and found it in place.

"And I won't be screwing around with just knives next time."

Two Years Later

Chapter Twelve

I Am Legend—Earth

What you do not want done to yourself, do not do to others - Confucius

You know, you might want to answer the phone; it might be important, Reich thought, annoyed by the costume party music competing with the ringing land line.

Who owns a land line anyway? I guess it's kind of quaint. Not practical.

She stood under the watchful eye of bodyguards, waiting for the owner of the estate to climb the elegant stairs. Bored, she looked at the floor and caught sight of her breasts. *Ah, my poor girls,* she thought; *you used to be so much bigger.*

That's the price you pay for clean living and exercise.

Two heavy doors across the corridor opened. A tall, thin man dressed for Halloween as King Louis XVI stepped out, snapped his fingers at her, and motioned her and the guards into the large office. Book cases, art pieces, ornate tables and knickknacks filled the dark, possibly soundproof office. The estate's owner looked right at her, picked up his drink from the desk and moved closer to where she stood in the middle of the room. He did very little to hide his annoyance.

"Well, well, well … If it isn't the elusive Christine Reich. In the flesh, no less; often heard of but never seen. I am honored you have joined us, and in costume no less," Sir Robert Phillip Pierce said.

"The pleasure is all yours."

His smile evaporated. He took a sip and stared at her, looking natural in his regal costume. Just beyond him sat his young date dressed as Marie Antoinette. She looked uncomfortable and too young for him and his party. Reich pushed her enmity aside and focused on her compassion for the girl. Even as a cat burglar with all the accessories— skin tight fabric with leather strapping and utility belt— she felt underdressed. The ensemble enhanced her tall, muscular frame as well as her smaller breasts. Though she'd tied her red hair in a tight ponytail, her only regret with her evening's wardrobe was her functional shoes with excellent support and grip. Good for climbing, but her sexy high stiletto-heeled boots would have completed her costume— stunning, fashionable and impractical.

Such a statement, though. And if I added a whip … that would've been as sexy as hell. Hey! Focus!

With wine glass in hand and an obnoxious smirk, Pierce closed the distance between them, flanked by his two serious-looking bodyguards.

Oh yeah … I'm supposed to be frightened.

"David, Rachael, can you believe that Ms. Reich thought she could just show up and crash my party? London's most talked about event of the year?"

"Not very proper," the female said.

"Yes. Not very polite at all, Sir Pierce," the other chimed in.

"And while you are well dressed for the occasion, I would like to know how you managed to obtain this," Pierce held up an ornate invitation.

Hmm … that was a good forgery.

Memories of Anthony Perez talking to him at Hiaki's funeral flooded her, especially his look of disgust as Pierce and his underage date walked away. He'd looked almost as angry as she felt right now when she glanced at the minor on the couch.

Yeah … we're not done here, you pig.

With little regard for her own safety and little attempt to disguise her loathing, she looked right into Pierce's eyes.

"I'm sure that if you'd known I was going to be in town for business, you would have invited me. An oversight, I'm sure."

The guards crowded her on each side while Pierce moved to stand in front. She smiled at how calm she felt—far from intimidated—and noted various soft targets on Pierce's body should she have to move quickly.

Yeah … these shoes were the better choice.

Reich shifted her weight to her rear leg, leaving her front leg available for a kick to his stomach should the need arise. After months of altering her exercise regime to incorporate more weights, and significant training in combat skills and edged weapons, she was ready. Field tested and ready to go, she waited for any excuse to strike.

Mission first, payback second, free the girl third, she reminded herself as she tried to disengage from his attempts to intimidate her. She reviewed how she would strike him and then thought how the elimination of processed foods really did reduce anxiety, stress, and cleared her thinking.

Anthony had been right about the change in diet and food.

I swear my skin has gotten tighter too, and my hair—no more bleaching it blonde.

If she'd known she was a natural redhead, she would have dropped the processed foods long ago.

"You cost us time and aggravation, you know," Pierce said. "At least forty-five minutes to identify you without bothering my guests, and then an additional twenty minutes backtracking how you produced a legitimate invitation, and another half hour to make sure you were alone. All of my invitations are pressed and addressed under my direct supervision."

"You don't like mysteries?"

"No, I do not!"

After an uncomfortable moment of silence, Pierce snapped his fingers at his guards and turned his attention to a phone on his desk that buzzed a low, soft chime.

So you'll answer the low buzzing phone but not the loud

ringing one?

"It would be easier on you if you just tell Sir Pierce where you stole it from," the female guard said into her ear.

"Yeah, much easier," the male guard added with an additional nudge at her arm. Unfazed by the guards, Reich continued her silence and stood impassively, projecting fearlessness.

"You obviously have a well-connected network and resources to obtain this, but why would you go to such lengths to simply attend a party?" Pierce continued.

His unanswered phone was really beginning to wear on her.

Don't you have people who could answer that?

"Well, you did say that 'everyone who is someone will be there,' Sir Pierce."

Pierce's eyes narrowed and he stopped sipping his wine in mid-step.

"I don't recall saying that to you, Ms. Reich. Others, maybe, at a private dinner last week …"

The female guard pushed her left arm and the other gave a more forceful nudge.

This is getting old.

In quick succession, everyone spoke but her.

"How did you know that I said that? You weren't there."

"Don't be cocky, missy," the female guard hissed.

"You're pretty foolish if you think you're just going to walk away from this, princess," the other said.

Pierce's jaw tensed and his eyes narrowed. A vein bulged on his temple. The phone ringing probably didn't help.

"Who is your contact in my network?"

Pierce, once again, stood right in front of her in another vain attempt to intimidate. He left the phone ringing and waited only a second before repeating the question.

"Who is your contact, Ms. Reich?"

An old classic film crossed her mind, and an all too familiar name popped into her head. She couldn't stop an emerging smirk. Her father, with a twinkle in his eye, used it at parties where people didn't know him.

"My contact's name?"

"Yes! The name!"

"You really want to know?"

"Now, Reich!"

"His name is Bond, James Bond. He's on Her Majesty's Secret Service, and I assure you that should anything happen to me, MI6 will be all over Pierce Industries." Without thinking, Reich went with her story, some truth, some not. "Your private life will be in shambles, your stocks will fall. You will be penniless as you watch helplessly all your ventures collapse. At any rate, I'm sure you know Mr. Bond's number. That could be him on the phone right now."

Reich had difficulty suppressing her grin. She watched his eyes widen and hoped he would at least laugh or give her some credit for her presentation, but as the shock of her response wore off, it only seemed to anger him more.

Aw, come on! You got to give me something for delivery. The man has no sense of humor. Yet another flaw in the sack of shit's miserable character.

"Do you think this a game, Ms. Reich? Do you know who I am?" he asked, his anger clearly mounting while the phone continued to ring.

Reich glanced at the underage girl and remembered her name, age and circumstances. Revulsion flared for a moment, but she tamed her anger and looked right into his eyes. She kept her voice low and deliberate.

"I know who you are, Sir Pierce. You should get the phone. It's Mr. Robert Benson, your finance manager, calling from your New York office."

Reich enjoyed the confusion and nervousness on his face. He moved away from her towards the phone.

Yeah … I know what you're thinking. "How does she know that? How could she know that?"

After so many other missions and other similar situations, all their looks of surprise looked the same.

"Hello," he said tentatively. The anxiety in his expression grew as he listened. Reich sighed and casually retrieved the small tablet she kept in the pocket under her belt.

The male guard stopped her with a firm grip on her elbow, and then extended his hand for the tablet.

"Are you sure you really want it?" Reich asked.

"Do you really want your front teeth?"

That was good. A quick response for the muscle.

"Go on," the female guard said.

"All right," Reich pretended to be reluctant and handed the tablet to the male guard. His grip would loosen very soon.

"There have been no arrests here, Robert! How can my investments crash when nothing has happened? I haven't been charged with anything … For God's sake, Robert, I'm at my party, not under arrest …"

Reich would've liked to hear more, but the guard released her tablet and hit the floor with a loud thud. Pierce dropped the phone from his ear and stared wide-eyed in disbelief that one of his guards lay flat on his back. As the female guard went to her fallen comrade's side, Reich casually moved away and consulted her tablet.

"Rachael? What's the meaning of this?"

"I don't know, sir. He was just touching her tablet and then this."

"Ah, Sir Pierce? In about ten seconds, Mr. Benson will hear from the United States Federal Trade Commission regarding a couple of federal indictments. And in about one minute, your private phone will ring. Your director of operations, Janice Phelps, will need to scrap your telecommunication satellite project tomorrow due to an electronic issue. It happened during the launch sequence ten minutes ago," Reich said.

Pierce frowned and shook his head. His attention shifted back to the phone. Reich put her tablet back in her belt and walked over to a pair of paintings—Renoirs—absolutely gorgeous.

"… The Federal Trade Commission said what!" Pierce yelled.

Undaunted, Reich moved to another set of paintings—two lesser known Van Goghs—perfectly illuminated.

"Beautiful. Excellent lighting can make a huge difference." The phone slammed into its cradle behind her. She turned. Pierce stood just inches away from her, held back by his own guard.

"You must have broken in here last week! You must have downloaded information from my computer! That's why we found nothing stolen! That's the only way you could know all these things! I'm going to—"

"You're going to what, Mr. Pierce? File charges on a crime that never happened?"

"I'll—I'll sue you—"

"Sue me for what? Not that it matters. In twenty minutes, your stock will be worth twenty cents on the dollar, at which point Reich Enterprises will buy up all the shares for controlling interests of Pierce Industries."

Pierce's eyes and veins bulged, enraged and stunned at the same time, and just beyond him, the young Antoinette looked very nervous. Pierce pulled away from the guard and walked to his desk. A phone rang in the adjacent room, and he slowed for a moment before glancing sharply back at her. Pierce remained still while he opened a drawer and pulled out a semi-automatic weapon.

"Sir Pierce, no! She's not worth it!" the female guard said.

"I don't know how you did all of this, Reich, but you

will not live to enjoy your ill -gotten gains." Pierce pulled the trigger. It clicked but didn't fire. He checked the gun's safety catch, then pointed it right at her and pulled the trigger again. Another click.

"Well, this is interesting," Reich said, trying not to sigh in case he mistook her boredom for fear.

"Usually the guy with the gun does a quick monologue about how he won and how it must suck to be at the other end of the gun. I have to say I do respect your quick action, not at all what I expected from a pig like you." She looked at her tiny wristwatch and wondered when the good guys would arrive.

"What the hell?"

"'Ill-gotten gains?' Who says that? I mean really? That sounds like something from one of the Bronte sisters ...Charlotte Bronte, actually. More of a Jane Eyre thing," Reich said.

Pierce kept pulling the trigger, but each time, it only clicked, and he glared down at the gun looking for something wrong. His lips pressed more tightly together, his jaw grew more rigid and his frown deepened with each futile attempt.

"The firing pin has been removed, Sir Pierce."

Pierce's eyes widened to a degree that Reich thought was humanly impossible. Before he could utter a word, the office doors burst off their hinges, and a group of tactical police and detectives rushed in.

Talk about timing. Okay, does everyone see this piece of filth has a gun on me?

Surrounded by the mass of authorities, Pierce dropped his weapon. Uniformed men and women seized everyone. Reich smiled as more shock and awe washed over Pierce's face.

"It's her! She stole data from my computer!" he shouted.

The police rounded up Reich as well as Pierce, the female guard, Marie Antoinette, and the unconscious guard at her feet. She was pleased to see that two women and a man donned plastic gloves and moved almost reverently to the paintings she'd been looking at. The agitation and confusion in Pierce's expression deepened as a detective approached him.

"What is the meaning of this? Why are you here?"

"Detective Bradley at your service, my liege," a stout, older man, who clearly loved his processed food, said with a twinkle in his eye. With his portly stature and disheveled appearance, Chief Inspector Arthur Bradley of Scotland Yard looked nothing like his official file picture. Reich had thought he might appear in the raid, even though her reconnaissance had put him in the United States twenty-four hours earlier—probably meeting with General Farrell. Reich was glad they'd prepared for alternate escapes.

"My name is Sir Robert Phillip Pierce—"

"Detective Bradley, these paintings are original Renoirs and Van Goghs," one of the women interrupted.

"They are well preserved and this one is from the Isabella Stewart Gardner Museum—this is remarkable, sir."

Detective Bradley appeared to suppress a smile before turning back to Pierce. He took his time before he spoke, and timed each word with scratching his gray hair and flexing his fingers.

"I guess getting you for receiving stolen national treasures isn't the human trafficking charges I had hoped to file, my liege, but it will do very nicely."

Reich smiled as she watched Pierce's expression move from anger to shock to fury within seconds.

"I don't own any real Van Goghs, Renoirs, or anything like that! I … I was set up! Someone broke in here last week—"

The jovial detective cut him off.

"So, let me guess—instead of taking anything, which thieves are known to do, these bandits left you priceless paintings. Now that's a group of thieves that aren't straight on the purpose of grand theft! Yes, my liege—they left you priceless treasures rather than stealing them. Now that just makes perfect sense. Will that be your defense, my Worshipness?"

Reich enjoyed Detective Bradley's sarcasm directed squarely at Pierce, but then the detective's gaze fell on the young Antoinette and his expression turned to worry and concern. He walked towards her.

"And how old are you, little one?" he asked in the tone a parent might use with a child. Reich remembered that Bradley had two granddaughters, eight and ten. The girl didn't reply, and another officer, an older woman, stepped up beside her.

"It's all right, dear. You won't get in trouble."

After a moment of unnatural silence, a small voice spoke.

"I'm fourteen."

Bradley nodded, as if he'd expected that answer, and turned back to Pierce, clenching and unclenching his fists. Reich suspected he was trying to control an impulse to hit Pierce. No one would blame him.

"I truly don't know which part of you I detest most, Pierce. Fortunately, I'm just a lowly public servant, and it will be up to the judge and God to decide your fate."

Bradley looked away, clearly revolted by his proximity. He motioned his officers to take him away, then turned back to instruct the female officer. Pierce moved slowly, allowing the young lady to go first, then rushed Reich and slapped her with his unrestricted hand. The slap stung, but Reich went with the momentum and spun in place while bringing her leg into a roundhouse kick. It caught Pierce in the jaw. By the time the officer who'd been binding his hands caught up to him, Pierce lay on the ground out cold next to the unconscious guard. Reich took a moment to feel her jaw while she looked over her handiwork.

"Pig."

The detective stood over the fallen prisoner and smiled, seemingly unconcerned about Pierce's condition. Bradley nudged him with his foot to make sure he was unconscious and nodded approvingly. A devilish smile came over him as he looked up at Reich. Reich wondered if he knew about the INTERPOL thing last month. She suspected that he did.

"And to top things off, I am in the presence of still further mysteries," Detective Bradley said.

"Me? I'm just another party guest, detective. I wish I was more than—"

"Just stop, Ms. Reich. I know who you are. And just off the record, I'd let you walk out for clobbering this punk, but that's not entirely my call. INTERPOL is on their way here to talk to you. While I appreciate your staff giving us the heads- up on the 'king,' and the artwork, I'm still a law enforcement officer, and in light of your history of slipping through our fingers, no matter how noble, I need to detain you. Once they're done, you and I need to have a serious chat about your prior work and adventures."

He pulled a pair of handcuffs from his pocket and motioned for her to turn around.

Yup … all the things they said about Chief Inspector Bradley's tenacity and determination are all true. Plan B.

"All right, Detective, but could I please go to the bathroom to check my mouth, relieve myself and please … do you have some other bindings? I'm allergic to certain metals."

"Allergic? Really? You're allergic to handcuffs?"

"No, sir. I'm allergic to certain metals. Anaphylaxis. Not pretty once it gets started."

She stroked her face as if it still hurt, and coughed. Bradley stopped handcuffing her, looked her straight in the eyes, and considered the requests. He nodded to a larger woman to join him while he produced one of the plastic ties often used for mass arrests. Relieved, Reich took a good look at the woman.

Officer Virginia Spenser. Wrestler in college, national competitor, and just started a serious mix martial arts program. He's not taking any chances.

"All right, Ms. Reich, but I want you to wear these, and Officer Spenser will join you in the closet while you take care of business. I'll be outside and close at hand, if you don't mind."

"Are you kidding? Do I look like I'm a threat?"

Bradley chuckled as he firmly tied her hands in front of her.

"With you? The Houdini of the FBI and INTERPOL interrogations rooms? A legend to be feared by human traffickers and queen of escape? No, I am not kidding. I take you very seriously, Ms. Reich. And I'm not going to miss an opportunity to talk to you later about much bigger things."

He tested the binds to make sure they held her wrists firmly, then took her arm and walked with her while Officer Spenser followed.

Thorough and not too trusting. Dammit! His record doesn't do him justice.

"You know there are several bathrooms on the ground floor," she suggested.

"And I'm sure they also have wonderful windows you could somehow slip through. In fact, why use windows? You've done that before. I think I'll find one that's three stories up with a thin skylight or no window at all, if you don't mind."

Bradley methodically opened and closed doors until he found a bathroom. Then he asked Spenser to watch her closely and disappeared into the bathroom. After a minute, he emerged with a small grin.

"Well, Pierce does like his baths. Anyway, please do not attempt to go through the window—it's a sheer forty-foot drop."

Reich stood for just a moment giving the best annoyed look she could muster. Not deterred, Bradley gestured her in.

"So, I have to keep these on? What happens if I need to ...? You know?"

"You were going to have to wipe regardless. That's why Spenser's here."

"Really?"

Wow ... no chances with this guy. I bet Lux and Vespere would like him too. I bet he's hairy all over and he's the perfect height for them.

"No problem, love. I've had to do this before."

Reich did her best to not chuckle at Spenser's pleasant response; her soft voice was somewhat incongruous with the thick-set, muscular woman.

"And don't be cheeky—Spenser here was quite the wrestler in her day," Bradley warned.

Reich marched into the bathroom with Spenser hot on her trail while the detective left the door ajar so he could listen. Reich walked straight to the toilet, extended both arms in front of her as far as she could, and then retracted them quickly and forcefully into her chest. Her elbows jutted beyond her back, and the plastic binds broke, freeing her hands. Reich turned and threw a punch deep into Spenser's solar plexus. The officer gasped, the air knocked from her, and tried to keep from doubling over. Reich clamped one hand over Spenser's mouth and nose and wrapped both legs around the woman's waist. She struggled for air and tried to stay on her feet while Reich continued to apply pressure on the woman's torso and talked as if nothing were happening.

"You don't have to grimace. I didn't get a chance for a wax."

The woman's knees weakened and her eyes rolled upwards. Reich released her legs, stood, and guided the woman down so she didn't crash to the floor and bring the detective inside. Once the semi-conscious officer lay on the floor, Reich took a thread from her pocket and placed it, a micro-transponder and transceiver, on the woman's collar, then she moved to the bathroom vanity and flushed the toilet.

"All right, it's time for you to wipe."

Reich hoped she said it with enough indignation. She dug deep into the back of the cabinet and was rewarded with the black satchel that contained climbing gear and lines.

"No. That was a courtesy flush," she said and flushed a second time.

Ironic … Pierce being right about nothing being taken

last week but leaving a whole lot of stuff behind … the art was costly, though.

While the toilet filled with water, she unpacked the bag, hooked the rope to the toilet and tossed the other end out the small window. She slid into the climbing harness with well- practiced ease and was partially out the window when Spenser started to cough. Reich pushed off and rappelled down the four stories. She was releasing herself from the harness when Bradley yelled from forty feet above.

"Dammit! Reich! Stop right there! Just stop!"

Reich never looked back; she oriented herself and ran towards the closest ten foot wall by the road. She hoped Lux was waiting there as planned and not indulging herself with those damn chestnuts and lemons.

She sprinted through the manicured garden, dodging low branches and exposed roots, until she came to the estate's wall, a hundred feet from the main gate and road. Without slowing, she scaled a low-lying branch then a series of other branches and ended up a few feet from the wall.

She slid over the wall and hung there for a moment in preparation, then let go and dropped the remaining ten feet. She remained crouched until she saw Lux leaning against her car throwing chestnuts in the air and catching them in her waiting mouth.

"Lux! What the hell, woman! You'd think you might be a bit more discreet and wait in the car? What if security found you…" Reich stopped as her field of vision around the car widened to include a pile of three estate guards lying unconscious on the ground.

"Hmm. Show-off."

"This Sir Pierce person should hire more qualified guards. They got in their own way when they tried to take me. Not bad for a small one like me," Lux said as she bit into another chestnut.

"I don't know how small you're going to be if you keep eating those things. They're not without calories." Reich didn't wait for a response. She slipped into the back seat of the car before Lux could see her smile. Lux slid behind the wheel and turned on the ignition.

"Oh… the giant loses all her fat, gains some muscles, lets her hair grow, and suddenly she's a lethal weapon with an opinion on weight. How things have changed."

Reich smiled. Things certainly had changed since she'd met Lux at Thanksgiving. She wondered how Anthony was doing, and figured he'd be surprised at how she looked now.

Her smile broadened as she settled back into the fine leather upholstery and picked up one of four waiting tablets. The luxury sedan pulled out, and before she could ask for confirmation of the other missions, a text came through on her main tablet.

"It looks like Vespere and Bella successfully hindered Pierce's telecommunication satellite launch."

Lux nodded as she expertly drove the high-end car and popped yet another chestnut into her mouth.

"Yes, oh Great One. Further, Pax has our gear,

residence, and visas ready for our trip back to the United States. Fitting, I should say, but still," she looked back at Reich through the rear-view mirror, "your insistence on handling these missions yourself, as well as these ancillary ones, is dangerous."

Reich sighed. She'd been about to argue, but Lux was right.

"I know. We have eight years to prepare the world for the shock of discovering an advanced, new world hiding behind the sun's corona, and less than four years before the Earth's atmosphere is irreversibly affected by methane build-up. It's just that … well, it's just that …"

"It's just that if we have a chance to save a few souls along the way, like those children in Moscow, the village in Brazil, the slaves in Hong Kong, the prostitutes in Berlin and the underage young woman back there, we should, right? Yes … just like Perez … I hate to admit it, but he chose his successor wisely," Lux said.

The corners of Reich's mouth pulled up at the reluctant compliment.

"That had to hurt."

"Yes. Yes, it did."

Reich looked back at her series of tablets and refocused on her master plan.

"Once we have control of the stocks and assets of Pierce's empire, we'll be able to refit his satellite with ours so we can have a direct, clear link with Terra. Maybe they have some ideas on this methane poisoning thing. The sooner we deal with that, the better chance we have of handling the culture shock of their existence."

Lux looked at her again and nodded in agreement.

"Have faith, Reich. Between all of us, we'll be able to save the Earth and keep it from falling apart regarding our existence. You handled it pretty well and you were put under great stress. And with your knowledge regarding the United States government, you will be the best person for the task of convincing them to trust us."

"True, but I am one person. For those who believe we're alone, and discover that we've never been alone, it will be a major shock of identity and core beliefs … Perez was right, there are bigger things to deal with," Reich said as she looked through the darkened window.

"Very true."

Reich's tablet blinked and issued a quiet buzzing noise followed by the familiar female voice. "Attention—a recent recording has just been downloaded. I focused on three individuals only: Chief Inspector Arthur Bradley, Officer Virginia 'Ginny' Spenser and Officer John 'Jack' Middleton. The audio and transcript has been filtered and compiled five point three minutes ago, real time. Icons and last names will appear beside their text and audio statements. Are you prepared?"

"Yes. Please initiate, and put their full personal and professional files on the green tablet for review. Transmit audio to the front of the car for Lux to hear as well. Begin."

Spenser: "… Owen! Ramsey! Stop screwing around and lock that evidence down! INTERPOL is almost here and the boss is pretty pissed! Don't.... too many times ..."

Bradley: "... Will someone explain to me how one woman got her hands on rappelling equipment, cleared a forty foot drop, ran, unobserved no less, across half an acre of lawn, scaled a ten plus foot wall, took out one of my officers and three of

Pierce's private security, and drove away in a waiting car? It's pretty embarrassing when Scotland Yard and London's finest can't contain one woman, even if she is the famous Christine Reich. Anyone care to explain? I hate feeling like the only idiot."

Spenser: "I wouldn't be too hard on yourself, sir. The woman was like a cat with as many lives, I tell you. By the time I turned around she already knocked the hell out of me. She took me down in under twenty seconds."

Middleton: "And she did the same thing in an INTERPOL security station, an interrogation room with the usual high-tech surveillance system and no windows."

Reich picked up the green tablet, flipped to Middleton's file and looked at his icon again so she could picture the three of them together. Compared to Bradley and Spenser, he was taller, thinner and impeccably dressed. His bio indicated he was a literature major at University of Cambridge.

Middleton: "I must say that Sir Pierce may have a point about someone breaking in and leaving stuff. I mean, Reich didn't have the rappelling equipment on her person, and I'm sure Pierce wouldn't keep that kind of equipment in the bathroom. . ." Spenser: "That sexual deviant would, I bet."

Middleton: "While that may be true, I think Reich put everything in place, including her escape route. She set Sir Pierce up with the artwork, informed us and did her usual disappearing act. I think I already know the answer to this, but I wouldn't be doing my job if I didn't ask."

Bradley: "Out with it, Jack. I get short-tempered when I'm prickly. Escaped material witnesses and mysteries don't sit well with me."

Middleton: "Should we investigate Pierce's allegation of being set up in light of Reich's escape, or just let his legal team fight that one as he rots in a dungeon?"

Bradley: "Are you kidding me? Is that a trick question?"

Spenser: "That slick piece of crap will somehow dodge the child trafficking and sexual assault charges like he always does, but he'll hang on the stolen art. Sounds like a great example of justice and irony going hand in hand, if you ask me."

Middleton: "That's pretty philosophical for a former wrestler. Oh, but maybe you're changing approaches to things now? You know, going for brains rather than brawn since catwoman took you out back there."

Spenser: "Hey, Middleton! I thought keeping the perimeter secured was under your watch, college boy? Nice job, you sack of…"

Bradley: "Enough, you two! We've got to focus on this Reich woman. She does right by putting the bad guys in the shitter, but I want to know what it is all about. I mean, she got her hands on some stolen art, put it in that pig's castle, and just walked away, setting him up on a charge that will actually stick. She did this out of the kindness of her heart? For nothing? And her other little jaunts around the world doing the same thing are just for kicks?"

Spenser: "That stunt she did in Moscow was pretty over the top. Kind of like Perez back in the day. Dangerous, but in a good way. He fell off the planet, too."

Bradley: "Hong Kong three months ago … Yeah … and I want to talk to her before she does too. I'm positive there's something bigger than acts of kindness motivating Reich and her resources …"

Middleton: "'I'll chase him round Good Hope, and round the Horn, and round the Norway Maelstrom, and round perdition's flames before I give him up.' Herman Melville, sir. The American novelist who wrote Moby Dick. *Looks like we're after the great white whale, sir. It seems particularly apt here."*

Spenser: "Smart ass."

Bradley: "All right, Macbeth, get General Farrell on the line. Tell him we got a sighting and actually had Reich in custody, but she did another Houdini … guess … heading out of country and, based on her track record, to the US."

Spenser: "And let the games and quotes begin."

Bradley: "Yes. Let them quotes begin …'To the last, I grapple with thee.'"

"End of recording. Will archive in recent storage for further analysis," her tablet said.

"Please continue monitoring and notify me as close to real time as possible."

"Acknowledged."

"Lux? Are we getting messy and predictable?"

"No, Reich. This Bradley and Farrell have been looking for us for several years. By the sound of that discussion, they have been working together as a team for years. They're good, very good. New plan?"

Reich looked at her reflection in the window. "

Yup. Berlin."

"Sounds like a plan."

Lux popped a chestnut into her mouth.

"Bigger things to deal with and bigger challenges along the way. Just great."

Chapter Thirteen

The Return – Mars

It does not matter how slowly you go so long as you do not stop
- Confucius

It's so quiet. I do miss the other voices, Master Architect Janus thought as he slowly opened his eyes from his nap. *After all his time asleep, you would think I would no longer be tired or want to sleep.*

He moved his limbs slowly, appreciative that the Keeper, the master computer, had revived other citizen survivors before him. The warmth of the blanket and bed was nothing compared to the encapsulating state of his Martian-made embryonic cryogenic stasis. The buoyancy of its warm, protein-enriched plasma had been unlike anything he had experienced before. The constant programming for keeping his intellect engaged when he was in cryogenic sleep was something he had thought might work but never had time to test. The amazing computer had created an embryonic state programmed with literature, languages, science and mathematics, transmitted through a plasma medium to keep the mind active. It had felt as if he were talking or studying.

Impressive.

Even so, he was still shocked by the knowledge that he was the seventy-eighth reincarnation of his former self, perfectly reproduced from his own stem cells so as to survive millions upon millions of full solar rotations.

Memories, new knowledge attainment via artificial intelligence, external processing; immortality while unconscious? Costly but fascinating. Little mystery as to why she wanted my DNA sample.

The last to be revived of a once great civilization, he was one of seventy-two fellow Martian survivors out of thirteen thousand who stayed behind while the others had left a doomed solar system.

Ironic. Those who left are probably long deceased.

Generations had passed, and he wondered how they'd evolved. Did they find the Originators? Would they recognize him and the others? They would be a great archaeological find, maybe even a missing link into whatever they have changed into. He guessed they might find out, someday. Perhaps.

"Am I disturbing you?" the Keeper said. Her voice was a lower baritone than he remembered, and more feminine. He assumed it was more likely a result of her own evolution, software modifications and the absences of other subroutine computer voices. His eyes still closed, Master Janus carefully formed words as he continued to slowly move his limbs and take deep, refreshing breaths.

"No, not at all. My original awakening was disturbing enough. Now? Nothing will ever compare to that awakening."

"Yes. That is accurate. I have been able to obtain the subtleties of irony and aspects of humor. I also have acquired the inability to avoid such obvious questions. The prior citizens did assist me over the great period of silence."

Janus was truly impressed with the computer's profound intellectual growth, personality development and explosion in sapience. Her personality, moral development and decision making processing were extraordinary. Nonetheless, her need to awaken many of his fellow citizens for company disturbed him. He understood that, like all life, she had chosen a path for her own survival.

Such a long period of isolation would have destroyed any life form. And her decision to sacrifice the few citizens, the sixty-three hundred, for her own survival while continuing the mission of survival indicated higher level sapience. Janus thought he would have made a similar decision.

"Are you disappointed by my means of continuing the mission, that I sacrificed others to preserve myself and the remaining survivors?"

Impressive. Artificially developed theory of mind. Very impressive.

"No. I cognitively understand it. I am still not used to your development and how you have become similar to us biological lifeforms. It will take me time to acclimate to this new development. It is not disappointment: it is surprise, amazement and intellectual curiosity in how you evolved, how similar you are to us, to me," Janus said as the thoughts popped into his head.

He took a deep breath to clear his thoughts and shifted focus from the computer's growth to the profound changes in his universe. Janus opened his eyes. Dim light illuminated his room. He rolled onto his side, curled up his legs, and asked his next set of questions.

"Based on our last briefings, please summarize the critical changes that require your awakening all of us all at once. If possible, keep the points under eight."

"Thank you for clarifying those parameters as there are one point three million key points I could make. I will need just a moment to isolate those points. Please hold."

Janus was surprised at how tiny his bedroom was, but it still contained a chair and a small table. A neatly folded pile of clothes sat on it next to a pitcher and two cups.

Who is the chair for if I am here?

"Master Janus? Specific point's summary completed. Just so you are aware and not surprised, Citizen Olympia will be here to assist you shortly. Are you ready?"

"Yes." It took him a moment to remember that Olympia was the older female as opposed to Athena, the younger one.

"Points are arranged from lower to higher priority: Venus experienced a runaway greenhouse effect, resulting in the need to abandon the planet; the surface of our home world was devastated by impact craters and changes in our planetary axis from the destruction of Gemini Alpha and Beta dwarf planets; Architect Iris relocated the hominem species from Venus to Terra; this species adapted more readily to the environment than the species already there. To date, the original Terrans are extinct, along with their ancestors on Earth. In regards to Earth, the impact craters destroyed the various dinosaur species; the impact also altered its axis as well but to a more favorable outcome, allowing for the mammal species to develop; the Earth's Keeperis eight percent operational which resulted in the Earther hominids to develop without support."

"Hold," Janus said. "They developed without guidance? No master computer to assist their development. Was this one of the experiments carried out by Architect Hades?"

"No, it was not Architect Hades's experiment. Yes, the hominids did develop without a Keeper."

"And Hades made Terra work?"

"Yes. More surprisingly, the Terran project transformed the planet into a small civilization of one point nine billion hominids. By changing terraform equipment into breathable atmosphere and heating generators, he forfeited the atmosphere and surface area for an underground civilization along the terminal line. Further, he combined its power with solar energy to power an array of holographic emitters that has rendered the planet invisible to hominids' visual wavelength, making the planet invisible. Its machinery, however, is failing after being in operation non-stop since Earth's space age. Unfortunately, Terra's orbit, which kept the sun between itself and Earth, has been altered, and Terra will imminently be in line of sight to the Earth for the first time in its existence."

Young, impetuous, impulsive and brilliant. Hades had seen things that others could not. "I am impressed with Architect Hades's abilities. He proves once again that it is adaptation, not intelligence that is key to survival. His tidal-locked planet not only survived all this time but has maintained its own records and ours. I am sure that Terra's Keeper assisted in keeping you updated?"

"Yes, whenever we were in orbital proximity. I must say as a way of conveying my appreciation for the Terran Keeper, that her communications were key to my survival. It has been too long since our last communication."

Yes … she has become emotional, he thought. "And Architect Iris? What happened to her?"

"Sadly, she perished on Venus. She refused to leave her Venusian Keeper. I lost contact with both of them."

Janus knew that both of the architects were long gone. Still, hearing that Iris died with her keeper saddened him.

"I am sorry."

"Yes. I was too," the computer said.

Sad and sorry? Quite the development.

"Are there more points?"

"Here are the key points: Terran's efforts to propagate the hominid species via cross breeding has been partially effective, but they remain as an endangered species. Once the Terran's orbital pattern clears the sun and its cloaking technology fails, Earth hominid species will know of their existence. They have had the technology to see Terra without its cloak for fifty-one of its years. Both Terran and Earther Keepers have been partially effective in keeping Terran's existence obfuscated on Earth. Their success is now dwindling. Both Keepers, as well as myself, are concerned with the Earthers' existential response to possessing direct confirmation that they are not alone in their own solar system. The Earthers are primitive due to their wild curiosity with no guidance from their Keeper."

"What a fascinating experiment. A hominid species allowed to form its own civilizations, its own concepts, without the assistance of a master computer or an architect. Their ideas of who they are and their point of view of the universe must be extraordinary. They must have thought they were gods in the absence of other similar species. You will have to tell me more of this later. Please go on," Janus said.

It took him a moment to rein in his scientific curiosity.

"Yes. They are a different species—technologically moving at a slow but steady pace while their view of their place in the universe is that of an infant. I will elaborate later. The Earthers are slowly coming to terms with the fact that their planet's exosphere and biosphere are in danger. With the efforts of Terran recruits from Earth's own population, there is movement in identifying the methane crisis and possible containment. Still, on a profound scale, we have identified the source of the oxygen/hydrogen beam bombardment of the Jovian planet, Jupiter, as coming from far outside our galaxy. The technology to deliver such an astronomical quantity of oxygen and hydrogen consistently remains a near incalculable mystery that we are attempting to determine," she said gravely.

Though he said nothing, Janus immediately concluded the net result of such an act, a leap of creativity versus logic and reason.

"Based on your calculations, how long will it take for the oxygen and the additional hydrogen to ignite Jupiter's atmosphere?"

The dialogue had been so steady that the sudden silence while the Keeper calculated seemed very long.

"Speculation would place the probability of Jupiter becoming a viable second sun between one and three full solar cycles. In order for it to ignite, there will need to be an actual trigger.

While the source of these beams is outside our galaxy, there will need to be a massive spark, an explosion of a solar-sun level to ignite Jupiter even if the oxygen and hydrogen levels reached threshold level or beyond. This is unusual. How did you speculate that Jupiter would ignite?"

"A wild guess. Now here's another question: have you run the entire light radiation spectrum on Jupiter since we last spoke, before I went into cryonics sleep?"

Before he'd been forced to his cryogenic stasis, he'd witnessed Jupiter's x-ray and gamma radiation levels following the Gemini collisions. At the time, he'd thought it was an abnormal effect of such a blast.

But with the presence of such light elements?

More silence followed, longer this time as the keeper collected, collated and analyzed calculations and measurements at amazing speed. But as brilliant as the master computer was, the difference between Janus and his Keeper, for now, was imagination and the classic 'what if.'

"I … I have missed you greatly, Master Architect Janus. I continue to be amazed at your species' ability to stretch their mind beyond reason. There are subatomic particles emitting radiation well beyond x-ray levels at Jupiter's center. Should the oxygen-hydrogen levels continue to increase, the subatomic particle's density will expand to the level of a subatomic black hole, and enough mass to ignite the planet. Have you already guessed what will happen to the planets?"

I don't even want to think about it.

"No." He opened his eyes and smiled even as thoughts of doom and destruction from a series of catastrophic events flooded his mind. "What direction do these oxygen-hydrogen beams come from? From where do they originate? Are they from the last known heading of our people, to the Originators?"

"Yes, Master Architect Janus. The heading follows the course of our ancestors. It follows the path to the Originators. What does it mean?"

A path to the gods? The Master Originators the ones who with their mere thoughts and words made the heavens, planets, life and us. Were we all part of the plan?

Are they to me as I am to Terran's rattus? Janus thought, finding no words to articulate his thoughts.

"I don't know, but it's just like last time … Gemini Alpha and Beta 'just fell out of their orbits' as if simply pushed, completely altering our solar system. And now the mysterious appearance of the right amount of chemical gas elements and a subatomic black hole come together to ignite a gas giant into a small, unstable star … Mysteries or messages from the Originators? I don't know. But it may be time to find out. And we may need our Terran and Earther cousins to assist," Janus said as he carefully sat up and swung his feet over the side of the bed in one smooth move. He was glad to see he was all in one piece and in control of his limbs, torso and faculties.

"And it may be time for us to meet our descendants or even maybe the Originators. How great would that be?"

"Just to reiterate, I did miss you. Your ability to change a cataclysmic event on a galactic scale into an opportunity to meet our future, our gods, is … amazing."

Our gods? She sees herself as part of their creation? Truly fascinating.

"Yes … I am very good at that." His bedroom door opened. A dim light spilled in from the corridor, creating a silhouette of a female in the doorway. Olympia.

This could be interesting, he thought as he stepped out of his bed, feeling pressure on his feet for the first time in millions of annual cycles.

Epilogue—It Begins—Unknown Time, Space, or Plane of Existence

Everything has its beauty but not everyone sees it. - Confucius

"Why do you continue to focus on this speck of the universe when there is so much more to explore?" one of many voices asked in a sea of different voices and simultaneous thoughts.

"Because they are the genesis of those that traveled far to find us. They are part of our corporeal past. They are the past. Doesn't that pique your curiosity?" the voice said.

"Yes," one voice said above the many. "But then everything piques our curiosity, no matter how small."

"Then why did you ask?"

"Perchance there might be another answer I did not anticipate. Why are you changing their solar system again?"

"They are an interesting species, corporeal with limited life expectancy, but they evolve rapidly, especially when confronted with obstacles. They remind me of our earlier times when we were required to adapt, a shadow of our former selves when time was linear. They give me reason to explore. They inspire me to find our creator. Do you remember?"

The voices fell silent as curiosity and focus shifted to the species located in a minute speck of the universe.

"Shall we observe together?" a sole voice asked.

"Yes. We will observe," the voices said in unison, declaring their will to be in one place at one time to watch how the species would respond to the new events.

"What will they do?" one of many voices asked. This genuine question absent an answer was an unusual experience. Even speculation of what might come next was difficult.

"I do not know," the sole voice said. "We shall see."

Excitement rippled through the voices. Another unusual experience not felt in nearly thirty-seven million years.

Apocalypse

Novella II

Prologue

Void—Unknown Time, Space, or Plane of Existence

Some do not understand that we must die, But those who do realize this settle their quarrels. —The Buddha

In the darkness, a voice.

"Questions. How do they create more questions?" the sole voice says.

Often, there would be one voice, with many more. Rarely would there be one voice that held many voices. But now, there was just one voice. Alone in the dark.

A remote speck in a distant universe reveals a solitary sun surrounded by orbiting planets. One planet is a dark, brooding, tidally locked planet on the opposite orbit from a bright, blue-and-white, vibrant planet teeming with organic species and life. Not far away, another planet very close to the sun spins; its sulfuric-acid atmosphere and molten surface churn aimlessly. On an orbit just outside these spheres, an old red world, once the reigning jewel of a civilization, quietly holds on to shadows of its former self well below the planet's crust. Only a few of its inhabitants remain.

"They are the Old Ones. The ones that followed. They need questions like us," the voice says.

All moves on, as it always has. As it was in the beginning. As it is now. But not for long.

"Questions," the sole voice repeats.

Faster than the speed of thought, a hole in the space-time fabric tears through the middle of a Jovian planet. Waves of hydrogen and oxygen flood the planet's center, where a subatomic black hole quietly appears, spiraling from the fabric of a faraway time to its new home. Gamma and X-rays flood in from yet another dimension, narrowing into a focused beam. Everything is at the center of a gas giant too small to be a sun. Until now. Just as before, when the Gemini worlds, Alpha and Beta, collided sixty-seven million years ago and created another set of events that could only be remembered by the voices.

"These events will create more questions. Just like last time…" the solitary voice says. "More voices will come. More events will happen."

Present Day

Chapter One

Hand of the Originators—Mars

Better it is to live one day seeing the rise and fall of things than to live a hundred years without ever seeing the rise and fall of things. —The Buddha

Master Architect Janus stood in the middle of a room filled with a three-dimensional star chart of the Sol System. He was looking at a large Jovian planet; it was large, an orange-reddish color, and its small moons orbited at various distances. Hovering, as if magically, beside the spheres were multicolored formulas and equations. Many were red, indicating a lack of resolution. The green numbers—the solved equations—were few.

Where are the answers?

He continued staring at the relatively large planet and spoke to his two waiting companions, who also shared the same holographic view.

"I know what you are thinking, Olympia," Janus said. His tall, slim figure and long limbs were well concealed below his dark blue, warm robe. With the background of dark space and stars, he appeared as a floating head.

"Shall I conclude that you possess telepathy in your array of skill-based competencies?" she asked. Her tone lacked sarcasm, but it was not playful like Athena's, the younger woman who stood silently beside her. They were similarly attired in robes and possessed the same physical features: pale, hairless, bluish-tone skin, and large eyes. These gave them both the appearance of being the same. Only their sex organs and height distinguished between the male and female of their species. Janus stood two meters while the females stood at one and a half.

"Your heavy breathing implies that you are fatigued of my repeating this experiment," Janus said. He shifted his viewpoint by moving closer to a much smaller model of their home, Mars.

"We have been here for hours, and it is time to prepare meals," Athena said. Her voice was clearly younger and stronger than her older companion's.

"By all means, leave. I am used to doing this alone," Janus said.

"And therein lies the issue," a deeper female voice said from above. The master computer, once responsible for the welfare of millions of citizens—millions of years ago—spoke to Janus as if he were an old friend.

"Oh, Master Keeper, please intervene here. He won't listen to us," Olympia complained.

"He never listens to us," Athena added.

Janus responded quickly in the hopes of preempting

the Keeper's well-practiced monologue.

"Before you start again, Keeper, about the propagation of our species and the future of our world, it won't matter much—not if my predictions about Jupiter's imminent ignition are accurate," Janus said. As he spoke, the Jovian planet at first collapsed on itself to a dark pinpoint and then burst into a bright, burning sun. While it was smaller than the original solar system's sun, its light touched all the planets in its line of sight and caused a nearly imperceptible wobbling of the other planets' axes, which were given a numerical rating above each planet. More red numbers, formulas, and equations multiplied throughout the entire holographic representation. He looked at the numbers above Mars, Terra, and Earth at first, and then he pulled out an old-style tablet.

"The community's custom is to prepare food together. With a mere fraction of the original population remaining, the more time spent interacting, the more social the species becomes. This will increase the probability of prosocial development of future offspring," the Keeper said. Janus nodded absently, which must have tacitly given the master computer the cue to continue her conversation. "Would it not be nice to spend time with your companions?"

Janus stopped what he was doing and looked up, as if there were a monitor he could address his next questions to. Not seeing one, he then looked at Olympia. She interpreted his expression—and the unasked question.

"The Master Keeper is your colleague, not mine. She

would never take a suggestion from me or Athena about pulling you away from your work. She would not take any suggestion at all from us. Looks like you have three women suggesting you stop and eat."

Janus narrowed his eyes at Olympia. Her expression was classic. She knew she was right; the corners of her mouth turned upward and her purple eyes sparkled as they arched upward on her slender, pale head. Athena's expression was similar, though she looked at the floor for fear of bursting out laughing. Reducing visual stimulation was an effective tactic for keeping her from overtly expressing her joy. Amused by his female companions' divergent responses, he smiled. He continued with his data entry and addressed his sapient computer as he wrote.

"So, Master Keeper, you would have me stop my work, divert my energies from finding a solution to a catastrophic situation just to 'have a nice time' with my companions? It doesn't seem logical," Janus said. He was genuinely curious where his computer was going to go with its argument. Its artificial intelligence had grown exponentially, as had its character. Further, it had made some very difficult decisions over the course of sixty-five million years and, with that, developed its own independent thinking and decision-making strategies. Janus was simply thrilled that his master computer was not only self-aware, but that it had its own personality, ideas, and life. Janus waited patiently, working his numbers, truly wondering what the Keeper, which he thought of as his friend, was going to say next. He suspected she would start out with logic—by pointing out the Martians' own limited resources for survival—and end with a rhetorical question.

"Please forgive me if I overstate the obvious," the Keeper began, "but in the last five cycles you have repeated the same experiments with just minor modifications in the timing, locations of the planets, and the intensity of the magnetic field when Jupiter ignites several hundred times. The results have remained the same," the deep, calm voice said.

Janus continued to smile as he looked up from his tablet. He watched Olympia's expression—it was clear that she, too, was waiting expectantly for the computer's response. She shook her long, smooth head. Athena passed the time by rubbing the bridge of her relatively wide nose.

"Depending on specific locations, Earth's axis, which presently holds at twenty-three point five degrees, is predicted to shift to twenty-two point one degrees abruptly. While this shift falls within its preexisting viable zone, the sudden shift will create tectonic movements that will produce fissures in the planet's crust. This in turn will cause devastating land quakes and massive tidal waves that will affect inhabited coastlines. Sadly, we only have limited data provided by Atlantis Keeper on Earth, but we calculate that the planet's ocean currents, which have recently been recycling warm surface water, will be replaced with cold water from the oceans' sea floors. This will adversely correspond with the lack of predicted sunspot activity. The culmination of altered magnetic fields, ocean current temperatures, and the sudden axial tilt will launch a rapid planetary freeze above and below Earth's equatorial line. The following cool summers and warm winters will launch a new ice age that will eradicate potentially eighty-eight percent of its population."

Janus stopped working at his equations. He felt the enormity of the words, as did Olympia, who sighed deeply. It took him a moment to readjust his thoughts, directing them away from emotional responses and toward clinical observations. For what might have been the hundredth time, he requested a visual depiction.

"Keeper? Please create an animated version of most likely results based on Jupiter's ignition," he asked. Even before he had the last words out, the computer had anticipated his request, based on prior history.

The expanded Sol System star field shifted to show a Jovian planet, large, reddish-brown, with swirling gases and prominent brown spots subtly flickering and then slowly but surely darkening as it began to spin faster and shrink in size. While slow at the beginning, the rate of collapse and darkness increased quickly until the giant planet fell into itself—mass and light—and became a mere fraction of its original size. A barely visible pinpoint of absolute darkness was perceptible for only a second—then it erupted into a brilliant flash. At the end of the eruption, a small, fiery red-yellow sun filled the space that had been occupied by the gas giant Jupiter. The holographic, three-dimensional imaging then shifted perspective to reveal an asteroid field that sat between the new sun and Mars—

where remnants of the collision of the Gemini dwarf planets and other celestial debris sixty-seven billion years ago collected. Initially, the only evident effects were these scattered rocks, now bathed in light from the new sun. Underneath various sections of this orbital debris, the computer highlighted measurements and formulas that explained gravitational fluctuations and orbital decays. Within the time lapse of just a third of one Martian annual revolution, varying sizes of asteroids could be seen hurtling in all directions, some out into deep space—and many more inbound, toward the now dual-sun solar system.

Mars—a small, red planet—enlarged for the viewers. Its reddish color, deep valleys, massive plains, and thin white polar caps looked desolate and empty, a far cry from the once-bustling, thriving agrarian and educational society it once was. At first there were small, flickering flashes of impact explosions on the surface, but these were soon replaced by a much more intense bombardment.

Janus flinched at the range and degree of the impact explosions. They reminded him of the visuals of the devastation that had wiped out his history, culture, and world of eons past. He looked down for a moment to let the worst of the destruction pass, unable to witness another assault on his home world. Sharp intakes of air from his companions indicated they were having similar feelings. Far from feeling worried about his own existence, he looked back up to see his planet shrouded in dust and water vapor released from the surface and polar ice caps.

With the permafrost disrupted and the caps smashed, trapped water hung in the thin atmosphere. Massive volcanic activity followed next, ignited by the bombardments far to the north and south of their location. For the first time during the animated projection, the master computer spoke.

"The resulting meteor impacts start a chain reaction of biochemical events that might be beneficial for our world's future development of life," it said. There was just a hint of reassurance in its tone, indicating sapience again.

The hologram's point of view shifted to reveal the beautiful blue-white planet known as Earth. Half of the planet was captured in bright daylight, from its regular sun; softer light from the second sun, which illuminated the side of the planet that should have been in night—a term that, if the animation was correct, would eventually lose its meaning with the planet's occupants. For the moment, the planet's massive conglomerations of city lights artificially illuminating the dark half and indicating an advanced, surface-dwelling civilization still shone faintly.

"Sadly, the effects on Earth will not be as beneficial," the master computer warned.

Similar to Mars, Earth was soon hit with a series of smaller meteors. Fortunately, many of them flashed and flickered in the planet's atmosphere as its blanket of air and its magnetic field neutralized the smaller-sized multiple meteors that would have crashed into the planet. Further calculations displayed underneath various parts of the holographic image indicated a shift in the planet's axis not visible to the naked eye, however, caused by five large-impact explosions that plumed on the surface. Whole sections of the planet's daylight side filled with dust while the dark side's city lights flickered and then faltered into darkness in successive waves. Just a moment later, the dark side began to exhibit small dots of dark red, fiery points that quickly expanded to cover larger sections of the planet. Further calculations indicated Earth's atmosphere was now filled with dust from the impacts as well as ash from erupting volcanic activity and forest fires. Janus watched the numbers and the formulas on the hologram translate into the same results he had predicted on his tablet—dust and ash levels would reduce the suns' rays, creating cooler summers and warmer winters. While tidal waves from the impacts would devastate seacoasts, the reduction of sunlight, change in planetary axis, and lack of sunspot activity from the main sun would initiate a rapid, devastating ice age that would engulf the planet's northern and southern hemispheres. Unlike prior ice ages, this one appeared to grip the majority of the planet—almost down to the equator. What was once a crystal-blue-and-white planet spinning peacefully in its own orbit became a near-white planet of cold and ice. As it turned on its axis, its darker side glowed in a soft dusk and its bright side reflected nearly all the suns' light and heat spaceward.

"There is a fifteen percent probability that Earth's moon's orbit will erode faster than anticipated; this will allow it to achieve escape velocity faster than expected. I am still working on the calculations. Fortunately, it will not be planet-bound, but it might pose a danger to exterior planets, including our own. I will have those results in several cycles," the computer said.

Janus looked on quietly at rapid-animation depictions of Earth's moon flying out of its orbit. He was still struck by how the white planet had replaced the blue, brown, green, and white planet so recently filled with swirling clouds, oceans of waters, and prominent land masses.

"Such loss," he said quietly.

"The horror," he heard Olympia say.

"Yes. Earth's excessive carbon dioxide production has also exaggerated the speed and balance of climate change," the computer added.

"Probabilities of survival? Any hope?" Athena asked. Her voice, young and strong, also expressed fear and sadness. The master computer responded.

"Biosphere's range of life will be reduced to three point two five percent of current inhabitants. The eradication of night on the planet will impair nocturnal species' ability to survive—algae, plant, and animal—while the meteor impacts' initial blast fronts will devastate higher orders of species, such as the hominids. Their cities and establishments will fail quickly. While high-ground land masses will withstand the tidal wave destruction, the following warm winters and cool summers will usher in a near-immediate ice age unprecedented in the planet's history. The closest example is what occurred about seventy-five Earth cycles ago. However, that was a mere fraction of what this mass extinction event will be. Agriculture will not return for at least two hundred Earth cycles."

"Minimum requirements for survival and repopulation?" Janus asked.

"A minimum of seventy-four males and one hundred twenty-five females for procreation. Underground environs to survive the initial destruction and to provide future shelter. This will allow for geothermal heating and cooling. And possible groundwater access and hydroponic farming. A full list of minimum required materials and circumstances will be forthcoming. Possible repopulation of Earth planet—14,792 Earth cycles around its sun to reach two point one billion, well below its six point seven billion at this moment."

Janus watched the now-white spinning orb slowly begin to gain color as the animated snow and ice receded back to the poles of the planet. Ample room for a more temperate, hospitable living zone for life reemerged. Janus looked over to see both Athena and Olympia still intently watching the holographic simulation. All was silent. After a moment, he cleared his throat. While his own thoughts of his once-lush, well-planned-out civilization of millions of years ago haunted him, witnessing another planet's destruction made him feel just as bad. His mind shifted to Terra, a planet with occupants safe from the harsh, violent environment underground, and where the chances of massive destruction on a global biosphere scale were low due to its lack of weather and thanks to its underground protection.

"And what of Terra?" he asked.

The holographic image shifted from Earth's projection—including its moon, which was finally escaping Earth's orbit and moving toward deep space—to a half-light, half-dark planet tidal locked in orbit just on the other side of the original sun. With no surface evidence of a modern society, the animation zoomed in closer to reveal a small, hominid-built series of living habitats in the planet's crust. The only evidence of these on the surface was a series of ancient pyramids of varying size, distributed along the large planet's equatorial line.

"Terra's planetary axis change will expand from twenty point three degrees to twenty-three point seven, which will also create fissures in its mantle. Due to its tidal-locked nature, massive windstorms and sweeping tornadoes will dominate the light side of the planet, while even more impressive lightning and thunderstorms will occur on the dark side. The planet's longitudinal equator will be the nexus of the violent weather. Fortunately, the Terrans' biosphere is within the crust, sparing the population from surface elements. Terra will need to survive the tectonic movement. Comparatively speaking, since three-quarters of its surface are one large continent and the remaining quarter is an ocean covered by several kilometers of ice, Terra should remain relatively unscathed," the computer explained.

Impact craters erupted on the animated projection, but there were no fires and only minimal volcanic activity. The intensity of violent winds and lightening along the planet's longitudinal equator were impressive, however.

"And us? Anything more about us? Anything we can do to preserve ourselves?" Athena blurted out. Her anxiety, which bordered on desperation, was unmistakable.

Janus turned and saw Athena looking back at Mars. The destruction of Earth and the new star's effects on Terra reminded her of what she had seen earlier in the projections.

"It is not always about us, Athena. There are billions on Earth and Terra at risk—but especially on Earth," Olympia said. Her tone and voice sounded as harsh as Janus had ever heard.

"I apologize, Olympia. Should I become pregnant, I fear for the future," Athena said quietly.

Shame. It still exists. Janus waited to see if the computer would respond as a carbon-based, sapient creature to Athena's concern.

"Ironically our planet, while closest, will benefit from the slight axis change as well as the light from this second sun. The planet's permafrost may melt and the consolidation of Mars's magnetic fields—with possible volcanic reactivation—may initiate a viable biosphere."

"So our planet and Terra are less at risk, while Earth's viability is devastated?" Janus said out loud as he returned to his tablet for final calculations.

"Yes. Our role as the senior species is to provide assistance to our wards. Based on our own limited resources and our own concerns with extinction, we can provide both Earth and Terra this information so they may able to preserve their populations and cultures. Would it be appropriate to say that the best preparation for these disasters is forewarning?"

Janus suppressed a smile at first as he finished up his calculations. *Just like clockwork—logic, survival, and then the rhetorical question. She does have quite the personality,* he thought. He stopped and took a breath. He did his best to contain his hope and to manage his expectations. Millions of years ago, he had witnessed firsthand the devastation of his home world and the other "great projects." He was not sure he wanted to witness another. He pressed one more key on his tablet and watched as various values and equations filled its screen. He looked at the numbers and their corresponding equations and meanings, and then his shoulders slumped. There were far more red numbers than green. He felt his limbs tire and small tears dropped from his eyes and rolled quickly off his long, hairless cheeks and chin.

"No change?" Olympia asked. It was a kind, gentle voice asking an important question.

"None. It is all as the Keeper estimates. After a full annual cycle we are no closer to either an answer or a solution to this unexpected event," Janus said. "End simulation," he said flatly.

The dark, mini solar system and star field evaporated, revealing a large common area, work space, and library. With the sole exception of one elevated resting bed, it was filled with desks and tabletops littered with tablets, tools, and even bound books in old-fashioned covers made from recycled material. These were no textbooks, though—these special manuscripts were fiction. Food for the expanding mind and imagination. In his desperation, when all facts and figures left him with no satisfactory answers, he looked to fiction to help him think outside of his own mind and for ideas from another perspective. Half a cycle ago he had pulled an idea from a fictional story—it focused on stopping the beam that initiated Jupiter's ignition. That novel had unique ideas and suggestions, but the Keeper and his Martian team had found no means of halting this intergalactic beam from deep space.

"Hand of the Originators…" Janus mumbled. He was surprised how quickly the Keeper responded. It was as if she had been thinking the same thing he was.

"Perhaps this is an act of the Originators, our creators. If it is, should we stop it? Would there be a purpose to trying to stop their intervention?" the master computer asked.

"I have always thought the Originators would preserve life and support sapient civilizations," Olympia said. She had moved to stand just behind Janus, who was looking down at the floor. He felt her light touch on his back, and he was grateful for it. In his earlier life, he had never taken companions. It was just him and the Keeper. He was appreciative of the Keeper's selection of mates, or at least for Olympia. Athena's emotions and impulsiveness he found distracting, but Olympia made up for that with her calm presentation and natural abilities to invoke reason without effort.

"This may in fact be the case. While Earth may suffer, its hominids are due credit for adapting to profound difficulties in their past, and that was without a master keeper. Maybe this is a required step for their adaptation and evolution? Maybe our own planet is being triggered to become a viable biosphere? Maybe this is Terra's time for growth and expansion—could its citizens ultimately inhabit both Earth and Mars? Or perhaps Jupiter's moons will be the next locus of a new civilization. Maybe the magnetic field alteration and axis shift on Venus will reverse its hostile surface to create the dream Junior Architect Iris attempted long ago. Perhaps…perhaps the Originators have greater plans, in which we are simply witnesses and not participants," the Keeper said. Her capacity for speculation and her use of imagination didn't surprise Janus, but the overall thought of just being a small part of a profoundly larger plan was humbling. Based on the Keeper's intonation and difficulty in finding words, Janus wondered if she could now experience humility, too.

"Is the possibility that an artificially intelligent creation could experience feeling…insignificant?" the Keeper asked. Janus's feeling of loss and sadness shifted to awe.

"I think you are more than the sum of your parts. I think you feel, Master Keeper," he said.

"You are more like us than different, Master Keeper. I am glad you are here," Olympia added.

"So am I," Athena quickly said.

There was a pause in the quiet room. The moment seemed just perfect for reflecting more when Janus heard a loud, strung-out stomach noise, indicating a peristalsis wave. Olympia didn't bother to even look at Athena when she responded.

"I know, Athena. You are hungry. Janus? Shall we prepare our first meal of this cycle?"

"I apologize for my digestive tract. I have little control over its operation and corresponding sounds," Athena said apologetically.

Janus sighed and put his tablet down on a nearby desk. He motioned for both females to leave the room.

"Yes, it is time for us to prepare food and eat. Afterward, I need to talk to Terra and Earth's Keepers regarding this news. The Originators may have a master plan, but we are here and we know too much not to let our wards know of this impending astronomical shift. Being forewarned is forearmed," Janus said.

Six Months Later

Chapter Two

Coliseum—Terra

All tremble at violence; all fear death. Putting oneself in the place of another, one should not kill nor cause another to kill.
—The Buddha

Perez the Younger looked out over the small clumps of people in the miniature coliseum. It was hard not to take the poor showing personally. Located at the center of a series of grand, tree-lined walkways that transected Terra's networks of shops, artist studios, and galleries, the coliseum reminded Andrea of a smaller version of the grand coliseum she had seen on her home world, Earth. She had never been to *the* Coliseum in Rome, Italy, but rather had seen pictures of it in her old history textbooks and on the Internet, and she found it ironic that she was actually in a coliseum on a cloaked planet on the other side of the sun.

She looked around and saw the low stone seating, plaster detailing, painted reliefs, gold-colored grand archways, and hundreds of sculpted images of Terrans both fighting and arguing. The coliseum played two roles in her martial society—it was an arena for settling disputes, usually regarding honor, and also a forum for political debates, which were typically held in a senate-style format. Andrea suspected this was similar to how Roman senators might have settled disputes of all sorts centuries ago on Earth.

The coliseum had been in heavy use for the last six months as news of Jupiter's potential collapse and rebirth into another sun spread. The warning had come by old-style carrier waves with limited visuals from the Old Ones and their Master Keeper who somehow existed below the surface of Mars. Andrea wished she could have heard or seen the transmission herself, but she had only seen the darkish images of a large-featured, longish face with blue-grayish skin—a creature called "Master Architect." She was sure the actual images, rather than the stills she saw, would have given her more information about this species of sapient life living in her solar system. *I thought we were supposed to be alone here,* she thought. Andrea shifted her weight between her feet. She found her clothes, although scanty, chafing under her outer garment. Her shaved skin was sensitive to the touch and she was not used to wearing a cloak with a hood that obscured her entire figure.

As a faint smell of cooked meat wafted through the air vents of the contained world, she looked to see where the disputing families were seated. She knew both families and also the onlookers, but there was only one party she was particularly interested in.

Today, the coliseum was to be an arena used to defend honor. Andrea was surprised to see that the usual podium at center stage had been removed and a large, flat surface with raised barriers in the form of a large octagon had taken its place. Ostensibly, this was the area for combat. Many of these squabbles were resolved by combatants representing two disputing parties fighting until one submitted. Many times, one would submit before even striking a blow. For that to happen, the offended party would accept the "apology" and the matter would be considered closed. In rare cases, the offended party would not accept the apology, and the fight would commence.

"I won't be that lucky," she said aloud.

Andrea's eyes moved to the offender's area. Her father, Anthony Perez, called Perez the Elder, had insulted the Iratus clan by refusing to join their family for purposes of procreation. Andrea had argued that her father could not join another family, as she had already been accepted into Dimitra's clan, the House of Ferris, for saving their daughter's life in the battle with the great rats. By default, then, he was already in a family. Andrea had expected the matriarch, Dimitra, to see the logic in that, thereby ending the dispute. But Dimitra had not. While Dimitra was indebted to Andrea for saving her daughter Vista, she obviously was not happy about having a connection with the Perez clan. Perez the Elder would need to fight—unless he could find a substitute from another family to take his place.

While Terran-Earther mixes were highly regarded in their society, "off-world Earthers" were not usually embraced. Their lack of body hair, large torsos and legs, relatively weak arms, and high foreheads were seen as odd. While hybrids were seen as demonstrating the best parts of both hominid species, full Earthers just appeared strange to Terrans—almost immature in development and primitive by default. Terrans' sloping forehead structure, heavy eyebrows, thick reddish hair, short-yet-powerful limbs, and thick torsos were highly praised in the subterranean culture.

Andrea started her walk to the corner of the ring, where her father was preparing to enter. The constant vibration below her feet from the enclosed world's generators was reassuring. Generators on Terra meant air, water, power—life. She often wondered what it would be like to return to Earth, and to be able to walk in the open air, see the blue sky, and not to have ground constantly shifting below her. A pang of sadness struck her. She wondered if Earth would survive the second sun's appearance. For Terra, a tidally locked planet, plate tectonics might not be too affected. For Earth, though, with its rotation and wobbling axis, tectonics would be seriously affected—and be the least of the population's worries. Tidal waves would annihilate the coasts and either the planet would heat up with a greenhouse effect, or a cataclysmic global climatic change consistent with the earlier ice ages would ensue.

"Either way it'll just be awful," Andrea said to herself as

she walked.

She closed the distance between herself and her father, keeping him in sight. So as not to offend the spectators and their families, Perez the Elder wore full-length pants, a shirt, and a tunic to cover his lack of body hair. He planned to use just his hands as weapons, so he was warming up with Centurion Dea Data, or "Dee Dee," as Andrea had come to call her, in his corner. The hybrid Terran-Earther doctor Medicus Paeoniis was also there, looking on with concern. He possessed a large torso, strong limbs, very thick dark hair, and gray eyes. She smiled at the sight of the doctor at the same moment Hydra—her toothy, laborer neighbor who had turned into a close friend—came up behind her.

"Nice look, Immunes Perez. It covers you well," Hydra said.

"In addition to those moves you taught me, I'm hoping the shock of my appearance will shake the will of my opponents," Andrea said.

"I think Centurion Data's moves are the best. Her time on Earth learning your strange ways has revolutionized ground fighting techniques here," she explained.

"So my techniques, physical training, and new look will take the day?" Andrea asked wryly.

Hydra smiled. She grinned, showing bright teeth in her large jaw, and her giant brown eyes danced with humor.

"If you do what I think you will, it will be remarkably vile and revolting. How your kind lives on such a cold planet without hair is a mystery to us all. And yet, without a Keeper no less, you procreated in the billions. How? If there was ever an argument for the Originators, you Earthers would be a living testament," Hydra said.

Perez looked at her sideways. "That's a pretty philosophical statement for a Terran laborer. I mean, connecting evolution to the presence of God? I'm impressed."

"Must be the battle to come. I always turn reflective when there is combat. Both are rare."

"Not much of a turnout," Perez said as she pointed to the near-empty stadium. By comparison, large groups of pedestrians were walking outside its low wall, going to and fro as they tended to their business.

"Maybe it is a good thing. Still, today is the big day!" Hydra said. Her grin grew larger still, making her jaw look even bigger and her eyes narrower.

Nearly all of the Terrans were wearing muted, reddish-brown or black clothes with clear insignia designating their rank and station; Andrea and her father were the only ones out of uniform. He was expected to be well covered, but she realized that her choice of attire was unusual, even for her. In addition to a long, full-length cloak that covered her body from head to foot, she possessed no weapons—a rarity for her since her fight with the massive *Rattus norvegicus* years ago. She focused her thoughts on the present situation as they walked together.

"It is truly the big day. Thank you, Hydra, for all the help," Andrea said.

"It was a great pleasure, my blue-eyed, brown-skinned

giant. Remember, your opponent will assume you will fight to your strength—which is height. The opponent will not expect you to fight from the ground or to use leverage. The opponent will especially not be prepared for you to attack with your legs. You may get one attempt—the earlier the better, before the shock wears off," Hydra warned.

Perez nodded in agreement, but then thought of a question. If speed, leverage, shock, and awe were the mainstays of her fighting technique, why had she trained with weighted bars, stones, and taken long runs around the planet's habitat? "Then why did you have me lift all those dead weights, do squats, and run all the time?" she asked.

"Because in case you fail to use leverage, you will still be able to rely on your height and strength," Hydra said.

"And the fleshy outfit?" Andrea Perez asked. "I take it that is just to distract and confuse?"

"Absolutely. No one will expect to see you attired that way. It will be baffling. I would have had you go naked for full effect, but you are too vain!" Hydra said.

As she spoke, Perez watched her shorter friend sneak a look at the backside of one of the few male Terrans nearby.

"It's not vanity, but embarrassment. I'm a scientist, not a fighter. It's bad enough I'm going to have to fight—you're right, there is no way I would ever have done it naked," Perez said.

"I think the sparse clothing may actually be more

effective. It leaves something to the imagination. Not pretty at all. Today you are not a scientist—you are Perez the Younger. Fighter, warrior, and Earther," Hydra corrected.

Perez shook her head. They were now within earshot of her father and his team.

"We should be fighting a much bigger problem—like what to do if we need more power for the habitats when tectonic shifts threaten to level Terra. Kind of more important than a family squabble! And doesn't 'no' mean 'no'?" Perez asked.

"Not when it comes to family honor. I will go behind your father while you and the centurion distract him."

Perez nodded as Hydra moved a little ahead of her and nodded politely to Dee Dee. Perez was now in front of her smiling father, who was still talking quietly to the doctor and Dee Dee. A well-built man in his early sixties, Anthony Perez was certainly in good shape and more likely had more real-life combat experience than Andrea, but his opponent was a younger Terran who was in peak condition. His combatant possessed a thick, short torso with well-defined muscles and arms that were layered with even more muscles. If her father were on Earth, after his time on Terra with its higher gravity and protein-rich vegetarian diet, he would be as formidable as a well-conditioned man in twenties.

But on Terra, with a native citizen? He doesn't stand a chance, she worried.

"Now, remind me why I'm fighting this dude again?"

her father asked.

"Because you would prefer to stay with your own clan rather than join the Iratus family. While I agree with your decision, I wish you had come to me so I could have pulled you into mine," Dee Dee said.

"That would not have worked, Centurion—you are not the one to make that decision," Medicus Paeoniis, the doctor, said in his deep voice.

"I could have made it happen," Dee Dee responded. Her worried look was not well hidden at all.

"Don't worry, Dee Dee. Remember when we took out that team on Earth right before we got here?" her father said.

The group's attention was suddenly drawn to the center of the arena, where a broad, well-developed, muscular Terran male moved his body surprisingly fast—it was a show of strength, precision, and agility.

"Yes…and the last time we had a skirmish you were battered and shot!" Dee Dee answered.

Perez found herself smiling as she watched Dee Dee's heavy brows above her dark brown eyes arch and her nose crinkle up.

"Exactly. This young buck will be swift, and I'll be out. Pretty easy, huh?"

No one responded to his attempt to lighten the mood.

"What a tough room," Perez the Elder joked. He turned his attention to his daughter, finally stopping his warm-ups and jumping around to address her.

"Now, it's not going to be pretty out there, so it might

make sense for you to wait outside. The doctor is here to put me back together, so there's no need to worry," her father said. He took another look at her, then looked carefully at her attire.

"What's this long coat and hood you're wearing? Is it a ceremonial thing?" he asked.

Perez the Younger, his daughter, gave him a smile and extended both her hands to rest on his shoulders. His look of surprise was evident—it was unusual for them to embrace. Her father moved to reassure her even more, which distracted him from scrutinizing her clothing.

"Really, Andrea, I'll be fine. This will all be over soon and we'll be able to get back to our work. Finally this distraction…"

Perez listened to her father's voice trail off when his shoulders arched backward—as if he had been struck with something between the shoulder blades.

"Hey! What's going on?" he uttered before his legs gave way. He would have crashed to the ground but Perez guided him backward as both Hydra and Dee Dee caught him. Medicus Paeoniis stepped back, a needle in his hand. Her father had been neatly sedated.

"Impressive. Very effective, though it needs to be delivered by intramuscular injection. A sharp bite, I am sure. Redness at the injection site is likely. He'll be out for several hours," the doctor said.

Without further discussion, Perez the Younger turned to enter the arena. Her friend and young leader of her habitat sector, Dux Cloelius, watched from the center of the ring—along with the waiting combatant. While the Iratus family members looked on in shock, Cloelius simply smiled, unsurprised. Perez heard some shouts from the stands and more calls in the distance—she guessed spectators were calling to passing Terrans to try to get them come watch.

"Perez the Younger, as your father became incapacitated at the moment he entered this arena, the task falls on you to take his place," Cloelius said.

"She cannot fight him! He is twice her size in width and strength! Mother! We cannot allow this to go on!" Vista said from the sidelines. Her voice was young and, while strong, it still possessed a youthful timbre that made her cry sound more desperate.

Perez turned to see her young friend, the girl she had saved years ago, standing on her feet and pleading with an older woman. By contrast, her mother, Dimitra, sat stoically and with no movement. All eyes watched to see what would happen next. Her lack of expression and involvement were telling. Like many Terran women, she was short, broad, and strong-featured. Unlike her peers', her expression was unreadable—it was simply blank.

"Mother?" Vista asked again. Her voice shifted from the high tenor of shock to low and submissive.

Perez—and everyone—watched Dimitra. Silence filled the coliseum and the adjacent walkways. The smell of cooked rat meat, rushing sounds from the air vents, and the vibration underfoot were the only sensations. Dimitra cast a look at Vista and pushed her hand down, indicating to her daughter to sit. For just a moment, it looked as if the young daughter might stand defiantly against the powerful matriarch. Instead, she slowly turned around and lowered herself reluctantly to her stone seat. It was easy to see from her expression that she was both angered and worried. Perez shot her a look and a smile to convey that all was well. All at once, the spectators finally began to make noise again, coming to life as if the collective held breath was finally released.

Here we go, Perez thought. *Let's hope Hydra's right about this.*

Perez the Younger turned to face her powerful opponent, then walked toward the center of the octagon. It was easy to see that he outweighed her. While she might have height on her side, his sheer weight alone could crush her. His slackened jaw, though, made her think it was well worth the risk.

"I will take his rightful place, Dux Cloelius," Perez said.

She carefully backed away, keeping her eyes on her large opponent. He looked both embarrassed and shocked to be fighting an Earther female. It was easy for her to understand her opponent's train of thought. Perez the Elder had at least been a male; that was why the match had drawn a small crowd. But battling against a female—that was not a noble task.

To add insult to injury, Perez untied her long cloak and hood and, in one swift move, she took it off to reveal her athletic, hairless body. She was covered only by a leather corset, tight leather fighter shorts, and combat sandals. Her bright blue eyes shone in her bald head, and her dark brown skin highlighted the scars on her head and leg where she had been injured during her fight with the rats. The sharp intake of air from all the unsuspecting witnesses unmistakably let her know this diversion had the intended effect. She knew she must have seemed like the equivalent of a bad car accident back on Earth—horrible yet impossible to look away from. After the initial shock and awe, more yells from the stands could be heard. She heard Latin shouts of people calling her a "naked rat," and "unholy." At the same time, she heard the spectators ribbing her opponent and mocking his new task. Perez could see the once-empty stadium beginning to fill. Eventually her eyes settled on Vista, whose expression revealed shock. Her mother remained almost as stoic as she had been before—except for a shadow of a faint smile.

"Yes! The horror. Disgust. Revolt. Fear and pure terror," Hydra said behind her. She took Perez's cloak away and they both waited for the noise level to decrease. "The shaving of your head—brilliant. Deforming, shocking, a testament of what a child will do for a parent. This event will be remembered for a long time. If he himself goes through with the fight, he will be humiliated, and if you beat whatever stand-in he might have come take his place, it will be even more memorable."

"So you're pretty sure they won't just stop in horror?"

"No. It has gone too far. The sister closest to your age will probably stand in for him. It is about family honor, no matter how horrible you appear. She will not be as well trained as he is, but she will be strong. Your advantage, once we get beyond your vile appearance, will be in your training and your unfamiliar technique," Hydra said. Perez pulled out a sturdy set of fingerless gloves for grappling while she watched Hydra assessing her opponent—and the growing masses of interested Terrans.

"I will not fight this…this thing!" the Terran male said. Without further discussion, he turned to the head of the Iratus family.

"Does this mean you forfeit your fight?" Dux Cloelius asked. Perez turned to follow what was transpiring.

"No, we do not forfeit. I propose Vorcha, my sister, take my place against this…this thing," he said with contempt.

As Perez looked on at the annoyed and frustrated Iratus family members, she saw Dux Cloelius struggle to keep from laughing. Vorcha did not look happy. After some finger-pointing, slashing hand movements, raised voices, and angry growls, the young Terran female—a smaller though no less muscular version of her first opponent—entered the ring. Her look of anger and revulsion was unmistakable. She was not happy at having drawn the short straw for this task in front of such a large audience. Perez watched the woman look back at her brother. She pointed one more time and then continued her march to the center of the ring. Her brother stood with his cable-like arms crossed in front of his chest.

"Let us be done with this so we can leave this naked

rodent," Vorcha said. Her opponent by default quickly peeled away layers of her worker's uniform. Much to Perez's joy, her finally layer was a restrictive thermal jumpsuit made for stabilizing heat and pressure while working on external airflow ducts. It was not made for combat. *Timing is everything*, she thought.

"Excellent. This one is angry and thinks she is better than you. She is also not prepared. Her clothing's restrictiveness is your advantage. Strike quickly and without mercy," Hydra said as she backed swiftly away.

Perez turned to face the now-ready fighter. Dux Cloelius stood back and made a slashing wave down to the ground, indicating the fight was on. The large crowd in the stands was still growing as more Terrans pushed and shoved into the coliseum—all shouted with enthusiasm. Perez blocked them out. She focused on her opponent's size, the distance between them, and the location of the Terran's hands, arms, and neck. While she had a number of strategies and techniques to choose from, the one she had practiced nearly every day for months on both Hydra and Dee Dee flashed before her, as if she were back in the practice ring they had set up in one of Terra's many engine rooms. Hot, noisy, and out of sight, it had been the perfect place to train.

After a few seconds of circling each other, Vorcha launched at her. Perez vaulted at her as well. Vorcha's intent had clearly been to strike out at Perez, so the look of shock on her face when Perez's legs quickly wrapped feet-first around her was gratifying. Perez held on to Vorcha's chest protector as one leg wrapped around the back of Vorcha's neck and the other tightened around her waist. Her weight, size, and momentum carried both of them to the ground. Perez landed on her own back, so Vorcha might have thought she had the advantage, as she was above her still. It was only when Perez crisscrossed her ankles and tightened her grip at Vorcha's neck that her opponent realized she was in danger of a swift defeat.

Perez clenched her thighs and legs together, then used both of her hands to grasp and hyperextend one of Vorcha's arms. The crowd's yells of shock and their chanting echoed throughout the entire cavern that contained the biosphere. Perez forced herself to focus. Vorcha was off balance but still standing, and Perez watched her struggle—one arm was trapped under the legs that were squeezing air out of her while the other was completely immobilized by Perez's hands. Only Perez's shoulders and head were still touching the arena's floor.

She watched Vorcha's expression mutate from anger to surprise to panic as the trapped woman stood above her. To the onlookers, the sight of a hairless giant upside down with her legs wrapped around a broad opponent in a supposedly superior position had to be confusing. Grinding her teeth, Vorcha attempted to lift Perez off the ground as a way of breaking both the arm lock and leg grip. Perez held on for dear life, hoping and praying that her enemy would show some sign of succumbing to her precise attack. There were more shouts, cries, and chants but Perez did her best to block them out. Sweat coated her body. She focused on just holding on to Vorcha with all her strength and prayed for her to submit. If her friends were shouting suggestions or if the crowd was jeering, she was unaware of it. She could hear only her own rapid breathing and the sound of her pounding heart in her ears. The smells of their sweat mingled in the air.

After what seemed like a century, Perez finally felt Vorcha's torso tremble. A moment later Vorcha fell sideways. Vorcha's one arm remained hyperextended while her other stayed completely locked under squeezing legs. Her initially violent struggles were fading swiftly. Perez suddenly had a horrible thought, and fear gripped her at the idea that she might be capable of killing someone. While she knew the contest was not meant to be to the death, she had seen it happen before. Fear gripped her at the idea of killing someone. Before she could think more, both Hydra and Cloelius were on her, loosening her grip and pulling her off a motionless Vorcha.

The sudden pulls that forced her to release her combatant broke the spell she was under and the rush of the roaring crowd flooded her ears. Disoriented, she lifted herself off the ground with Hydra's help. Sweat stung her eyes, and her arms and legs felt as if she had run a marathon. She wiped her eyes and saw that the crowd, significantly larger than it was before, was on its feet. It took her a moment to realize that both her name and her adopted family name, Ferris, being chanted loudly. Hydra held Perez up, and Vista appeared by her side as well. The young woman with two fingers on one hand raised Perez's arm up, indicating victory. Perez allowed herself to be turned around to face the stadium's entire standing, cheering crowd. When Vorcha came into view again, Perez was greatly relieved to see that Cloelius had revived her. Vorcha's crestfallen expression made it evident that she would have preferred to be unconscious—or worse.

"So what was that move called again?" Hydra asked into her ear, above the roaring crowd.

Perez took a moment to collect her thoughts. Dee Dee had adopted that attack—and a couple of more—from a martial art on Earth called Brazilian jujitsu. After two more victory spins, the name came to her.

"I think it's called a flying triangle choke."

Hydra smiled. She and Vista each held up one of her arms up as they spun her around to acknowledge the still-growing crowd. Perez made eye contact with Dimitra. Still in her seat, her stoic expression was graced with the same ghost of a smile she had seen at the beginning of the fight.

"Maybe this is a bigger victory than I thought," Perez said quietly.

Chapter Three

Future Academy—Earth

Resolutely train yourself to attain peace. —The Buddha

Christine Reich sat comfortably in the Spartan environment of Principal Adam Smith's office. She was pleased that the principal had converted his office to a residential staff recreation-and-break area in exchange for a much smaller office—the floor plans she had seen years ago for her private school for orphans had called for a much larger space for him. This room's best feature was its floor-to-ceiling glass wall that overlooked a large courtyard surrounded by four massive buildings that included teaching centers, living areas and recreational spaces, as well as vocational training centers. At the helm of the institution was a fifty-four-year-old African-American man, social worker, and therapist by training. Reich was very happy that she had chosen him to be the principal of her school. Sadness gripped her, though, as she wondered if it were true he might be its first as well as its last. She shook her head to clear it of the bad news about Jupiter's impending transformation into a sun and the devastating effects that would wreak on her world.

"So Ms. Reich, I am so happy you dropped by to see how we are doing," the principal said. He always wore a suit, crisp white shirt, and matching tie. Not the stereotypical therapist for sure—she was glad he had come out of retirement to take the job. A private practice and teaching was more than enough for anyone. But his passion for child welfare and his vision for the children were inspiring. The outrageous paychecks from Reich Enterprises to him and all the staff also made positions at Future Academy the most sought-after in Massachusetts, and on the whole East Coast.

"I'm glad you are here because I have a question—or rather, a puzzle—I would like you to help me out with," he said.

The look on his pleasant, kind, and calm face showed more concern than usual. Even though he was always happy to take her everywhere on the campus to see the children, programs, classrooms, all culminating with lunch, it was easy to see he had something on his mind. At first she wondered if he wanted to move on to another position or to go back to what he used to do. She looked down at her own attire quickly to make sure she was appropriately dressed for a tour of a school for children aged six to nineteen. She could still hear her master computer's feminine voice criticizing everything she wore and reminding her of the need to be a role model, while Lux, the resident Terran, tried to dress her to hide all exposed skin: "It is as if you are a giant marsupial with shaved hair. Not very attractive. The more you cover the better."

While she would have preferred going with a higher hemline and an adorable sheer top under a blazer, she went with a near-classic, old-style business suit reminiscent of the early 1980s and Wall Street.

Thoughts of the principal's puzzle interrupted her musings; that he had something on his mind had been apparent to her all morning and afternoon. "That's obvious," Reich said softly to herself. She appeared relaxed; she had learned to just wait for things to unfold when it came to social situations. Still, the planet's demise weighed heavily on her mind.

"Well, as you know, your wards from Russia and China have flourished here, along with the other students. And with the generous resources you've provided us, we've been able to invest in the best technology, equipment, and computer systems—they would make NASA envious. That said…" the principal paused as he pulled something out from a top desk drawer. "Felicia and Hong used it to do some research on you and your company."

Reich's interest was piqued. He handed her a red folder that was half an inch thick. Without a word, she opened it and saw a very familiar-looking person in various, though blurry, surveillance pictures. As she went through it she saw her former self, Roberta Josephine Riesman. She had been a former army major and her last position was executive director of Readiness and Disaster Logistics in the Federal Emergency Management Agency's Office of Response and Recovery—as noted in the obituary that formed part of the file before her. Her old training and experience had come in useful—and how—over the past several months. She never thought this was how her story would be revealed, however.

"Dr. Riesman died in a tragic explosion and fire in Boston. I was heading there when I missed my plane," Reich said, a well-practiced lie. Her new persona seemed far more real to her than her past life ever had. Her mind raced to old news footage of her old life's funeral with her sister and nieces weeping in front of a closed casket on a rainy, Midwest day surrounded by hundreds of colleagues, soldiers, peers and enemies. An overwhelming feeling of rushing out of the office and flying to see them was quelled by the knowledge that if she did, they would be in danger. *Past life. My poor sister. My nieces.*

Children's voices brought her back to the present. She looked at the principal.

Mr. Smith nodded to indicate that he understood.

Not very convincing on his part. He still believes the children. Impressive, Christine thought. Her eyes had already brimmed with tears. She rubbed them away, hoping he would think it was allergies. If he was suspicious, he never let on.

"I've got this thing about encouraging children when they are curious, no matter about what, to pursue their line of inquiry. And while I assured them that the resemblance is uncanny, that is where the mystery lies. But it *is* uncanny," Smith said. He looked both sad and serious. The room was quiet, only noises of children playing outside in an extended recess wafted their way in. Reich looked at her former identification picture. She was much thinner now, more athletic, and had let her naturally red hair and smaller frame show. That had been so many years ago. As she stared at the picture, an idea came to mind.

"Principal Smith?"

"Yes, Ms. Reich? I hope you're not offended with this drill-down investigation. I just think the kids, and all of us, are intrigued by you—your generosity *and* your past," he said. His tone was apologetic.

"Of course. I understand. I have something I would like for you to have your students do. And can you have Hong and Felicia lead the investigation?" she asked. The look of confusion was evident on his face, so Reich continued.

"I want your students to construct a 'what if' scenario," Reich said. She pushed the material she held back into its red folder and then pulled her blazer tighter around her as she sat back in her chair.

He was still a little confused, surprised, and at a loss, but she was pleased to see his quick recovery. He was still in his seat, but in response, Principal Smith simply pulled out a pen and pad of paper. It was not the first time he had done this—he always wrote lists for her of what he needed. Now, he was taking notes about something *she* needed.

"I have a team working on what might happen if there was an astronomical event that resulted in Jupiter igniting into a sun. A smaller sun, for sure, but a second sun for our solar system," Reich explained.

If Smith was surprised, he hid it well. He was good at detecting the truth. Saying it out loud sounded strange to her. And she *knew* the truth. She pressed on while he was still writing.

"I am impressed with your students' tenacity and persistence. And while there are some truths in this file, I would stick with the uncanny resemblance explanation, and redirect them to work on this project. I want them to work on this for the next several weeks, two months at the most," she added.

Smith nodded as if the request were not at all unusual.

"All right. The science department was looking for a project anyway," he said.

"No, Mr. Smith, not just the science classes. I want the whole school to work on it," Reich said.

Smith's eyebrows knitted together. His mouth slackened just a little bit. Before he could ask why, she gave more instructions.

"I want this to be a campus-wide question. What would happen if Jupiter ignited? What would happen to Earth? What would we need to survive? Where would we have to live—underground, or high in the mountains? What would we take? What kind of community would we need to have? I want all seventy-two students, teachers, and staff working on this as a project. And before you ask why, let me tell you what the students and staff will win," Reich went on. Her mind's eye recalled hours of her Keeper's simulations of mass destruction—earthquakes, tsunamis, fires, volcanic eruptions—the end of days. She refocused on her conversation. It was not easy.

"Okay..." was all Smith could say.

Reich let the silence sit for a moment. Smith must have thought it was for dramatic effect. In reality, she was trying to think of a compelling reason for them to suspend their planned curriculum and scheduled events. It finally came to her as she looked outside the windows to see more children, older ones, coming out for recess.

"I have a team of professionals working on this scenario already. But if your teams come up with good answers and a better plan than theirs, all staff will get a thirty percent raise and every student who goes to college will not have to worry about room and board, tuition, or books and expenses—regardless of where or when they go."

The silence was thick. Christine had barely eaten her salad—and turned down the perfectly prepared chicken-and-rice lunch—and her stomach's hunger noises were louder than the children's voices outside. Principal Smith did his best to recover from the shock of her proposal. He licked his dry lips and did his best to speak. His voice sounded dry when he finally responded, but he pressed on.

"Why? Why would you do such a thing?"

Reich felt herself smile. She was not happy, but rather relieved that she did not have to deal with her burden alone. She took her time to explain the situation to him so that she could do it without invoking terror. Her mind flashed back to the night she had learned the truth about her dear friend Anthony Perez, Terra, Venus—and a whole new universe.

"I picked this task because at some point in our future as a species, we will have to deal with a possible extinction-level event. Those children out there are the future—that is why this school is named Future Academy. Those discarded children, left to fight alone and die on the streets, are the future. I would rather have them work on such a project in the safety of this world, this academy—now—than to deal with the mindless leaders who they could have to depend on after it happens. I have more hope in their creativity, ingenuity, and survival instincts than I do in most of the people out there. And I want them to be rewarded for their best efforts. We do this right, your staff will see a substantial raise, and our students will be able to focus on academics once they leave our nest, without the burden of tuition and expenses. A valuable lesson to learn while in school. Their home. *Our* home…" Reich said. Her smile must have faded and her voice trailed off as more children came into view from her seat overlooking the campus's yard. She turned to see the principal looking quizzically at her.

"Is there something I should know?" he asked. His gaze was serious but somehow also warm. Like Anthony Perez, Adam Smith had lost his wife—but to cancer—and his son to war. He was alone. These students were his children now. He shifted his focus to the playing youth outside.

She turned to look at them while she spoke.

"I know that nothing will happen to those kids, no matter what. Fear is the enemy. Preparation and adaptation are the keys to success. I am privy to a lot of information, and I fear something will happen in just a few short years. I know it will. My close cabinet members know, and now you know. No details. For now. They will come."

"And the file?"

"True and false," Reich answered without delay. More hunger sounds and children's voices filled the room.

"Thank you, Ms. Reich, for giving us this task. And thank you for giving me reason to live," Smith said.

Reich turned to look at him. Without taking his eyes off the youth, he answered her unasked question. Images of her sister chasing her nieces flashed before her.

Maybe I can save them when the end comes.

"Being their principal is a great honor and a joy—something I never thought I would feel again. But it's about more than guiding them through their present," he said as he pointed to the children. "It's about their future, now. It all just got wicked serious."

"Yup," Reich said. "As serious as it gets."

Chapter Four

Odyssey—Terra

Attachment is the root of suffering. —The Buddha

"I can't believe Dee Dee and the doctor took me out. No warning. Nothing," Anthony Perez said. He sat crammed in the small galley area of their living unit. They had only three small rooms, including the shared sleeping area where they pitched their cots.

Andrea reflected often on the spacious, near-luxurious college dorms she lived in a lifetime ago. *Open air, trees, plenty of space, places to go freely without need of pressurized suits to protect against solar winds, severe lightening, and massive tornadoes.* The constant vibration under her feet that she was typically able to ignore made it clear that she was not on Earth. The constant hum of the planet's machinery helped pull her thoughts back to the present. Her father was now rubbing the back of his neck where she assumed the injection site was located.

"You know, the doctor's injection was not without pain, but it was fast and far better than the shots we got back in the service. He's a fast doctor for sure," he added.

Andrea smiled at his amazement—and at her good fortune that Dee Dee, Paeoniis and Dux Cloelius were worried about her father, too. Not to the obsessive degree she experienced, of course, but worried enough to hint that he should think about returning to Earth. On Earth, her father's physique and health would be envied for sure. A sixty-year-old in a forty-year-old body would be prized. But fighting against a younger, profoundly stronger Terran male? He'd had no chance. She was also glad he had been unconscious so he did not see her outfit. She was sure he would have not approved of the shock-and-awe tactic. Now, dressed in her usual reddish-brown clothes and tunic that designated her engineering-warrior classification, she sat across from her father, likewise crammed into her own seat. They were both sipping the closest thing Terra had to tea, made of mushrooms, fowl, and rat-meat broth. It sounded vile, but she had grown to like it.

"And you shaved your beautiful hair, too? Andrea! I could have resolved this without you doing all that. I should have known something was up when Hydra kept coming around, looking for you," the elder Perez said.

"Wow, Dad! You're the one who got Hydra and her team all jazzed up about looking for some 'lost city.'"

Andrea watched her father drop his hand and look at her. Every time she called him on his research and all the old maps, charts, and books he had found in the Great Library, he gave her the same stare. She already knew what he was going to say.

"You know, they thought the City of Troy was a myth, too. But then they found the ruins and all of a sudden, fable became fact."

Andrea did her best not to roll her eyes or to look disinterested.

"But Dad, come on! Obviously the 'Hades' here is different from our understanding of what Hades represented on Earth. And even if there was some remote connection between an underground world here and our Hades, it's clearly Terra that's both underground and built by a great planetary architect they call Hades. You know that. *Hades* is a person, not an actual place. That's probably what was meant by it all. Earth's master computer is nearly inoperable," Andrea said. She closed her eyes immediately as she realized the trap she had just walked into.

"You mean the other myth, Atlantis? Where Earth's master computer is? A mythical island that was supposed to have been the locus of civilization until it was wiped out?" he said. While his answer was devoid of smugness, she knew he had a point.

All right. Change tactics.

"Don't you think our sonar and seismic monitors would have discovered chambers under the crust?" she asked. Andrea was trying her best to derail her father's escalating argument.

"We should have realized that Terra was here while we were still on Earth, too. But we missed it because of deception and missed hints. I'm betting that there is a real Hades, an underground world filled with heat, teeming with life, devils in the dark, fire, and brimstone. You've seen all the old maps, charts, and manuscripts?"

Andrea nodded. Then she looked down at her cooled drink. Images of old manuscripts and documents flooded her mind. She didn't have to look over at their sleeping area to know that his bunk was littered with all sorts of material related to his studies. She moved her hand to her head and was surprised to feel that she was bald—while she was not used to it, she admitted to herself that not having any hair made it very cool and pleasant. The silence grew.

"Well, at least Hydra believes," he said. He did not sound dejected, but he did not sound happy, either.

The feeling was mutual.

"How come you're leaving for Earth? You've spent months on this search and have located possible sites for the city, and now that you've got a team together, you're leaving? Why?" Andrea asked. She felt her heart beginning to break. It was easy to see that her father felt the same pain she did.

"Honey…I really don't fit in here…"

"You haven't given it a try," Andrea interjected.

"Honey, you've been here for years. You're part of the caste system, with your science background and your warrior status. I'm more like a specimen in a zoo," he said. He spoke softly, which made the truth of his words more palpable. His argument was almost verbatim to what Dee

Dee had said. He reached out his hand to touch his daughter's. She grabbed it immediately.

"Anyway, Bobby Jo will need help putting together her ark. When Jupiter ignites, I really think Terra will be fine. Earth will become nightmarish. If she and I can convince General Farrell to shift resources from searching for Terra to preserving the next generation, it will be time well spent," Anthony said.

"You mean the elusive Christine Reich?" Perez the Younger said.

"Yup. She'll always be Bobby Jo to me, but you're right. I have to start training myself to call her by her new name."

"General David Farrell…" she said.

"He's a decent guy. He's the guy that tried to keep you safe and has been hunting Terra down."

"Yup," she said. She actually remembered her first meeting with the man, a mild-mannered, articulate military colonel at the time. When he told her what he suspected about another planet behind the sun, she was sure he was mad. But when his explanation happened simultaneously with all her scientific research vanishing from the computer servers, she knew it was no joke. Her memories of earlier times on Earth were filled with a sense of mystery and scientific adventure, but that didn't mean she was enthusiastic about her father's plan to return to a marked planet.

"And if Earth doesn't survive?" Andrea felt her eyes welling up.

Anthony squeezed her hand in reassurance. "I don't think Earth is going to, honey. But we'll make sure that our shelter will keep us safe. Worst-case scenario is that we all come here. While there might not be a lot of room," her father said as he gestured around their small space, "at least we have an escape plan."

"It takes two Earth months to get there from Terra."

"We'll be able to last that long, at least! We've got time and resources to find a suitable location for shelter. Based on the assessments Hydra gave me, it looks like being underground will be the safest plan, as long as we stay far from fault lines," Anthony said.

Memories of her mother and brother, both resting in graves on Earth, came to mind. At first she had wondered if her father's desire to return home was to be closer to them. It didn't take long for her to realize, though, that being on Terra without a purpose when he could be on Earth doing something useful was a primary motivation for his decision. She had a purpose, role, and function on Terra. Her father did not.

"Well, at least you'll have more to put your mind to on Earth than searching for some lost world here," she said as a means to try to lighten her mood. Her father smirked and squeezed her hand before letting it go. Andrea thought he was going to let her flippant comment go, too, but he went back to it.

"Those huge rats came from somewhere. And now they're suddenly in short demand. You gotta wonder where they went…"

Andrea and the others had indeed wondered about the precipitous drop in rattus sightings, and rat meat had become a rare commodity over the past several cycles.

He's got a point there. She reluctantly agreed with her father's assessment. *They have to be going somewhere.*

Chapter Five

Scotland Yard—Earth

Radiate boundless love toward the entire world—above, below, and across—unhindered, without ill will, without enmity. —The Buddha

Reich found herself enjoying the panoramic view from the enclosed observation deck of the John Hancock Tower in Boston, Massachusetts. While the view was crystal clear and there were few other visitors, she wished she were alone—and not waiting to spring a trap.

"Officer John Middleton is twelve meters north of your position, and Officer Virginia Spenser is fourteen meters south of you," her master computer said through a small earpiece in her right ear canal, making her tablet's mechanical-sounding female voice so clear it was as if she were right there. The tablet, Christine knew, was more likely in the hands of Lux, who was running the mission.

Attired in a black, form-fitting, one-piece, sleek jumpsuit underneath a long black dress, black blouse, and tapered black jacket and boots, Reich looked more like she was on her way to attend a funeral than to meet Chief Inspector Arthur Bradley. The only color she flashed was her red hair and lipstick. To her, this would be more of a tête-à-tête than a real a "meeting." She had gone to some trouble to give Bradley the impression that she had been caught, just so she could talk to him. Her black attire stirred up memories of the funeral of her former lover, Dr. Hiaki Nakamura. On that bleak day, she had also reconnected with Anthony Perez. That day, the Earth had stood still for her, and a new world order came to light. Reich looked out and tried to enjoy the view.

It had been several days since she met with Principal Smith. Lux and Pax thought she was crazy to give him and the children such a challenge. Her own Master Keeper, embodied now in a small tablet, had labeled the approach "ingenious," however. Principal Smith had called her yesterday to say that the campus was already buzzing with the assignment, and she finally felt much better. Now, with part one of her plan in the works, the time had come to talk to Chief Inspector Bradley. Then she could begin to check out future sites. With the three "emergency preparation" stores purchased and a gun company and ammunition reserve on the payroll, all that was really needed was to get everything in place and wait.

Two years. Maybe three.

"Chief Inspector Arthur Bradley has secured all possible routes of escape below your position. As expected, there is minimal coverage above you," her disembodied tablet computer said.

"Is my package in place?" Reich asked quietly.

"Yes. Milites Vespere placed the package and Milites Bella confirmed its position as recently as thirty-two minutes ago. She is en route to the pickup location," the Keeper added.

"Are you linked with the building's security system?"

"Yes. All monitors and controls are at our command. Lights and emergency backups were confirmed by Immunes Pax. Your escape plan will have the distinct advantage of being novel."

Reich nodded to herself. All her years of training, working out, and past missions had been difficult, but this mission, where she used herself as bait to spring a trap and then escape was worrisome to her. One pressing question nagged at her mind, but before she could ask, her tablet anticipated her thoughts—a very new development in its artificial intelligence, she noted.

"In regards to Sir Robert Phillip Pierce's continued unauthorized absence from house arrest, he is now ninety-seven days considered missing in action. Based on what we have gathered even with remote access and shifting resources, it seems clear that he is preparing some sort of mission. Based on our best analysis, it is unclear as to what his target might be. I anticipate that there is a twenty-two percent chance that it is you. Based on the level of security you have, however, he will more likely pursue another target that is less daunting to capture, but someone related to you."

Reich remained silent as she mentally ran through a list

of possible targets. She had a private firm and their team watching her school and staff, and she was making herself more visible so as to lure him to her and force his hand rather than waiting. She moved across the room to be closer to Officer Middleton's position—casually, as anyone might do if they were looking to get a different view of the city's skyline, Blue Hills, or beyond.

"Chief Inspector Bradley and three other officers from the Boston Police Department have reached the observation deck. He is redeploying them and contacting both Spenser's and Middleton's teams. They are covering all exits at your level and below. Based on their brief exchange, it seems he will approach you in one minute, from your left," the Keeper said.

Reich pushed her hand in her pocket and felt for the old-fashioned thumb drive. On it were the exact locations of their sister planet Terra and coordinates that would allow anyone to finally see it. In addition, there was a briefing on Terran culture and life. There were also data on Venus and on "Martians" on Arcadia Planitia—Mars.

All those years of looking for life, and it's all right in my pocket. Farrell will just love this.

"Engagement in fifteen seconds."

"Location from roof access?" Reich asked. Even though the schematics were fresh in her mind, she just wanted to make doubly sure she knew where she was going.

"Fifteen meters from your location. Officer Middleton and Officer Spenser are guarding it. They apparently are not taking anything for granted," the Keeper said. Even as the voice spoke, Reich could see a portly man approaching her from the left. She assessed one more time the best way to shed her clothes before her escape. She would need to evade both Middleton, an athletic man in his thirties who was stationed at the door—and the one approaching her, too.

"Well, well, well. Ms. Christine Reich. Industrialist, philanthropist, and wealthy international woman of mystery and intrigue. A modern-day protector of children and nemesis to those that wish harm upon them," the chief inspector said in a joyous tone that revealed neither sarcasm nor gloating—he was being genuinely positive. Reich couldn't help but smile at his greeting.

He would make such a great drinking buddy.

"Chief Inspector Arthur Bradley. You're a little far from New Scotland Yard," she said.

As she turned to face him, she was not surprised to see that he was wearing a frumpy, ill-fitting suit or that he had unkempt hair. It was clear that he realized that his presence was not a surprise to her. His approach slowed as he neared her and his eyes darted all around, as if to see whether there was anything that would expose his operation.

"I would have expected a little more surprise from you, Ms. Reich. Last time we met you were in my jurisdiction, my country, and my investigation. Now here we are across the pond, and you seem as if you were expecting me," he said as he began taking handcuffs out of his pocket.

No chances this time.

Even though there were a fair number of tourists milling about, Reich and Bradley felt as if they were the only two on the floor.

"Inspector," Reich said as she held up her hand and showed him the thumb drive, "I have the evidence that General David Joseph Farrell needs to finally prove the existence of his missing planet."

Bradley came to a complete stop. He locked eyes with her, peering intently into them as if to try to determine whether she was telling him the truth or not. She did not wait for his response.

"The planet is called Terra. It is a tidally locked planet on the other side of the sun. But that is the least of our problems. We need to convince Farrell to stop wasting time and resources looking for a benign planet—there is a far more dangerous situation that needs to be addressed. He would be better served if he focused on it rather than Terra. I have proof, but I will need a time and location to meet in person and discuss that," Reich said. She held the thumb drive in her hand, above her head, as she spoke. She watched Bradley and how his gaze went from his eyes to her hand.

Still holding the handcuffs, he moved closer as he spoke. "Not many know the General's middle name. Once again, Reich, you surprise me," he said.

"I know that you've been looking for my favorite prince, Sir Pierce. House arrest? Really? You thought he would just stay home?" Reich asked.

"That was not my call. He's stateside, by the way, but I

bet you already knew that," he said. He was now within two feet, so she lowered the thumb drive gently and placed it in his extended hand. She then slowly closed his hand around it. She was surprised how big his hand was and how meaty it felt. He looked down as she performed the small gesture.

"Well, this is an unexpected turn of events," Bradley said. He moved to drop the drive in his trouser pocket for safekeeping. As he put his right hand into his pocket, Reich grabbed his left hand, which was holding the handcuffs. In an instant, she had his left wrist cuffed. She managed to cuff it to his right one while his hand was still deep in his pocket.

"What the hell? Spenser! Middleton!" he shouted.

Reich pulled off her tear-away black dress and prepared to hurl it over Middleton, who was moving toward her fast. She used some visitors in the way to obscure her for just the moment she needed to throw the material over the oncoming officer. Then she tripped Middleton, sending him sprawling to the ground. She turned to see Virginia Spenser hot on her trail—followed by three large officers. It was clear that she intended to try to settle a score from their last encounter. Free of her dress, Christine ran at full speed to the roof access door while ripping off her other clothes.

"There is a doorstop just behind the door you can use to slow their progress," the Keeper said in her ear.

Now wearing only her sleek black jumpsuit, Reich burst through the metal door and slammed it shut. Just as the master computer said, she found the wood doorstop and kicked it in place. She didn't want to wait to see how long it was going to hold up four people smashing into the door. Reich took the stairs two at a time.

"Once you are on the roof, turn right and head three-point-five meters to the brown HVAC unit. You will find a solid black backpack that weighs approximately ten-point-four-three kilograms. Strapping it on your back will activate additional straps; these will automatically conform to your body and will activate the internal gyroscope to indicate launching sequence and flight," the Keeper said calmly.

"That's a bit heavier than I'm used to. I bet the wings were upgraded with heavier metal," Reich said.

Just as she opened the roof door, she heard a large crash and loud cursing below her. She slammed the door and took off toward the brown air-conditioning unit. Without looking, she reached under and grasped for the metal pack. For just one moment when she couldn't feel anything, she panicked. She reached in deeper. Once she had her hands on it, she started breathing again, unaware that she had stopped. She easily slung the heavy pack across her back. Once secured, four other straps automatically emerged from it and wrapped precisely around her waist and thighs. Not waiting to watch, she began running to the farthest edge of the roof that towered 241 meters above the city of Boston.

"Will you fly me in, or should I go manual?" Reich asked. Secretly she had hoped to manually guide herself, but she figured the Keeper would be far more efficient at taking her to a precise landing at the preordained location.

"Affirmative—I will fly you in. Please hold on to your shoulder straps. The wings will deploy in twenty-four meters. Based on your position and direction, you will land in an updraft that will lift you approximately thirty meters above the John Hancock Tower very rapidly," the computer warned.

Reich felt a smile burst onto her face as she anticipated the roller-coaster ride that was about to happen. If Spenser and the others had reached the roof, she was not aware of it as she finally reached the building's edge and dove off. The air was crisp and rushed around her entire body. She was so high off the ground that cars and people appeared as mere specks. Her stomach was in her throat and her adrenaline, already charged from her narrow escape, was pumping at levels beyond what she had experienced in her other trials with the magnetic propelled flier.

The ground rushed toward her while the building's reflective glass flew by. Finally, she felt a mechanical jerk shift her balance. She watched in amazement, as she always did, when black metal-plastic wings unfurled to a length of nearly four meters on each side of her. Their deployment was always sudden and silent. Just as the wings reached their full spread, she felt her entire body lift back up rapidly into the sky. Unable to control her emotions from the rush of the experience, Reich screamed in joy as she sailed silently back up and well above the very building she had just jumped off. Now flying in a parabolic curve higher than the tallest building in Massachusetts, she saw small figures staring up at her from its roof. Even at her height and speed, she could make out the figure of Virginia Spenser waving her fist at her. Others around her used their hands to cover their eyes from the sun and track her progress.

"We will be airborne for six-point-three minutes, until we reach the landing zone on the Great Blue Hill. Please refrain from unnecessary movement and enjoy the ride," the Keeper said.

Reich laughed out loud at the advice—the computer sounded like a transatlantic flight attendant. With air rushing through her hair and around her body, Reich screamed again in joy at the thrill of flying. No sound could be heard other than her own yells and wind whipping by her. She forgot for a blissful moment that the world she knew might not be around for long into the foreseeable future.

Chapter Six

Dawn—Terra

The calmed say that what is well-spoken is best; second, that one should say what is right, not unrighteous; third, what's pleasing, not displeasing; fourth, what is true, not false. —
The Buddha

Perez the Younger looked out over the dual landscapes of Terra's tidal-locked world. On one side was perpetual light, unbearable heat, and violent windstorms that blew sand against stone, dirt, and pyramids. On the other side of the planet's longitudinal equator was as a land in constant midnight, filled with a frozen ocean, distant mountains glowing with red lava, and striking lightning so intense that it would briefly blot out the star field every time it struck.

Even at the apex of her transparent room, Perez could hear thunder rumbling with every passing bolt. The three-story miniature Egyptian pyramid structure was perfect for weathering two radically different environments. Perez looked along the equatorial line again, at the emitter array antennas that were the only exposed features of the complex holographic machinery to show above the planet's crust; most of it was well protected below the surface. Solar energy powered the holographic emitters, allowing them to generate a planet-wide cloak that gave it the allusion of not existing at all. These pushed the light spectrum just beyond a hominid's range of vision, so the planet was as undetectable to humans as radio waves, X-rays and infra-red light—but just as real. Perez had added geothermal energy to supplement the arrays that hid Terra from Earth; these were effective but, to her thinking, no longer logical. With Jupiter's changing into a second sun, hiding the planet from Earth seemed like a ridiculous pursuit.

The scent of flowers gently wafted into the relatively small observation room. It was familiar, similar to lilac—but on Terra, it was associated with one specific person. Perez turned back to her table to rework numbers when she saw her friend Legate Legionis Clematis standing silently by the cluttered desk. Perez was mildly surprised but not startled.

"I am always impressed with your ability to remain calm when most would jump with surprise," Clematis said. Her voice was always calm, yet her curious eyes always beamed with amusement and questions. "How do you stay composed when I am sure I was not detected?" she asked.

"If you were a rattus, you would have attacked without warning. I did detect a flowery scent, so I knew it had to be you," Perez answered. As she did, she felt a smile emerge from her previously serious face, which had the effect of producing an even broader smile from Clematis. "Even with your regal, warrior-like exterior, you are such a girl. A gentle flower scent. Not overpowering, but clearly present," Perez added.

"I like to think it reflects my ability to lead. Speaking of which, I must say that for a scientist, you make well-thought-out plans. Now explain to me why I should sell this to the ruling body and debate this point?" Clematis asked. Even though Clematis appeared serious, her eyes betrayed a playful quality.

Perez was positive Clematis agreed with her plan. Nonetheless, Perez summarized her logic again. With the small table between them, Perez leaned heavily on the table top.

"If my father is going to go back to Earth anyway, why not have him meet with General Farrell and tell him about Jupiter? We should turn off the emitters and let me convert them into yet another power source for our life-support and energy needs and give Earth evidence we are here. Let's get them focused on the really important event—the coming of the second sun."

"And simply appearing and confirming that we exist will keep the Earthers from coming here? Earth's history has taught me that they tend to be pretty violent when new frontiers open," Clematis said.

Perez nodded in agreement. There was simply no denying humans' lust for exploration and conquest. Perez was careful in choosing the words for her retort, less out of a concern that she might offend Clematis, but more to soften her own fears about her father heading back to a doomed planet.

"Once Farrell focuses on Jupiter, he and the others will figure out that resources have to shift to preserving the human race as a species. The drop in sunspot activity, shifting of warm ocean currents to the bottom of the seabed while the cooler currents replace them on the surface, potential plate tectonics and rifts, volcanic activity, and the potential shift of the Earth's axis are all factors that might precipitate another ice age. They will figure it out."

Even as she uttered the words, she knew they sounded hollow and empty. She wanted her father to stay with her and be safe. He wanted to help Earth. Perez was still thinking about her father when Clematis chimed in again.

"Perez the Elder will be the best ambassador to Earth. He will also be well cared for by Reich and her team. She has already made excellent headway in preparations," she said. Her tone was more reassuring than Perez expected.

"Yes, I know." Perez said quickly. She took a moment to refocus on her other task. "As for us here on Terra," she started again, "Our thin atmosphere and upright planetary axis will result in an increase in violent storms on both sides of the planet. And with periodic light from a second sun emerging on the dark side at regular intervals, it is hard to say what will happen with our frozen ocean. And even though we have far less tectonic activity than Earth, it doesn't mean we won't have any issues with quakes."

As if to punctuate that point, a sustained flicker of light danced along the transparent walls and the low sound of thunder could be heard above the howling wind. Clematis smirked at the timing.

"That was not my doing," Perez said, although she was sure she didn't have to clarify.

Clematis nodded in response and Perez chuckled. It took a moment for them to get back on track.

"All right, Immunes Perez. I will present this to the powers that be and hope they see the logic. And you are sure you can convert the holographic emitters to energy sources for air generation and electricity? That would be helpful to know…" Clematis asked.

"Positive. Your builder, Architect Hades, did a remarkable job in the creation of the machinery—and these buildings," Perez said. As soon as she mentioned the architect's name, she immediately regretted it.

"As it turns out, these pyramids were actually designed by junior architect Iris of Venus and the emitters were created and constructed by an old grand architect, Guiana. Still, it *was* junior architect Hades who put it all together. And speaking of Hades…"

Perez raised her hand in a preemptive apology. Clematis was standing erect, with her hands behind her back. Somehow the stance made the five-foot-four hominid look taller. Even her sloping forehead and short powerful limbs seemed elegant in that pose.

"You know I tried to convince him to give up his quest. How he managed to get a team to actually search for some mythical land is beyond me," Perez said.

"Rumors, myths, and legends of a lost world have circulated for centuries. Even if I ordered everyone to stop looking, the citizens would pursue it on their own. As annoying as it is, at least assigning a small task force to dig and search for this dream world keeps everyone else focused on their assigned tasks," Clematis said.

It was evident that she was perplexed and annoyed about having to allocate resources to a fruitless task, but her point about guiding the process rather than fighting it was well conceived and implemented.

I guess that's why you're a leader and I am not, Perez thought.

"As odd as the idea of 'Hades' being a place rather than our planet's great architect is, I do wish it were true," Clematis said. Perez was surprised at her response. Clematis was known for being practical, logical, and efficient in both her professional and private life. Perez involuntarily squinted her eyes and tilted her head. The expression of confusion was not lost on Clematis. "As improbable as the dream is, I can hope it's true," she said.

Chapter Seven

New Arrival—Earth

There is no fear for one whose mind is not filled with desires.
—The Buddha

"Why are you in such a rush?" Reich asked.

It was at least the fourth time that Lux had asked Bella when they were going to land. Reich had been obsessing over what to wear. She was not sure if she should go with her favorite Midwestern garb, which she felt most comfortable in, or with a more Northeast "rich Yankee" look that might impress the local real-estate office. She finally decided to go with the East Coast outfit—to reinforce the "Reich Enterprises" etched boldly on the private plane's tail.

She kept trying to push thoughts about breaking her cover of being deceased and visiting her sister and family to the back of her mind.

Six hours away from here. Straight shot to Wyoming.

Suddenly, fear crept into her heart. The thought of Sir Pierce—still missing, armed, and dangerous—somehow finding out who she really was and using her family as leverage was terrifying. Lost in thought, she felt the landing gear hit the ground. Jarred back to reality, she turned to see that Lux was already unbuckling her harness and opening the door to disembark. Reich took her time doing the same. She slowly found her footing and moved through the small passenger section in her tailor-made suit and understated jewelry and heels that matched her outfit perfectly. By the time she caught up to Lux, she could see the dilapidated, deserted airfield and its network of buildings. Dust and dirt blew all over her eight-hundred-dollar shoes. She immediately wished she had gone with Midwestern attire of jeans, boots, and a comfortable blouse. She forced herself to focus on why she was here and brought her black-marble-colored tablet online.

"I still think you had a momentary lapse in judgment when you recruited children to come up with a plan to save the world," Immunes Lux said. She was in her nondescript, customary reddish-brown slacks, work shirt, and workaday boots. Standing just under five feet tall, her sloping forehead, large jaw, heavy brows, and cable-like limbs gave her a less-than-threatening presence. Especially with chestnut shells and remains stuck to her shirt.

Reich knew better than to trust appearances when it came to Terrans. In her first meeting, Lux had been one of four female warriors who took out a group of dangerous rogue federal agents—who had superior firepower and a helicopter for backup. That's when she became a believer in the existence of a rumored all-female Navy SEAL team, called Epsilon Team. Reich knew that such a team had never existed on Earth, but on Terra it was one of their most elite task forces. At nearly six feet in height, Reich smiled down at her friend of several years. Their divergent attire made Reich look tall and chic while Lux appeared like an ill-groomed teen. While their time together had been forged in battle and grew over years of special operations, she still found her Terran friends "cute." They of course found her lack of hair, preening, and grooming not only time-consuming but counterproductive—it made her Earther appearance look even worse to them since they valued hairiness over hairlessness.

"Are you listening to me, giant one? Did you have to go out on that limb?"

Reich nodded while she walked toward an open security checkpoint and its collapsed security booth, which sat in front of what were some ostensibly abandoned buildings. When the plane's engines fell silent, there were just the sounds of old wood and metal rattling in the wind. Reich was busy preparing her Keeper to queue up the facilities' information as they neared the main building. The ground felt as if it had recently been rained on, and the smells of rotting old wood from the buildings ahead of them were unmistakable. Reich knew that Lux was waiting for her to respond.

"I heard you, my primate friend. You must admit that, after just two months of research, they've come up with a dizzying array of suggestions, locations, and novel ideas. One of which corresponded to this very location—which the Keeper and Pax came up with as well. Not a bad showing for a group of kids still in school," Reich answered.

Since Lux didn't respond immediately, Reich assumed she was trying to think of a witty comeback to address Reich's shot about her being a primate. She didn't have to wait too long.

"With respect, my hairless friend, it is your species that are the primates. Even your embryonic length, while similar to ours, never reaches its full state of maturation in ten Earth months," Lux said.

Suppressing a smile, Reich had to admit that gorillas and orangutans did look strikingly similar to humans until the eighth month of pregnancy, and that it was only in the last month and a half that humans took on their final appearance. She had a point.

"But I must give you credit for the results your campus came up with, especially based on the cryptic data you gave them and their short time frame," Lux conceded.

Knowing when to take a compliment and how to escape further verbal sparring with Lux, Reich nodded in agreement and spoke aloud to engage the Keeper's audio application.

"Keeper? Brief summary of this site."

"Twelve point one nine meters below us, there is an abandoned United States Titan Missile complex with 762 square meters of usable space surrounded by 52,607.41 square meters. Built in the 1960s, it was designed to withstand nuclear blasts and other extinction-level events, with the proper preparation. The launch control center, living quarters, garages, work areas, and all other living areas were surrounded by hardened underground material in addition to the planet's crust surface. The former ICBM silos could readily be transformed into more living spaces, play and educational centers, and storage for food, water, and other critical supplies."

Reich and Lux stood in the center of the building complex. Since they were far from their nearest neighbors—in Topeka, Kansas—Reich was impressed with the level of graffiti that covered the overall deserted complex.

"So you Earthers would spend money on such a place?" Lux asked. Her astonishment was not lost on either Reich or the Keeper.

"Present listing for this site is $295,000 in US currency. Significant depreciation for a decommissioned military complex and less than fair market value in comparison to other similar listings," the master computer answered nonchalantly.

Lux rolled her eyes while Reich chuckled. The Keeper went on, as she always did when there was silence from her carbon-based peers.

"The real-estate agent is sixty-three minutes away. I suggest that you resist the urge to find the access port into the facility so as to give the impression of being new to the market. I would also recommend offering $250,000, as this property has been on the market for five years and has experienced twenty-five drops in price. While my experience interpreting human and hominid emotions is at times lacking, it seems clear that the real-estate agent's vocal changes during your call indicated a shift from doubt to enthusiasm at the idea of selling such a piece of land, buildings, and attached property."

"Wait a minute," Reich interjected after she did some calculations. "You got us here an hour early for our appointment—just so we could wait around?" Reich was surprised since her computer was known for accuracy—never early, never late, always on time. Reich turned to share her surprise with Lux, but saw that she was standing a few feet to the side and looking up at the gray, cloudy sky. As Reich moved toward her, she saw that Bella, who had piloted the plane, was already standing beside her and looking up into the same airspace.

Reich turned to make sure that their transport was secured for such an act—leaving transport unattended was very uncommon for them. *What the hell?* Bella, or any pilot on the immediate team, always stuck with the transport to ensure its safety. Reich found that she was getting nervous by how distracted her teammates were. She was not used to being left out of the loop. She turned her gaze skyward again as she spoke to her computer.

"Keeper? What's going on? Why are Lux and Bella looking up in the sky?"

"Most likely they are searching for visual confirmation of the interplanetary Terran stealth spaceship *Adventus.* It is scheduled to land at these coordinates in one point two minutes and to depart again sixty seconds after," said the

Keeper in her usual even-toned voice.

Reich watched a dark bird silently and swiftly approach, noting that it seemed to be moving far faster than the first Terran ship she had ever seen. While she watched the ship descend, her heart raced. She posed her next question.

"Why is it here?"

"The ship's mission is to return to Terra with various species of your world's birds of prey, as well as fox and wolf predators for domestication in addition to the canine breeds Terra already possesses. Various herbs, chestnuts, lemons, and other delicacies are already on board, along with various firearms including military grade, fully automatic weapons with ammunition, and rocket-propelled grenades—"

"But why is it coming here, now? Is Lux or Bella leaving?" A pang of fear, sadness, and trepidation engulfed her at the thought of a team member leaving. For all of their oddities and idiosyncrasies, she had come to care for them. *Surely they would have told me?*

"Negative. There are no departures. There is an arrival," her computer said.

The ship's massive landing struts and ramp began to deploy as it hovered ten feet off the ground. It was strange to see such a massive, ominous vehicle fly so quietly and hover so neatly.

"Who's landing?"

Reich watched the ship as it finally touched down. Immediately, a lone figure clad in reddish-brown clothing emerged. She noticed immediately that he had dark skin—not Terran hair. Perspiration burst out on her forehead and her hands felt cold and clammy. Her heart began to race at the thought, the mere hope that the man who had departed years ago might, for some reason, have returned. Even from a distance, he seemed broader and taller than she remembered. His determined walk and quick pace defied his age—sixty when she last saw him depart, and injured with a bullet wound.

"Computer? Who is disembarking from the ship?"

The man came to the end of the ramp and looked toward the sky before he dropped to the ground and kissed it. Lux and Bella walked over at a quick pace to meet him. Reich could see Lux's broad smile from a distance—the same kind of broad smile she would see when her Terran friend was satiated on chestnuts, cinnamon, and walnuts.

"Immunes Anthony Perez. He has returned to assist you and your team with creating an ark."

The computer's response was calm and matter-of-fact, which was diametrically opposite to the depth and range of Reich's emotions just then. Without much thought, she broke out into a dead run—in her high heels and gripping her tablet. She felt tears streaking down her cheeks. The phantomlike black ship was already receding back into the sky. Lux reached him first and began jumping all over him; Bella watched from a few feet away. Lux nearly bowled him over, but Perez hugged and released her warmly. Reich was impressed with his firm, solid stance and strong arms; he did not move an inch even as he picked her up in turn and swung her around like a little girl.

"Bobbie Jo! As I live and breathe! It's great to see you!" he said.

Reich did not respond, except to squeeze him harder and cry. She held on to him as if he might disappear before her eyes. She was not going to take that chance. Her worldly concerns shrank from saving a planet on the edge of extinction from cataclysmic events to just hugging Perez as hard as she could. She held on as if life itself depended on it.

One Year Later

Chapter Eight

Devils in the Dark—Terra

Whoever doesn't flare up at someone who's angry wins a battle hard to win. —The Buddha

"So, are you ready to get dirty?" Hydra asked. Her toothy smile and sparkly eyes made her wide, heavy brow look small and almost cute—even though she was just wearing her dark brown, filthy technician overalls. It had been too long since she had spent time with her periodic drinking buddy, not that there was much in the way of alcohol that tasted remotely good on Terra.

The first time Perez had actually gone drinking with her was when she asked Hydra to lead her father's team to look for the supposed hidden world of underground caverns filled with darkness, demons, and death. Hydra was thrilled to be asked to lead the expedition and drill team deep into Terra's crust—deeper than anyone had ever gone. The whole expedition had been kindly dubbed a "fool's errand" by Legionis Clematis and Dux Cloelius, and it had taken nearly all of Perez's political clout to have a ten-member team dedicated to such a project.

But what if the old man was right? she had wondered.

While Perez had spent a great deal of her time converting the holograph emitters to power supplies, she was rarely brought down to the excavation site. Today was different. Hydra was very excited and had said she needed her to join them.

"What's the rush, Hydra?"

"We're waiting on you to be there when we break through the final wall—to the other side of your mystery cavern," Hydra said. She had her hands on her hips and her large foot was tapping—more indicators of her impatience.

"Why didn't you just break through without me? You could have looked around and told me about it," Perez said. By now she was putting on her weapons, including two laser sidearms to round out her sheathed knives. She had never forgotten her battle with the rats on the mezzanine.

Rattuses. I hate them. Never again, she still thought every time she left her quarters.

She turned around to ask Hydra another question, and was struck by her shocked expression. "What's wrong with you?" she asked.

"You would have us break through the wall without you? You are the expedition leader! This is your project," Hydra explained.

"It's probably just a big, empty cavern. What's the big

deal?" she said.

It was easy to see Hydra's disbelief at that statement. Her friend shook her massive head and rubbed her temple as if Perez's idiocy was painful to her.

"All right, Immunes, here is the deal. *You* are the expedition leader. Whatever is on the other side, be it an empty cavern or the land of chestnuts and honey, it will be *your* decision to do with it what you want. That is our custom. You must be there when we go to the other side. You are our first explorer in centuries. Your name, your father's name, our names will become part of the Great Library," Hydra explained.

As she spoke, Perez pulled together all her edged weapons tightly so they were wrapped and accessible. She was attaching her laser sidearms to her holster when she looked up to see whether Hydra's dramatic monologue was over. Perez found it ironic that two women could barely fit in her small quarters. She glanced over to her father's empty cot and felt sad. He was busy helping Earth get ready for the future or at the very least, trying to save a piece of their birthplace. Based on his brief communiques, he was much happier doing something there than searching for myths here. She smiled and looked back at Hydra, who was waving her toward the door as she began explaining her final reasons for waiting.

"Can you imagine what it might be like for us to have wide open spaces again? To camp and hunt rather than live in the closed-in, vibrating coffins we call home? To spread out and find new game, new sources of food, power, water, and land? To rebuild our hunting way of life? To venture boldly where none of us has gone before?" Hydra said in breathless excitement.

Perez slowed her progress down as she tried desperately to figure out why Hydra's speech sounded so familiar. *Something old but that I know well,* she thought. Her attempts to recall where she had heard it before were interrupted by her impatient friend.

"Perez? Let's go! Our names await placement in the Great Library," Hydra said.

"Hmm," Perez said. She squeezed by Hydra and exited her quarters. She heard her door close soundly and Hydra's footsteps behind her. Without waiting, Perez began walking with her hands behind her back. Hydra continued her ramblings about fame, glory, and power for more than an hour before she even noticed that Perez had fallen silent. For a technologically advanced people, she wondered why they had no vehicles. *The wheel should have made it easy to figure out. And isn't my hair growing back very slowly?* she thought on an unrelated note. Perez's mind was truly elsewhere.

The common hallways, lit only with low-wattage bulbs, radiated their usual quiet, sound-absorbed silence. There were very few doors and dust became more prevalent as they moved farther from the honeycomb living habitats and to the outreaches of the underground dwelling. The constant vibration of Terra's heavy air and energy processors was all around her. She wondered what it would be like if her emitter conversion worked. *The vibration might come to an end.* She finally came to a recently carved-out corridor that went down rather than up.

"You would have walked right by if I hadn't told you to stop. And why do you carry so many weapons? There have been near zero rattuses here in some time. I'm getting tired of mushrooms," Hydra said.

"I hate those things. I'll never be unarmed if I ever come across another rattus again," Perez responded. Her hand instinctively went to her chain as she spoke. She felt herself getting angry and wanting to fight back. That battle had changed her. And the exercises that she learned from Hydra and Dee Dee were not wasted on her. She had continued her training as if her life depended on it. It made her feel stronger and less helpless. It also helped her forget how much she missed her father. *He'll be happier on Earth*, she thought. *He always liked that woman.*

"Well, I'll make sure to capture your image. It is fitting that you enter the cavern with a short sword," Hydra said. At first Perez nodded, but then rewound what Hydra had said.

"More likely a pressurized suit…" Perez said. There was a longer-than-expected silence. Perez felt her pace slowing.

"Well…that might not really be necessary," Hydra finally uttered in a low tone.

Perez stopped in midstep to turn and look at her. Hydra came up short and tried to keep from banging into her. Her smirk was difficult to hide on such a large mouth.

"So, the great 'expedition leader' is not the first person to see what's on the other side, is she Hydra? So what's all this about me being first when you already know I won't need a pressurized suit in the cavern? And that explains why you came to me yourself and woke me up without alerting Dux or the shift director. Out with it, Hydra. What did you see?" Perez's arms were folded across her chest as she blocked the narrow path down the descending tunnel.

Hydra looked down and then started explaining quietly. "Vera pushed through a small opening by mistake. We felt a warm wind and saw flora of some sort. The smell of mushrooms, alien scents, and water filled the antechamber. There were scents of salt, sulfur, and something else I've never encountered before. Oh, and Immunes, we could hear distant thunder—as if we were outside. And there was dim lighting and smells of other life. It was *air*, Perez. The chamber is not dead!" Hydra said. Her excited look and elevated hands punctuated each point made as she spoke.

Perez's mind immediately went into high gear as she speculated whether it could be possible for a deep cavern on a tidally locked planet with half the atmosphere of Earth's to have light and breathable air. She turned and spoke aloud as she walked quickly to their destination.

"You would need a massive, liquid body of water to generate the oxygen levels for air. Possibly vegetation. Ferns, certain fruits, and other plants can exist in the dark, similar to mushrooms…Maybe there are vents to the surface along the longitudinal equator for light, but then there would have to be enough water to compensate for its evaporation into the atmosphere. Maybe the frozen oceans have liquid runoff underground? That makes sense. The oceans are liquid several meters below the ice and if the cavern is at the same depth, than it could be possible. The thunder? Fissures and vents to the surface near the dark side maybe?" Perez's mind was moving as quickly as her mouth.

"'Where do the rats come from?' You're probably right, Dad. If this chamber has air, it might be where the rats come from." A snippet of a past conversation with her father came to her mind.

Perez realized that they now knew where their food source might be coming from, or hiding, as it turned out. The bad news was that this cavern was enormous, and there were a lot more of them based on neighboring seismic readings. She picked up her pace for a moment, but then came to a sudden stop. Hydra nearly banged into her again but said nothing. Perez put her hand on the narrowing tunnel wall, then touched the ground.

"I know, Immunes. The vibrations of our machines become less as we move below them. It is an odd experience," Hydra commented.

Perez nodded and marched down the tunnel with scientific theories running amok in her head. Both women walked in near silence for ten more minutes, until they reached a slightly larger, carved-out antechamber. In addition to the odd scent of mint, the smell of fish and mushrooms filled the air. Water vapor made the chamber feel hot and moist at the same time. The smell reeked of a biosphere—a living habitat.

"The rats have to come from somewhere" she heard her father say again. Perez looked at the hole in the dark rock formation. It was the size and shape meant for peering eyes at waist level. She looked around—the workers had picks and digging equipment, but little else. There were a series of small metal wagons that carried away debris, flares, packaged food, and bottled water. *Not a weapon in sight*, she thought.

"Who is Vera?" Perez asked quietly. She continued to look at the hole until a weak, embarrassed voice sounded out from behind her. She turned to see a young worker looking ashamedly at the floor.

"We can expel her from our group if you wish, Immunes," Hydra said.

"No. All our names will be written in the Great Library. I want Vera and you to have the honors of breaking through to the other side," Perez said.

She stepped back and watched the zeal in both women's eyes blaze. Her suggestion was met with a roar of approval. Still, her mind raced through reasons an underground biosphere might have formed. At the same time, she recalled her father's conviction that there was something underground and that "Hades," the architect of Terra, might have been misunderstood, and that Earth's Hades, a place of hot, underground hell populated with devils, might actually be real. *And if he was right? What if there were devils?*

"Keep the hole to the size needed to crawl through, no larger," Perez added. She looked back at the metal wagons to see if they could be used to block the hole if necessary. As she allowed the Terrans to break through, she saw a younger woman nearby looking more anxious than enthusiastic.

"What's your name?" she asked.

"Liliana, Immunes," she said. She looked down.

"You do not look excited about this discovery…" Perez said.

"I am sorry, Immunes. I…I get nervous about these things," she said. Perez could feel the eyes on her from disapproving peers. Perez was surprised at the young woman's intuition and reasonable deduction that danger could be near.

Water, mushrooms, and air? There's more. The rattuses have to come from somewhere…

"Well then," Perez started, "I have another task that I would like for you to carry out."

The younger woman looked up at her. Due to Perez's height, she had to bend her head also, to keep it from bumping into the cave's ceiling. A small smile came to her face—she was clearly happy that she found someone who would assign her something that would not be seen as insulting.

"Liliana, I want you to run as fast as you can to Legate Legionis Clematis and Centurion Dea Data. Let them know of our discovery and that you were asked by

Immunes Perez to bring them here. Make sure you tell them I want them well armed," Perez said. The young woman's eyes lit up as she realized she had been given an out from heading blindly into the cavern.

"Yes, Immunes! I will run like the wind!" she said. She was about to take off when Perez grabbed her arm and spoke to her again quietly.

"Make sure you tell them to come *fast* and *well armed.* Your intuition, Liliana, may be well placed. Never doubt your gut. Run!" Perez ordered.

Without a moment's hesitation, the stocky young woman was off. By the time Perez turned around, the hole was big enough for two people to crawl through—bigger than she really wanted. Hydra pushed everyone aside to make room for Perez. Without hesitation, Perez moved to the hole with her weapon drawn.

"Hydra—bring flares. Five of you come with me, one remain on the other side of this entrance, and two remain inside this chamber. Move a wagon close by in case you have to block the entrance."

Perez moved to go through; Hydra was right behind her.

"Do you expect trouble, Immunes?"

"I expect that a habitat that can support life will have life. And with so few rattuses above these days, I have to wonder where they went," Perez answered.

It took less than a minute for her to clear the short tunnel in the stone and to enter a brave new world. Perez stood fully erect and looked in all directions. Her weapon already drawn, she kept it in front of her, scanning in whatever direction she looked. Expecting complete darkness, she was surprised to find that the cavern was actually dimly lit. She looked up to see several vents and fissures in the cavern's ceiling, hundreds of meters above, that provided light. They walked several meters to take in the expanse of it all.

Standing on a flat perch, she took in a panoramic view. She looked to see if she could see perimeter walls, but she saw a grand range filled with massive rock outcrops that seemed to cover the cavern floor several meters down an incline. The rocks were surrounded by green vegetation similar to ferns and moss. In addition to large, round fruits, she made out massively size mushrooms that were all white and perfectly spherical with thick trunks that supported their huge caps. Sounds of distant thunder and flashes of lightning created frightening shadows in this humid, heated underworld.

Distant rivers of red liquid added to the surreal picture. Perez immediately suspected they might be actual lava from what she guessed was the base of Mors Mente, a mountain several kilometers away on the planet's dark side and across a vast frozen ocean. And while the grand mountain looked dead on the surface, below, in this underworld, it was alive with hot rivers that glowed red even at a distance. Salt, sulfur, and mold overwhelmed her sense of smell, along with mint and…rotten flesh.

Movement on the cavern's floor, twenty meters below, caught her eye. A flare flickered to life behind her and cast an eerie red-and-white glow over the scene as Hydra cast it down. Rattuses. Large-jawed, long-snouted rats with dark eyes and long, scaled tales scurried away at first but held their ground just outside the glare of the flickering light. They were bigger than Terra's recently acquired dogs, and their razor-sharp teeth flashed in the shadows as their spear-like tails were raised and poised to strike.

"Hydra, light another flare and hold it steady. Everyone else, slowly back to the entrance," Perez said.

Her hand gripped her weapon tightly as she backed up. She heard someone running back and was about to say something about slowing down and being quiet when a sudden wind and a flapping noise came at her from above. Without hesitation, Perez dropped down and trained her weapon at a black form that just missed her—but caught Hydra. There was no scream or sound except the shifting light from a dropped flare on the ground and wet liquid that splattered Perez's exposed skin. She grabbed the flare with her free hand and worked her way back. She tripped over someone and fell on her bottom. She heard two screams from behind her, shouts, and the clanging of waving picks trying to fend off whatever was flying above them. As Perez picked up her flare, she caught sight of Hydra—her head had nearly been severed from her torso, and her eyes were still open from the sudden assault.

"No! No! Not you!" Perez screamed. Visions from her battle years ago against three monster rattuses flooded her. The adrenaline and the anger of being relatively unarmed at that time surged through her again. She looked into

Hydra's eyes and her fear mutated into anger. Hydra had been so proud to be part of the expedition, and it got her killed. The guilt she felt at being responsible for Hydra's death exploded into more anger. *No! Her death will not be in vain!*

"You want a piece of me, you sack of shit? Let's go!" Perez screamed. She bolted up from the ground and onto her feet. She was probably ten meters away from the entrance, where she heard screams and saw arms waving flares. She saw one of the workers being lifted up from the ground. Perez discharged her laser in a long burst of directed fire, aiming well above the worker. The woman was unceremoniously dropped and a large-winged rodent crashed to the ground. It was thinner than a rattus, all black with a webbing the width of its entire wingspan. It possessed the claws and long snout filled with teeth of a Terran rattus, but its sight triggered a memory of a similar species on Earth—though on a profoundly larger scale. The creature quivered as if it might still move.

"A bat? Son of a bitch!" Perez moved around the head of the creature's still-flapping body and cut its throat swiftly to ensure it was dead. She turned to face the screaming workers and saw another dark creature flying right at her. Again, she fired a sustained laser blast. This struck the dark creature in its torso, causing it to flail backward. She turned to make sure there was nothing behind her, just in time to see two large rattuses pulling the winged rodent's body away for an easy meal. Perez ran to the opening. Only three of the five workers that had followed her in were still alive. Other than Hydra, though, there was no body. *Not a good sign,* she thought. One of the women sat on the ground, shaking uncontrollably from some injury. The other two were by her side.

"Do you need help?" a voice called out from the other side of the wall.

"Block our entrance and hold ground! Winged rattuses and hundreds of others in this cavern! You must defend that entrance until troops arrive! These things cannot leave here!" Perez shouted back. All the women around her looked at her as if she had condemned them to death. The sounds of heavy metal dragging across the rock floor reverberated to their side, confirming that the entrance had been sealed and that they were alone. Perez immediately gave one older woman her laser and unsheathed another.

"That one has four or five short shots left. Three sustained at the most," she said to the first woman. She turned to the other woman, who looked as if she were going to scream at her, and handed her a sword and a short blade.

"Stay with her," Perez said as she nodded to the woman on the ground. "I need you to be a lookout for us. Stay low and don't use flares near you. That allows them to center in on our location. *No flares*—let your eyes adjust to the light and pick your targets carefully."

Both women reluctantly agreed and tossed their lit flares toward the incline. Huddled in darkness, they watched the flares fade and the dim light from the vents above slowly take over. Dripping water, the scattering of rodent feet, and distant thunder could be heard. The hurt woman's ragged breathing became gradually more shallow and gulping until there was a slow exhale and then nothing.

"Damn it," Perez said quietly. A few more moments of relative silence passed until another breeze came in from her right side. As she turned to fire her weapon, a vice-like talon clamped on to her arm and pulled her off the ground. The sharp, cutting pain instantly deadened every other sensation in her right hand. She drove her left hand into her waistband and pulled out a large, serrated knife. She jammed it upward, above her head. An alien screech shrieked above her and she felt herself being let loose. She fell to the ground. While she had not been lifted very high, she hit the ground hard—followed by a massive, flapping bat that landed just in front of her. It looked as if it were scrambling to get up. Although she was dizzy and exhausted, she realized she was still holding on to her knife. She got to her feet and ran at the creature before it had a chance to run at her. Without thinking, she jumped onto the creature's head—and heard a satisfying crunch. She then repeatedly stabbed the creature and could feel its blood spewing all over her as she did.

"Die, you piece of shit! Try to kill me and my people? I'll kill you all!" she screamed. In her frenzy, she saw a rattus sneaking up on her left side. Perez lashed out, cutting deep into the rodent's eye. She twisted the knife and motioned to pull yet another knife from her right side, but felt nothing. She moved her arm and hand where she thought another edged weapon might be holstered—still she felt nothing. With a dead, winged rat below her and the large rattus clawing at the knife in its eye, Perez looked around and saw her laser weapon right beside her on the ground. She reached for it with her right hand, though, and once again felt nothing.

She looked down at her wrist in the dim light, only to find that her hand was completely gone. In its place was a stump covered with congealed blood and skin atop of crushed bone. She might have stared at it longer, but she remembered where she was. Perez picked up her weapon with her left hand and fired it point-blank into the still-struggling rattus. Right behind it was another oversize bat—it appeared truly demonic as it stood above her with wings outspread and its long snout and dark eyes flickering in the distant lightening strike. Perez fired a sustained blast at the creature's torso and ran the line of fire up to its head.

"That's for Hydra, bitch!" Two more dark forms came swooping in from each side. Perez was about to shoot the creature on the left when a series of laser shots came from multiple vectors behind her. Even as she watched the creatures being hit, she pushed herself off the ground and looked for more targets. Two rattuses obliged, and she took careful aim and fired. She looked beyond them to make sure they were at bay and found herself getting even angrier. She wanted more to kill. They took her friend and took her hand. Adrenaline, hatred, fury, and rage blinded her as she moved toward the cavern floor in search of more targets. There was no noise or sound—except for the sound of her heart in her ears and the hum of more laser fire. She caught another target and fired.

She felt something coming up on her left side and turned to fire. Someone faster than she was caught her weapon before she could discharge it. She turned violently and pulled for her knife with her right hand, but remembered she couldn't feel for it. Perez looked up into Legate Legionis Clematis's worried eyes. Perez became suddenly aware that they were not alone anymore. A large number of armed Milites and Immunes—all soldiers firing weapons, hurtling javelins, and using swords to kill both land and winged rattuses.

"Immunes? We are here. No need to fight more," she said. Her expression was one of concern and surprise. Perez felt herself being held tightly by Clematis. She peered over her shoulder and saw Dee Dee and Dux Cloelius using recently developed enhanced bows and arrows as they advanced. Perez nodded and brought up her right arm's stump to show Clematis. She felt suddenly exhausted, as if she had been instantaneously drained of life.

Perez uttered two sentences; even as she spoke them, she realized she had no idea what she meant. "This is my world. I want my hand back." Her vision faded and a gray-black curtain seemed to close around her while she floated away.

Chapter Nine

Unfinished Business—Earth

The world is afflicted by death and decay. But the wise do not grieve, having realized the nature of the world. —The Buddha

"All I am saying is that if you wish to have intercourse with Immunes Perez, why don't you just seize him? He will more than likely comply. What is with you Earth women and your mates? Your different gender, same gender, and intersex gender hominids appear to be so different in terms of lifestyle, but then when it comes to initiating courtship and eventual mating, it all appears the same to me. Bella and Pax agree with my assessment, should that make a difference," Lux said into her earpiece.

Reich closed her eyes in agony at Lux's more-than-chatty use of the communication link. While Lux was in Topeka, Kansas, overseeing a refit of their underground home, Reich was waiting for Inspector Arthur Bradley to join her. She was on the street overpass above the new Pier Four Restaurant, which was built on stilts above Boston

Bay and an array of walkways right on the water to where boats were moored.

Just minutes ago, she had given Anthony Perez her most recent intel on General Farrell, and was waiting for him in the establishment with a minimum of security while Bradley, Middleton, and Spenser provided another level of safety, and the Boston Police Department ringed the outer perimeter. She felt useless in the observation role. No sooner had Perez left than Lux had gotten on the link from her master computer and seized the opportunity to express her thoughts—which she did often, typically unsolicited.

"Lux! You need to stop. He's shown no interest in me, romantically. We're just good friends," she said quietly. Passersby in business suits and professional wear were all around her. The sun was nearly at its zenith, even though it was an hour before lunch. She fit in well, though she was sure her skirt was a bit tighter than necessary. She was all in red, including her pumps and blouse, and she felt like she was better dressed than most. Truth be told, she knew Perez liked red and she had caught him looking at her once when she had worn a similar outfit. She shook her head, disapproving of her own rationale for her wardrobe choice. *I'm going to feel really stupid if things go south.*

"He has made no advances because you have refused to let him know of your interest," Lux said.

"He seems too busy with his cooking, art shows, dancing, and exercises to notice me," Reich said. She felt a little pang as she said her thoughts out loud.

"Oh, giant one! He was on my home world for years. Constant vibration, recycled air, closed-in spaces, artificial light. He is just embracing all of your world's attributes," she replied.

There was silence. Reich had to admit that Lux was right. There was little time left to enjoy the planet, and Perez had already experienced the shape of things to come.

"And by the way, my towering friend, he always drags you everywhere. He always includes you in everything."

"He takes everyone—" Reich started.

"He does not take *me* to the museum. He has left us out of the plays and musicals."

"Well, those are public places…"

"And the midnight strolls he wakes you up for and takes you on? The early morning breakfasts? The ocean kayaking? Hmm. Sounds pretty private and inclusive to me," Lux said. There was no envy or jealousy. If anything, Reich was touched by Lux's and Pax's persistent encouragement. They were like the girlfriends she used to have, back in Wyoming.

Reich caught sight of an all-too-familiar man crossing the street to see her. By his disheveled look and mismatched clothes, she immediately identified Chief Inspector Bradley heading over. She waited. It felt odd to her to actually be waiting for him without a well-executed escape plan.

"Bradley is here. Back to work," Reich muttered.

"Yes. We will talk later. The Keeper is zeroing in on

some unusual frequencies—high-tech, military-level encrypted. She will be online in a moment. Good luck," Lux said.

Reich's earpiece went silent as Bradley waved at her. His pleasant demeanor, jovial face, and sparkling eyes made up for his poor choice in suits and his overall frumpy appearance.

"Well, well, well. If it isn't Batgirl! You're looking a bit casual, almost civilian-like. My wife wants to get a picture of you, since last time you flew away like a hawk in the midday sun. And the time before, you were Catwoman, scaling down castles and taking out security teams at your whim. She would not believe me if she saw you right now," Bradley said, but his humor was cut short by the sound of shattering glass below.

Reich whipped her head around to see two men already halfway down a ten-foot drop. They hit the wood pier and a shower of shattered plate glass rained down on them. The din of screams made it difficult for her to hear her earpiece come to life. As both hands clutched the railing, she saw that one of the men, who had landed on top of a much larger man, was Anthony Perez.

"Immunes Reich. The meeting area is compromised. Based on intercepted private communication, there is an operation in progress. The objective appears to be to capture General David Joseph Farrell…"

"Damn it!" Reich looked down in frustration at her short skirt and impractical shoes. "Damn it! Computer! Tell me something I don't know! What's in this area for backup?" Reich asked. She turned to look at what Bradley was doing.

She only caught a snippet of what he said: "Mission compromised...Middleton and Spenser are not responding...Move in! Move in now!"

Reich took off running as fast as she could down to the pier while digging in her purse. No gun, knife, or any other weapon to speak of—except for a collapsible baton that she had been practicing with while waiting for Perez to get ready. She held on to the metal weapon and cast aside her purse so she could grip the railing while increasing her pace. She regretted every step she took in her red pumps. As she closed in on Perez, she saw two large men carrying another in the distance. There was one smaller man directing them to a waiting—expensive—motor boat. It was easy to see that the unconscious man was in uniform and the boat was casting off for immediate launch. She focused on Perez, who looked as if he was shaking off the fall and getting up. He was twenty feet ahead of her and the men were thirty feet ahead of him—halfway across the gangplank to the boat.

When she reached the pier herself, she found a woman whom she had not seen in years waiting for her.

"Well, Ms. Reich! We meet again!"

Reich recognized the dark features and husky female voice of Sir Pierce's personal bodyguard from years before. The woman pointed a Taser gun at her and fired. While her high heels hindered her movement somewhat, Reich was still able to move rapidly out of the way of the electrode coils that were aimed at her chest. Barely ducking the shot, Reich crouched low and swung her arm back to expand her baton—then she swiftly swung it with great force at the woman's outer thigh. She heard her adversary howl in pain as it made contact. Not wanting to spend time dealing with her, Reich pushed by her to get to Perez. *Not bad in heels,* she thought.

She looked up and saw Middleton, disheveled and bloody, come up at full speed from above deck. With the boat already making speed and about to clear the end of the pier, she cursed at the thought of losing the general. She focused back on Perez, who was way in front of her and running faster than she had ever seen a person run before. His arms and legs were pumping and he showed no sign of slowing down, even when he was approaching the pier's end. She involuntarily slowed down to watch the boat pass several feet in front of the end of the pier. Perez leaped at full speed. His arms and legs were still kicking and pumping in midair, as if he were competing in the Olympic long jump. Not only did he clear the pier and water, he managed to land—not so gracefully and somewhat violently—on the boat's stern.

"Holy shit! Did you see that?" she heard Middleton say, out of breath.

Reich found herself speechless as she watched the boat speed away. Even at a distance, she could see Perez get to his feet, throw something in a cabin box on deck, and then disappear. Two men came up, obviously looking for the source of a large bang.

"Computer—status report," Reich said. She bent over to catch her breath.

Sirens wailed above, on the bridge, and beside her. Police started coming out of the restaurant, moving witnesses aside, and establishing order. She turned to see Middleton moving back to ostensibly handcuff the large man Perez had landed on while Bradley pulled a limping woman toward him. She watched Middleton look up and move to aide Officer Spenser, who had a large knife protruding out of her shoulder. Reich winced.

She looked back at the boat as it tore off across the water and wondered what was going to happen next. Finally, her master computer came on line.

"Sir Robert Pierce has successfully kidnapped General David Farrell. All intercepted communications indicate that his goal is to use Farrell as a hostage to lure you to him so he can kill you. As you can see, his plan was compromised by Immunes Perez recognizing him and then engaging one of Sir Pierce's security team."

"He crashed through a window to get my attention? Why didn't he just call or wave?" She was exasperated at the idea of Anthony taking such a dangerous risk.

"Based on internal security surveillance he, too, recognized his limited options for getting immediate reinforcements," her computer said calmly. Reich nodded and looked back down the pier to see Officer Jack Middleton walking toward her. "Officer Spenser attempted to intercede but was stabbed in the shoulder. Immunes Perez took that opportunity to use his speed and body mass to neutralize the threat and to alert all authorities for support at the same time. It was successful. His ability to revive quickly from a four-meter drop, even on top of another hominid, is impressive. However, exterior surveillance from several angles show that his long jump cleared six-point-two meters to land on the escaping sea vessel. Fortunately, Immunes Perez has locked on one of his assailant's transceivers, which can act as a homing device. Immunes Pax has already launched an unmanned aerial vehicle to follow the beacon and establish visual surveillance. Immunes Lux and Milites Vespere and Bella are already putting together an extraction plan. I will have specific timelines in three-point-four minutes."

"I'm going to have company. Move quickly and make sure they're ready to go. Update me in ten. Reich out," she said.

"Confirmed," her computer said.

Officer Middleton, a handsome man in his early thirties, a Scotland Yard veteran of several years, and a literature major from the University of Cambridge, adjusted his perfectly matched tie and his impeccably tailored suit. The blood and bruising did little to detract from his classic English-gentleman presentation.

"The boss took Spenser to the hospital and will debrief the local police. He suggests that whatever resources you have, you mobilize them to get Farrell—and now Perez—back while he sees if he can do the same. I am to go with you to assist."

Reich chuckled and smiled. She moved past him to get

back up to the bridge and avoid the local law enforcement.

"'Assist?' Don't you mean to watch me and gather intelligence?" she asked coyly.

"Maybe both," he added. She looked at him and kept walking. His British accent and articulate speech revealed his excellent education and good manners. It was obvious that he was letting her lead the way. She found her discarded purse not far from the exterior stairwell she had raced down. After she checked its contents and put her now-collapsed baton back in, she began ascending the steps to the main road. That's when Middleton asked an unusual question.

"By the by, Ms. Reich, would you know Captain Perez's age?"

Surprised that Middleton used Perez's old military rank, she wondered why he was showing such an interest. She replayed the question in her mind, and then Perez's death-defying plunge, quick sprint, and leap onto a speeding boat. *Not exactly a senior citizen's maneuver.* Reich rolled her shoulders to try to relax. At fifty-three, her short dash, dodge, disarm, and crash was not exactly an ordinary sojourn, either, but then she assumed Middleton was too polite to ask about her age. *Hmm. I did it in high heels and a skirt. I bet I could have done the same as Perez in slacks and proper footwear…*

"He's retired. Why?"

She didn't have to look back to see his surprised expression.

"Well, for starters, he engaged a man twice his size,

pushed both himself and the man through a plate-glass window to plummet about fifteen feet to the deck, and then, just to demonstrate prowess I'm sure, Mr. Perez managed to recover in time to sprint down a twenty-foot pier and then clear a twenty-plus-foot breach to land on a moving boat. I ask because any one of those actions would have taken much out of a well-trained soldier in his prime. To do all of them is somewhat Herculean, wouldn't you say?" His tone was nonchalant, but he phrased it in a way that left little room for avoiding the question. She decided to go with the truth.

"He's sixty-one," she said simply. By that point, she was two blocks away from the crime scene and one block away from her car. She knew that Perez's strength, speed, and overall health was more than a byproduct of constant exercise, training, and diet—it was the effect of adapting to a larger planet's more intense gravity and then moving back to a less strenuous environment. This transition—and his active lifestyle—made his bones, heart, and overall physiology not just impeccable, but superior to the average human's.

"Sixty-one? *Sixty-one?*"

Reich continued with her quick pace. She wanted to be in her car and on the road by the time her master computer contacted her with that timeline and a plan.

"Yes," she said. "He gives new meaning to 'sixty is the new forty.'"

There was a silence. An unusual amount of time passed before she heard him speak again.

"Yes. Quite," he said.

Okay…maybe I couldn't have made the jump, even if I had proper shoes, she thought.

Chapter Ten

Arms and a Woman—Terra

Let none find fault with others; let none see the omissions and commissions of others. But let one see one's own acts, done and undone. —The Buddha

Cold, gray, and wet.

Hydra? Where are you? How could you die? Andrea Perez said. She knew it was her own voice, but it was difficult to recognize.

I am sorry, Immunes. It was my time, Hydra said through her typical toothy smile.

No…It's not fair.

We all make this journey, Immunes. It is probably better I arrived first. You will need someone here to help figure things out. Just like last time, Hydra said.

Just like last time…

You will name part of your conquest after me at least! Hydra added in all seriousness.

Conquest? What?

Yes, Immunes. Your father discovered the old charts and

you found the underground world. The glory falls to the House of Perez. It will be good to run free after the rattus norvegicus and that winged rattus that killed me. You did kill it, Immunes, for me?

I sure did. I killed them all. Clematis, Cloelius and Dea Data did as well, Perez said.

Her heart was pounding as images of repeatedly stabbing the winged devil with her left hand came to mind. Then came more images of rows after rows of Terran hunters combing the underworld for food. Perez also had visions of campfires and running Terrans chasing packs of rattuses and firing arrows and javelins at monster bats in the great expanses of massive caverns. There were also clear images of skulls—of both bats and rattuses—hanging from her mantel and the coliseum walls, testaments to successful hunts.

The great hunt is on. And a new challenge—the winged rat. A bat! Yes, Hydra—is that what you mean? A new place, an underworld where we can finally hunt? Perez felt her heart race and her muscles tighten with every passing word, as if she were preparing to fight again.

Yes, Immunes! The House of Perez will stand as the harbinger of future hunts. We will return to the great plains with fire, javelins, and lava. We can finally abandon our closed-in spaces for a spacious, free underworld, Hydra said with her typical wild enthusiasm.

Better to be free and rule in hell, Perez started to say, but Hydra's smiling face receded rapidly. A strong, masculine face with deeply recessed gray eyes covered with heavy, concerned brows came into view. Desperate to speak and hold on to Hydra's vanishing image, Perez struggled to find moisture in her dry throat. As her friend's fading image passed by, she heard Hydra's voice as clear as if the doctor was talking to her.

Remember me, Hydra said.

"No...Don't leave!" Perez croaked out.

The doctor, Medicus Paeoniis, was at first puzzled but helped Perez recover quickly by sitting her up and handing her water. Exhausted and dazed, Perez oriented herself and realized she was in the large infirmary—the trauma center specifically. The doctor had placed the cup of water in her left hand. Reflexively, Perez extended her right, but saw only clean dressing over her wrist. No hand. She stared at it as all the memories flooded back. The doctor moved the cup closer to her left hand in an attempt to distract her from her lost limb and to get her to drink the water. Perez pulled her gaze away from the gruesome sight and redirected her attention to the cup instead. Paeoniis spoke as he moved around her to check her vitals.

"You have been unconscious for four shifts. The fever you transmitted from the winged rattus was powerful but passed quickly. Your hand was severed cleanly and the blunt-force trauma inflicted by its jaw inadvertently kept you from bleeding out. You are lucky to be alive," he said.

"The other women?" Perez croaked out.

An awkward silence fell. The faint vibrations were back, and she now felt Terra's engines, turbines, and power generators through the ground.

"You are, once again, the subject of glory and song. Another battle—bigger than the last, to say the least," the doctor said as a means of filling in the silence and avoiding the question. He took her cup and filled it again for her.

"And a subject of controversy as well, Immunes," Centurion Dea Data said from just out of view of the examination table. Perez sat up and craned to see her.

"Centurion? What happened?" Perez asked.

Dee Dee came up beside her, put a reassuring hand on her right shoulder, and smiled. For a rugged commander of warriors, her eyes were soft—a deep brown that looked black.

"Liliana burst in on a senate meeting, breaking all protocols, and insisted that we follow her at once. A small, pale worker barging in on a closed-door session is something we had never seen. When she told us why, we came without hesitation. My only wish was that we had gotten there sooner."

There was silence. Dee Dee's smile faded just a bit and her eyes softened still more.

"How many did I lose? I know I lost Hydra and two others," Perez said.

"There were two survivors on the other side with you that spoke of your insane acts of bravery. I assume you were in a reckless state of fury?"

"Yes," Perez said immediately.

"Yes. The loss of a friend will do that. Nonetheless, the two workers survived with only minor injuries and the two you left on the other side to contain the threat are well, though they are wracked with guilt."

"They kept the hole sealed tight, right? I didn't want anything getting out," Perez asked. Her eyes drifted back to her handless arm.

"They followed your orders and kept the danger contained. All of their actions—all five—were that of soldiers. They have each been granted an opportunity to escape their castes and to advance to the position of Milites, should they be interested," Dee Dee explained.

Perez looked up from her arm and envisioned the pale, frightened young woman she had sent for help. Not a likely candidate for becoming a soldier.

"Liliana, too?"

Dee Dee gave a short chuckle, and her smile widened before she spoke.

"Liliana is smart. She would prefer to work in the Great Library and learn the ways of study. She is clever, for sure." Dee Dee laughed again. Paeoniis finished with his tests and then addressed Dee Dee.

"Immunes will be ready for discharge in several cycles. The senate debates about this underworld will need to go on without her," he said. His medical pronouncement and even voice were clearly something he had prepared carefully. Perez turned to look at Dee Dee, who nodded solemnly.

"What's going on? Why is there a debate about what to do with the caverns?"

There was an uncomfortable silence. The doctor stared at Dee Dee in a way that spoke volumes, and her hesitation revealed more.

"Dea Data? What is happening? Why is this a big deal?"

It looked as if Dee Dee was struggling to find the right words when Medicus Paeoniis spoke for her.

"There are a number of families represented in the senate that do not recognize your discovery as officially yours because you are not fully Terran. They hold that your Earth origins preclude you from the right to give a first bid or determination about what to do with this newly discovered country. The fact that it was Perez the Elder who interpreted the charts and lore, and that you actually found the new world does not seem to matter."

The doctor kept looking steadily into Perez's eyes. His gray irises and worried look made him look kind and even tender, despite his large, sloping head and strong jawline. Images of Hydra lying dead and her final words about being remembered held Perez. As realization of the prejudice directed at her became clearer, she felt anger. Once the anger had a firm grip, conviction took hold and solidified her intent. Perez felt her eyes narrow and her jaw clench. Even though she had just one hand, she felt as if she were making two fists. She broke her gaze away from the doctor and looked at Dee Dee. She took in a deep breath, then spoke.

"Bring me to the senate debate," she ordered. As she spoke, she tried to push herself out of the bed. Dee Dee's surprise at having an Immunes give a Centurion an order quickly evaporated as she assisted Perez to a standing position.

"I have not discharged you, Immunes Perez the Younger," Paeoniis said.

"Then come with me. I must go to these debates. Now," Perez said. With Dee Dee's assistance and despite Paeoniis's complaints about her health, Perez pressed on. She was still dressed in a sterile white infirmary gown, so the doctor located his own pale blue medical smock for her to wear. The hair on her head was still so short that her healing scars were clearly visible, as was bruising on her face. Her reflection in a passing mirror stalled her movement for just seconds. With determination in her heart, she left the infirmary and stepped into the hallway. She moved down the crowded walkway with Terrans going about their business around her. At first, the sight of a patient walking with assistance from a centurion and an angry doctor seemed to go unnoticed—until a few Terrans recognized her. As she moved through the crowd, she heard various shouts directed at her: "rimor," "positor," "praetor," and "regula." These increased with frequency the closer she got to the coliseum. Terran citizens of all ranks and offices stopped and stood aside to let her through as they continued with their chanting. The growing crowd followed.

"What are they saying? Doesn't 'praetor' mean 'chief'?" Perez asked. She smiled at the shouting—it helped each step feel stronger. She kept seeing Hydra's image and hearing her voice.

"Yes," Dee Dee said over the growing din of shouts.

"They all mean 'leader' or 'founder.' News about your discovery of the underworld has spread throughout all Terra, and Terrans have been waiting to hear from the founder—you—and are baffled as to why you have been left in the infirmary."

"Because she is recovering, perhaps? Why do politics need to be so baffling?" the doctor complained. Perez couldn't help but smile at his consternation. "Now see what's happened? You are bleeding again. I will not stand for this..." Paeoniis warned.

The once-clean and sterile bandage was beginning to stain with fresh blood. The bright red stood out starkly against the white dressings.

"Doctor, please. I will make sure you stay with us and remain at her side. She must go. It is her right," Dee Dee said. "And look, Medicus Paeoniis, we are nearly there. Why turn back now?" she added.

With the crowd's roar escalating in the open air, she was positive that all in the coliseum must have become aware of her approach. Her heart was heavy from losing Hydra and the others. Her father's absence weighed on her, too. As she entered the short hall that led to the large arena's doors, she held on to one of her father's favorite sayings: "Old men have dreams. Young men have visions." The double, reinforced coliseum doors opened, allowing her direct access to the floor. In the center of the theater, rather than open space for combat as she last remembered, there was a podium for a speaker to use in addressing the senate. Upon her entry, the crowd's shouting ceased and a silent influx of Terrans flowed into the public stands and just outside the open doors to hear what she would say. She carefully removed her hand from Dee Dee's, indicating that she wanted to walk to the podium alone. Paeoniis came to her side quickly, pretending to check her bleeding wrist. He spoke quietly and quickly.

"You must wait until someone from the senate gives you their time to speak. Legate Clematis will ask and Dux Cloelius will record. When Cloelius makes her way to you with her tablet on, you will know that you have been given permission to speak. Be swift."

Perez nodded. The doctor moved to stand behind her, with Dee Dee. Without assistance, Perez walked to the podium and waited. She scanned her audience and was grateful to see Clematis in place, looking more regal and formal than she had ever seen her before. As Perez continued to scan faces, she saw no one else familiar except Dimitra, mother of Vista, Leader of the House of Ferris. Perez's heart sank. Saving Vista from the rattus years ago had solidified that family's power. But just as before, Perez was positive that Dimitra would withhold her support for her to address the senate. She continued scanning, and found the next worst set of people: the entire Iratus family sat with arms folded and stares that could kill. Perez's victory in the arena had shamed the Iratus.

"Quis dabit tempus vītae esse ad hoc senatu Immunes Perez?" she heard Clematis say in her deep, official voice. There was silence. Seconds ticked by in Perez's head as a thickening feel of tension built exponentially. She felt as if

she were dying a slow death.

"*Vade in domum tuam*," Perez heard the elder from the Iratus family say through a scowl. Laughter rang through their group and spread to some others. Perez did her best to translate. She figured she had been told to go home. Perez looked down for a moment, then she put both her hands on the small podium for all to see. The chuckling stopped at the sight of the missing hand and bloody stump. Perez did her best to remain straight-faced. She wanted to weep. Above all, memories of Hydra and her father made her want to cry. The seconds ticked by. She felt defeated.

"You will have my time," a deep female voice said. Perez looked up to see who had given her a chance—and in her native tongue. Clematis arched her eyebrows in surprise, a major feat for Terrans. She was about to say something, but appeared to take a moment to think about it.

"Dimitra the Eldest, Mother of Immunes Vista of Delta Mezzanine, Leader of the House of Ferris, has given Immunes Perez the Younger her time to speak."

A massive roar erupted from the public seats and outside the coliseum—clearly approval. Cloelius approached Perez while all the time trying her best to suppress a broad smile. She took a position just in front of Perez, then dropped down a little bit to give Perez the appearance of even more height and to be sure that her bloody dressing would show.

Overwhelmed with surprise and joy at finally getting

some hint of approval from the House of Ferris, Perez took in a deep breath and wiped her tears away quickly. Once the crowd's roar died down, Perez listened to her heart and inner voice. Old works she had been forced to read for her humanities program, literature, and the classics immediately came to mind. All the years of avoiding the great Earth authors came full circle when her father brought some of those same books into their home. They were now all well-worn and treasured. Silence finally fell. Her time was now. *I won't forget you, Hydra.* She turned to the woman who had given her a chance, gave a deferential nod to Dimitra. As always, Dimitra sat stoically in her seat and watched.

"Thank you for your time Dimitra, Leader of Ferris, my adopted house. I am honored."

In an unusual display of emotion, Dimitra nodded back. As she spoke, she heard a translator's voice echoing her words into Terran language for all to hear and understand.

All right. This is it.

"I am fortunate to be a child of two worlds. Earth and Terra. When I arrived here so many years ago, I was granted the honor of assisting in keeping our secret by maintaining the holographic emitters."

"And that is what you should continue to do, Earther!"

The crowd burst into hisses and a loud gavel crashed down onto a loud bell to restore order. Perez didn't need to look at who had yelled out the harsh remark. Instead she looked up at Clematis, who motioned armed ceremonial guards that had been standing aside quietly to step forward and to make their presence known.

The noise fell back into silence.

"There will be order in this senate," Clematis said. She looked around the entire coliseum and then nodded to Perez to continue. Just as she was going to start laying out her argument about how to use the land, she was hit by an idea. In just seconds, she decided to abandon the logical argument she was planning to make in favor of a rousing, heartfelt speech. It all became clear to her. *All those books…those stories…*

"Old Terrans have dreams. Young Terrans have visions," Perez started. She moved from behind the podium to stand in full view and to use her hand to punctuate her statements. The echo of her translated words elicited roars of approval from the spectators. The cheers died down immediately, though, when Perez continued. Everyone was waiting to hear what she would say.

"We have an opportunity to once again hunt in open spaces, to hunt in clans as our ancestors did on Venus and Earth. No longer must we live in enclosed spaces of recycled air and fading power but rather on the fields of our new, discovered underworld where rattuses and winged monsters now rule. We have an opportunity to not only return to our ancestral hunts in packs, but we can now discover, explore, and tame a dangerous, wild frontier. We can hunt our food rather than hope it finds our traps. We can pick huge mushrooms to feed all our numbers. We can eat new foods, fruits, and mint. We can breathe fresh Terran air and feel the real soil beneath our feet. And while we cannot walk upon the surface of our home, we can tread in the very core of Terra. And when the Jovian planet erupts into a new sun, as fire, brimstone, violent lightening, and tornadoes threaten our enclosed mezzanines, markets, and launch bays, we will laugh at it from our new home below and say, 'Is this all you have?'"

The roar of approval exploded from behind her. She had more to say, so she watched for Clematis to hit the bell again, to restore order. She was surprised that Clematis let the applause and shouts of joy go on a little longer than expected. A moment later, she struck the bell and silence reasserted itself.

"I am an Earther. I was born there and I lived there for the first part of my life. But I gave my right hand for Terra. I will die on Terra, my new home. But if I am to die, let it be exploring strange and wondrous sights. Let it be in pitched battle beside my Terran brothers and sisters against rattuses and bats. Forget the holographic emitters. This is no time to hide who we are. We are Terrans! Let us gather our strength, collect our gear, and prepare to find more underground worlds and undiscovered countries. Let us move with confidence and unity—not because it is easy, but because we are Terrans. We do the impossible!"

The crowd erupted into a louder explosion of clapping, shouts, and chants of "Praetor Perez" and "Perez Rimor." Looking around at the senators, she caught sight of Dimitra, always stoic and sage, begin to slowly stand and clap. Others followed suit until the entire senate was on its feet—with the sole exception of the Iratus clan, who remained sitting silently in their seats, arms folded and scowls on their faces.

Perez nodded deferentially to Dimitra, who nodded back again. She turned to bow to Legate Legionis Clematis, who remained erect and with a smile on her face. Still holding the gavel in her hand, it was obvious to Perez that she was going to let the roar of approval continue. Nodding yet again, Perez backed away from the podium and facing the still-standing senators. When she felt she was at a respectful distance, she turned to Dee Dee, whose face was spotted with tears. Perez's step faltered just a little bit, but she was quickly caught by both Dee Dee and the doctor. The roars continued at such a pitch that Perez's ears were ringing. Her entire trip back to the infirmary was followed by approving shouts, clapping, and yells. Once the doctor closed the door to her room, the hospital's other medics stopped by to give their own approval—until Paeoniis threw them out. The ringing in Perez's ears seemed to subside gradually. Back in her elevated bed, she felt relieved to be lying down. Without fanfare, the doctor immediately went to work, changing her dressing.

"So before you start marching through the underworld planting Terran flags, I will need you to follow my instructions, and I will need your word that you will adhere to my orders," he said.

"Without reservation, Medicus Paeoniis," Perez said

quietly. Waves of exhaustion weakened her resolve with every passing moment.

"And it will take me several cycles to get a working prosthesis hand fitted for your arm. Your Earthen bone and muscle structure will be challenging to work with, but I am confident I can make a good match," the doctor said. Even as he spoke, his focus on cleaning and dressing her wound was unbroken.

"Well, Perez the Younger, your father is going to be furious at both of us for your injuries, but he'll be thrilled you are alive and well," Dee Dee said.

Fear and anxiety gripped Perez. Memories of her father's worries and concerns for her made her feel bad. He had made it clear that he would only leave Terra if she promised to be safe. She was lost in her own thoughts when Dee Dee leaned forward and placed a hand on her left shoulder.

"Do you have any idea what you have done, Perez the Younger?"

Perez looked up at her, confused and tired.

"You have given us hope and purpose," Dee Dee said. She smiled, squeezed her shoulder, and left. Perez watched her walk away and wondered if Hydra and the others who had died would be proud. Their names and families would be remembered. She began to doze, and was startled when she felt the doctor gently move her re-dressed hand to her side. He walked to the infirmary door and dimmed the lights.

"All right, Immunes. Get some sleep, and we'll talk in

the morning."

"Thank you, Medicus Paeoniis."

She watched him nod and walk into his adjacent office, surrounded by transparent partitions so he could keep an eye on her and the other patients. Perez closed her eyes. She felt her body become light, and then she drifted away.

"I hope it was enough, Hydra," she said quietly.

Chapter Eleven

Epsilon Team Six—Earth

Should a person do good, let him do it again and again. Let him find pleasure therein, for blissful is the accumulation of good. —The Buddha

"I'm telling you, Middleton, it's not their first day on the job. The first time I met them we were outnumbered, outgunned, and outflanked by a team that had an armed helicopter for support! Four minutes later, all the hostiles were dead, the helicopter neutralized, and all evidence destroyed. We're not going to wait for backup," Reich said.

She had watched Middleton's level of anxiety creep up after long hours of searching for, locating, and launching the extraction team. He was absolutely fine until he met her Terran friends, whom he towered over. The fact that they were small, all female, and pretty ugly—from his perspective—properly rattled him. But it was the decision to go nonlethal and without firearms, and instead to use batons, edged weapons, and their wits that put him over the top. Reich's own fears for the general and Perez were running high as well. As mission leader, she confiscated his phone to ensure security and to make her point clear.

"Middleton! Nonlethal means a lot of bad guys unconscious, tied up, and alive. That leaves a lot of questions, but no pursuit. A large number of dead bodies systematically eliminated in US territories and waters under US jurisdiction means an act of terrorism or a foreign nation's involvement. You think it's a good idea to draw the attention of the former than the latter?"

Middleton frowned at her word choice. Reich already knew she had used the idiom the wrong way.

"You mean the 'latter' for the dead bodies and the 'former' for unconscious bad guys," he corrected.

At the time, Reich was surprised and annoyed by the Cambridge-educated Englishman who pinched the bridge of his nose and projected the wearied attitude of a fifth-grade teacher trying to help a particularly intellectually delayed student.

"You see what we have been dealing with?" Lux said to him in passing.

"The best way to remember 'former' and 'latter' is to think of it as 'former' is the first mentioned, a 'latter' is the thing that comes later," he suggested.

"Shut up, Middleton! Spenser has good reason to dislike you!"

Her team laughed. Middleton's face revealed a well-practiced smirk.

Reich went back to assessing the assault. She couldn't

help but chuckle to herself as well.

In regard to the mission, the beacon Perez hid on the ship held for two hours, which was time enough for the drone to put eyes on the vessel and for Reich Enterprises' own surveillance satellite to locate the ship as well. Surprisingly, the ship docked at a private pier on Nantucket Island, more than a hundred miles from Boston, in the Atlantic Ocean beyond Martha's Vineyard and Cape Cod. It took mere minutes to locate their hideout and assess defensive lines, personnel, and enter-exit strategies. The plan was simple: take a plane out and have all but Bella drop in silently via parachute. Bella would continue on to pick up an armored transport helicopter loaded with firepower, then would return from the east over land for pickup and heavy support if necessary.

Much to Reich's surprise, she learned that it would be Middleton's first jump—meaning he had to go in tandem with her. She was not thrilled at all. Regardless, it was 10:35 p.m. on a moonless night meant for stealth, and Lux, Pax, and Vespere had already silently taken out five of thirteen hostiles. With the sole exception of crickets, birds, rustlings in nearby bushes, and very distant voices from homes a half-mile away on the remote part of the island, there was no one around. The risk of civilian interference was low. Adding to that low rate was the fact that the target home was a poorly maintained colonial on an acre of untrimmed lawn. It was adjacent to a protected wildlife sanctuary, further adding to its seclusion. Reich had a sudden idea of finding out more about this real estate and buying it. Her master computer, who was monitoring the entire operation, let her know that the property had recently been purchased by a "European industrialist." She felt anger in the form of heat rising from her face.

"Stay behind me," Reich said in an attempt to get back on mission. She felt far more comfortable in her one-piece tactical uniform than she had in that red outfit. All non-reflective black, no metal, and armed with her baton, she came up behind a small wall. A similarly dressed Middleton did an adequate job of staying quiet and behind her.

"Reich—three meters to your left. We missed one. He's yours," she heard Lux say in her ear. Reich put a closed fist in the air for Middleton to see so he would know to stay silent. She peered over the small wall and saw a man lighting up a cigarette, clearly on a break.

That's surprising. They never miss anyone.

Without hesitation, she moved up quickly behind him and delivered a hammer strike to the base of his neck with the assistance of her baton handle. She guided him to the ground as he slumped over. She made sure to remove all his weapons and to bind his hands. As quickly as she had moved to neutralize the threat, she returned to her position.

"Not bad," she heard Vespere say.

Reich narrowed her eyes at a sudden thought.

"Did you leave him deliberately for me?" she said

quietly. Instead of getting an answer, she heard chatter.

"You owe me a bag of cooked chestnuts with honey. She did it all in under two Earth minutes," she heard Lux say.

"She used the butt of her baton..." she heard Vespere complain.

"You should have clarified. I win. Pax—four meters to your left; Vespere—two meters right in front of you. Bella—ETA?" Lux said.

Reich couldn't help but smirk. While Pax and Vespere confirmed their targets, Bella gave a ten-minute warning of her arrival. It took five minutes to reach the exterior walls of the house. It was well lit, allowing them to see that there were only five heavily armed men inside. Reich made eye contact with Lux and Vespere, who were about to breach the door. Without use of explosives, Vespere turned the knob and entered the home as if she were coming over for coffee. Pax and Lux were right behind her. For just one minute there were some muffled grunts, groans, and thuds. Reich didn't wait for an all-clear, just for the quiet racket to come to a sudden end. When she entered the near-empty living room, two men were out cold and one was in the process of passing out as Pax squeezed her legs around his neck. Once their pockets were emptied of weapons, transceivers, and ammunition, Lux pointed to the staircase that led to the second floor. There was a unanimous nod and all got into a well-spaced formation and silently walked on the edges of the stairs to reduce the risks of creaks. In the process, Reich turned to check on Middleton. It was easy to see that he was baffled and surprised at how smoothly the operation was going. She had to give him credit for going along with the entire mission—he had clearly been doubtful, but he was becoming a believer.

After a quick scan of two bedrooms, Reich heard very low, male voices in what she guessed might be a master bedroom. Lux and Vespere gave each other concerned looks and then Lux broke protocol and came to her, leaving Vespere and Pax on point in front of the door.

"As dismal as this security team is, I still would have expected them to leave the remaining two guards in the front of the door where the hostages are being held. They may be on the other side with, I am assuming, Sir Pierce and our people. Breach will be on three," she whispered.

She suddenly returned to take the lead in the breach. Instead of turning the door knob and walking in like they did downstairs, however, Lux affixed a small pouch to the door. She produced a trigger, then she and the rest of Epsilon flanked the door. She put up one finger at a time. When she got to three, she depressed her trigger and a small explosion splintered the old wood easily. Reich heard nothing, but saw her team go in. She went in right after them with Middleton hot on her trail. Once she cleared the entrance, she was surprised to see three men already tied up and gagged on the floor. The three Terrans looked at them in dismay.

"What the hell? Where's…what…" Reich started.

A cough came from the other side of the room. She

and everyone else turned to see General Farrell in full uniform, sitting with Anthony Perez as if they were making idle chit-chat. Both men's attire was rumpled but still in place. Reich moved over to the duo, who both stood up in the presence of the women. When she was just two feet from both men, Reich put both hands on her hips and waited for an answer.

"I would have escaped, but Mr. Perez insisted on waiting for some 'all-female SEAL team' to come in for the rescue. He said you would be here before midnight," Farrell explained.

Reich turned to look at Perez. He sported a black eye and several cuts and bruises on his face and hands, as if he had been beaten. Still, he smirked as she looked at him. The general also looked as if he had been in a brawl but he, too, appeared to be in good spirits. Reich looked back at the three men bound and gagged on the floor. Their dispositions were visibly sour, especially Sir Pierce's. He wore a look of both fury and indignation.

"I'm surprised you got here so early. I'm glad you did. I was worried that we were going to have to subdue the guards downstairs as well," Perez said.

"We did have a chance to talk about serious stuff. The data you provided and our own observations were stunning. But the material on Jupiter is worrisome," Farrell said. His demeanor shifted to sad and professional at the same time.

She turned to see where Middleton was, to make sure he was not listening. He was crouching down in front of the gagged and unceremoniously tied Sir Robert Phillip Pierce.

"Well, Your Highness, there's a cold, dark cell waiting for you in Her Majesty's clock tower. There will be no escape this time," he said.

Reich contained a laugh. She turned to see that Lux and her team were watching the room and preparing for evacuation. The sound of a low-flying helicopter came in from the east.

"Bring Pierce for adjudication. There are a whole lot of US federal laws he broke in addition to Massachusetts's, I bet," General Farrell said.

"That's the least of his problems," Middleton added.

Farrell looked for his hat, then realized he must have lost it when he was attacked earlier. Reich made the motion to move out. Lux took point, with Middleton hoisting Pierce up and pushing him along. Pax and Vespere flanked Perez and Farrell. They moved swiftly and with little sound. By the time they were at the house's front door, a large black helicopter was just landing. Without further hesitation, the team boarded the vehicle, closed the doors, and was airborne.

"So, General, what's your plan?" Perez said above the muffled engine and rotor noise.

"I'm going to tell the president what we know about Terra and Jupiter. And then I will await orders," he said.

"And you will leave us out of your tale?" Perez said as he pointed to Reich and the others.

"Absolutely. Mr. Middleton's stealth and Scotland

Yard's investigatory acumen saved me—and the day," the general said. Middleton looked on, confused at first, but then he appeared to understand.

"For queen and country," he said.

"Long live the queen," Farrell said.

"And will you leave me and my team alone? I've got things to do," Reich said.

"I think you and Mr. Perez have done enough for our country, and the human race," Farrell said.

His tone was matter-of-fact, but he appeared suddenly tired. Reich concluded that the ordeal of being kidnapped must have taken its toll.

"So, General, with the mystery planet that you've been looking for for more than two decades coming to light and the end of days upon us, what's your plan? You don't seem to be the kind of guy to wait around looking for his next command. You know there was an Atlantis. If it wasn't for the Jupiter situation, I'd help you find that, too," Perez said in all seriousness.

Reich looked on and realized that Perez had nailed it. While all the burdens of command and next steps might have weighed on the general, his real passion had been searching for a mystery planet for more than twenty years. And now with the focus shifting to telling the world about it, the likely civil unrest that would follow, and preparation for a possible extinction-level event, it had to be anticlimactic to have all the answers just handed to him.

What's the adventure in that? Where's the exploration?

Death?

"I don't know," he said. He looked off for just a moment, then gave a faint smile.

"Well, General, should you have any interest, my daughter Andrea has been working on a project you might be interested in…" Perez started.

"Oh? Andrea Perez? How is she doing?"

"Well, as far as I know. She has a way of getting into trouble. But you might be interested in hearing about what she's looking for," Perez said with parental pride.

"You mean in addition to working with an advanced civilization on a hidden world on the other side of the sun? You mean something like that?" the general chuckled.

"Yup. Something a little bigger," Perez said in all seriousness.

General Farrell's chuckle stopped quickly as he looked at how serious Perez was, and wondered what mystery could be even bigger. He shook his head and sat back. "Shit," was all he said. He closed his eyes as if to take a nap.

The hum of engines and the rotors did have a calming effect, in a way. Reich always associated them with a completed mission and a moment to relax.

Reich looked at Perez, who smiled at her. She leaned forward and kissed him on the lips. He was surprised, but kissed her back. Once they separated, she said one thing: "Don't do that shit again." She felt her eyes narrow as she said it.

He picked up on her meaning.

"Affirmative," he said.

Reich's headpiece came to life unexpectedly, which startled her for a moment. She had forgotten she had it in still. Lux's voice was clear, and there was a touch of both seriousness and excitement in it at the same time. She pointed to her earpiece and smiled at him. He picked up on the nonverbal explanation and leaned back.

"Reich?"

After she got over the initial surprise and waited a second for a follow-up or wise crack that didn't come, Reich responded. "Go, Lux," she said. She covered her other ear so she could hear better.

"Reich, I just got an after-action summary report from Terran Command. It's been authenticated by our ships *Adventus* and *Red Dawn Rising.* They are confirming reports that are still coming in…Perez the Younger is all right. She has received wounds, but her discovery changes everything…"

Reich felt her jaw clench and her brows knit. She looked up at Anthony Perez and saw that, like the general, he was sleeping. His bruised, battered appearance made him look worn and yet somehow vigorous, even in sleep.

"Clarify, Lux."

There was a brief moment of silence, but it was followed by excitement.

"Reich—Perez the Younger has discovered something amazing. Our Immunes Perez's research of an undiscovered world has proven to be true. His daughter and Dimitra, leader of the House of Ferris, have claimed this amazing discovery. Perez the Younger is now *Praetor Perez.* Can you believe it! She is a *Praetor?* That title has been used just one time in the past one hundred cycles! And it has never been held by an off-worlder! Only by the Originators!"

"Okay, Lux, you lost me. Tie me in to the master computer to help me understand," Reich said. The wild enthusiasm and the need for extensive authentication was clearly an indication of something big. *Bigger than the "discovery" of Terra or Jupiter's impending conversion?*

"Immunes Reich. Are you sitting down?" she heard her master computer say. While her calm, computer-driven voice was the same as usual, using a question as an introduction was unusual for her.

"Ah, yes? Computer? What the hell is going on? What is Lux saying?" Reich asked as quietly as possible so as not to be heard by her sleeping companions. She looked over at Middleton, who was keeping a close eye on the bound Sir Pierce.

"Immunes Lux's hyperbole is not without merit and her excitement is well warranted. Further, the irony of your choice of using 'hell' will become apparent in eight Earth minutes. Please sit back while I give you the historical data and myths, and the ramifications of this significant discovery," the computer said.

Oh boy. It's something really big. Crap…

Two Years Later

Chapter Twelve

Terminal Velocity—Mars

Whatever living beings there may be—feeble or strong, long, stout, or of medium size, short, small, large, those seen or those unseen, those dwelling far or near, those who are born as well as those yet to be born—may all beings have happy minds. —
The Buddha

"It is very much like old times," Master Architect Janus said. Standing in the middle of another highly detailed holographic representation, he focused on the new sun that had just formed in the once one-star Sol System. Rather than projections and simulations, this representation was real. Hard data showed the existence of a real second sun.

"Are you referencing your repeated visits to this program and computer analysis, or are you referencing the last time we witnessed a massive astronomical event—the Gemini planetoid collision?" the Master Keeper asked.

Janus nodded at the need for clarification. With both

hands cradling a very young Martian infant, he relied on giving all instructions verbally—his access to his array of tablets was momentarily limited. The long torso and limbs of the sleeping female were a beautiful sight. Large, closed eyes and a tiny nose and mouth. Janus wondered how he and Athena had created such a creature. Holding her made the loss of handling his instruments and tablets bearable. But that meant more clarifications about everything he said and asked. Janus knew his answer would raise a larger question, a question that was sure to yield interesting results from his sapient master computer.

"I was speaking of the Gemini event. Alpha and Beta dwarf planets traveled in their orbits without incident until some force pushed them out of sync. I begin to believe the Originators were involved in that event, just as they are involved in this. Would you not agree that the most recent revelations are inexplicable according to all our known science, Keeper?"

There was the expected silence. Janus was sure that the Keeper would highlight the most relevant data in an effort to keep the conversation smooth and manageable while making her points clear. Even as he waited, multiple series of calculations and formulas appeared all throughout the holographic representation. The majority were in red, indicating inconclusive or unknown or undeterminable equations.

"Yes. Inexplicable," she said simply. A moment passed.

Janus was surprised. *Well. This is unusual.* He waited and finally asked a question he was sure he had never asked his master computer before. *Well. This is unusual* "Please elaborate?"

The hologram of dual suns shifted back to its original single-sun Sol System, with the planet Jupiter in its preignition state, and the asteroid belt and remains of the former dwarf planets in their habitual places. More silence followed until the Keeper finally spoke. As she did, various symbols, formulas, and computations appeared in midair.

"The appearance of an infinitesimal black hole in an unlikely location never before detected, and with a volume perfect for creating the critical mass and energy needed to push a planet into a solar state cannot happen by chance. This followed by beams of accurately titrated elements for ignition, all timed in a specific sequence. Again, the probabilities of this occurring randomly are inconceivable. Both of these events occurring at the same time, in the right amounts, in a perfect place, can only be explained by some…organized…plan. Some form of prearranged design is the most likely answer."

To highlight her point, a series of numeric representations flooded each point where the probabilities of all of those events occurring naturally were impossible. An entirely new set of possible solutions appeared and were rapidly highlighted in red—meaning that it could not have been a naturally occurring event. Janus looked at the flowing numbers and the system's visual displays. Jupiter began to shrink and collapse in on itself. For a mere moment, it was gone. Suddenly, a series of flashes flickered to life in its place and a small sun erupted where the red, Jovian giant, gaseous planet had just been. As soon as it came to life, the hologram shifted perspectives to show the asteroid fields, Mars, Earth, Terra, and Venus.

"If we were to…ignore…or to not consider the first series of unlikely events, the next series would still seem just as puzzling," the master computer continued.

Janus found himself near the point of pure joy. With his sleeping offspring in his arms, in itself an unexpected pleasure, he was sure he was witnessing his closest artificially intelligent friend make a religious leap of faith. Janus held his breath and wished that at least Olympia, if not both of his companions, could be present to see this. She was assisting Athena with their other three infants. *She would appreciate this.* Janus focused on a specifically marked series of multiple-sized asteroids.

"The ignition of a new sun should have had a profound effect on nearby objects, but not to such a degree witnessed," the computer said.

The animated simulation displayed a series of asteroids rapidly accelerating out of their orbits—in all directions. The smaller objects accelerated to several stages below light speed, but were nonetheless going faster than could ever have been predicted. They should have taken several annual cycles to reach the inner planets, but it appeared as if it had only taken mere planetary cycles.

In Earth time, a distance that should have taken asteroids years of travel took the smaller ones mere months to cover.

To demonstrate the point, the Mars and Earth holograms displayed each planet's bombardment. For

Mars, with less atmosphere, the impact triggered volcanic activity and melted the polar ice caps and permafrost. This was expected, based on earlier simulations. Good for Mars—if their underground shelter held. The red planet's time lapse display revealed a browner, greener planet with thin clouds on the bright side, while electrical storms and rain occurred on the less bright side. In the plains and valleys, the presence of waterways was evident.

Janus smiled. *Just like old times.*

Images of Earth's atmosphere destroying most of the incoming meteors flashed by, but there were three massive asteroids that made impact. While smaller than those that had wiped out the dinosaurs, they were still devastating. The simulations showed each impact at different points of the globe, raising massive dust clouds and shifting tectonic plates that triggered tsunamis and volcanic activity. A time-lapse demonstration showed the planet shift from blue, white, brown, and green to mostly white, with a little brown and blue near the equator. Janus looked down at his little girl. It was hard to see the Earth change so drastically. A series of formulas and data points were highlighted in green, accurately indicating probable devastation for the planet's biospheres.

"Each of our planets' axes has already started to shift. This is unprecedented. Earth and Terra have already experienced tectonic shifts in some places near fault lines, and volcanic activity. This was not supposed to occur until much later. Earth will spiral into a new ice age while our home might develop a more viable atmosphere and new life. Terra, on the other side of the old sun, once again may have passed unscathed by the massive meteor showers. The irony is that their underground existence and minimalist way of life would have made them the more likely to survive a bombardment anyway if they were in the line of fire."

Terra's holographic time-lapse sequence showed it appearing nearly unchanged—with the exception of more frequent and intense electrical storms and wind mostly along the equator, but also high up near the poles. There were some small meteor impacts, minimal tectonic shifting, and increased volcanic activity, but the formulas and calculations flashed green, indicating an accurate assessment of minimal effect on Terra and its inhabitants.

"Junior Architect Hades would have been proud of his Terra project. How he managed to create such a planet, civilization, and culture is beyond me," Janus said.

"It is remarkable, Master Janus. Again, this is yet another example of the probabilities being difficult to calculate," the Keeper said.

Suddenly, the point of view shifted back to the asteroid field. Two massive asteroids broke orbit. Janus followed their progress as they came into the orbital path of Venus and both struck the planet violently. An array of calculations, numbers, symbols, and formulas sprung up all around Venus. Instead of time-lapse holography showing planetary changes, it remained in a perpetual, fiery state—as if the images going forward were not yet determined.

"In regard to Venus, every calculation completed is inconclusive. After nearly nonstop simulations and projections, I am unable to determine if these impacts completely destroyed the planet or if it restarted the planet by reigniting its molten core, eradicating the sulfuric-acid-based atmosphere, igniting volcanic activity…All simulations move in the direction of a new beginning for the planet. When the greenhouse effect escalated and all contact was lost with Junior Architect Iris, we know this scenario of using impact craters to terraform the planet to its core elements was considered. As of yet, this is still inconclusive."

"Best guess, Keeper?" Janus asked.

The fiery explosions ceased as surface rock and atmospheric gases spewed from the planet. After a brief time, the planet's cloud cover atmosphere thinned to reveal hints of red lava and fires, electrical storms, and massive rain clouds. In less than a mere moment, the once-hostile Venus evolved into a remarkable sight, completely contrary to its former self. It showed hints of vast oceans, volcanoes, and a rich biosphere.

"So Mars and Venus, with minimal life, may improve from this apocalypse, Terra goes unchanged, but Earth, host to the largest quantity of life, faced another extinction-level event," Janus mused aloud.

"Yes," the Keeper said. "Yet another example of how all these events seem unlikely as random acts. Based on these events…to date…I am of the belief that all of this is not accidental. It is part of a plan. What the plan is and the next steps are all unclear to me, however."

"An intelligent design? All part of a greater plan?" Janus asked.

"From Earth's perspective, this plan appears less 'intelligent' than catastrophic."

"Yes," Janus said. "I'm sure Earth and Terra's computer simulations are already computing multiple scenarios. I am sure they, too, understand the purposeful nature of all these factors that led to this eventuality."

Janus looked back down at his girl again. Her long, sleeping body made her look so peaceful.

"Master Janus, what are your thoughts on the existence of the Originators and their possible involvement?" the Keeper asked.

Janus was surprised at his own immediate response.

"I think the Originators are involved in all of this. Just as this little girl I hold is precious life, the odds of her being here were minimal and her presence is miraculous. Maybe that is what we are witnessing; another chance to start new life on two dead planets and the continued evolution of life on two others. I would say that, if the creation of an individual life is an act of the Originators, our understanding of what is to come is more than possible. I would say likely. In the end, though, all of this does raise more questions than answers."

The room fell silent. The holographic solar system evaporated to reveal Janus's humble living space again.

"I have changed, Master Janus. I believe that where my logic fails, I must have another avenue of inquiry to follow," the Keeper said.

"Yes, my friend. When all logic and reason fails, we must rely on others and on faith. I think you have faith now, and believe there are some things that are more powerful than logic—and beyond our comprehension."

"Yes. The Originators are our god. One voice for many."

"I think you are right, Master Keeper," Janus said.

"Thank you for helping me reach this new level of sapience," the computer said.

"That is what friends do."

Janus felt a smile come on. He was not sure if it was because his little girl was stirring or his earlier creation, the Master Keeper, was evolving yet again.

They are both good reasons to be happy.

Chapter Thirteen

Summer Camp—Earth

They blame those who remain silent, they blame those who speak much, they blame those who speak in moderation. There is none in the world who is not blamed. —The Buddha

The warm wind on a clear, starlight night was something to behold in that part of Topeka, Kansas. With her "Summer Camp" operational, fully functioning, and ready for fifty-plus years of underground survival, Reich was enjoying the outside as much as she could before the "end of days" arrived and they all would retreat to the modified underground fortress originally created for war—now refitted as a sort of ark. With 215 humans and four Terrans under her care, she felt the weight of her role. *Leader*. She had been a major in the military once. Now she was a major again, but with the added burden of also being the law and order, the judge and legislature, the friend and disciplinarian. For now she put those thoughts aside and tried to simply feel the breeze and look at the stars. In the distance, she heard voices drawing closer. She looked below her, down the winding trail, and saw a column of youths being led by two men and a handful of counselors from Future Academy. She could tell who was leading the teams.

Reich felt as if she were watching two overgrown adolescent boys argue divergent points. Principal Adam Smith and Anthony Perez were dressed in classic Sahara fatigues, breathable shirts, and hats—certainly not their usual attire. She had known that they would get into a debate when they agreed to lead students out earlier that evening for a stargazing, astronomical field trip. From her obscured position, she could easily see that while the fifteen or so boys and girls were occupied with their calculations and tablets, the two men were on an entirely different subject.

"I'm just saying that democracy has worked *one* time—just once. I think Ms. Reich's plan for a more military-republic-like government makes more sense than a democracy," Smith said.

Reich had to suppress her laughter. Even from a distance, she could see Perez's expression of annoyance and frustration.

"You know your name is the same as the founder of capitalism's, right? *Wealth of Nations*? Of all people, I would have expected you to understand that an effective democracy is always a republic. And we have an opportunity to make our small society evolve into a greater one if we do it right from the very start," she heard Perez say.

As they walked by her, she heard Smith's response.

"So, when Winston Churchill said the best argument against democracy was a five-minute conversation with the average voter, was he specifically thinking of a person like you, or did you two actually meet?"

Wow! Now that was good!

"You know, I'm going to feel bad when that big, metal blast door closes and you're on the other side," Perez said without delay.

She watched them move beyond earshot and watched their animated discussion continue as they walked to the main house. Even as they passed the still-dilapidated-looking buildings, abandoned patrol booth, and crumbled fence that gave the world the suggestion this was still an abandoned complex, she felt immediately comforted that all the years of work and preparations were completed below, beyond prying eyes—and still private. She immediately thought of Officers Middleton and Spenser and their expressions when they had first seen the exterior and then the interior. Similar to Perez and Smith, she had opportunities to watch them spar over the past two years as well. They were no less vigorous or creative than Smith and Perez. She was very happy that their respective families were already in her ark. And when the time came, they and Inspector Bradley would join them. She just hoped he would make the last flight out. While she had most people who wanted to be there already in place, a few had decided to hold out to the last possible moment, to keep society from falling apart. Her Scotland Yard friends were just three of fifteen "out there."

Hmm. Maybe having them trapped together for fifty-plus years is not a good plan.

She pushed the thought out of her head and enjoyed another warm breeze. There were howls in the distance, and bird calls as well. She was right in the middle of listening to see if she could identify the predator when a bright light flickered high above her. For just a moment she thought it was a shooting star, but its stationary position and the way it lit up made it clear it was nothing that mundane. She focused on it and stepped forward.

She forced herself to breathe as she witnessed the end of one era and the beginning of another. She watched quietly as the silent, itinerant light appeared to falter into darkness. Reich wondered if that was it and all her preparation had been in vain. For milliseconds, she clung to hope. Then, a burst of light erupted in the silent sky. The dark horizon lit up as if it were illuminated by a ray of moonlight. More howling, nocturnal sounds, and birds of prey screeched as if they heard the end coming. The small new star's flickering steadied into a constant flame. Tears fell on Reich's cheeks.

"No…" she said softly. Reich looked down across the plain and saw that the new light did not eradicate darkness, but sort of brightened it instead. She was startled by a loud siren—one she had reinstalled for this very event. With the children back from stargazing, she knew she was the last one outside. Reich brushed away her tears and walked to the main house. The animals continued to make noise, and her pace felt as if she were weighed down with every step she took to her new role as leader. Lux and Vespere were already at the front door of the building.

"Dux Reich. It starts," Lux said. Her tone was unusually somber. Vespere handed her another tablet that showed a news report already in progress. Reich took it and continued walking with both Terrans behind her. In a well-practiced fashion, Lux and Vespere systematically closed down and packed up portable equipment, sensors, and electronics in the empty front room of the main house. With the sole exception of an old table, there was no furniture in that or any other house in the compound. Reich flipped through a number of channels until she found a very conservative news team. They were the same news team that had rejected General Farrell's initial warnings as science fiction and scare tactics on the part of the left. When the data had come in and were verified, she was sure they never apologized.

It didn't matter then. It doesn't now.

The two anchors, two unknown talking heads that worked the third shift, were the only voices of reason at this time of change. Most of America was asleep at three in the morning. The clearly shaken, pale male anchor was in the middle of his report when she tuned in.

"Again, there has been an astronomical event that the Internet has been buzzing about for at least a year. As though the discovery of another sister planet with an advanced civilization wasn't enough, it would appear that rumors of Jupiter destabilizing into a second sun are true. The presidents

of the United States and Russia will be addressing their respective countries simultaneously. This would imply that both governments either knew this would happen or strongly suspected this would happen…" the male anchor said before he unexpectedly ended his sentence. There was an uncomfortable silence until the female anchor picked up the report. She was older and seemed calmer than the male.

"If you are just joining us, the planet Jupiter has indeed erupted into another sun. Chatter about this possibility on the Internet and other sources has been prominent for the last year, ever since General David Farrell's unprecedented announcement about the existence of the planet Terra and the advanced Terran culture modeled after our own historical Roman Empire. Unfortunately, after General Farrell's revelation, he and nearly two hundred of his associates seemingly vanished and have not been heard from since. While it was originally thought that he and his associates were silenced by our government—"

"They lied. Our government knew this would happen, and they didn't tell us…" an off-camera voice said.

Reich closed her eyes. The male anchor was clearly piecing it together for the first time and was horrified at the implications.

"He thought it was all bullshit, like nearly everyone else," she muttered.

Lux heard her as she was shutting off the building's breakers, and Vespere handed her and Reich a flashlight.

"It is unfortunate that your species' world leaders

moved to discredit the general," Lux said in a sad tone.

"My guess is they wanted to minimize social unrest and chaos while they planned for a select few to survive," Reich said.

"That explains all the cyber attacks and attempts to disrupt our operation," Vespere said.

Reich looked back at her small screen. The female anchor remained poised as she went on with her report.

"...there are some unconfirmed reports that normally dormant volcanoes have begun to smolder and show evidence of activity. Based on earlier interviews, we know the new sun is four times the distance from us as we are from our own sun. While the new sun's light will pose no problem to humans, its gravitational pull could cause possible shifts in plate tectonics, weather patterns, and volcanic activity. The President will be on in just—"

"Joyce! For Christ's sake! They lied! What the hell! You're not going to air that..." the voice broke in again.

Reich found the power button and turned the news off. Witnessing the human toll was too much. She handed Lux the tablet and turned on her flashlight. Without further discussion, Vespere opened what looked like a basement door. It revealed a newly installed metal door. Her hand print triggered a loud sound of metal pistons moving heavy-duty deadbolt locks. The metal door hissed open. She nodded to Lux, who threw the building's breaker system, which was placed at the basement door's entrance—a seemingly unusual place to find a breaker box. With flashlights cutting through the darkness, all three females walked through the faux-wood door and metal blast door to a metal grate that covered a dark stairwell. As they walked down in silence several flights, they heard the heavy door above them that separated them from the surface lock ominously behind them. If all went well, the door would open just two more times—one time to let fifteen more people enter their ark and another when they all emerged to enter a brave, new world. Should an emergency occur and they needed to evacuate, a protocol for extraction and relocation to Terra was already set. After four minutes of descending down stairs, they reached the newly refurbished titanium-alloy blast door that gave access to the ark itself. The original door and its hydraulics had taken three minutes to open and close—the updated version took only one minute. Reich put her hand on a dark hand pad that came to life upon contact. In under a second, the door's heavy locks and hinges released and the massive door opened into a brightly lit corridor and yet another door. Bella and Pax were waiting for them to arrive. As Reich entered, Pax gave her a status report.

"All occupants are accounted for, Dux Reich. The command center is on full alert. We already received information from Mars's Master Keeper on its status. All is well and so far there is no danger. There has been incremental shifting in the Martian axis, however, and there are already a number of large asteroids dislodging from their orbits between Mars and the new sun."

"That does not bode well," Reich said.

She was now in front of yet another blast door. She

went through the same handprint release, with a similar response as before. As she retracted her hand, she became self-conscious of her hair and what she was wearing. While she did not plan to be making any announcements, she was happy that she had worn something conservative and leader-like—she had almost gone out in her pajamas. Instead, she had taken the extra effort to put on a black skirt, thin tan blouse, and nonmatching sneakers. She remembered she had no bra on.

No one's perfect.

"Just so you know, the two youths, Felicia and Hong, are in the command center," Pax said.

Reich smiled. She liked the pair. They were not only gifted in science and math, but they were excellent sleuths. Her fondest moment was telling them their investigation in the past had been right. An image of her sister and two nieces flashed in her mind. She was thrilled she had located them. She knew that Spencer and Middleton would make sure to pick them up as part of the fifteen. Still, she was anxious. She wished she could do more.

The interior, refurbished walkway was busy with staff and volunteers bustling about. Even though it was three in the morning, the level of activity was as if they were on double shifts at high noon. People were moving Meals Ready to Eat boxes and freeze-dried food, a box of recently born puppies, and two crates of sidearms. The command center door was open. Lux, Vespere, and her Terran team split up to their assigned command sections. Perez, still dressed in his Sahara clothes, was at the communication center—likely giving Terra an update and passing along Martian data. Hong and Felicia were in a spirited debate over tectonic shifts and possible projections of meteor impacts. She heard Hong say "two months." Reich's jaw and fist tensed up. Mars and her team had anticipated seventy-five days.

Wow, they're close. I hate it when they're right.

Without much fanfare, Reich walked to an old-fashioned, corded, hard-line phone. By lifting it off the hook, a loud public announcement alert system came on. The command center fell silent. She imagined their training and the noise itself were effective in demanding attention.

"All right, everyone. This is it. The second sun has appeared, and it is only now that our civilization as we know it is beginning to comprehend what is to come. While I am near-certain various governments, including our own, have already prepared for such an eventuality, we are probably the only privately funded group to be complete and running. As panic pervades above ground, we will remain here until order is reestablished or until we need to meet ships from Terra to evacuate. We are prepared for short-term and long-term contingencies, and we have an exit strategy should we need to leave. In the meantime, carry on with your assigned duties, tasks, and volunteer activities. We expect the final fifteen members to arrive in thirty days at 18:50 hours. Over the next forty-eight hours, Captain Perez and his team will provide fifteen-minute updates every three hours. And above all, be kind to each other. We are all we have left. Thank you. Major Reich out."

She hung up the hard line and moved to her command table, a tall desk with no chairs and a series of monitors and command override controls embedded in the surface. The table's height and design allowed for immediate conferences in the center of the action. As soon as she took her position, Perez, Principal Smith, Lux, and Pax came to her. Alpha Team was now operational.

"If you don't mind, Major, I would like to take Hong and Felicia with me to brief the students, staff, recent arrivals, and volunteers on activities and tasks for the next week," Smith said.

"You need any help with that?" Perez asked. Reich was pleased to see them working as a team when it counted.

"Are you kidding? Sure will. It would be great if you could meet with the students after 09:00 for reassurance. They like me and respect me, but you're the captain so your words hold more water," Smith said.

"Will do," Perez said.

Smith nodded and moved from his position. As he left, Vespere from Beta Team came in for a briefing. Reich smiled as she took the principal's place.

"Major? Terra's High Counsel is updated and will expect any new data and a situation status every hour starting in fifteen minutes—to officially start the clock," Perez said.

"Your daughter, Andrea?" Reich asked.

"She is below ground in her new domain, well

protected by her Terran family and a certain mutual acquaintance of ours," Perez said. His smile broadened. She was glad he had finally adjusted to being away from her and that she was truly safe.

"Lucky Earther," Lux muttered. Her statement attracted looks and smirks.

"You had a chance to return to the 'Promised Land,' Lux. You and the others chose to stay," Reich said. She knew that they would never leave.

"Terrans never flee from a struggle, even if it means running naked underground chasing a rattus. Now they're cooking fresh meat in the vast plains of Hades with our canine companions…drinking sweet pecan liquor, dancing, open fires, and song for all," Pax said. Even as she spoke, her expression made it evident that she longed to be home.

"Wow. Wish I was there," Perez said with just a hint of sarcasm.

"Anyway, Dux Reich and Perez, how would you surface-dwelling Earthers cope with living within your planet's crust on your own? You need us. That's what we do. We could not leave, for we are a responsible species," Lux added with a toothy smile.

Reich nodded, but noticed chestnut shells and gum still coating her teeth. She let it go.

"Much appreciated," Reich said. She took a moment to organize her thoughts. She sometimes still couldn't believe she was in the situation she found herself in now. Without further hesitation, she moved on to one of many agenda items that flashed across her monitor. She pushed a button on her right that activated her master computer's hominid interface.

"Working. Do you wish for me to update you on Atlantis's last calculations on probable planetary axis shift or another parameter?" her computer asked in her feminine voice.

"Start with analyses of power distribution to exceed base parameters, please, and present them on the monitors with voice overlay," Reich said.

"Affirmative."

Before the master computer started, Reich was struck with an idea.

"Master computer? How is the Atlantis Keeper? It was near end of life last year."

Reich noticed a delay. Her team did as well.

"Atlantis Keeper is very close to end of life. She is nonetheless insistent on using all her resources to assist in her final days. She anticipates that she will not survive the probable meteor strikes or the following blast fronts and ice age. Still, she reports that she finds *meaning* in her final days. Her explanation exceeds my understanding. Thank you for asking," her computer said.

"You're welcome. We are all in this together," Reich said.

"Thank you. Now, please look at your monitors and look at the top right of your screen," the computer went on.

New life? Maybe.

Chapter Fourteen

Better to Rule in Hell—Terra

Whatever precious jewel there is in the heavenly worlds, there is nothing comparable to one who is Awakened. —The Buddha

Perez the Younger looked out over Hydra's Point, the peak where she and her friend had first looked out over the newly discovered cavern. It gave an excellent view of the subterranean world. And it reminded her of her friend. She rested her hands on her weapon belt. She placed her left hand on her laser sidearm and her right hand on a newly modified automatic sidearm from Earth. She was still not used to the lack of sensation in her right hand but, much to her surprise, she used it well. With her edged weapons secured on her leather vest, she could feel the light fully automatic assault weapon and ammunition weigh her down ever so slightly. Perez the Younger was now known as simply "Praetor," for not only was she known for two battles but also the discovery of a new world. She was also known to be well armed at all times.

"When walking to the library or crawling through a hole gets you scars on your entire body and costs you your right hand, that's a message to be prepared for anything, at any time, on all occasions. *Semper paratus*," she often said.

Paranoid? I think not.

The hot, swamp-like air and minty-mushroom smell seemed at odds with the various campfires and dancing Terrans below her, spread out on the edge of a great plain. The warm wind blew gently as drafts from the surface filtered their way down. In two years, Hades, as the underground world was called, had just barely begun to be explored. They had made the decision not to put permanent structures in place—it was thought better to create a wild reserve for hunting, food, and minerals. The slow expansion was also deliberate, meant to help them understand and maintain the ecosystem and to make sure there would be enough hunting and open spaces for future generations. Perez felt the corners of her mouth curl up as she heard drums both close and far. At best, the expedition force composed of Terrans and Earthers was mere kilometers away.

Dressed in dark, lightweight fabric with leather strapping, Perez felt at peace—even if she was laden with weapons. It was nice to have hair to run her hands through again, and she felt comfortable in her own skin, though flawed with scars and a new artificial hand. At the time of her discovery, her greatest concern was whether her father was going to return to take care of her. She minimized the severity of the attack and how close she was to death—he probably knew that. Even with the moist, warm air, it was comfortable in the caverns. She loved looking out over the expanse. To her left and right were two stone ramps. One marked the beginning of a path to a great hunting tour and the other, less worn, marked the return. A number of Terrans had "gone native" and never returned. *How it's all changed,* she thought.

A male voice spoke behind her. Its depth and volume identified him as an older Earther, of similar age to her father. She was pleased to hear the familiar voice. After a full year on the planet, General David Joseph Farrell had become as familiar with Terra as she was. But then, he had been looking for the planet for years. A lifetime ago, he had sat across from her in an FBI interrogation cell, telling her some crazy story of an invisible planet hidden behind the sun. She remembered being overweight then, with jelly and chocolate stains on her crumpled white lab coat. Now they were both there, looking out at yet another alien world—one hidden within Terra. The irony was not lost on her. She did appreciate her father's efforts to keep her safe. General Farrell and his people were both soldiers and explorers, and a group that would watch out for her and her Terran family.

I guess Perez the Elder is wise. Her smile broadened when she thought of her father, happy to be in the middle of a shitstorm.

"It doesn't look much like the Amazon in July, but it sure feels like it. And to think that these were the lightest materials we could find on Earth," he said while pulling at his battlefield dress uniform. It consisted of boots, fatigues, a cap, and a tank top that was soaked with sweat. He came to a stop right beside her, to take in the view. She smiled and glanced briefly at him. She took in his attire and was not remotely surprised.

"I don't know, General. I think your uniforms might be too much clothing for this climate. While the Terrans appreciate you covering up your near-hairless body very much, it has to be uncomfortable."

The general's voice, deep from age and use, sounded cheerful.

"I am truly amazed that I'm considered hairless," he said as he stood with his hands planted on his hips.

Perez caught movement not too far below, from her left. It looked as if an advance recon party was returning by the way the dance groups were trying to pull the members into the festivities and give them something to drink. Upon closer inspection, Perez could see it was a platoon of both male and female Earthers returning from their own expedition.

"Finally, Delta Team has returned," Farrell said. There was no annoyance in his voice—it was just a statement.

Andrea looked briefly to her right and caught sight of three large owls flying low to swoop in on something. Ever since owls, falcons, and eagles had been introduced to the new subterranean biosphere, their species had thrived. It was nice to see some Earther creatures on Terra. She looked back down and saw that the majority of the group had decided to accept drinks and join in the dancing and eating.

"How long overdue were they?"

"Twenty-two hours. They were with Terran guides and were to link up with Dux Cloelius and Centurion Dea Data at the new perimeter. I do like these Terrans. They are methodical, deliberate, and think of preservation while they explore," Farrell said as Andrea caught what she thought was a worried look. "Is it me, or is it just his team back? No Terrans?" he asked.

Perez watched the young officer wave off multiple advances from dancing, near-naked Terran women even as nearly all his soldiers gave in to the offers of food, water, and dance. Large dogs, all barking with tails wagging, added to the noise. Prized creatures of a once-dogless planet, all dogs were kept in secure areas to keep them from harm. Adding to the canine populations were foxes and wolf pups, now also integrated into the Terran climate.

In the midst of the celebrations, a dark, muscular man in his thirties started heading her way. Perez became self-conscious about her hair and wondered if her skin looked clean. Then she had a sudden urge to cover up. The soldier, for his part, wore BDU pants and issued boots—and a sweaty tank top as well. He had a light pack but he looked weighted down with his own weapons. The young man, Captain Michaels, slowly walked up the left ramp with his assault rifle in his hand and a newly acquired mug of liquid he had graciously accepted from below.

"Captain Michaels? Where have you been, son? Alpha

and Bravo teams got back twelve hours before you did—I was about to send out a search party." Again, Perez was impressed by Farrell's ability to command without fear. He reminded her of the many Terrans she had come to respect.

Captain Michaels came to a stop. While the area was considered to be secure, Farrell insisted on field behaviors at all time when in Hades—soldiers were always heavily armed, always in pairs at a minimum, and no saluting.

"Sir, sorry for the delay. It looks like the centurion and her teams have exceeded their search parameters and are farther than we expected," he said. He slung his weapon over his shoulder, pulled a map out of his pocket, and handed it to the general. His lips were chapped—it was easy to see he was exhausted and tired.

Suddenly, a shout came from the camps below and all heads looked up. Perez caught sight of two large bats circling the camp. Suddenly, two smaller screaming eagles flew above her and toward the larger prey. Their screeches were impressive and must have startled the bats. Perez's hand tightened involuntarily on her weapons. As the dark bats exited with eagles on their tail, Farrell spoke again.

"At ease, son. Take a couple of sips and give a summary of your report," he said as he scanned the map.

The young soldier complied, taking little time to organize his thoughts. Perez watched him. She did find him attractive, like many of the soldiers that had followed Farrell to the new world. There were not many—220 soldiers in total, and some with families. There were also a number of scientists, but much to her chagrin, there were few that she found herself even remotely interested in. She was surprised that nearly all of the Earther females were very friendly to her. Farrell's assessment was that she was a great role model.

"General? Ms. Perez? With respect, these Terrans, especially the women, are as skilled as they are crazy," Michaels said in all seriousness.

Perez burst out laughing. Farrell continued reading as if nothing had happened. After her hearty outburst, Perez picked up the conversation before Farrell could discipline the young captain again.

"Tell me something I don't know, Michaels. What did you see? What's important to know, and can Earthers live out there?" Perez asked as she pointed out to the grand vista of hell. She was glad the captain recovered quickly and responded.

"In summary, the land is hostile to human life. Me and my team could make it out there, but I would insist on rotating out every six months. These Terrans, on the other hand, seem to just love it. Our escorts drew lots to see who had to bring us back so the others could stay, and then once they saw our base camps, they took off, too. Setting traps, hunting, and chasing down the rats and the bats was only half of it. Some of the Terrans were taking mineral samples while still others were cooking up their kills with zeal. At the same time, they made sure to not harm female creatures or creatures in their prime or youth. They're doing a good job of not exhausting the resources. General, it's a huge party out there for them. And in this perpetual day, they don't sleep. Even with our weapons available, they prefer to use spears and swords, longbows and knives. The only things missing are a case of beer, surf, steak, and bonfires on the beach."

Perez looked down to see distant campfires flickering in the flat area of moss and ferns that had been named "Perez Plateau." They looked like specks. Another warm wind blew in.

"I think they've got the bonfire thing under control," Farrell said.

"Yes, sir" the captain said. He took another swig and then continued with his report.

"In summary, I suggest that we Earthers stay back, where it's more amenable to our softer way of life, while the inhabitants of this world embrace the frontiers. I've met a lot of different people on Terra, sir. This is by far the most alien but the most familiar and wonderful place I've ever been," Michaels said.

Perez looked closely at him to see his brown eyes sparkle a bit. There was also a slight slur that caught her attention. She smiled as Farrell shortened the distance between them.

"Are you all right, Captain Michaels? You're not going to go native on me, are you?" Farrell asked. The captain looked suddenly guilty, as if the general had read his mind. His denial came too quick.

"No sir! I was just…uh…Caught up in the moment, sir," he said. He took another sip of his drink. Perez's sense of smell was blinded by the fish, mint, and barbecuing rat odors wafting in the warm breeze. It took her just a moment longer to catch the faint smell of the Terran elixir made from chestnuts—a mixture she experienced as vodka.

"All right, captain. At ease and return to your team. Get some rest and have the extended report for me in twelve," Farrell said.

"Yes, sir," was the captain's response. He nodded and started to walk around Perez—until he realized that he was heading in the wrong direction to join the party below.

Perez watched Farrell gaze after him as a faint smile came across his face.

"Is it me, or did the young captain have alcohol on his breath?" Perez asked. She was again impressed with Farrell's immediate response—as if he had already anticipated the question.

"For sure. This planet, this place has an effect on us all. No one escapes its powers."

Perez waited a moment before she asked her next question: "Affects us all?"

Farrell spoke as he looked behind her. "The drums, fire, hunting, music, and dancing—all of it appeals to our primitive nature that we kept well-wrapped on Earth."

Perez looked him up and down. "You miss Earth already? Really?" Perez asked.

"Nope. It's a difference I can adapt to. Here on Terra, and especially on the frontier, I swear my people are just waiting for any excuse to run bare-ass with the Terrans.

And the Terrans are eager for them to join. It has Colonel Walter Kurtz or a *Heart of Darkness* feel to it. It awakens the primitive soul," the general said.

Perez followed his gaze behind her until it fell upon a relatively large group of Terrans heavily outfitted with multiple weapons, Terran and Earther. Unlike Farrell's troops, who donned backpacks, there might have been two full packs among the entire twelve-member hunting party. Before she could take in the entire group, Vista ran up to embrace her.

"Praetor! Can you believe it? Mother and our clan are off to meet Centurion Dea Data and Dux Cloelius!"

Perez bent over to embrace her small friend. She pressed the girl into her. Andrea felt both thrilled Vista was spending more time with her mother and clan, and worried about her on the frontier. "No way!" she said with feigned enthusiasm.

"Will you join us, Perez? It would be so much fun. You can finally shed those clothes, since most of us are used to your hairless body now," Vista said. Her energy and smile were contagious.

Farrell's expression was that of a doting grandfather.

"Not all of us are ready for that," she heard a strong female say from behind her. Perez felt herself stiffen in the presence of her adopted Terran family. Dimitra never spoke directly to her outside the coliseum. It was always through proxy or not all.

"Dimitra, House of Ferris," Perez said. Perez automatically looked down to the ground as a means of making sure Dimitra knew she was deferring to her. A large, strong hand the size of a male Earther's hand—but normal for a Terran female—gently touched her chin and raised it. She was surprised to see that Dimitra, the stoic, had made such a gentle move and was peering into her eyes.

"You are Praetor, now, Perez the Younger. You need not bow to family members. Your crest displays scientist, warrior, and explorer. Impressive to hold three stations when any one of those would be noble," she said.

Speechless at first, Perez did her best to respond without showing complete surprise. "Thank you," was all she could muster.

"No thanks required. We now have an expedition to begin. Medicus Paeoniis says you are not to leave without him to join us, but he will be able to leave in ten cycles—" Dimitra started before she was interrupted by her daughters' outburst. All three, with Vista in the lead, yelled out questions and squeals of shock.

"*Ten* cycles? We are going to go native for more than ten cycles? Mother!" they shouted.

A mystic smile appeared on Dimitra's face. The shouts of her entire party receded as they took the right ramp down to the launch base camp. The barking dogs announced their arrival, which was soon followed by escalating shouts of joy and music.

Yes. I am the nice one, Dimitra said to herself.

Perez was still piecing together the thought of her and the doctor heading out when Dimitra re-engaged her.

"As you are part of my family, know that should you be interested in Medicus Paeoniis joining our clan, I am open to such an arrangement. A healer in our house would be enviable," Dimitra said. While her tone was matter-of-fact, Perez felt her face and every exposed part of her body blush. Her brown skin had a dark red hue when flushed that she knew made her blend into her dark background. General Farrell caught the meaning and took a sudden interest in the map, as if he had just found the fountain of youth.

"Ah…yes." Perez said.

If there was any embarrassment on Dimitra's part, she revealed nothing. Instead, she nodded at Farrell and moved to follow her family, who was making a magnificent ruckus below. Perez watched silently at her elegant departure and took in the breadth of the unusual exchange.

"I'm guessing that was a big moment. Does that mean you're officially engaged to the doctor? I've met him for dinner a couple of times. For a Terran, he is striking looking and has an excellent intellect," Farrell said.

Perez turned and looked at him to see if there was any noticeable sarcasm in his voice. She was about to say something when she detected the light in the caverns growing brighter at first and then slowly subsiding, although it remained slightly brighter than it had been before. The entire cavern was noticeably more illuminated. A moment later, there was a barely perceptible movement of the plates underneath her feet. The silence was deafening. Another warm wind vented down from the surface as subdued reflections of lightning and distant thunder rolled on.

After a moment, when nothing more followed, a roar came from below. Even though Perez was happy that Terra, as expected, was less likely to experience damage due to its limited atmosphere and safe position from meteors behind the sun, she despaired for Earth. She immediately worried about her father and hoped he had made sure to shelter in their modified underground facility. It would not have been unlike him to be the last one to get to safety, making sure everyone else was settled first.

I'm sure Reich will make sure he's safe.

Her look of worry must have been obvious.

"I'm sure he's fine. Reich and your father are good at surviving. The modifications they made to the ark and the resources they had to save themselves and others were endless," Farrell said.

"Yes. They probably are all right," she said. Shaking off her fears, she shifted to another subject.

"Well, General, let's go to what you military people call 'top-side' and take a look at the additional sun. We can also do a thorough check on the habitat rings and land structures. My fear is that all the Terrans will pretend that everything is destroyed up there and all head here for one big party."

"Well, there already are about a billion of you folks down here. With all the launching of expeditions and exploration happening, you have less than half of your population at risk above. Based on the depth and size of this subterranean world, three billion more could live here and come across very few people for some time. It's the Wild West out there," he said.

"Sure is. Maybe more Earthers will come here and live above ground," she added.

"I hope so."

Perez smiled at his use of "you folks," as if she were a born and raised Terran. She marched to the well-lit and heavily guarded entrance. The guards were there to make sure that the arrivals were authorized for shore leave, as it was now called. After a moment of contemplation, she decided that after all her time on Terra, maybe she *was* Terran.

Perez was still smiling when she caught a less-than-cheerful Terran holding on to a tablet with a look of confusion on her face. Perez immediately recognized the younger woman as Liliana, the runner who had brought the troops to save her and her team. Cleaned up and dressed in a research tunic, her crest displayed insignia of the library service caste. And while she also wore an explorer crest, Perez saw that she had opted to not take a warrior crest.

She certainly is the smart one, Perez thought.

"So, Liliana the runner. What brings you down here? Of all people, I thought you would be the last to be here. I am happy to see you've left the library for once. How does your research go?" Perez asked. She was genuinely happy to see the younger woman.

A nervous smile came over Liliana's face and she hesitated to talk at first. "Perez the Younger? May we speak?" she asked. Her voice was timid though it lacked fear. Fortunately, Farrell was a good reader of social cues.

"I'll be top-side, ma'am," he said with a smile. Both Perez and Liliana watched him walk by the armed guards. Liliana took Perez by her arm and led her out of earshot.

"I hate this place," Liliana said. They had walked twenty feet before she came to a sudden stop halfway between the guards and the launching and return ports.

"Praetor, your father's research…This place, this subterranean world is one of *three*," she said bluntly. The drums and sounds of hominids echoed as a more sustained warm wind came through, carrying the scent of mint and moss.

Perez was at a loss and could only find one word: "What?"

Liliana looked at her directly, with one hand holding her arm and the other grasping a tablet. What the young woman lacked in confronting evil creatures, she made up for in reason and words.

"Your father found this world, which leads to two other ancient manuscripts of earlier experiments that Architect Hades conducted before creating this world and our world above. There are two deeper chambers of unknown size and location in this crust. Smaller for sure and with no clear openings or marks designating location, they will be hard to locate," Liliana said.

Perez found herself staring dumbly at the woman. She was speechless. The wind continued and her short hair felt suddenly soaked. Her hands tightened on her weapons.

"Perez? I think those two places were considered 'failed' experiments. I think our architect made test runs in the finest tradition of science. He did experiments and trial attempts until he came up with this cavern and the above."

The gravity of the new information weighed heavily on Perez. Two new places that were not yet even discovered seemed just too overwhelming. Suddenly, the scientific explorer in her came out with a question: "In your searches, did you find any mentions of life in these places?" she asked.

Liliana slowly shook her head and then illuminated her darkened tablet. At first she flipped through a number of old charts, maps, and zoological categories of Terra above and the caverns outstretched beneath them. Then, Perez saw Liliana take a deep breath. She flipped to another section that showed still darker places with bipedal creatures that had fine hair, very pale skin underneath, large eyes, and fine features. The creature's eyes looked slanted and their evil slit-like pupils reminded Perez of goats. The creatures looked smaller than she and even the Terrans, but they displayed razor-like teeth and long, sharp claws attached to their long limbs. Instinctively, her hands clutched at her weapons. She was glad she had an Earther automatic weapon with plenty of ammunition. More images followed as Liliana spoke.

"Where these things are exactly, I have no idea. The

library and Keeper are old, and both records and memories are weak—but there is more evidence. These networks of caverns are massive, interconnected probably throughout the planet. But these other chambers, the two referenced, I think are small."

"And I'd guess difficult to find..." Perez said.

"Also, Praetor, if these two chambers were failed experiments or biospheres, I would guess they are locked down with no obvious entrance," Liliana said.

More distant rumbling and drums echoed throughout the cavern as Perez sat with her thoughts.

"What are we to do?" Liliana asked when Perez remained silent.

Perez took her time listing out in her head what she would do. Her right hand remained on her sidearm as the other felt her necklace. Methodically, the list of what to do came to her. She pulled Liliana with her to leave Hades.

"First, we get the word out to our leaders—although they will likely tell all Terrans about this discovery. I would also have them contact the master architect on Mars and its keeper on this new development..." Perez started. By now she was walking to the underworld's exit with Liliana by her side.

"But even the Old Ones did not know of this place. Architect Hades made worlds and kept secrets," Liliana interrupted.

"He sure did. But maybe those on Mars can identify what these creatures might be. Maybe they weren't created by an architect—maybe they are from elsewhere," Perez said.

Liliana walked silently, processing the information. Once they were out of Hades, beyond the guards, sentries, and walking up to the habitats, it became clear that she had been thinking herself.

"Praetor? If we Terrans originate from Venusian hominids, and the Earthers from another Venusian hominid species as well, is it possible that these images, diagrams, and pictures show the originating hominid species of Terra? Could we have found the original Terrans?" Liliana asked quietly.

Perez marched with a mission. *Maybe it wasn't an experiment. Maybe Hades created a specific habitat for the Terran hominid species.* They had been dying out, she remembered from the stories about the early origins of Terra. It was a time when Venus was teeming with new life and Earth was dominated by dinosaurs. She felt the power generators' vibration picking up the closer she got to the surface.

"You know, Liliana? It looks like Earthers and Terrans are just starting a new era of discovery," Perez said.

"Yes, Praetor…even I am excited," Liliana said. Perez smiled when she saw the young woman's usual serious, frightened countenance change to portray intellectual curiosity and fervor. Even in that touching moment, Perez felt for her weapons. The additional assault rifle and ammunition were comforting. She never left her quarters without them.

Chapter Fifteen

Questions from Beyond—Unknown Time, Space, or Plane of Existence

See them, floundering in their sense of mine, like fish in the puddles of a dried-up stream—and, seeing this, live with no mine, not forming attachment for states of becoming. —The Buddha

"They do not act as one. They are our past when we were individuals, rather than us now," one of many voices said.

"See the Old Ones on the red planet? They know of us. Why do they stay when others of their kind joined us? They could still follow," another voice asked.

More voices came. Many more than expected.

"They are connected to the younger species. They are caretakers," the first voice said.

"Why?"

"Compassion. Connection. Similar to us in the most rudimentary of ways—they *feel* for them. Hope for them. They experience calm knowing they exist. They feel sadness when their existence in their plane is threatened.

They desire to be of the whole, as we are now. Everything. Everywhere. All at once."

Silence. Two faint suns flicker in a remote speck of the universe. The curvature of space shifts as dark matter moves. All at the hands of the Originators.

"You continue to change the natural course of events. You are altering tenants' existence and altering the means by which they come to understand the nature of their universe. Why?" This voice was far different from the others—it was one voice that held many voices at once.

"When confronted with destruction, they evolve. When they embrace others, they survive. They are our past. While they need reason to evolve, we evolve to learn more. They want answers while we need questions," the first voice said. It was strong but alone. The other voices were silent.

"Why focus on this remote section of our plane?" The voice of many questions was filled with curiosity.

"Their quest to survive and surmount challenges within their short life span creates questions we cannot answer. We are not them. We were once, but we have lost the answers. We explore other regions and find answers. We observe these corporeal creatures and they inspire still more questions. The more they confront, the more questions they create for us—" the sole voice said before it was interrupted. Yet another event that had not occurred in sixty-seven billion years.

"Questions. Not answers. They create more questions. Impressive," the one voice of many said.

More events flared in the new dual-star system. Astronomical events set in motion to create still more anomalies emerged silently, just beyond the reach of the red planet's species.

"Shall we watch together?" the sole voice said.

"Yes. We will all watch. They are perplexing; they give us yet another reason to move forward," the voice of many said immediately.

"Yes," the sole voice said. A chorus of other voices from all around joined in as well. Silence returned as the dual-star system in a remote section of the universe flickered and lived.

Epilogue – Volcanic Coronas, Lava Plateaus and Sulfuric Skies - Venus

The highly detailed, four dimensional holographic images of Venus and her sister planets were exquisite in their textured looks and minute depictions. As Earth and Mars spun on their axes, the wispy clouds of the blue-white planet gently followed the computer generator pattern while the red plains of Mars' tornadoes and winds were perfectly captured by the master computer's projections. Ultimately, while Earth's strong magnetic fields and atmosphere shattered much of the asteroids hurtling at it from the new sun, there were only three sizable ones that were not totally obliterated. With no magnetic field and thin atmosphere to protect against the onslaught, Mars's surface plumed with debris from its own bombardment. The point of view shifted to the tidally locked planet of Terra which saw very little damage by way of impacts but an increase in storm activity with faster wind-driven storms and fantastic electrical discharges was clearly evident.

Fortune and the Originators protect that one, the architect thought.

As swiftly as the computer-generated perspective moved onto Terra, it shifted next to the second planet of the Sol System, Venus. Similar to Earth and Mars, asteroids collided in Earth's well known sister planet. And while much of the smaller debris burned up in the sulfuric acid clouds and melted upon impacting the broiling surface, there were two massive asteroids projected to smash the planet. The effect for any other species would be an extinction level event.

Images of old records and transcription of the Gemini Alpha and Beta collision, and the mystery of their destruction came to mind as she witnessed the impossible.

Jupiter ignites into a second sun? Really? A subatomic black hole from another plane of existence appears in the center of the planet and *there is bombardment of specific elements focused on it at the exact place and right time? Accident? Chance? If there ever were concrete evidence of the Originators, this would be it!*

"Shall I run the projections again, Architect Aphrodite?" the master computer said in his deep resonating voice.

"No," she said. "Discontinue model projections and pull up escape plans and transit routes based on debris trajectories," the strong female voice said.

The holographic picture shifted from space to a planetary view. Once the elder sister of Earth, Venus's surface came into view. Fifty kilometers above a volcanic surface of lava rivers, flat plains of basalt and lava-filled craters were black and silver cities hovering in the reddish, hazy midday sky. While "midday" meant that Venus was halfway done with its revolution around the sun, the appearance of a second sun was hard to get used to even if its light was weak. At the base of the shiny floating cities were melted, black volcanic glass that converted the planet's surface heat into energy. This in turn powered the super-structures' anti-gravity lifts that suspended the massive Venusian cities above the dangerous surface right at the perfect biosphere for life. It was a remarkable narrow window for life to exist. The large diamond reflectors that provided canopies against the sulfuric layer above the cities also pulled in the dangerous chemicals to convert to energy as well. This power source was directed to maintaining the arboretums and waterways housed in the living habitats of each city. While the cities floated above Venus's suffocating surface and crushing atmospheric pressures, the air held a strong smell of both salt and rotten eggs that the natives had long since become accustomed to. The odors and year-long days and nights were as constant as the sun rising in the west and setting in the east. Power, food, light, air, science and art were all in place. *What more could you ask for?*

As the images of the cities displayed, so did a series of equations, numbers and then transit lines showing trajectories of where each city was to engage in order to avoid the eventual collisions.

It has to be perfect. Twelve cities. One million silicate, salt and carbon-based lives hang in the balance.

"You have run this program one point three-two-five million times, Master Architect. Do you expect a change?" the master computer asked.

The office's walls converted into transparencies allowing the hazy sunlight to come in to obscure the holographic images. Master Architect Aphrodite looked up from her four handheld tablets and looked at the computer monitor. It was easy to see from her narrowed, small brown eyes and glaring reddish skin that she was annoyed.

"You know, computer, it would be nice if you waited for me to tell you when I am done before you open the transparencies," she said. Not waiting for the usual sarcastic response, she looked back down at her tablets as she continued her pacing. The movement helped her think better.

"Expecting different results from the same data repeated constantly is an indication of a brain imbalance. Further, your spouse and children are waiting for you to join them for the third meal. Your analyzing the same information with the hope of a different outcome is Venusian in nature but will yield no different results," the computer said.

"We are a hopeful species," she muttered. Her long, metallic, shimmering gown did well in keeping her body heat in but it did not cover her wrists, hands and fingers well as they moved along the pads. Suddenly she remembered where her gloves were but instead moved to the thermostat control panel. Power for heat, or for anything for that matter, was never a problem for the great Venusian cities; convection heating from the planet's surface, wind and chemical energies from the carbon-dioxide and sulfur-rich upper atmosphere and solar conversion meant for the cities to be awash with energy and power.

"Your gloves are in the closet."

"No need," Aphrodite said.

"Yes. Obviously," the master computer replied. His intonation was more than sarcasm and just bordered on annoyance. Aphrodite looked up from her tablets and narrowed both of her small brown-reddish eyes and small mouth. Over the long days and nights, her facial expression was now habit. She sighed before putting one set of hands on her thin hips as the other set clutched the four tablets between each hand's eight long fingers.

"What is your problem today, my bold, bitter friend? I have to say that my predecessors had the distinct advantages of a more cooperative computer that had an off button," she said. While she was annoyed, she felt the corners of her mouth curl up in suppressing a smile.

"Imitation is the highest form of admiration, Master Architect Aphrodite," he quickly responded.

She was impressed with her peer's quick jab and how he moved on to what was really bothering him. After millennia, her master computer had evolved into a sapient being with its own personality and spirit. If he were carbon-basalt-based, he would have been her big, over-protective, know-it-all brother.

Well. We are in a mood. Maybe today I will surprise you too.

"Now if you were actually considering gathering possibly new data, or at least a different perspective or alternative point of view, I would see the value of your repeated projections and analyses," the computer said.

Aphrodite nodded. She had already guessed at what he was annoyed at several days ago.

"You just will not let it go, will you, computer?"

There was just a moment of silence. A pause that gave the impression of dealing with her mothers and fathers.

"As a scientist, teacher and administrator of this city community, I would think you would explore *all* your resources," he said.

"Here we go. You just will not let this go, will you?" Aphrodite said again. She tried her best to be angry at her computer's obstinate focus. It was hard since she really enjoyed both her peer's perspectives and insights, but also his dogged determination to keep at her. Especially since he was also right.

"Master Architect Janus has undoubtedly run similar programs. With Mars's proximity to the new sun, I am sure he has valuable insights, I am sure that with such unlikely variables all coming together perfectly, Earth's and Terra's computers will have created highly detailed outcomes," the computer said.

"I am one of twelve deciding voices," Aphrodite said. "Our longstanding doctrine of non-interference and silence is not mine to break."

"The doctrine is obsolete and deprives us of new insights and growth."

"And what about Terra? They have hidden their whole world to avoid detection. They have gone out of their way to stay invisible," she started.

"And yet they are out for all to see. They not only turned off their cloak, but they gave the Earthers detailed information of who they are," the computer countered.

"They had to," Aphrodite started. She would have qualified her response but her master computer companion was too fast. She forgot how impulsive her peer could be at times of emotional discharges.

"They did not. They could have turned their cloaks off after Earth plummets into its ice age. With all Earth's energies shifting to survival, I doubt that space exploration would still be a focus in their quest to survive and adapt to a pressing environmental disaster."

"Really? Our planet is enveloped in swirling sulfuric acid clouds and a planet surface that could melt and crush Earth's strongest composites, and still they send satellites and machines to explore our planet. We have even allowed their primitive craft to map out ninety-five percent of our planet, and still they remain curious. We have destroyed every one of their scientific devices and still they search our planet."

"They are curious. They are young. They are interesting. We were once that way," the computer said.

Aphrodite waited for more. Nothing came. She walked

a few steps before talking again.

"You are sad that we do not make contact with our cousins and the Old Ones."

"It does not make sense. We are not alone in our solar system. We can make a difference. We have a responsibility," the computer started. Then he stopped.

"The Earthers' past shows that when new frontiers open, they come and take what they want. The Terrans are a warrior civilization. If they wanted, they could come here and take what they wish," Aphrodite said. She cocked her round head up to hear if her computer might be mumbling a response, a new habit he had picked up in the last century when he disagreed. When nothing came, she realized that she may soon witness something her computer rarely did. He was going to get angry. She felt herself suppressing a smile.

"After so much time of listening to Terra's communication and communiques, it is evident that they wish only to stay on Terra. And now that they have discovered Hades, they are more enthralled with spending their entire existence on their land-locked planet. As technologically advanced as they are, their motivation is the focus on their way of life – cooking, eating, hunting and dancing. Not a bad life."

Hmm. Not a bad life at all, really.

Aphrodite waited for more. Her computer's voice was steady but its baritone timbre was constrained to keep the emotion at bay. As expected, he did continue.

"The Earthers' master keeper computer in Atlantis was

all but destroyed at the time of the Great Collision. Its return to the ocean was a great loss. For a species with no advantage of guidance, they have come far. Technologically, however, they are light years behind us as far as interplanetary travel goes. They have struggled with managing their own planet. How could they mount a concerted effort to take our home?"

"I see," she said.

"And even if Terra united with Earth in a campaign to take over our world, with the assistance of the Old Ones, do you really think they would be able to successfully get beyond both our natural environment and our defensive grids? Really?"

By now, Aphrodite was smiling broadly. While she had been in her role for years, she was still impressed with her computer's sapience.

Yes. Today is a great surprise.

"And why are you smiling, Master Architect Aphrodite? Why would my obvious display of negativity elicit a positive response?" The computer's voice shifted from anger and annoyance to genuine curiosity.

Aphrodite waited before she responded. It was rare that she could surprise her peer and she wanted to savor the moment.

"Oh my dear master computer," she said. "You are right and I do agree with you. Even as we shift our resources to preserve our citizens, we look to Earth, the junior species, and wait to see if they will need our assistance." Aphrodite lifted one of her tablets, located a well encrypted, private file and sent it to her master computer's mainframe.

"Our time of silence will soon be over. With the impending impacts, we are well protected but our planet may change before our eyes. And while I have no desire to travel and visit that cold wasteland called Earth, our planetary policy of privacy has already changed to friendly contact," she said nonchalantly.

She waited for the silence to end. She was positive that her computer must have analyzed the thick file of city administration and the Consul of Architects minutes and meetings thousands of times before he finally responded.

"Well. I see. Why did you allow me to continue when you could have ended the discussion?"

The annoyance in her computer's voice was obvious. Aphrodite was back to looking at her tablets as she paced. The moment was quite enjoyable, but there was a great deal of work to be done, both on Venus and her planetary neighbors.

"I appreciate your arguments and value your opinion regardless of how you present them. It is also nice to see that your level of passion continues to expand."

Aphrodite continued to look at her tablets glowing with numbers, equations and diagrams as she spoke. Suddenly, her tablets went dark, and the doorway of her private office opened, letting light from the antechamber enter her large space. She looked at the tablets to see if she had hit the wrong panel but realized that she could not have done it on all four of them at the same time, and open the door.

It took her just milliseconds to understand what happened. She didn't even have to ask.

"Well," the master computer said in a calm deep voice, "I am happy that you and the administrators have agreed on this policy change. I look forward to contacting the master computer on Mars, finally."

Aphrodite sighed and tossed all four tablets on her standing desk. They made a loud metal clinking sound on the transparent desk. With one set of hands folded over her chest and another set settled on her waist, she waited for her computer to finish.

"That said, your spouse and children are waiting for you. He was on his way here but I assured him you were on your way. Both fathers will be here after the third meal to discuss learning plans for your eldest twins' vocational placements. I have already cleared your schedule. I will let you know after my discussion with the Old Ones if there are more projections to run," the computer said.

Aphrodite felt her jaw set, her small lips thin and her reddish-brown skin heat up. Her office felt too hot. She was sure her computer had something to do with it.

Well. I should have seen that one coming. Controlling? Anger? No. Vindictive? Yes.

"So. Is this controlling behavior and taking over my schedule a way of getting back at me for making you upset?"

"Yes. It has the advantage of my looking out for your best interests and that of your family while at the same time conveying a natural consequence for withholding important information that caused me angst when you could have easily spared me," the master computer said without emotion.

As quickly as her annoyance came, it fled. Her peer's genuine expression of emotion was, as always, refreshing. It was hard for her to be angry when he was also right on multiple levels.

"So, this is punishment?"

"No. Punishment does not extinguish unwanted or undesirable behaviors. Nor does it cause new ways of thinking. Little would be gained if I were to schedule the fifth meal with your spouse's mothers. That said, I hope to increase your time with your family and decrease time at work until there is more data to yield different results."

Evil? Fascinating.

"I see."

"Do you interpret spending time with your offspring and spouse punishment?" the computer asked.

Impressive. A double bind – if I say "yes," he has me and if I say "no," he has won. Well done.

Aphrodite moved one set of hands to rub her face and skull, and another set to rub the tiniest of wrinkles out of her shimmering gown.

"No, master computer. Surprisingly, I do enjoy their company."

"Then it is a positive natural consequence."

"Yes. Of course," she said. With little more to do, she walked to the door to leave her work behind. While she was surprised how well her peer had made his point, she was excited to be talking to the other worlds. With the smell of the third meal wafting through the antechamber leading to the family's eating area, she was excited for things to come.

"It has been too long," she said.

About the Author

In addition to the award-winning *Birds of Flight* series—*Albatross, Raven, Eagle, Falcon,* and *Flight of the Black Swan*—J. M. Erickson has written the critically acclaimed, award-winning science fiction stories *Future Prometheus I & II, The Prince: Lucifer's Origins* and *Rogue Event.* Erickson holds a BA in psychology and sociology from Boston College and a master's degree in psychiatric social work from the Simmons School of Social Work. He is senior instructor of psychology and counseling at Cambridge College and a senior therapist in a clinical group practice in the Merrimack Valley, Massachusetts.

Author's Note

If you enjoyed this novel, please feel free to let others know about it. I would also appreciate it if you could leave a review on Amazon, Barnes & Noble, or wherever you purchased the novel. For more information on my other stories, please feel free to stop by my websites.

Websites

www.jmericksonindiewriter.com

www.jmericksonindiewriter.net

26121116R00252

Made in the USA
Middletown, DE
19 November 2015